Too Many Suspects

A Mystery/Thriller

by

Ken L. Burke

Ken L Burke

DANCING CROWS
PRESS

Copyright 2020 © Kenneth L. Boekhaus

ISBN 13: 978-1-951543-99-0

Library of Congress Control Number: 2020908129

Cover design by Colin Wheeler, MFA, ABD

Strikenbrow.com

DEDICATION

I dedicate this book to Labetta, my lovely wife of forty-eight years, for her support and encouragement during the writing and editing of this book. As the first person to read the entire book, she helped me see serious weaknesses in the story leading to a rewrite that changed the perpetrator. It is a better book because of her.

ACKNOWLEDGMENTS

I am a blessed man who has a number of people to thank for their support writing and publishing this first novel.

Thanks to the members of the Carrollton Writers Guild for helping me develop my writing skills. Special thanks to the Just Prose critique group for providing moral support and challenging me to become a better writer. When I began writing in earnest six years ago, I thought I was a decent writer. The guild helped me see how deficient my fiction writing was and then helped me to learn the craft. Writing fiction is far different than writing business letters, reports and emails.

Many thanks to both my Beta reader, Karen Gordon, a neighbor and close friend, and to my editor, Val Matthews, for pointing out where the book could be improved. Thanks also to Donna Johnson, Drug Addiction Counselor, and Wayne Wheeler MD MPH for sharing their insights into the struggle of opioid addiction and withdrawal.

Finally, thanks to Elyse Wheeler and Stephanie Baldi of Dancing Crows Press for guiding me through the publication process and editing this novel.

Without the help of the above people, this book would not have been possible.

Chapter 1

My plan unfolded in the exact way I had envisioned . . . until it didn't. Her surprise confession turned my world upside down, and my life would never be the same. The background noise in the busy diner evaporated as the universe collapsed to just me and her.

"What?" Sitting bolt upright and struggling to maintain composure, the question escaped a mouth now devoid of all moisture.

Her eyes turned frigid. "When you disappeared, I was pregnant with your child."

"What are you talking about?" My outburst, too loud for this public setting, silenced all conversations at other tables.

The missing youthful sparkle in her lovely dark eyes returned, but not for me. Lights reflected off tear-filled eyes. A white paper napkin became a tissue and stood out against her olive complexion as she dabbed under her glasses. "We had been talking about getting engaged after graduation. I wanted you to ask me because you wanted to marry me rather than because you felt obligated. So, I waited to tell you until after you proposed. Instead, you blew out of town and abandoned me without even a goodbye. I never heard from you again." The edge in her tone cut through the layers of protection built up over years of painful relationships.

"The way I remember it, you were the one doing all the talking about getting married. Besides, how can you be sure it's mine?"

Her eyes turned dark and her jaw clenched. "How could you even ask that? You were my first and only, until after you left. I thought you knew me better than that." Tears again pooled in the corners of her dark eyes. I longed to take her in my arms and tell her how beautiful she was, but fear of rejection mixed with self-disgust paralyzed me.

Her words reverberated inside my head without congealing. Nothing made sense. How could this have happened? Was the child mine? I needed certainty. "I don't understand. We always used a condom."

Ronnie recoiled and shook her head. "Condoms aren't a hundred percent."

Her unexpected revelation brought back memories that had haunted me for twenty long years—memories of dumping her out of a haunting fear of commitment. She had wanted to get married. All I knew about marriage was the hell I went through for seven long years before my parents ended their misery, and then the nightmare of my own failed marriage.

My marriage had been doomed from the start, a victim of my suppressed passion for this gorgeous creature who sat across from me. My wife was nothing like Ronnie and never could live up to my memory of her. My obsession drove me to the edge of insanity or at least crazy enough to believe I could waltz back into Ronnie's life now after all these many years and sweep her off her feet.

In an instant, I formulated a revised plan—I would pick up the pieces and become a role model for this child I had fathered years ago. "What's his name?" Macho me assumed I would have had a son, to carry on the bloodline, name and all.

"We had a girl. I named her Lorelei." Her words seemed forced.

I knew nothing about fatherhood. Mine had been an absentee parent, travelling on business most of the time. But it seemed only logical a good father would show interest in their child. "Can I meet her?"

Ronnie couldn't speak for a moment. When she did, sobs broke through. "She died about a month ago. The sheriff's office classified it a suicide."

Her grief reminded me of war scene pictures where a heart-broken mother clutches the lifeless body of her child in grief. I searched for words to demonstrate deep empathy for this woman I still loved. "It sounds like you don't believe it was suicide."

"No, I don't." She set her eyes and spoke with conviction. "Lorelei was too full of life to shoot herself. She hated guns and would never touch one."

"I'm so sorry, Peaches." It slipped out before I could catch myself, but it felt good to use my old pet name for her.

Her eyes locked on me in a harsh glare. I had crossed a line and scrambled to recover. "After all these years, why tell me now?"

I studied her lovely face. She had aged well over the past twenty years. Lines and crow's feet highlighted a face that had lost the sharpness of youth. Red-framed glasses, imposed by the wages of life, masked the true beauty of her dark eyes. She no longer matched the sexy femme fatale in my detective novel based on her. As she brushed her long hair back, big penetrating black eyes softened. Those eyes were what first attracted me. They still captivated me.

I laid my hand on hers to offer comfort. She recoiled, a diamond ring scratching my hand. I hadn't noticed her modest engagement ring and accompanying wedding band. The last I knew, she had divorced and was single. Had she remarried, or was she just wearing the ring from her failed marriage to ward off unwanted male attention? I hoped for the latter, but the timing didn't seem right to inquire. She had recently lost a daughter and was still grieving.

I tried to process her blockbuster surprises. "I'm so sorry, Ronnie. You appear to be in a lot of pain over your loss. What can I do?" I wanted to take her in my arms and console her.

She sat bolt upright and assumed a more formal air. "I realize it's asking a lot, especially after so long without connecting."

"What, Pea . . ." I caught myself. "What do you want me to do?" Hope surged. Maybe she wanted me as much as I lusted for her. I felt the need to help her but couldn't offer her counsel. Not having children, I couldn't share any experiences or offer any advice. I sucked at marriage as my ex-wife would testify. What could I do for her but love her? How could I let her know how much I cared?

"Would you look into Lorelei's death? Would you do it for me, for old times' sake? As a favor, I mean." The meekness of her smile exposed discomfort in asking.

The request stunned me. "You mean investigate her death? Ronnie, I'm not a detective. I'm a washed-up dentist with foolish dreams of becoming a best-selling author. What makes you think I could investigate your daughter's death?"

"*Our* daughter's death." Her silence scorned me more than her verbal admonishment. The sudden discovery I had fathered a daughter needed time to sink in. I didn't have a clue how to respond.

"I read your book. It's all about this detective who solves a murder. So, you must know how to investigate a crime. You researched for the book, right?"

"Not really, unless you count binge-watching Pink Panther movies. A detective who reviewed my book said I should be arrested for impersonating a mystery writer. You've read it. It's awful." I wondered if she suspected she was the lead female character in my book.

"It's not that bad. Besides, the poster promoting the book signing said you're a bestselling author."

I laughed and shook my head. "Ronnie, I'm self-published. No self-respecting publisher would touch my book with a ten-foot pole. My books are 'Print on Demand.' On the rare occasion when someone orders one, they print and ship it. I tried to order one-hundred copies for book signings, like the one today. I accidentally ordered a thousand copies on a slow day. For about a minute the book was a top one-hundred seller on Amazon. I'm sorry, but I can't. Have you asked the sheriff to take a second look?"

She gazed at me and flashed her long dark eyelashes. "Yes, but he won't. I think he's involved and protecting someone. You won't need to do a full-blown investigation. Just prove it was murder, not suicide. You don't even have to catch the culprit. The sheriff will do that once he's forced to reopen the case."

I longed to help her, but a lack of self-confidence prevented me. "Why don't you hire a private investigator?"

She pursed her lips and gazed down at her hands. "I looked into it. We simply can't afford one."

Behind those glasses, her candlelight eyes drew me in and cast a spell over me. My love burned deep for this woman, and I would do anything to spend more time with her.

I started to agree, but reality stepped in and trumped lust. "Ronnie, I'm sorry, but I can't do it. I manage a dental practice in Savannah and need to be back at work on Monday. The local book store's request to do a book signing flattered and intrigued me. I decided to make it a long weekend, catch the homecoming game, see a few friends and, if lucky, sell a few books along the way. I need to clear them out of my closet."

She smiled like the cat that ate the canary.

"Wait a minute," I said. "Did you have something to do with my book signing here?"

She sat upright and looked away as a slight blush shown over her face. "The book store owner is a good friend of mine. I asked her to set it up so I could see you."

It all fell into place now. The call from the book store had set off a series of events leading to this moment. The idea of returning to Talmadge stoked my old flames for Ronnie. When she appeared at the book signing, I fell in love with her all over again.

I briefly considered honoring her request to investigate our daughter's death but feared I would be in over my head. Others were far more qualified than me. "I'm sorry, Ronnie. I can't." Guilt swelled inside me because I was rejecting her all over again.

She looked away as if summoning strength. "Tim said you wouldn't do it. He said I was asking too much."

"Who's Tim?"

"My husband." Those two words cut me worse than any knife thrust.

"I thought you were divorced."

"Tim's my second husband. We've been married for two years. Ray, my first husband, and I divorced when Lorelei was three."

Not good news. This whole trip, which I couldn't afford, had been planned in the hope of reigniting my old relationship with this woman. Now my dream had been dashed.

Chapter 2

Parenthood had never been in my plans. I struggled to get my arms around what Ronnie had just divulged. I had fathered a daughter, a daughter I never knew, nor would ever know. Visions of my child played out in my head—cuddling with her on the sofa in front of a warm fire on a cold winter's night, a young girl blowing out seven candles on a birthday cake through gapping front teeth, me teaching her to ride a bike and later to drive. I now shared this woman's loss.

"I'm sorry to spring it on you like this." Ronnie's words brought me back to reality.

Bliss transformed into anger. "How in God's name could you not tell me about my daughter? I had a right to know. You cheated me from knowing her. Besides, if I had known, I would have done the right thing and married you."

Ronnie flinched. Mascara ran as tears erupted anew. She grabbed a dry napkin, removed her glasses and blotted her eyes. "I'm sorry. When you left, my world collapsed. I didn't know what to do—ask you to quit dental school and come back here? That wouldn't have been fair to you."

Her pain became my pain, and I resented it. "You could have gotten an abortion."

Her head shot back, and her eyes became hate-filled slits. "You mean murder an unborn child? How can you suggest such an atrocity? I thought I knew you better than that."

I had stepped in it and didn't have any idea how to recover. "You're right. I would never have wanted you to do that. I'm just angry you didn't tell me. We could have been a family." I wasn't sure I could have delivered on that claim.

"You made it very clear you didn't want to marry me when you deserted me."

"Don't you understand? You talked about marriage *all* the time. 'When we get married' this and 'when we get married' that. It scared me. I panicked. I wasn't ready to settle down but couldn't bring myself to tell you. So, I ran away." Did this sound as lame to her as it did to me?

"I was a fool and thought you loved me and wanted to get married, too. But I guess you just used me for sex."

Her accusation held an element of truth long ignored. Could I love her more now than when I left? That idea disturbed me. "Why didn't you tell me about our daughter? I would have come back for you." I wasn't sure that was true, but it bought me time to set aside my pain and come to grips with the fact I had fathered a girl I would never meet. This changed everything and nothing.

"How would a child have made a difference? I was angry. Maybe this was a way of getting revenge. I don't know." She stood and grabbed her purse. The diner went silent again as if someone had hit "mute," and all eyes focused on us. "Tim said it was stupid to ask you. I should have listened to him."

I watched the love of my life leave the coffee shop, bawling. Glued to my seat, I reflected on my disappointment. My grand plan to win her heart back had failed. I now understood how she felt when I walked out on her and hated myself for it. My conscience refused to stand by and let it happen again. I chased after her.

She pulled away from the curb in an older Toyota Corolla with a noisy muffler. I dashed into the street to cut her off, waving my arms. When she didn't stop, I dove for the curb, but her car grazed me with enough impact to send me tumbling head over heels.

Tires squealed in complaint as the car skidded to a stop, and she jumped out. "Tanner! Oh my god! Did I hit you? Are you hurt?"

I sat up and took a quick inventory. "I'm okay. The car just brushed me. Guess I'm not as agile as I once was." The dive had tweaked my bad back. Severe pain made standing a difficult challenge. One of my OxyContins would dull the pain, or as I called them, Oxys.

She held out a hand to help me stand. "I'm so sorry. I didn't see you. Why did you jump in front of me like that?"

Masking my pain, I stood somewhat upright and looked her in the eyes. "I changed my mind. Since I'm staying for the game on Saturday, and have nothing else planned, I'll look into Lorelei's death over the weekend." By then I hoped to know if she still held buried feelings for me. My rare optimism surprised me. Hope felt good after the hole of my drab existence.

She wrapped her arms around me in an exuberant hug, causing warmth to shoot through my body and sharp pain to run up my spine. Any anger I had felt evaporated. I never could stay mad at this woman.

I longed to kiss her, but she gave no signal she wanted me to. I so loved this woman. I had a weekend to convince her she still loved me.

CHAPTER 3

All eyes followed us as we returned and took a clean booth in a far corner. I needed a stiff drink, but this diner didn't have a liquor license so more coffee would have to suffice. Ronnie ordered water because caffeine made her jittery.

She loaned me a pen to scribble notes on a paper napkin. Over the next few minutes, Ronnie shared details of Lorelei's all too short life, illustrated by photos on her smartphone. Images of Lorelei revealed a cute, precocious child. The young tomboy blossomed into a woman, slender tall. Every bit as beautiful as her mother, she could have been a fashion model.

I've never cared for children so didn't know how to relate to them. But this was different. She had been my child. A small hole opened deep in my heart.

"I'll airdrop some of these pictures to you," she said.

"Sorry, I don't understand what that means. I'm not good with computers and electronics. It's all I can do to use this thing." I retrieved my old person's flip phone from my pocket and displayed it with false pride.

She chuckled. "How did you get through dental school? That's okay. I'll send some of them to Walmart to print for you. I should have them for you tomorrow."

The thought of seeing Ronnie again so soon brought a smile to my face.

Ronnie laid out everything she knew about our daughter's death, which wasn't much. She died of a gunshot wound to the head. The sheriff's office had publicly declared her death to be a suicide. According to her, she and Lorelei were close—more like sisters than mother and daughter. She swore there had been no sign her daughter might be considering taking her life. Might a doting mother have overlooked the warning signs? I expected an investigation might take one day, but planned to milk it as long as possible to spend time with my Peaches.

A quick read of the police report would have been the logical first step, but Ronnie did not have a copy. She suggested I start with Amy Hall, Lorelei's best friend and a fellow student at Central Georgia who had discovered the body. Ronnie phoned her and scheduled a meeting for me at the Central Georgia University Student Union at five-thirty.

My planned investigation would be short and sweet. After meeting with Amy, I would work with Ronnie to get a copy of the police report or, at the very least, talk to the investigating officer.

Ronnie pressed me to visit Lorelei's apartment. That didn't promise to be very useful since a month had passed since her suicide. Odds were, her apartment had been cleaned and occupied by a new tenant. Time is money.

Frequent shifting of my weight did little to relieve my raging back. I obsessed on Ronnie while forcing my craving for an Oxy to the back of my consciousness.

"So, you're here for the weekend? Where are you staying?"

"Ballard Inn on Seventh Street. It's not much but was the only thing available on a homecoming weekend at such short notice." The truth was, I couldn't afford anything better.

"Never been there. Is it nice?"

"Only if you're a cockroach."

She chuckled. "You said something about attending the game on Saturday. Do you have a ticket?"

"Not yet. Thought I'd go the route of the scalpers. They still scalp tickets, don't they?"

"Only online, I think. We have season tickets. Tim played for the Fighting Owls when he went to school here. I haven't been able to make myself go since Lorelei's death. Why don't you use my ticket? It'd give you a chance to get to know Tim."

The thought of hanging with Ronnie's husband roiled my stomach. Best not to know the husband you are trying to cut in on. "You may change your mind. I'm sure I can get a ticket somewhere. As I recall, the Fighting Owls rarely sell out."

"Some things never change." She checked the time on her phone. "I better hit the road. Tim wasn't crazy about me coming to see you. Knowing him, he's counting the minutes until I get home. He probably thinks you kidnapped me by now. You have my number if you need anything." She half stood before sitting back down. "One other thing, everyone in town thinks my first husband, Ray, was Lorelei's real father. I'd rather keep it that way, if you don't mind. It would create a lot of problems if the truth got out. Okay?"

Her request stung. I found out I'm a father—or rather, had been a father, and now couldn't tell anyone. Oddly that hurt, but I choked back my emotions. "Yeah, sure." I wasn't sure I could keep that promise. Now that I knew about Lorelei, I was strangely proud to be her father.

Ronnie stood and said goodbye. I stayed planted in my seat, not wanting her to see me wince from pain when I stood. I coveted the Oxy in my car.

She leaned over and kissed me on the cheek. I turned to kiss her back but my lips caught only air as she breezed out the door. I savored the peck on the check for a moment before sucking it up and shuffling back to my car. People gave me a puzzled look as I limped out of the diner. Once in the car, I washed down an Oxy with a glass of sweet tea snuck out of the diner.

CHAPTER 4

A third check of my watch in the last fifteen minutes confirmed Amy was late. I pulled out the paper napkin with my notes taken at the coffee shop and dialed the phone number Ronnie had given me. After ringing for a minute, the call rolled over to voicemail. Amy's recorded message revealed a gruff, sexy voice with a Georgia rural twang.

"Hello, Amy. This is Tanner Nole. Veronica Mason scheduled a meeting for us at five-thirty at the north entrance to the student union. I was calling to confirm our meeting time and location. I'll wait here about ten more minutes. Thanks."

I stood, stretched my back, and then paced to loosen it up. Another Oxy would have helped, but there was no water fountain nearby. I didn't dare leave my post for fear of missing her.

Another glance at my watch showed six o'clock. Enough time wasted. I spun toward the door and collided with a pale young woman with short, straight black hair. She recovered her balance and took a step back. "Are you Mr. Tanner? You're, like, much younger than I expected." The gravelly voice matched Amy's voice mail message.

"You must be Amy. Nice to meet you." Her tan blouse and brown slacks seemed in conflict with her dark makeup and hairstyle. Silver hoops hung from her pierced ear lobes, accompanied by two more silver studs running up each ear. A small silver stud adorned the right side of her nose. She was cute, despite the hardware and gothic influences.

14

She shook my hand with a firm but clammy grip. "Sorry I'm late. Got hung up and couldn't get away." Her speech held only a hint of the southern drawl I heard on her voicemail message as if she were trying to suppress it.

"Ah, yeah, sure. Thanks for meeting me. I want to ask some questions about Lorelei's murder."

"You mean 'suicide'." She avoided eye contact and appeared nervous. "This isn't a good place to talk. There's a bar up the street where we can have some privacy."

"Boy, things have changed since I went here. You have bars on campus now?"

"Things haven't changed that much. It's just across the street from campus. Come on." She waited for me to open the door for her which didn't fit her rebellious image.

Walking the five blocks to the bar, we labored to make small talk. I learned her major was computer science or IT as some would call it. She met Lorelei in a journalism class. I tried to build rapport before asking her personal questions about my daughter. The growing hole in my heart created by Ronnie's pictures of Lorelei needed to be fed. Amy's answers were short and vague, her gestures quick and jerky. She appeared uncomfortable talking about her deceased best friend. And, we hadn't even gotten to questions about her death.

The bar was called The Barking Owl Pub after the CGU Fighting Owls. The dimly lit establishment and a stench of stale beer brought back fond memories of my college days.

A rich baritone voice called out from behind the bar. "Hey, Amy. You working tonight?"

"Hi, Jake. No. I don't work again until Monday. I'm a customer tonight. How about a Pinot Grigio? What'll you have, Mr. Tanner?" She sat on a bar stool and I did likewise.

15

Jake looked me over hard. "What's your pleasure, *Mister* Tanner?" His emphasis on "mister" hinted scorn and distrust.

"Jack on the rocks. Make it a double."

He poured our drinks and slid them across the bar. "It's happy hour, so drinks are half price. Enjoy."

Amy grabbed her wine glass and glided toward the back of the bar. "Come on. It's more private back here."

The bartender looked at me and smiled a crooked smile, as if on the verge of exploding in laughter. "That'll be ten dollars, Mr. Tanner." He took my twenty without offering change. Oh, well, a starving college student needed a few dollars more than I did. I snatched a bowl of mixed nuts off the bar. In my mind I had paid for them.

Few customers occupied the dim bar. Amy slid into a booth in the back corner and I sat across from her. Setting the nuts down, I took a long sip of my Jack while I pulled out a pen and the napkin from the coffee shop with my notes on it. Amy chose a Brazil nut and chomped on it very unladylike. Fear showed on her face. This interview took on a new level of importance.

"Thanks again for meeting me on such short notice. Earlier, when I suggested Lorelei had been murdered, you corrected me. So, you believe she shot herself?"

She stopped mid-sip and banged her glass down on the table, spilling a little. "I found her, you know? I'm no expert, but it looked to me like she shot herself. I hear the sheriff's department came to the same conclusion. Why would you think it was murder?" Between fidgets she picked up her glass and swallowed hard.

I took a sip of Jack while collecting my thoughts. "Her mother's convinced she could never have killed herself. I understand you were her best friend. Did she say anything about wanting to hurt herself? Did she seem depressed to you?"

Amy took a gulp of wine. "Yeah, I think she was in a funk. I mean, I didn't see it then, but in hindsight, she was depressed."

"What was the cause of her depression—grades, boyfriend or . . .?"

"That asshole Reggie wanted to marry her and threatened to evict her if she wouldn't."

"Marry her? Reggie and her were a couple?"

She took a long drink that emptied the glass and paused a moment longer. "Yes, I suppose you could say they were a couple."

I had agreed to this investigation to pacify my Peaches and stay near her, but now clarity exploded in brilliant radiance inside my head. She had identified Reggie Braun, the richest guy in town, as the likely killer, but I hadn't probed her about that—a huge mistake. I hadn't taken this investigation seriously enough. "You're not sure they were a couple?"

"No, they were a couple. It's just that he was married." She tried to sip from an empty glass.

Ronnie's pictures of Lorelei had painted an image of innocence and purity that Amy had just tarnished. My daughter had been sleeping with a married man. Now I understood Ronnie's suspicion. You always look first at the people closest to the victim. But then, why hadn't Ronnie mentioned this important fact? What else was she keeping from me?

I trudged on. "You said Reggie threatened to evict her if she didn't marry him. Was he her landlord?"

Amy tapped on her empty glass with long, white fingernails with black widows painted on them. She held her empty glass up again and looked for her bartender friend, but his back was turned toward us, mixing drinks. "Yeah, he owns the apartment building where she lived."

I dropped my pen and drained my drink in three huge swallows. "Tell me what happened the night she died."

Amy picked at the mixed nuts. "I called her like four or five times, but she didn't answer and didn't call back. That wasn't like her, so I went by her place to check on her. And, there she was, lying on the floor near the table, soaked in blood and everything. I barfed right there on the floor next to her. It was totally disgusting and all." Amy shuddered and turned a shade of green as if ill.

"Was she expecting anyone that night?"

Amy paused for a moment. "You know, now that I think about it, her table had been set for two."

"And *you* weren't invited to dinner? Any idea who she was expecting?"

"I don't know. Maybe Reggie."

"How did you get in her apartment? Did you have a key?"

Amy jerked in response to the question. She emitted a muffled cough and laid her left hand flat on her chest just below her neck. Her face turned bright red as she hacked hard. I rose from my seat to play the hero. Reaching around her from behind, I locked my hands below her breasts and applied the Heimlich maneuver. On the third squeeze, a nut dislodged from her windpipe and shot across the table.

As she drew a long breath, the bartender appeared out of nowhere with two more drinks and another bowl of nuts. "Amy, are you all right?"

She snatched the wine from his hand and drank half of it down before catching her breath. "Yeah, I'm okay. A nut caught in my throat. No big deal."

I sat back down, "You scared me for a moment."

I gave the bartender a ten this time, which he snatched from my hand while collecting our empties and then disappeared.

"Are you sure you're okay?"

She took a gulp of wine. "I'm good." She leaned in. Expecting gratitude, her next words shocked me. "Did you enjoy feeling me up?"

I don't blush easily, but I felt a warm flush explode across my face and neck. I cleared my throat and summoned up the willpower to continue. "Let me see, where were we? Oh, yeah. How did you get in the apartment that night?"

"It wasn't locked." Her strained voice was weak. Clearing her throat didn't help. "I knocked, and when she didn't answer, I tried the door. It opened, so I went in. The lights were all on. Oh, my god! The image of her lying in a pool of blood on the floor is burned in my brain forever. I wake up nights with that scene exploding in my head." Grieving eyes showed through a tormented face.

Her earlier inappropriate question was forgotten and forgiven. "Did you notice anything unusual about the position of her body on the floor? Anything out of the ordinary?

She nibbled on nuts again. "No. Well, maybe. Something didn't look right, if you know what I mean."

"No, I don't know. Describe it to me."

"It just seemed odd the way she was lying there with the gun still in her hand. It just didn't look right. I guess I don't know how a suicide victim should look."

I fought back a tear as I pictured my lovely daughter lying lifeless on her floor in a puddle of blood. My stomach turned. I had to push on before I broke down. "What happened next?"

"I lost it. Like I told you, I threw up and collapsed on the floor. The next thing I remember was this scary-looking guy wearing a bathrobe asking me if I killed her. I freaked out."

"Who was he? How did he get in?"

"His name was David or Daniel or . . . Donald! His name was Donald. He lives in one of the apartments there and had heard a gunshot."

"Were you still there when the sheriff came in?"

"Yeah. A female deputy arrived first. The sheriff and another deputy arrived later."

"Was there anyone else there that night?"

"A medical guy and paramedics showed up, but much later. They examined the body, you know."

"What did the deputy do when she first got there?"

"She checked for a pulse and then shook her head." Amy gulped the rest of her drink. The empty glass tipped over when she set it down. "When the second deputy arrived, he took me into the front room and asked me questions. After a while, the lady deputy took me home because I was in no state of mind to drive home."

"Any idea where Lorelei got the gun?" Amy stirred the nuts with one finger but did not respond. I repeated the question. "Do you know where Lorelei got the gun?"

She pushed the bowl away. "From me. It was mine."

My napkin filled with notes, I took a fresh one to continue. "Your gun? How'd she come to have your gun?"

"She totally freaked out about some guy hitting on her, I mean, really hitting on her. She was terrified. I made her take it, for protection."

"Why would you loan her a gun if you thought she might be suicidal?"

Amy looked away for a moment. "I told you, I didn't realize she might be suicidal at the time, only looking back now."

"When did you loan her the gun?"

"I don't know, maybe two weeks before her death."

"Did she tell you who was scaring her?"

"She may have, but I don't remember."

"Did she know how to use a gun? Had she ever shot one before?"

She looked up. "Why? Do you think it might have been an accident?" A glint of hope showed in her eyes.

"I'm just beginning the investigation, but I doubt it was an accident. You don't normally shoot yourself in the head accidentally unless you are cleaning the gun. Wait a minute. Did you see the entry wound? Where had she been shot?"

Her face tightened and darkened. She stared as if seeing the scene in her head. "On the right side of her head."

"You mean the temple?" I pointed to mine and Amy nodded agreement.

I chastised myself for jumping to a conclusion. "Are you certain? I think most suicide victims stick the gun in their mouth. They only shoot themselves in the side of the head in movies."

She looked at me as if I had struck her. Tears flowed, her words weak. "Yeah, I'm sure."

"What model was the gun?"

"It was a Tokarev."

I wrote that down. "I don't know much about firearms. What caliber?"

Amy squirmed in her seat. "Didn't you say you write murder mysteries? Don't you need to know about handguns?"

"I didn't say I was a good writer. Most of my victims are readers who die of wordiness and poor grammar." My weak attempt at humor fell flat.

"It's a 9mm with an eight-round magazine, nine if you have a round in the chamber."

"Did she ever fire it?"

I half expected her to say, *Duh? She shot herself with it, remember?* Instead, she said, "I pushed her to go to the gun range with me to practice, but she refused. She hated guns. They scared her."

"So, to the best of your knowledge, she didn't know how to use it?"

She fidgeted with her empty wine glass, as if stalling to formulate an answer. "Not that I'm aware of, but maybe her dad took her. He hunts, so he knows all about guns and shooting."

"By dad, I assume you mean, Ray Adams." She nodded.

I took a long sip of my bourbon to buy time while racking my brain for other questions. Amy had blown my mind with her revelations. "I can't think of any more for now, but is it okay to call you if I think of something?"

She sat up as if preparing to escape. "I'm sorry, but I'm busy with midterms and all."

"I promise I won't take much of your time."

Standing to leave, I grabbed the table to steady myself. My head spun as a result of alcohol and pain-killer in my system. I threw a five on the table for a tip and followed Amy to the door. The bar had filled up with female patrons who all glared at me as they jumped to an erroneous conclusion about my relationship to this young coed.

I turned toward the student union, but Amy didn't. She motioned in the opposite direction. "I'm headed to my apartment. It's the other way. Thanks for the drinks, and for saving my life in there."

On the way to my car, the truth weighed on me. My daughter had been a whore. I couldn't think of any other word for it. "Kept mistress" didn't describe it. Paid whore did. My anger shifted to Ronnie. It was her fault our daughter turned out this way. Grief and regret consumed me. If I had been there for her, things might have turned out different. No. Things *would* have been different! So, in the end, maybe it was my fault, too.

Self-guilt fueled growing anger toward Ronnie. I questioned how well I knew her and wondered how my soulmate could have failed our daughter. In college everyone was sure Ronnie would make a great mother. How could we have been so wrong?

The walk to my car helped clear my head of alcohol and Oxy. I remained unconvinced Lorelei had been murdered. But if she had, the list of suspects was growing.

It was Amy's gun, and she had seemed nervous talking about Lorelei's death. Could she have killed Lorelei?

And then there was Reggie, the jilted sugar daddy. Ronnie believed he murdered her. If he loved Lorelei enough to ask her to marry him, this had been more than casual sex to him. Could he have killed her in an angry reaction to being turned down? I needed to question him about this.

There was something suspicious about the timing of Donald's appearance. It seemed too coincidental.

And finally, the new wrinkle of an unknown stalker. That thought sent chills down my spine.

Unable to afford another DUI, I drove to my hotel using extreme caution. Visiting the sheriff's office should wait until I was sober.

Chapter 5

On Friday morning the Oxy from the previous night made waking difficult. I fought a strong urge to roll over and go back to sleep. It took an ice-cold shower to clear my head enough to get moving. I was eager to meet with my Peaches again and needed something to update her with.

Just before noon I located the sheriff's office in a new building on Main Street. During my college days, the office had been in an older building across the street. It brought back memories of bailing out my college roommate after a bar fight I had somehow avoided. Everything inside had been old and gray—the peeling walls, the floors, old weathered steel desks and chairs. A general lack of windows and burnt-out light bulbs added to the grayness. The lack of color, combined with the dim jail cells, carried on the dark, depressing theme. I had wondered how anyone could work in such a drab environment.

By stark contrast, the bright new office shined among those older buildings lining Main Street. Glass along the front illuminated an open, expansive lobby. A beautiful oak desk, like those in a law office, served as the duty desk. Beyond the lobby, pastel walls bore framed prints of local scenes. Fixed-wall offices with high windows lined one side of the building. A large fishbowl-type conference room dominated the opposing wall. In the middle, short walls divided the open space into cubicles populated with wooden desks and plush brown leather desk chairs. Gigantic flat-screen computer monitors, keyboards and printers dominated messy desktops—taxpayer's money at work.

A dark-haired woman in uniform, wearing a badge, worked a keyboard at the duty desk. When she looked up at me, her beautiful smile brightened my otherwise dull existence that morning. Large, dark eyes sparkled in the bright light. "Well, hell-o, there, honey. Y'all must be new in town because I know all the good looking men living in Greene County. To be honest, there aren't that many." Her Southern drawl was elegant, like from Savannah or Charleston. Southern belles with Southern accents have always been my weakness.

I blanked for a moment, stunned by her pulchritude. The tag on her blouse identified her as Deputy Russo. Her facial features hinted Latin blood. When she tilted her head to the left, sunlight glinted off a tight French bun. "Cat got your tongue, honey?"

"Oh, hi. Yeah. No wait. I mean no." I tripped over my words. Shaking my head did little to clear it. "I mean, no. A cat doesn't have my tongue. My name's Tanner Nole. I went to college here, but now live in Savannah." Busy typing on her keyboard she didn't notice my hand extended for a handshake. My hand fell to my side in embarrassment.

She stopped typing and looked up. "Pleased to meet you, Mister Tanner. I'm Deputy Mallory Russo. Now, what can I do for you this fine morning?"

The "mister" made me feel old. She was only ten, maybe twelve years younger than me. "I'm here to pick up copies of the police and coroner's reports on the death of Lorelei Adams."

Her smile faded into solemnity. "Are you a detective, Mister Tanner?"

"No."

"P.I.?"

"No."

"Are you a member of Lorelei Adam's family, then?"

I wanted to say, "Yes. I was Lorelei's biological father." but realized she wouldn't believe me. "No. I'm a friend of her mother, Veronica Mason. She asked me to pick up a copy for her."

"Sorry, Mister Tanner. We can only give police reports to immediate family, their counsel or other law enforcement agencies. Privacy, you know."

I screamed inside my head. *I am family, damn it.* Instead, she heard me say, "Her mother asked me to investigate Lorelei's death. She can't accept the suicide classification."

The deputy shot a pensive glance over her shoulder in the direction of an open office door. "I don't understand. You said you aren't a detective. Then, why'd she ask you to investigate her daughter's death?"

"Well, you see, I wrote this murder mystery. For some reason, Ronnie thinks that qualifies me to be an investigator. As an old friend, I'm doing her a favor by looking into it."

"A writer, huh? I read a lot of detective stories. Tanner—Nole—that name's not familiar. What have you written?"

"I've only written one novel. It's called 'Black Widow's Revenge 2."

Her bright smile returned. "If you only wrote one, why is it called *Book Two*?"

"I planned to write a prequel, but the first one isn't selling, so it may be the last."

"Sure am sorry about that, but I don't think writing a book qualifies you as an investigator."

A youthful red-headed man of slight build exited the open office door. His uniform still showed ironed creases as if it had just come off the hanger. Neat as it was, it didn't look right on him. A $1,000 banker's suit would have better fit the air of culture he exuded by his grooming and mannerisms.

26

He stood next to the lady deputy, looked me in the eyes with a gruff smile and held out his hand. "I don't believe we've had the pleasure of meeting. I'm Deputy Daniel P. Lowell, a descendant of John Lowell of Newbury, Massachusetts."

That explained his unusual accent—a Yankee, for sure.

The lady deputy must have read the puzzlement I felt. "Deputy Lowell here is a descendant of the Mayflower Lowell's."

"Direct descendent," he corrected her with an overblown smile.

Her reaction hinted humorous doubt. "Daniel, this is Mister Tanner Nole from Savannah. He's a friend of Veronica Mason, the victim's mother, and she asked him to look into her daughter's suicide."

Deputy Lowell's smile collapsed. "Is that right?"

"Mr. Tanner came in to request a copy of the police report."

"We can only provide that to immediate family." His pleasant tone turned flat and less friendly.

"I am fam . . ." I checked my words. "I'm not asking for me. Mrs. Mason sent me to pick up her copy."

Mallory smirked at my answer. He shrugged dismissively. "Mrs. Mason will need to personally sign for her copy. Besides, the report's not released yet. We're waiting on a revision to the coroner's report."

"What do you mean a 'revision'? Is there a problem with the coroner's report?"

Deputy Lowell gazed at me for a long moment. "I'm sorry. Are you some kind of expert on police reports, Mister . . . Mister . . .?"

"Nole," Mallory said. "Tanner Nole."

27

Deputy Lowell frowned at Mallory for an instant before staring at me. "Mister Nole, the report has not been completed. We will contact Mrs. Mason when it is, and she can personally come in to pick up her copy. Good day, sir."

I looked to Mallory for a hint of support, but she studied the papers on her desk. I walked away, my head sagging forward in defeat.

Why had I gotten myself into this mess? I knew why. I was still madly in love with Ronnie and would do anything to win her back.

CHAPTER 6

I grabbed the napkins with my notes and headed for Lorelei's apartment. A call to Ronnie rolled over to voicemail, so I left a message. I alerted her to my failure to get the police report and requested she try to get a copy when it was finalized.

On the way, I enjoyed a McRib sandwich from Mickey D's and vowed to break the fast-food habit with a decent dinner—maybe IHOP for a change. My body craved Oxy to calm my raging back, but I resisted to maintain a clear head.

It had been a month since the alleged suicide. I hoped they were having difficulty renting the apartment. In a small town everyone would know about the tragedy that had occurred there. Potential renters would deny being superstitious but would still bow out while giving some contrived excuse.

The beautiful two-story brick apartment building sat between two identical buildings on either side. They looked very nice—far too nice for poor college students. This complex appeared to target young, upwardly mobile professionals. I crammed a few clean napkins from Mickey D's in my pocket for note taking.

The building's front door was locked. A keycard reader and a panel of buttons with names blocked entry. The absence of a name next to the button for Lorelei's apartment gave hope it remained vacant.

I pushed buttons at random until Delilah Morton in apartment 1D responded. "Who is this?" The stern, gravelly voice created the image of an elderly woman who had smoked most of her life.

"Oh, hello, Ms. Morton. I'm here to see about renting apartment 2D."

"It's not ready to be rented yet."

"Are you the building supervisor?"

"No. He's in apartment 1A. Bother him instead of me." Her tone took on the harshness of scoldings received in third grade from Mrs. Black.

"He doesn't seem to be home. Are there any other apartments available?"

"How the hell should I know?" She nearly shouted the words.

"Would you please buzz me in to look around the building?"

"Go away! There aren't any apartments available in this building."

"Excuse me." The baritone voice came from behind. I turned to see a young black man dressed in a light brown sport coat, pastel blue sport shirt and navy blue dress pants with a keycard in hand. When I didn't respond, he motioned for me to step aside.

"Oh, hi. Do you live here?" I asked.

"Yeah," he said with disdain as he used his keycard.

"Well, I am Detective Nole. I'm here to look at the apartment of the deceased, Lorelei Adams. She committed suicide a few weeks ago."

He looked me up and down and frowned. "No one has been in that apartment in a month. Why the renewed interest?"

"I just started with the sheriff's department, but have a lot of experience with suicide cases. Sheriff Sykes asked me to take a fresh look at the evidence." I was skating on thin ice here. If the apartment had been cleaned, he would realize I was a fraud. "It's my first week, so it'd be a big help if you could let me know."

"You need to speak to Donald, the apartment super. He works nights so he should be in."

"He was supposed to meet me here but didn't answer when I buzzed his apartment. Something must have come up. Maybe I could ask you a few questions." It impressed me how I could improvise such fiction on the fly. Why didn't it come this easy when I wrote?

"I don't know anything about the suicide. I was out of town on business and missed all the excitement. Do you have a key to the apartment?"

I showed him my house key while concealing the other keys on the ring with my hand. He fell for my ruse and held the door open for me. We shared an elevator to the second floor and both turned to the right. I stopped at the door to 2D and he walked on down the hall. He dawdled at his door and watched me put on rubber gloves purchased at Walgreens. I wished they sold something other than hot pink. Hot pink didn't look police issue and hurt my manhood. My key slid into the deadbolt, but would not turn. To my surprise, the door opened anyway. "Thanks," I called to him and slipped into the apartment, closing the door after me.

CHAPTER 7

The smell of death greeted me the instant I opened the door and stepped in. An expansive great room with a high cathedral ceiling reminded me of a photo I'd once seen in Restoration Hardware's catalog. Stylish white upholstery and rich wood accessories produced a balance between formal and casual. Artworks on the walls were original oils with lights at the top of each frame to highlight the painting and draw out the colors. The room smacked of success and wealth, not the residence of a struggling college student from a poor family.

My daughter had lived well. I imagined her greeting me at the door and showing off her apartment with pride. But a dark shadow fell over my vision. The two of us yelled simultaneously in a heated argument about her shameful behavior that yielded her such luxuries. Truth be told, I hated that I could never have provided for her like this even at the height of my dental practice.

A large glass and chrome table with six high-backed leather upholstered chairs dominated the dining room. Two place settings were neatly set on the table. It looked as if Lorelei expected a guest for dinner but only one setting had crystal.

Then, I saw the bloodstain on the leather seat and back of that chair. This must have been the spot where my daughter died. I fell to my knees. A chilling wind of reality swept through me. I rocked back and forth, weeping. "Oh my God! Lorelei, I'm so sorry you're gone and I'll never be with you." I had had a child and lost her before discovering she existed. It was more than I could tolerate.

After minutes of weeping, I collected myself enough to stand. I couldn't face this without help. I chewed an Oxy to get it in to my bloodstream faster. I washed it down by drinking from my cupped hand under the kitchen faucet to avoid using a glass and contaminating it with my DNA. I leaned against the cabinet to let it take effect and scanned a kitchen that would be the dream of any home chef.

Stainless steel fronts on the Bosch appliances and a Sub-Zero refrigerator/freezer gleamed like mirrors. The range sported six gas burners under a voluminous stainless-steel vent hood. Pots and pans hung from a rack over the center island, looking new and unused. Gleaming black marble countertops held every convenience appliance imaginable. White cabinets with glass inserts in the doors revealed shining glassware and bone white china stacked with precision. The countertops and Carrara marble floor were coated with dust, indicating the place had not been touched in weeks.

When I could feel the soothing flow of the Oxy in my bloodstream, I resumed my search. The decorating in the bedroom stood in stark contrast to the opulence of the living room and kitchen. In a way it reminded me of a medieval torture chamber. A massive wooden four-post bed dominated the center of the room. Each corner post had large black metal rings at the top and bottom. Massive nightstands either side of the bed matched the medieval motif of the bed. Its drawers held the normal things like sleeping blindfold, magazines, Tylenol. Another drawer contained handcuffs and soft ropes that likely were used with the bedpost rings.

Oddly that was the extent of the furniture in this room. There was no chest or dresser.

The massive closet could have been a picture in a California Closet catalog. Designer clothes, shoes and purses were packed so densely she would have needed to take some out to add anything else. In contrast, one short wall section was bare as if someone had moved out. Another wall was covered with drawers containing her undergarments, sweaters and other clothes.

At one end, a wall safe stood open, its cloth-lined jewelry drawers empty. In Ronnie's photos, my daughter always wore expensive-looking jewelry. I wondered if her death had resulted from a burglary gone bad. I took a picture of the empty jewelry box and added to my notes on the napkins.

A small section of the closet stood out from the designer clothes. It held an odd assortment of what I could only call costumes—black leather lingerie, a shorty nurse outfit and a deep V-necked police uniform, to name a few. A box on the shelf above contained sex toys. I became embarrassed at my daughter's depravity.

I took notes and snapped pictures with my flip phone. After an hour, I had examined everything and prepared to leave. I froze at the sound of a key entering the door lock, not knowing whether to hide, run or stay to face the music. Before I could react, the door swung open.

"Hey! What the hell are you doing in here?" Words tripped over a thick tongue and passed through thick lips. His shrill voice matched his short stature but contradicted his tattooed muscular body and shaved head. Harsh, brown eyes projected an image of someone to fear.

"I'm investigating Lorelei's suicide. Who are you?" My response was delivered too weakly to be convincing.

He stared at me, taking longer than expected to formulate an answer. Clearly, he was not college material despite his youth. "You don't look like a cop."

"I'm not. I'm a private investigator. Lorelei's mother retained me to look into her murder." Again the lies flowed like silk.

"Murder?" The stranger's eyes bulged, and muscles tightened. For a second, I wasn't sure if he would vomit or flee, but then he collected himself. "The deputy said it was suicide, an open and shut case. Why'd you call it murder?"

"Actually the sheriff's report isn't finalized. That's why I'm here. Lorelei's mother is convinced she was murdered. I'm trying to find enough evidence to prove it one way or the other."

His eyes blinked, and his head moved in quick short movements. "Look, you can't be in here. The deputy told me to not let anyone in this apartment. You gotta go."

"Are you the apartment supervisor?"

"Ah, yeah. I'm Donald Wirth. Who are you? And how the hell did you get in here?"

"My name is Tanner Nole, Private Investigator. I'd like to ask you a few questions about that night."

"How can I be sure you're what you say you are? Show me your fuckin badge."

"PI's don't have badges. The state issues us a license." I flashed my Georgia Weapons Carry License by him with my index finger masking the words "Weapons Carry," so all he could see were the words "Georgia" and "License". I slipped it back into my wallet before he asked for a second look. "So, you see, I'm official. Now, I'd like to ask you a few questions?"

"Already talked to the deputy. They're done investigating. Said it was suicide, so I ain't answering any questions from you. Now get the fuck out of this apartment, asshole."

"I'm sure you did answer a lot of questions from the sheriff's department, but I collected a retainer from Mrs. Mason and can't afford to give it back. How about helping a guy out and answering a few questions? What's the harm in that?"

"I need a Benjamin then."

"What?" I asked.

"Give me a hundred dollars, and I'll answer your questions. I'm a little tight on cash right now."

When leaving Savannah, I emptied my paltry bank account for the trip. I had hidden a hundred-dollar bill deep in my wallet for an emergency. This seemed to be one, so I pulled it out. He snatched the bill and held it up to the light, flipped it over and examined the other side. "Is this real?"

I doubted this guy had ever seen a hundred-dollar bill before. "Sure, it's real. Let's start with some background questions. What kind of a tenant was Lorelei?"

"She never made any trouble. It just got a bit noisy here some nights, if you know what I mean."

"No, I don't know what you mean. Did she throw loud parties or something?"

He laughed. "Nah, I meant her and her guy used to get pretty noisy some nights. The neighbors complained."

"Noisy? Like, playing loud music, arguing, what?"

He laughed and shook his head as if I had said something stupid. "No, I mean they got loud with their sexual activities sometimes."

Embarrassment washed over me. "And who was this guy? Her boyfriend?"

He paused a minute, likely to forge a response. "Yeah, I guess you could call him a boyfriend." He snickered as if it was a punch line.

I paused while he composed himself. "And the alleged boyfriend's name?"

"Reggie Braun."

I took notes and felt like a real detective. A shadow of fear appeared across Donald's face. "Uhm, you need to leave now."

"I haven't got my hundred-dollars worth yet."

He shifted weight from one foot to the other and studied the floor. "Okay, but no more questions about Reggie. Ask me something else."

I put a large asterisk behind Reggie's name because mention of him generated fear in this man. "Tell me more about Lorelei."

"She had a rocking hot body, I'm telling you."

My strong glare must have intimidated him because he rocked back on his heels. Only my fear of him saved me from trying to smash his arrogant face.

After several more unfruitful questions, I concluded he didn't know much about Lorelei, so I shifted my questioning to her death. "Did you hear the gunshot that night?"

"Oh, no. I was in the shower. Mrs. Gordon from 1D knocked on my apartment. I wrapped a towel around me and answered the door. She pretended my level of undress shocked her, but I saw her eyeballing me. I made her night." His proud smile and bravado made me sick.

He continued. "She said she thought she heard a gunshot from upstairs. I expressed my doubts, but she persisted. I threw on my robe and grabbed my master key to check. No one answered my knock, so I unlocked the door and went in. I found Lorelei, lying on the floor by the table. It was awful."

"Wait a minute. I thought Lorelei's friend, Amy, discovered the body."

"No, I did. I ran back to my apartment to grab my phone. When I returned, Amy knelt beside the body, sobbing and talking with the 911 operator."

"So, Amy called 911, not you? Are you sure?"

"Hell yes, I'm sure. She called before I had a chance to."

I jotted down that Amy had called 911, not Donald, as she had said. I underlined this note to remind myself to follow up on this discrepancy.

"So, did Amy know you had found Lorelei's body before she arrived?"

"I don't know. I guess I never told her. She was a freaking mess."

"What did you do until the first responders arrived?"

"I tried to comfort Amy. Wow, was she hot! I love that gothic look." I noted his remarks about Amy in very personal terms. It made me wonder if there might be a connection there, so I probed.

"How well do you know Amy?"

"Not as well as I'd like to, if you know what I mean."

"Did you two talk while you waited for the sheriff?"

He paused for more than a minute, so I repeated the question.

"Not really. It took the sheriff's department forever to arrive. Amy drove me nuts asking, 'Why? Why did she do it?' over and over again. I tried to put my arms around her, you know, to comfort her, but she pushed me away and screamed at me. I guess it wasn't a good time. We didn't talk much after that. Okay, you got your hundred-dollars worth. I've got things to do. I've got a cleaning woman coming to get this apartment ready to rent."

"One last question. Why has this apartment remained untouched for so long, and now suddenly you seem eager to clean it up?"

"I don't know. My boss just told me to have it cleaned ASAP. Maybe Reggie's got a replacement to move in."

"What do you mean?" Heat surged in my body as adrenalin flowed.

"Hey, interview's over." He grabbed my arm and escorted me to the apartment door. "Now get the fuck out and don't come back." He stood at the door and watched me get on the elevator. On my way out the front door, I discreetly crammed an unused McDonald's napkin in the door latch to defeat the lock.

After hanging around outside for a few minutes, I re-entered the building without being seen. I tapped on the door to 1D. Mrs. Morgan opened her door to the length of a security chain and glowered at me through the crack. "How'd you get in the building? Whatever you're selling, I don't want any. Go away!"

"Donald, the super let me in to interview the residents. I'm a private investigator hired by Lorelei's mother to look into her death."

"Who in God's name is Lorelei?" Her voice reminded me of fingernails on a chalkboard. A strong smell of curry oozed from her apartment, making me nauseous. I hate curry.

"Lorelei. She lived in apartment 2D. Donald said you heard the gunshot the night she, ah, committed suicide. He said you knocked on his door. Is that right?"

"Oh, my. That poor child. Yes. I did hear the gunshot. My eyesight may not be the best, but there is nothing wrong with my hearing. That idiot Donald was more frightened than I was. I had to practically drag him to her apartment. He must have a thing for older women. He let his towel gap a few times to expose himself. He didn't seem too interested in what I heard."

"Did you see or hear anything else?"

"Huh?"

"Did you see anybody leaving her apartment or maybe hear something else?"

"No. I didn't see anything. It took me a while to find my cane and put my robe on before going to Donald's apartment. I heard shouting just before the gunshot."

"From Lorelei's apartment? You mean like a warning, disagreement or something?"

"Huh?"

"Was there an argument in Lorelei's apartment?"

She mulled the question over. "Yeah, I heard two people arguing upstairs and then glass breaking. These apartments are pretty well insulated, so they must have been yelling at the top of their lungs. A few minutes later, it sounded like a firecracker."

"You heard glass breaking before the gunshot? Are you sure?"

"Yes, I'm sure. I told you there's nothing wrong with my hearing."

The missing crystal for the one place setting came to mind. A quick mental review of my search of the apartment confirmed I hadn't found any signs of broken glass, not even in the trash cans. More evidence someone had cleansed the crime scene. "Do you know who was arguing?"

"Not a clue. I wanted to stay out of it, and don't want to now."

"Can I come in and ask more questions?"

"I don't know you from Adam. Look, the deputy got all this that night. Check with him. I heard arguing and then a gunshot. That's pretty much it. Goodbye."

I stuck my toe in the door's crack to prevent her from closing it. For an elderly lady, she exhibited impressive strength. Pain shot through my foot and up my spine. "Did you tell the deputy you heard people arguing before the gunshot?"

Thankfully, she let the pressure off my toes while considering my question. I pulled my smarting foot back.

"Of course, I did. Well, now that you ask, I'm not sure. I have to admit I was pretty rattled that night. Just like that fool Donald. What a mess. Well, goodbye."

The door closed. I didn't dare stick my swelling toe in the crack again.

CHAPTER 8

The door to Lorelei's apartment stood closed. After listening for a few minutes, I tried to open it, but it was locked. Even Donald wouldn't make that same mistake twice.

Donald wasn't about to let me in, so I considered my options. I could go outside, climb up to her balcony and break a window. With no other viable option, I resigned myself to entering a criminal life and headed to the building exit. The building door lock clicked and the door swung open.

A weathered middle-aged woman holding a bucket full of cleaning supplies and a mop blocked the doorway. She presented a possible legal alternative to breaking and entering. "Oh, thank goodness. You must be the cleaning lady I called. Hi. I'm Donald Wirth, the supervisor here." I prayed she had never met Donald in person.

"You sounded different on the phone."

I coughed into my sleeve and cleared my throat. "Excuse me. I've been fighting a cold."

She took a step back and scowled as if I were Typhoid Mary. I stepped aside for her to enter and trailed her to Lorelei's apartment. She opened the door using a key, and I followed her in.

With her first whiff of death stench, she covered her nose with a forearm. "Oh, my god, did something die in here?"

"Yes." One word said it all

She gave me a puzzled look and surveyed the apartment. When she spied the bloodstains, she dropped her bucket and mop. "Oh, my god. Something awful must've happened here. I didn't come prepared for anything like this." She crossed herself. Her lips moved in what must have been silent prayer. I can't clean up that carpet and chair. You'll have to have someone replace those."

After a few minutes, she recovered enough to begin cleaning the bathroom. I put my rubber gloves back on and searched the other rooms employing greater diligence this time.

As I noticed before, two formal place settings adorned the table, short one wine glass. The cabinet held ten wine glasses rather than standard twelve. Mrs. Morgan had heard breaking glass, but where were the telltale signs of it? After turning on the dining room lamp and walking around the table, I noticed a small glint of light in a seam in the floor tile from a glass shard. Every trash can in the apartment was empty. Someone had collected the trash after the murder.

Returning to the master bedroom I searched it again. A reexamination of the left end table revealed a small secret drawer hidden between the tabletop and the other drawer. Buried beneath unused condoms I found a prescription bottle containing Secobarbital. Barbiturates like this are rarely prescribed anymore because of their potential abuse in suicide. The label identified Dr. Goldman as the prescriber and that it had been filled only once, six months ago. A quick count showed twenty-nine of the original thirty pills remaining. I stuffed the condoms in my pocket and snapped a picture of the bottle in the drawer to preserve it as evidence.

It appeared she had obtained this drug legally, but how? Maybe Reggie pulled strings. Why hadn't the sheriff's department collected this bottle as evidence? Maybe they had also missed the secret drawer. Why would Lorelei shoot herself instead of just popping some pills and going to sleep? Neat and painless.

Standing at the door, I took one last scan of the apartment. A tiny glint of light shone from under a flower pot containing a withered plant, tucked back in the corner. Upon closer examination, it appeared to be a fancy silver safety pin with diamond chips adorning the clasp. I deposited it in a sandwich bag retrieved from the kitchen and stuck it in my pocket. It appeared to be something a well-kept woman might own, but I wasn't sure of its purpose.

CHAPTER 9

While driving back to my hotel, I reviewed the facts and arrived at a startling conclusion. Ronnie was right. Lorelei had been murdered, and the sheriff appeared to be covering it up. A call to Ronnie's cell phone went right to voice mail, so I left a message. "Hey, Ronnie. It's Tanner. I've got some news for you. When can we get together?"

Desire drove me to say more, but caution intervened. Shifting my position did little to relieve pressure on my aching back. I resigned myself to taking an Oxy when I got back to my hotel.

Returning to my room, I opened the curtains to let in light before collecting my prescription bottle and counting my trove of the precious drug. Five pills, barely enough to make it through the weekend at my rate of consumption. A quick read of the label yielded bad news—no refills left. A call to the prescribing doctor would be futile. On my last visit, he refused to renew my prescription until I committed to rehab, something I had tried once and swore never to do again. It was time to find a new doctor.

Sitting cross-legged on the bed, I employed a meditation technique learned in rehab to mitigate the pain rather than take a precious Oxy.

After twenty minutes, my pain subsided to a level I could tolerate. Now able to concentrate, I reviewed my notes. Halfway through, back pain resurfaced with a vengeance and demanded an Oxy. After taking one, I laid on the bed with a pillow tucked under my legs and waited for the pain to ease.

I awoke to a dark hotel room. The clock showed 7:15 PM. I chastised myself for wasting over three hours. A shake of the head pushed the fogginess back enough to check my cell phone. Ronnie had called and left a voice message. I must have been out cold to not hear it ring. Oxy will do that to you.

I checked the message. "Hey, Tanner, this is Ronnie. Sorry to miss your call. I'm anxious to hear what you've learned. Tim and I are on our way to the pep rally. Don't remember if you planned to attend, but if you do, let's connect there."

My return call rang several times before rolling over to voicemail. The pep rally would have started at seven, making it difficult for her to hear a call. I longed to see her and tell her in person she was right about Lorelei being murdered.

To save time, I skipped a badly needed shower but rinsed my face, brushed my teeth and applied a half bottle of cologne to cover my body odor. Generous sprays of Febreze did the same for my wrinkled clothes. Ignoring severe hunger pangs, I rushed off to the pep rally.

After parking six blocks away, I jogged to the pep rally. Walking often aggravated my back and jogging was even worse.

A raging bonfire cast an orange glow on the maroon and gold-clad throng, squeezed into a tight ring around the fire. The crowd was larger than I expected, but then enrollment had more than doubled since my days here. My eyes burned when the wind shifted my way, carrying smoke laced with the pleasant smell of burning hardwoods.

A quick scan of the crowd failed to locate Ronnie. It should be easy to spot a middle-age woman in this sea of youth. A familiar mannerism attracted my attention to a shapely young woman with purple highlights in her dark, cropped hair. Working my way around to get a better look, I soon realized she was Lorelei's old roommate, Amy.

When she glanced my direction, I turned away for fear she might think I was stalking her. Embarrassed, I blended into a group of people walking by. Looking back to see if she had recognized me, I collided with someone bigger and heavier than me.

After steadying me with bear-sized hands, he released me and stepped back. "Ya been drinkin, son?" He wore a uniform similar to the deputies at the sheriff's office but about a size too small and wrinkled as if it had been slept in for more than one night.

"No, I was distracted by someone I recognized. Sorry."

"That's quite alright. No harm done. Don't think I know ya. I'm Sheriff Matthew Sykes." He extended his right paw and we shook. "Ya here for the homecomin?" I tried to mask the pain from his vice-like grip.

"I'm Tanner Nole from Savannah. You probably don't remember me, but you and I met twenty-two years ago when I bailed my college roommate out of jail."

He paused as if searching for a faint memory. "Can't say I remember. That was a long time ago." He tapped his finger on his right temple. "But then the old rememberer ain't what it used to be. Stayin in town for a while or headin home after the game tomorrow?"

"I'm going home to pick up a few things and then come right back to investigate the alleged suicide of Lorelei Adams. You remember that case?"

He flinched and thought for a moment. "Sure, I remember it. My rememberer ain't that broke. We don't get that many suicides here. Damned shame, it was. What exactly ya investigatin?"

"Her mother questions that it was suicide. She can't believe her daughter could kill herself."

"Been sheriff here for nineteen years. Parents never believe their youngin could kill themselves. If they admit it, that would reflect badly on their parentin." He held out his hand to shake again. I reluctantly submitted my right hand to torture a second time. "Let me know if'n there's anythin I can do to hep ya."

My crushed hand ached. "Actually, there is. I need a copy of the incident report."

"Ya'd need to see Deputy Thomas bout that cause he's the one in charge of that investigation."

"I did. He said it hasn't been finalized yet."

"Well, there ya go. Stay outta trouble, now, ya hear?" He drew close to the left side of my face. "Best be careful. Ya'r rattlin some trees best left untouched. There are powerful forces at work there, and this county don't need no trouble like that."

His warning chilled me to the bone. He turned and rambled off.

The pep rally ended, and the crowd dwindled to a trickle. I abandoned my search for Ronnie and headed for my car, feeling disappointment. On the way, I tried phoning her again. For the third time, it rolled over to voice mail, "Hi, this is Ronnie Mason. When you hear the beep, you know what to do. Have a blessed day."

Instead of a beep, it was an artificial voice. "This voice mailbox is full and cannot accept any more messages. Please try your call again later. Goodbye."

I slammed my flip phone shut and wondered where the hell she was.

"Hey, aren't you Mr. Tanner?" I heard a feminine voice laced with Southern drawl.

Shading my eyes from the flashing blue lights of a parked sheriff's car, I recognized the lovely face of the deputy from this morning, controlling traffic at a pedestrian crossing. After releasing the waiting traffic, she approached.

I returned her warm smile. "Oh, hi. Sorry, but I'm terrible with names. It starts with Deputy, but I forgot the rest."

She chuckled, more out of politeness than overpowering humor. "You got that part right. It's Deputy Russo, but you can call me Mallory. Where're you parked, Mr. Tanner?"

"You're still calling me Mr. Tanner like I'm old and decrepit. Please call me Tanner."

"Oh, sensitive type, huh? I normally don't mesh well with the sensitive type. I'm too strong-natured for them."

"Is that what we're doing here, meshing?"

"Not yet, but if you wait a few minutes, I'll be off duty, and you can buy me a cup of coffee."

"I see what you mean about being a strong woman." She was too young to be interested in me as a suitor. Maybe she was just lonely. I certainly was.

Amy had mentioned that a lady deputy investigated the scene the night Lorelei died. There couldn't be that many female detectives on such a small force as Greene County's. She might have information I needed about Lorelei's death.

"You know, I am kind of thirsty now that you mention it. I could use a drink."

"Yeah, I bet you could." She walked to the middle of the street, stopped traffic for a few stragglers, and then returned. She grabbed both points of her shirt collar and wiggled them. "Hel—lo. Uniform. Can't be seen drinking in my uniform. It's coffee or goodnight."

"You know, I was just thinking I could use a cup of hot coffee. Know someplace serving good Joe this time of night?"

"Good, no. Hot, yes. How about you meet me at Baker's Diner in ten minutes? You should know where that is. It's been around forever."

Baker's Diner. I was becoming a regular there again.

49

CHAPTER 10

Bakers' Diner seemed grungier than I remembered. The floor needed a good mopping, and the sticky tabletop begged for a clean rag. Gray duct tape repairs on the maroon bench seat did little to prevent the cracks in the vinyl from cutting into my butt. Maybe I was paying more attention tonight without my Peaches to distract me.

I ordered a cup of coffee with cream and sugar. Waiting for the deputy to arrive, I realized I was nervous about this meeting. I told myself this wasn't a date, just coffee with someone having facts about Lorelei's death. Feeling inadequate as a detective, I became increasingly nervous.

It had only been five hours since my last Oxy. I needed one but couldn't spare any pills right now. I needed to remain sharp to get information from the deputy. Two cups of coffee later there was still no sign of Mallory. My anxiety morphed into dejection. The absence of a police report made it critical to glean information she had about the sheriff's investigation.

After three cups and a visit to the men's room, I gave up and stood at the register to pay. Over my shoulder, a woman said, "Sorry, Mr. Tanner. I got a call on the way here."

I turned around to a smiling but embarrassed deputy. "Well, good evening, Deputy Russo. I thought we were going to lose the 'Mister.' Let's start over. Hello, my name is Tanner." I stuck out my hand to shake. "And you are?"

She slapped my hand away and showed me a playful smile. "Okay, you win. Tanner it is. In return, promise me you'll lose that Deputy part and call me Mallory." I loved her accent.

We returned to my earlier booth and sat across from each other. "Sorry for the delay. I got a domestic violence call on the way here. Lucky for them, I didn't want to stand you up, so let them off with a verbal warning. It's not like there was any blood or anything. Otherwise, I'd be doing paperwork until midnight." She ordered coffee and cherry pie. "Try the cherry pie. They make it here fresh every day, or at least that's what they claim."

With the mention of food, my hunger pangs returned with a vengeance. I ordered cherry pie with two scoops of vanilla ice cream in the hope it would neutralize the building acid from three cups of bad coffee.

She reached behind her head, removed a hair pin and shook her head from side to side. Her French bun fell into long shining black locks that kissed her shoulders. The restaurant lights sparkled in her dark eyes. She looked very different with her hair down. Even with minimal makeup, she was stunning.

"Wha—at?" she asked with a lilt in her voice.

When her question snapped me out of my trance, I caught myself gaping at her with mouth wide open and tongue nearly hanging out. A sudden flush came over my face. I reminded myself of our age difference and collected my thoughts.

Our order arrived to spare me further embarrassment. "You're right," I said. "Pie looks delicious." The warm blush on my face faded with the coolness of the ice cream.

"Guess you don't get out much."

"Hate to admit it, but you're right." This young lady was easy to talk to, but I needed to focus on extracting information from her.

51

We chatted while we ate. I inhaled mine and ordered a second piece. I watched her eat and listened while waiting for my seconds. Mallory was fourteen years younger than me. She had never been married and wasn't ready to settle down, but that could be because she hadn't met the right guy. She claimed to be a bad judge of character. According to her, being a deputy did not attract guys like a nurse, flight attendant, or even an administrative assistant. It was a small town, so everyone knew her occupation.

She asked about me. I told her about my disastrous marriage and subsequent divorce but did not mention Ronnie or my reason for returning to Talmadge. Best no one knows too much about our connection from the past. Word gets around.

I told her about managing the dental practice in Savannah but withheld that I had been a practicing dentist until my back problems led to heavy Oxy usage. Losing your license due to drug-induced malpractice charges is not something you want to discuss with a cop, even one as lovely and easy to talk to as Mallory.

"Amy Hall, Lorelei's friend, said you were one of the deputies who responded to the call the night Lorelei died."

Mallory stopped eating and set her fork down. "So, is this why you agreed to meet me for coffee? I thought you might be lonely being from out of town. You kind of remind me of my older brother. But all you want is to interrogate me?" Customers stared at us.

I kicked myself for being so undiplomatic. "No, no. I am lonely and really appreciate you inviting me for coffee. I'm sorry I brought up Lorelei, but that is how we met, and it's on my mind."

She took a long sip of coffee. "Okay, go ahead. Ask me your questions, Mr. Tanner."

Her return to the use of my more formal name set off alarms in my head. I pondered whether I should try to repair the damage already done or go for it by asking pointed questions about Lorelei's death. I took a deep breath and went for it. "You were there that night. What do you think? Did Lorelei commit suicide, or was she murdered?"

She paused and looked away. I couldn't decide if she was composing an answer or stunned that I bulldozed forward and interrogated her.

She pushed her half-eaten piece of pie away from her. "The coroner ruled Lorelei's death a suicide." Her words oozed contempt.

"That's not what I asked. Do *you* think Lorelei committed suicide or was murdered?"

"I can't talk about an ongoing investigation." She stood and turned to leave. "Like I said, I'm a bad judge of character." She stormed out the door.

Every eye in the restaurant fixated on me. I paid the bill and left to find a bar. I needed a stiff drink.

CHAPTER 11

I awoke Saturday morning to a flashing light on my room phone. Sitting up triggered a nuclear explosion in my head and raised bile in my throat. I didn't remember leaving the bar last night or how I got back to my hotel room. The phone message was from Ronnie.

"Tanner, sorry I missed your calls. I got a migraine and couldn't force myself to go to the pep rally, so I turned off my phone and went to bed. I just left a message on your cell but thought I'd try your room phone. Can you meet me for breakfast today at, say eight? Got to be at work by nine. I'll be at Baker's Diner. You used to love that place. I never understood why. Oh, well, see you there."

I forgot to put my phone on its charger last night, so the battery died. After a few minutes on the charger, the phone confirmed a missed call and a voice message from Ronnie. I saved the voice message so I could hear her sweet voice anytime I wanted.

The clock displayed a quarter to eight. I leapt out of bed, stripped and dashed into the shower without waiting for the water to get warm. The cold helped sober me but worsened my headache.

I arrived at Baker's Diner fifteen minutes late. Ronnie sat in the same booth Mallory and I had occupied last night. The half-eaten remnants of her full house breakfast roiled my uneasy stomach.

"You look like shit," she said between bites. "Hope you don't mind I went ahead without you. Have to go to work, you know." Her sarcasm winged me.

I slid in on the other side. "Good morning to you, too."

The waitress approached with a paper order pad, no iPads here. I ordered orange juice and black coffee for my hangover and dry white toast to soak up the acid.

"What no cream and sugar? You always drink your coffee with cream and sugar." Ronnie looked at my bloodshot eyes and sniffed the air. "Oh, I see. Hung over this morning, are we? What were you celebrating last night?"

Ronnie's chiding felt like a sledge-hammer pounding on my aching head. The waitress brought my order. "I wasn't celebrating anything! Just trying to forget I had a daughter you never told me about."

I must have spoken too loudly because the restaurant went quiet as the other patrons' eyes locked on me. Fortunately, I didn't recognize anyone from last night, but then last night's details were a little hazy this morning.

After a prolonged silence, she set her fork down with a large bite of pancake on it. Her lovely eyes watered. "Look, I said I was sorry. I should have told you about Lorelei, but I can't change that now. Why can't you forgive me? Maybe we should call off the investigation."

Her outburst reminded me how she could always push my hot buttons. I drained my coffee and swallowed my anger. The burning hot coffee made me feel alive. Still angry, I held the mug aloft to attract the waitress's attention. She appeared in an instant as if watching us like everyone else in the restaurant. She refilled my coffee and disappeared.

Ronnie dabbed her eyes and glared at me. "So, it appears you still have a drinking problem."

Choking on hot coffee, I wondered how she knew about my drinking problem from a few years ago. Did she know about my Oxy addiction, too? Maybe she had kept tabs on me like I had with her. Hope for the two of us getting back together blossomed anew.

"No. I don't have a drinking problem. I have problems, mostly with women, that drive me to drink occasionally."

"Am I one of them? Women that drive you to drink, I mean?" A quick scan of the diner revealed that the other patrons had gone back to their own business.

Her pouty expression thawed my anger a little. I never could stay mad at this woman. "You're at the top of the list, my dear—the top of all my lists." My smile exuded warmth, and she returned it in kind. The ice between us melted away.

She retrieved her fork. "Your phone messages last night said you wanted to tell me something important."

"As a matter of fact, I do. You were right. Lorelei was murdered."

Ronnie dropped her fork on her plate again. A bite of pancake bounced off the table onto the floor. "Oh, my god! I knew it. My baby wouldn't kill herself. Do you have proof? If so, we need to talk to the sheriff." Her excitement caused my head to ache even more.

"I don't think it would be a good idea for me to talk to Sheriff Sykes yet. We need more evidence before we do that. Were you able to get a police report?"

She looked away and bit her lip. "No. I called, but they gave me the runaround. They said the case hasn't been closed yet. That doesn't make sense because they stopped investigating weeks ago. I'll stop by the sheriff's office after work." She slurped her coffee, a habit that had always annoyed me. Did she do it on purpose to bug me?

"You said you have proof. Don't we need to take it to the sheriff right away?"

"Let's just say, I found some circumstantial evidence—nothing concrete. If the sheriff's office is protecting someone, I'll need more compelling evidence to challenge them."

She leaned forward and whispered. "So, what made you decide it was murder?"

Leaning in, I could smell her floral perfume—Anaïs Anaïs, the same fragrance she wore when we were dating. A quick shake of the head refocused my thought process. "I read somewhere that women overwhelmingly favor less violent means of suicide. Lorelei had barbiturates stashed in her nightstand. She hated guns, so why would she shoot herself rather than use sleeping pills?" My head cleared some, but the headache hung on in full force.

She took a deep breath. "So you think the sheriff is covering up for somebody?"

"Not sure. It could be the sheriff or that deputy of his, Thomas Lowell. Tell me about Sykes. Why might he want to cover up the fact that Lorelei was murdered?"

"He's a real asshole. You know what he said to me? 'Your daughter committed suicide. Accept it as fact and get over it.' I think he's treading water until he retires next year. A murder investigation would make too many waves for him."

"You mentioned before that you suspected Reggie Braun might have murdered Lorelei. Is that because she was his mistress? Don't you think you should have told me about their relationship?"

Ronnie stopped eating and looked at me with her best innocent look. "I'm sure I mentioned it. Did you check those notes on your napkins?"

"Yes, but I would have remembered that important detail. Look, Ronnie, you have to be totally open with me, or I can't do my job here. Why didn't you tell me?"

She looked away as if checking who might be looking. "If I didn't tell you, I'm sorry. It's not something I like to talk about. Okay?"

It wasn't okay, but I went on. "Tell me about Reggie and start with how they met."

"I don't know how she met him. We didn't talk much about him because it always ended in a shouting match. Reggie owns half the town and pretty much gets away with anything. That's why I think the sheriff is covering up for him. That's about all I know."

I sensed she knew more but didn't want to share it. She seemed to be dancing around the details of our daughter's relationship with this horrible man. I wanted to confront her but feared it might end my chances to collect more information from her. I now wanted to solve this crime, not just use the investigation as an excuse to see Ronnie.

"Okay, then. I'll start with Reggie."

She placed her hand on mine. "Oh, thank you, Tanner. You don't know how much this means to me."

Her touch and words sent a thrill down my spine and gave me hope we might reignite our past torrid relationship.

"Where would I find Reggie?"

"He has an office south of town—Braun Enterprises. You might start there, but they won't be open today or tomorrow. Didn't you say you need to be back in Savannah on Monday morning?"

I hate being confronted with reality. "Maybe I'll call in sick. I have sick days to spare." That was a bold-faced lie. I was on thin ice at work. Another sick day on a Monday would raise a red flag due to my history of opioid and alcohol problems.

She checked the time on her cell phone. "Oh, shit. I'm late." She slipped on her jacket, retrieved the check and stood. "I'll take care of your breakfast. It's the least I can do. Are you still going to the game this afternoon?"

"Don't have a ticket yet, but plan to go. It seems I can't do much on the investigation until Monday."

"Maybe I'll see you there."

"Wait, aren't you on your way to work?"

"We're closing early today because of the game. Tim has been pushing me to go with him. I guess it's time. Maybe we'll see you there and you can meet Tim."

My emotions were mixed. I reveled at the prospect of seeing Ronnie again but didn't want to meet the root of my jealousy.

"You said you'd go by the sheriff's office to request a copy of the police report."

"Oh, yeah. I'll stop by after the game, I guess."

"Please do. I need that report."

After Ronnie left, I realized how much my back and head ached. I downed an Oxy, not as much for back pain as for my aching heart.

CHAPTER 12

After a long, drug-induced nap, I drove to the football stadium and purchased a single ticket from the box office. Despite being a much larger school now, they hadn't sold out for homecoming, confirming the home team stunk as bad as always

My seat was decent but on the opponent's side of the field. I half-watched the game while scouring the Owl fan seats on the opposite side for Ronnie.

A father and his coed daughter sitting in front of me exhibited a closeness that created an aching in my gut. That could have been Lorelei and me. Even though I never met her, I missed her as much as if she had been an integral part of my life.

Pumped up for homecoming, the Owls played above their normal pathetic level and led by six points at halftime. Despite the lingering vestiges of my hangover, my stomach let out a loud growl. The fans next to me looked at each other and laughed. Blushing in embarrassment, I bolted for the concession stand to feed the raging beast in my gut.

I stopped cold at the unexpected sight of Deputy Lowell, sipping a beer near the door of an executive box wearing an Owls jersey and designer blue jeans. He stood, chatting with a middle-aged man dressed like a GQ cover model in a tan sport coat and an Augusta National golf shirt. The two talked with their faces only a foot apart as if they feared being overheard. Behind them, a striking younger woman in tight black leather pants, black low-cut Owls sweater, and six-inch stilettos looked as if she just stepped off a fashion runway. Oblivious to the two men, she scanned the crowd, reminiscent of a bird seeking prey.

Eyes glued to the deputy, I stepped backward and collided with a woman in a well-worn Owl's jacket. Before I could apologize, I heard Ronnie's sweet voice, "Tanner! I want . . ."

I hushed her mid-sentence with a finger to my lips, grabbed her arm and guided her out of the deputy's ear range. "Tanner, what are you doing?"

I relaxed my grip. "Sorry, Ronnie. I spotted Deputy Lowell and feared he might hear you. He was talking to a well-coiffed couple dripping money."

"Oh, really? Sounds like he was kissing up to Reggie and Tanya Braun. I'm sure he's pumping Reggie to fund his campaign for sheriff in the next election."

"They looked real cozy." Almost whispering in her ear, I caught a wisp of her familiar perfume, and my heart rate increased ten beats per minute.

A stocky man, wearing a jacket matching Ronnie's, glared at me as he approached. He slid his arm around her. Their eyes met and smiles spread across their faces. "Hey, honey. I'd like you to meet Tanner. Tanner, this is my husband, Tim. I'm so glad for you two to finally meet."

Tim's adoring smile for her turned into a scowl as we checked each other out like two foes probing for weaknesses in preparation for mortal combat. Several inches shorter and twenty pounds heavier than me, he appeared to be ten years younger. If not for my bad back, I felt confident I could take him.

While maintaining eye contact, he shook my hand with a punishing grip. "Nice to finally meet ya, Tanner. Ronnie's told me so much about ya." I looked to see if his nose was growing.

I hated this guy and suspected he hated me too. We aspired for the same prize, and both knew it. Still, I tried to be diplomatic. "Hello, Tim. Ronnie's told me a lot about you," I lied in return. At our meetings at the diner, I discouraged her from talking about her husband. The less I knew the less real he seemed. I had met my opponent. He was not only real but tough competition. Mentally I kicked myself in the ass for being so stupid.

"Ronnie says you have proof Lorelei was murdered."

"It's not what I'd call solid proof yet, but I am convinced Ronnie's right about it being a murder. My challenge is developing enough evidence to convince the sheriff to reopen the investigation. It appears they're covering for somebody, maybe Reggie."

Tim clenched his fists. "I hope to see that sleaze-ball fry fer this. He corrupted our sweet little Lorelei. Let me know if there's anything I can do to help nail that prick."

His affection for Lorelei made me jealous. The last two years he had filled my role as Lorelei's father, and I felt cheated.

The emptiness I experienced watching the father and daughter sitting in front of me returned with a vengeance. I trapped that emotion and stuffed it in a mental pigeon hole as men are prone to do. I couldn't show weakness in front of my adversary. "Ronnie said you were close to Lorelei. I may need to ask you a few questions as the investigation proceeds."

Ronnie likely sensed the tension in the air and strove to break it. "Why don't you call Tim later to set something up?"

We all knew I didn't have his number and probably would never call him, but we let that slide.

"Where you sitting?" Ronnie's eyes reached out to me and touched my soul. Tim noticed and nudged her.

"I'm sitting between the Owls' thirty- and forty-yard lines on the opponents' side about three-fourths of the way up."

"We're across the field from each other," Ronnie said. "We're on the Owls' thirty-yard line on the other side about halfway up."

Tim nudged her with his shoulder. Not wanting to witness their interaction, I gazed around. For an awkward moment they too looked about until I broke the silence. "Look, I haven't eaten yet today and need to find food before I pass out. Nice meeting you, Tim." I stepped forward and shook his hand goodbye. He squeezed my hand much harder this time, so I squeezed back as hard I dared without my face reddening. After grueling seconds, that seemed like minutes, I withdrew my stinging hand and locked eyes with Ronnie, "I'll be in touch." I may have blown her a kiss too, but if so, he didn't seem to notice, and she didn't respond.

"Tanner, thanks so much for looking into it. Tim and I appreciate it." They each put an arm around the other and headed back toward their seats.

Ronnie's amorous interaction with her husband served as a sobering slap in the face. Their embrace was a cold shower. Anger swelled inside me. I asked myself, *what in the hell am I doing here?*

CHAPTER 13

My jealousy tempted me to stalk Tim and Ronnie, but before I could act he stopped short and pulled her aside. I ducked behind a pillar and watched.

His face in hers, he glared at her. "You're still in love with him, aren't you?"

Ronnie recoiled as if stung by a bee. "What are you talking about? I don't love him anymore. He's just an old friend who is helping me—I mean us—by looking into Lorelei's murder."

"Ronnie, don't lie to me. I saw the way he looked at you. He's still in love with you."

Her head jerked back, and her eyes popped wide open as a small smile graced her lips. She shook her head and spoke in a shrill voice. "Tim, there's nothing there. I swear. We're just old friends. Yes, we were once lovers, but that's long gone. You are the love of my life. No old flame can ever change that. I love you."

I was convinced she was lying to him or at least hoped she was.

"Oh, yeah? Why's he doing this investigation for ya and not charging anything? He's doing it to get closer to ya. I'm saying he's still in love with ya."

Her mouth moved below gaping eyes like she was speaking, but no words came out.

He broke the silence. "Tell him to drop the investigation and go back home. I don't want him around ya because I don't trust him."

Tears welled up in her eyes. "What about trusting me? The sheriff won't listen to me. He's covering for Reggie, I know it. Tanner is our best hope to prove she was murdered. Please, give him a chance. You've got nothing to worry about."

"Let it go, Ronnie. She's gone. Nothing will change that. What does it matter whether she was murdered or killed herself?"

"It matters to me, and it should matter to you. I thought you loved Lorelei." She dabbed her eyes with a tissue.

"Honey, ya know I loved her as much as if she was mine. I just hate seeing this tear ya up so."

"Take me home. I want to go home. It was a mistake coming to the game. I'm not ready yet." She turned and marched toward the exit.

Tim breathed a large sigh and fished in his pocket for his keys.

I should have been elated at the discord in their marriage. It gave me the opening I sought. But for some strange reason, it disturbed me in a way I'd not expected.

CHAPTER 14

Hope of reconnecting with Ronnie was the sad dream of a sick man. What I saw in their interaction was her adoration for her husband, and it made me dislike myself for loving her. My appetite vanished, so I purchased two large beers with my dwindling cash and returned to my seat.

Early in the third quarter, the Owls squandered their halftime lead. It didn't matter anymore. As I drank my two beers, agitation and depression took hold and festered. I felt as empty as the two Dixie cups I crushed on the floor beneath my seat. At the end of the third quarter I had had enough of the game and self-pity. I grew to hate the loving father and daughter sitting in front of me. Swearing off women for the rest of my life, I bolted for the exit. All they ever gave me was pain. I needed another beer, or better yet, an Oxy.

In the parking lot, Deputy Mallory Russo appeared to be giving directions to an elderly couple. When they walked away, I approached from her blind side and tapped her on the shoulder. Surprised, she jumped and spun around to face me. With her recognition came a big sigh of relief followed by a scowl that indicated I was on her shit list.

She turned and walked away without speaking, so I called out to her. "Mallory, hold on, please. I want to apologize. I know I was an asshole last night."

She stopped but didn't turn around. I approached and laid a tender hand on her shoulder. She turned and looked me in the eyes. Her harsh facial expression softened to a look of indifference. "So, you were saying something about being an asshole last night."

"I met you for coffee because I'm lonely and you seemed lonely too. It was a nice gesture on your part, and I'm sorry for putting you on the spot with questions about Lorelei's investigation. That was wrong. I do want to be friends." I really meant it. A friend might share what they knew about Lorelei's death.

She scowled. "Friends? Now you want to be friends?"

"Hey, you said there weren't many good-looking guys in Greene County."

"Oh, so now you think you're good-looking. I think it was Tom Wolfe who said, 'The surest cure for vanity is loneliness.'" She smiled.

"Wow! A closet philosopher. Pretty and smart, too."

"Just to be clear, I just want to be friends. I'm not hitting on you or anything. It's hard to have many friends when you work the odd shifts I work. Understood?"

A naïve blush swept over my face. It hadn't occurred to me she might be interested in me romantically. As an only child, I had always longed for a sister.

Besides, I needed information from her but would be more subtle this time.

CHAPTER 15

That night I took Mallory to dinner at a moderately priced restaurant she frequented. Earlier I had scraped together enough small bills and pocket change to cover the check and an embarrassingly small tip to avoid the disgrace of a declined credit card. She must have picked up on that because, as we left, she snuck a five on the table behind my back to boost the tip.

When we reached her house, she asked if I wanted to come in for a drink and assured me conversation was all she was after.

I accepted because I had limited myself to one glass of house wine at dinner due to my cash shortage. Thankfully she had followed my lead on drinks, or I might not have been able to cover the check.

She served a dry white wine and then sat on an overstuffed chair. When I was a practicing dentist, and had money, I considered myself to be a wine connoisseur. Wines had changed since then, and all I knew was I liked the wine she served and told her so.

I sat across from her on the plush sofa. When she wasn't looking, I downed an Oxy.

She poured me a second, generous glass. "How's your investigation going?"

Finally, an opening to pump her for information. "Slow. I really need that police report. When do you think it will issue?"

"Another week, maybe two. The coroner suddenly resigned in the middle, so we now have a new coroner, and he's still coming up to speed. How long do you expect your investigation to take?"

That seemed an odd question to ask rather than how long I might be in town. "Until it's done." We were both playing it close to the vest. "Don't you think it odd that Lorelei shot herself in the temple rather than the mouth?"

"No, not at all. Research has shown most handgun suicides are in the side of the head rather than the mouth. Hollywood and the news media have created a misperception."

"In which temple did she shoot herself—right or left?"

Mallory's head jerked back and her eyes bulged for a brief moment before she regained composure. "Why do you ask?"

"I'm not an expert on the subject but would think it natural for someone to use the gun in their dominant hand. Am I right?"

Mallory tensed. "Statistically speaking, you are correct, but it's not a hundred percent. For some unknown reason, some use their recessive hand. What was Lorelei's dominant side?"

"I don't know, but I'll check with her mother." I did know but was holding things close to my vest and sensed she was doing the same. The standoff put the kibosh on conversation. Thankfully she changed the subject, but our conversation remained tense. The combination of alcohol and opioid soon made me drowsy. Rather than let an escaping yawn embarrass me, I suggested we call it a night.

We said our goodbyes at her doorstep. The investigation seemed a million miles away. It was just Mallory and me. The opioid and alcohol had eased my discomfort from the information exchange and erased my inhibitions. The raging depressants in my bloodstream distorted all logic. I moved closer to her. She pushed back. "Just friends, remember?"

Reality came crashing down. This sweet young lady had invited me into her home as a friend. In return, I had pumped her for information and then became a dirty old man.

I was in love with Ronnie. In a way, kissing Mallory would have been cheating on her. Depression weighed on me as I tried to stand without swaying.

I apologized for my actions and claimed to be a two-drink drunk. An awkward lull persisted as I considered what to do next. She rescued me from my deliberation by leaning forward and giving me a sisterly peck on the cheek.

I felt better about myself as I returned to my car.

Behind the wheel, I became even drowsier and fought to stay awake. How I made it back to my hotel without incident is a mystery to me. Thankfully I didn't get pulled over.

CHAPTER 16

On Sunday I awoke late morning, checked out and drove home to Savannah. Exhausted from the trip home, I set my alarm for an early start Monday morning and popped an Oxy to help me sleep. After a great night's sleep, I struggled to get up on Monday.

Savannah Advanced Dental didn't open until nine. Hot scalding coffee and an Egg McMuffin made the wait in the parking lot tolerable. My fast food obsession played hell with my health, but it was cheap, and my bank account was nearly depleted.

Dr. Neena Chiru parked in her reserved space, unlocked the door and entered the brick and glass professional building. I wiped grease off my hands and face, tossed the dregs of my cold breakfast sandwich into the paper bag and followed her in. Standing in her doorway, I watched her go through her morning routine, turning on lights and booting her laptop. I mustered enough confidence to tap on the door.

"Oh good, you're back. What brings you in so early on a Monday morning? That's so unlike you." She leaned over and keyed in her password.

Mornings are tough for me. Oxy makes getting out of bed difficult. Mondays presented a nearly impossible challenge following a weekend of heavy indulgence. Fortunately, it only came once a week, fifty-two times a year. I summoned all the humility I could muster short of kneeling. "Sorry to bother you so early, Neena, but something's come up, and I need a leave of absence."

She stood bolt upright, arms crossed in front of her, burning holes in me with glaring eyes. "Leave of absence? Hell, it's hard sometimes to tell that you work here. You're always calling out sick, especially on Mondays." She paused, took a breath. "Look, Tanner, we've been friends for what—fifteen years? You know I've always been straight with you. This is not a good time to be taking off. It's the end of our fiscal year, and you haven't kept the paperwork up, so our accounting records are an absolute nightmare." Her focus shifted to her laptop as she logged into our practice management system. "How long are we talking?"

I felt like a schoolboy being dressed down by his teacher. "Two weeks, three tops."

"Three weeks! Come on, Tanner, be reasonable. What's it been, three years since you were busted for opioid addiction and lost your license? The other partners and I felt sorry for you and threw you a lifeline. We bought you out at a generous price and created this practice management position for you. I'm constantly catching grief from the other partners about your performance, or lack thereof. They want to fire you, but for some godforsaken reason, I keep defending you. If I tell them you're taking a leave of absence, they'll insist we let you go. I doubt I can convince them otherwise this time."

Given my crumbling financial position, I needed this job. Courage waning, I pressed on. "Neena, I appreciate everything the partners have done for me, especially you. You've gone out on a limb for me time and time again. I wouldn't ask if it weren't important. You know that."

"Do I?" She dropped her arms to her sides in a sign of frustration, but her scowl faded somewhat. "Alright. What is so damned important that you need three weeks off? You aren't getting married again, are you?"

I chuckled. "No, nothing like that. If I were, you would be invited to the wedding, maybe even be my best man." She glowered in response to my weak attempt at humor. I pressed on. "This is different. While in Talmadge, I learned I fathered a child twenty years ago."

Neena snapped to attention, her face turning pensive. "Tanner, is that good news?"

I looked down. "Yes, and no. She died a month ago. The sheriff's office ruled it a suicide, but evidence suggests it might have been murder. They may be covering for some rich guy who owns half the town. It's up to me to prove it was murder. I've never done anything for my only child, so it's important to me to do this for her. If it were your daughter, you'd feel the same way." I realized the truth in my words. In spite of my strong desire to reconnect with Ronnie, my daughter had become my true motivation to look into her death. I felt committed to the investigation, and reconnecting with Ronnie became secondary.

Neena shook her head, and a tear trickled down her right cheek. "Tanner, I'm so sorry for your loss." She stared at me for a long moment before waving her hand as if brushing something away. "Oh, shit. Do what you need to do. No guarantees, but I'll do what I can to see your job is here for you when you get back. I'll tell them a week, maybe two. Just make sure it's not three. Okay?"

Relief surged through me. "Thanks, Neena. I owe you big time."

"You already owe me big time. Good luck with your investigation. Keep in touch."

We hugged for several minutes. We had been close friends for a long time. Old friends are the best friends.

Despite my exhaustion, I left for Talmadge right away, my Ford Probe packed with sufficient clothes to last two weeks. I didn't own enough for three.

My thoughts floated back to Mallory for some unknown reason. As I replayed our exchange about Lorelei's death, I suspected she was befriending me to spy on me. The question was, for whom—the sheriff, Deputy Lowell, or maybe even Reggie? It appeared Reggie had a broad range of influence, so it wasn't as preposterous as it first sounded. I needed information from her but pledged to be careful.

Nearing Talmadge, thoughts of Lorelei's death pushed Mallory to the sidelines of my consciousness. In reaction, the car slowed. Elderly drivers passed me, shaking their fists. One little blue-haired lady even flipped me off.

At the city limits, my thoughts swung to my Peaches and further distracted my driving. My obsession with Ronnie still thrived deep inside my being. My growing desire to see her forced my right foot down harder. As I re-passed some of those slow elderly drivers, I gave them a big smile and waved. The blue-haired lady got a special one-finger wave.

CHAPTER 17

I could have called Ronnie to let her know I was back, but insatiable desire drew me to her house. She didn't work Mondays, but Tim did. I parked two blocks from her house and walked just to be safe. In a small town, a strange car sitting in the driveway would generate juicy gossip. Logic dictated that nothing was going to happen. Lust fueled unwarranted optimism anyway. With each step, my pulse quickened.

To my surprise, an attractive, gray-haired woman opened the door and scrutinized me, her wrinkled eyes and nose hinting disapproval. Fearing I had the wrong house, I searched for a graceful way to get out of this uncomfortable situation without alerting a neighbor to keep an eye on me.

Her face turned harsh, causing my heart to beat faster. "Whatever you're selling, young man, we don't want any." She spoke in a slow, elegant Southern drawl, reminiscent of the old South.

From a distance, Ronnie's faint voice graced my ears. "Who is it, Mom?"

The lady shouted over her shoulder. "Not sure yet. He's either a sad excuse for a Jehovah's Witness or a serial killer—maybe both."

"It's Tanner," I shouted loud enough for Ronnie to hear.

The old lady's glare turned murderous. "Oh, my word. You're Tanner Nole? How in God's name do you have the gumption to bother Ronnie after breaking her heart all those many years ago?"

"Hold on. I'll be there in a minute." Delight laced Ronnie's voice.

"So you're Ronnie's mother. We've never met, but I see where her great looks come from." I extended a hand as a peace offering, waiting for her to volunteer her name.

"Ronnie said you were quite the bullshitter. Seems she was right. And then you possess the nerve to show up unannounced."

"Mother, let him in." The elderly lady stepped back to let me enter. After I passed, she poked her head out the door. "Where's your car?"

I summoned up the will to not look as guilty as I felt. "Uh, I parked down the street. I wasn't sure which house it was, so when I reached the neighborhood, I parked and walked."

Skepticism washed across her wrinkled face, and the elegance in her drawl turned edgy. "Hmm. That's about the dumbest excuse I ever heard. You look as guilty as sin to me. You wouldn't be waltzing back in here after all these years, intending to sweep my daughter off her feet again, would you?" I couldn't think of an appropriate response, so she resumed her diatribe. "I won't let that happen. I gauran-damn-tee it."

Ronnie, drying her hands on a dish towel, rescued me. "Mom! Please! Be nice." She gave me a warm smile. "Tanner, I'm sorry. Mother can be spirited." The word "cantankerous" seemed a better description.

"Mom, I asked Tanner to look into Lorelei's death so we can get her case reopened." Her eyes met mine in a smile, lacking the old sparkle in her eyes I craved. "We're about to sit down for lunch. Care to join us?"

Against better judgment, I agreed to stay. My earlier appetite vanished under the noxious gaze of her mother, who sent chills through me.

We dined on tomato sandwiches and guzzled sweet tea. Ronnie opened a bag of kettle chips to stretch the meal for the unexpected guest. She asked me to say grace, so I cleared my throat and somehow stumbled through it despite not having prayed in over a decade.

Conversation over lunch felt labored, to say the least. Her mother's name was Maggie Mae, like in the Rod Stewart song. She had lived in Atlanta when Ronnie and I dated, so I had never met her before. Her traits and mannerisms reminded me of Ronnie.

Maggie Mae's questions about my employment created anxiety. My work history is intertwined with drug and alcohol problems I didn't care to share. My back problem provided a convenient excuse for leaving dentistry without mentioning substance abuse. Technically speaking, it wasn't a lie because chronic back pain triggered my need for pain meds. Ronnie's cynical gaze suggested she might be more familiar with my history than she let on.

Maggie Mae's interrogation moved on to recent romances. I considered mentioning Mallory to test Ronnie's response but decided there was no upside. If Ronnie exhibited jealousy, it might send her over-protective mother into defensive mode. If Ronnie reacted indifferent, it would break my heart. Besides, my friendship with Mallory was part of my investigation.

Maggie Mae expressed concern about my lack of a romantic relationship with a woman in several years. She looked right at me with a straight face and asked, "Are you gay?"

Ronnie burst into laughter, spewing iced tea from her mouth and nose.

"No, I'm not gay. I just haven't found anyone as special as your daughter." As soon as I said it, I regretted it. Ronnie's face turned blank, not the response I had hoped for.

Her mother's snarl did not surprise me. It was clear she resided in Tim's court and considered me a threat to her daughter's happiness. I regretted my surprise visit and wondered how I could escape this uncomfortable situation with any self-respect.

After a short, uncomfortable silence, Maggie Mae resumed the interrogation. My crime investigation credentials didn't appear to impress her. She used the word "foolish" more than once in that discussion.

Tired of being on the defensive, I took advantage of a brief break in the questioning and changed subjects. "Can we talk about suspects for a moment?"

Maggie Mae stood and gathered her plate, glass and dinnerware. "I'll clean up while you two talk."

"But, Mom, you didn't finish your sandwich."

"All of a sudden, I'm not hungry. Besides, you can't buy good tomatoes this time of year." She dumped her sandwich in the garbage and placed the dishes and silverware in the dishwasher before attacking the kitchen floor with a broom and dustpan.

Ronnie shrugged and smiled. In a hushed tone, she said, "Mom never cleans my house. Maybe you should stop by more often."

The idea of stopping by again warmed me inside. I spoke in a soft voice so Maggie Mae wouldn't hear me. "She doesn't seem to like me very much."

"You broke my heart when you left. Things were rough with the pregnancy and all. She and Dad moved back here to support me. I don't think I could have gotten through it without them. She's very protective of me. Give her some time to forgive you, and she'll come around."

"Have you forgiven me?"

She looked away as if searching for the right words. "Yes, I guess I finally have. Otherwise, I wouldn't ask you to investigate Lorelei's death."

"I've lost my appetite too." Pushing my plate away, I pulled out the napkins with my notes and searched for a blank one. "Do you have a pen I can borrow?"

Ronnie stood and gathered our plates, both holding half-eaten sandwiches. "You know, Mom's right. You can't get good tomatoes this time of year." She took the dishes to the kitchen and returned with a pen and a note pad. "Here, use some real paper."

I took the pad and pen. Her pad of paper served as a blotter beneath my napkin. "Thanks, but I lose paper pads. For some strange reason, napkins are easier for me to keep track of."

Maggie Mae finished sweeping and wiped off the table, likely to eavesdrop better.

"Let's talk suspects. I know Reggie Braun is your main suspect, but who else might have killed her or been involved? I don't want to miss something important."

Ronnie did not hesitate. "I can't think of anyone else. Everyone loved my daughter. You would have, too."

The words stung like the lash of a bullwhip. She had said *my daughter* rather than *our daughter*. Her last words rubbed it in. Ronnie tilted her head toward her mother and mouthed the words to me, *"She doesn't know."* I sat in stunned silence. Even her mother didn't know the truth about Lorelei's true father. Anger swelled in me.

Maggie Mae perked up. "I don't know why you're wasting time looking into other possible killers. It was Reggie Braun, clear and simple."

"Why are you so convinced it was him? Is it because he was having an affair with Lorelei?"

There was an awkward silence. I gazed at one and then the other. "What are you not telling me?"

Staring at her mother with clinched jaw, Ronnie gave her a slight shake of her head before looking at me. "That's the reason we both think he did it."

Maggie Mae had to say more. "I think he was angry with her because she started dating that other guy."

"What other guy?"

Ronnie cast her mother a dirty look. "She's talking about Brandon."

"Yes, that's his name. Never cared much for that boy."

"Mother! You don't know him. You met him one time for about ten minutes."

"How many boyfriends did she have?"

Ronnie took offense. "Just the two and don't go passing judgment on her. She grew up a fine young lady. You, of all people, have no room to judge her."

A pert nod from Maggie Mae showed her concurrence.

There was obviously more to this love triangle, but I let it slide. "Who else should I look at?"

"You need to put Ray on that list," Maggie Mae said. "He hated her sin, that righteous son of a bitch."

"Mom, please. Ray loved her and would never have done anything to hurt her."

"That's Raymond Adams, your first husband, correct?" I should have said "and Lorelei's father" for Maggie Mae's sake, but couldn't do it. I added Ray to the list without an assigned ranking.

"What about Amy?" I asked.

"Amy?" Ronnie rocked back in her chair. "Amy's a sweetheart. She and Lorelei were thick as thieves. No, it couldn't have been her."

"I don't know—the way she dresses and all," Maggie Mae said.

Maggie Mae must not have approved of Amy's gothic look. Still, I added her name to the list without understanding why. "What about

Sheriff Sykes?" I wasn't sure if I suspected him, his deputy or both covering-up the murder.

Ronnie glanced at her mother. "What do you think, Mom? You dated him."

Maggie Mae glowered at her daughter. "Please. We had dinner twice before I discovered he was married. He's guilty of being a lying, adulterous asshole, but I can't see an officer of the law murdering an innocent young girl."

The sheriff went on the list anyway. "What about this Deputy Lowell? He seemed real tight with Reggie."

Maggie Mae said, "Word about town is Sykes will retire rather than run for reelection next year. Lowell has made it clear he wants that office and has been kissing up to Reggie to fund his campaign. I don't know if it is true, but some say he is related to Reggie—a second cousin or something. Others say they were fraternity brothers at some hoity-toity eastern school."

That could explain why he was sucking up to Reggie at the game. "Is there anyone else I should suspect or at least question?"

After a long silence, I laid the pen on the table, sensing the time had come to depart.

Collecting my napkins, I stood and stuffed my notes in my back pocket. "All right then, I'll get going on the investigation. Thanks for the delicious lunch. I haven't eaten a tomato sandwich in years."

Like a good hostess, Ronnie stood to show me out. "Sorry about the tomatoes. Where are you staying?"

"I don't know, maybe the Ballard Inn again. It's cheap."

Maggie Mae stood, face showing disapproval. "That place has become a dump. Who knows what you might catch in a place like that. Why don't you stay at my place? I've got plenty of room."

Her offer flabbergasted me. Why would an old lady who hated me, invite me into her home? Then I realized—she wanted to keep an eye on me. "Thank you. That's very generous, Maggie Mae, but I come and go at all hours. I don't want to frighten you. Where would you suggest I stay?"

Several hotel recommendations later, I thanked them, and Ronnie walked me to the door while her mother toiled in the kitchen.

Ronnie fidgeted in a cute manner. Although I couldn't see any sign of her mother, I could feel her eyes and ears on me from somewhere.

Taking her hands in mine, I gave Ronnie my best seductive smile. "The reason I stopped by is to tell you I'm all in on this investigation. I've taken a leave of absence from my job to be here until I find Lorelei's killer."

Ronnie's eyes bulged, and her jaw dropped. "Oh, Tanner, thank you." She closed the gap between us and hugged me tight.

I wrapped my arms around her. She laid her head on my shoulder, and her tears soaked my collar. It felt great! I prayed Maggie Mae wouldn't notice the instinctive rise in my pants. Ronnie must have felt my erection because she recoiled from the hug and looked down at my crotch. She grinned, blushing ever so slightly, and cleared her throat.

I turned and fled before Maggie Mae noticed the condemning bulge in my pants that would have validated her suspicions about my intentions.

CHAPTER 18

After exploring room rates for the hotels Maggie Mae and Ronnie had recommended, I realized I couldn't afford any of them. Ballard Inn, where I stayed last weekend, had no availability, so I checked into CrossRoads Inn. This place proved to be an even worse dump than Ballard Inn, but at least it was cheap.

The carpet was so dusty and grimy even the sickening-sweet spray cheap hotels use couldn't mask the stench. Poorly insulated walls did little to attenuate vehicle noise from the busy street below despite being one floor up. Parted curtains added daylight but no airflow from the frozen sliding window. What little light filtered through the murky window illuminated dust particles dancing in the air. I left the outside door ajar, hoping to air out the room. In the bathroom, gray grout, that may have once been white, framed faded blue plastic tile. A stained and yellowed shower curtain hung from half the normal number of rings on a crooked bar spanning a tub with rusty patches of cast iron peeking through gray-grungy porcelain, bordered by black mold. I made mental note to buy Lysol spray and shower thongs. Still, it would require some luck to not catch something from my room.

It didn't take long to move my stuff in. I left my clothes in the suitcase on the valet stand. Based on the thickness of the dust in the dresser drawers, no one had used them in a long time.

I took an Oxy, more for my aching heart than my sore back. While home, I had scraped together the dregs of Oxy I could find. Dosages varied from twenty to sixty mg. Some were outdated by more than a year but yet too valuable to discard. Still, there wasn't enough to cover my needs for two weeks, forcing me to cut back progressively and prepare myself for inevitable withdrawal unless a new source could be secured. I split them into three containers—a small pocket pill case to keep with me and two prescription bottles to hide in the room. The first bottle went into a Ziploc bag hidden in the toilet tank, and the other was duct-taped underneath a nightstand. Neither hiding spot seemed very creative, but a sparsely-furnished room provided few opportunities for concealing contraband.

By three PM, I had finished unpacking with enough time to conduct one interview before dinner. I called Reggie Braun's office to schedule a meeting. His secretary took my information and promised to call me back.

I next turned to Ray Adams, Lorelei's first stepfather and number three on the list. He worked as an auto mechanic at a small garage nearby. Ronnie warned me he didn't carry his phone when working, so I grabbed my car keys and headed his way without calling ahead. Stepping onto the open-air balcony, a deep cleansing breath triggered a wild coughing spree. I prayed that in time I would build up resistance to my slum of a room.

CHAPTER 19

The small repair shop where Ray worked did not live up to its name, Central Georgia AutoWerks. A cluster of dust-covered older cars and pickups surrounded a free-standing building badly needing fresh paint and its windows replaced or at least, cleaned.

The glass swinging door emitted a spine-chilling screech as it swept over its threshold. A strange mix of sulfurous transmission oil, aging rubber and sickening sweet antifreeze filled my nose, threatening another coughing bout. Overhead fluorescent lights created a shadowy environment thanks to a heavy coating of grime and several flickering or burned out lights. Years of automotive fluid spills had darkened and slickened the concrete floor.

A man wearing blue Goodyear coveralls leaned over the fender of a bronze Chrysler product, his head buried in the engine compartment. He beat on a wrench with a three-pound mall under the hood.

"Excuse me." The man kept hammering away. "Excuse me."

The wrench slipped from his grip and clanged several times during its fall through the engine compartment but never reached the floor. "Dagnabbit." The angry man stood, swinging his head to avoid hitting the hood, the move of an experienced mechanic. Shorter than I expected, he muttered under his breath while shaking his left hand like it was stinging. It seemed odd a mechanic would refrain from swearing under such circumstances. The wall held a large framed picture of Jesus knocking on a door with no door knob. Maggie Mae's reference to him as "a righteous son of a bitch" now made sense.

He set the mall down and wiped his stinging hand with a dirty, red shop towel. "Oh, hi. Sorry for my little temper tantrum there. Can I help you?"

"Hi. My name is Tanner Nole. Ronnie talked to you about my investigation into your daughter's death."

He scooped cleanser from a can and rubbed it over his hands. "Yeah, she called me. Your name sounds familiar. Have we met before?" He wiped his hands off on a shop rag and tossed it into a collection can made from a small oil drum.

"No, I'm an old college friend of Ronnie's."

"Oh, yeah. How could I forget? Ronnie talked about you all the time— I mean, *all* the time." A dark frown punctuated his statement. He offered his newly cleaned hand. "I'm Ray Adams, but you already knew that. Glad to meet you." He shook my hand aggressively. "You know, you broke that poor young lady's heart. I'm not complaining, though, because your loss became my gain." Ray smiled with a faraway dreamy look in his eyes, hinting I was not the only ex still in love with Ronnie.

My right hand felt greasy from residual hand cleaner.

"Oh, I'm sorry. Here." He snatched a clean shop rag off the top of a pile and handed it to me. "Are you a private eye? I've never met one of those before."

"No, I'm just an old friend who Ronnie asked to look into Lorelei's death."

"You mean, murder."

"So you agree with Ronnie it was murder rather than suicide?"

"Absolutely. Lorelei would never kill herself. She had too much going for her despite her sinful behavior."

"I understand you didn't approve of her lifestyle choices."

"Is that what they call it now, 'lifestyle choices'? The Good Book calls it prostitution. Satan prefers us to refer to things as a lifestyle choice. It's a more forgiving name for an unforgivable sin."

It hurt to hear him call my daughter a prostitute. I felt compelled to defend her honor. "I wouldn't call an affair with a married man, prostitution."

"I guess you didn't know about the business side of her relationship with Reggie. How did Ronnie refer to it?"

"She said Lorelei was Reggie's mistress."

"How do you think Lorelei attended school while living the high life? Tim and Ronnie don't have that kind of money and, as you can see, neither do I. Reggie put her up in that apartment, bought her fancy clothes, paid for all of her schooling. In return, she took care of his primal needs." He looked at the grimy floor and shook his head. "She said it was just business."

"It sounds as if you didn't approve of her, uh, business arrangement."

"No, I didn't, and I told her so. It's not just a sin, it's a mortal sin. As a believer, Jesus charged me with the responsibility to tell her so. She refused my offer to help her find a way out of the situation and told me to butt out and take my religion back to my church. That hurt a lot." He wiped his tears with a dirty shop rag. "I told her I loved her no matter what, but I couldn't watch her destroy her spiritual life like that. I tried to convince her to come to church with me, but she refused and kicked me out. Eventually, she stopped taking my calls." More tears and another swipe with a dirty rag.

"I thought you were the one who broke off your relationship with her."

"Oh, no. I'd never have deserted my daughter. I loved that young lady and hated to see that terrible man drag her down into the gutter."

"When did you see her last?"

"I stopped by her apartment the morning before her death. We got into a heated argument." Ray looked at the floor and shook his head. "Every time we got together, it was the same argument about her sinful ways." He looked up with bleary eyes and a set jaw. "She told me she never wanted to see me again. My only daughter and she wanted me out of her life. It stabbed me in the heart."

"I'm sure it was painful for you. Did you go back later to confront her a second time?"

"No. That morning was the last I saw her or spoke with her."

"So, if you think she was murdered, who do you think did it?"

"Reggie Braun. There's no doubt about it. I tried to confront him at his office once, but he had me thrown out. As a believer, I try hard not to hate anyone. Hate just eats your guts out. It hurts you, not the person you direct it at."

"Still, you hate him, don't you?"

His animosity radiated from him in waves. I knew because I shared his feelings. "Yeah, I must confess to you and the Lord. I despise that poor excuse of a man with all that's in me."

"I'm sorry, Ray." I laid a gentle hand on his shoulder. "Is there anyone else you think might have murdered her? I don't want to lock on to one suspect too early in the investigation."

"As sure as I'm standing here, Reggie did it, or maybe his wife. Never been introduced to her, but I'm sure she hated his business arrangement with Lorelei too. Word on the street is she has a dark past. Oh, I shouldn't say that. That's gossip, another sin."

"Lorelei's best friend, Amy, said Lorelei told her some guy was stalking her. Do you have any idea who that might have been?"

"Sorry. I don't have a clue. We didn't talk much at the end, just argued."

He clearly loved Lorelei. We shared the same pain for her loss. I patted him on the shoulder in a lame attempt at comforting him. "I'm so sorry, Ray. Thanks for the interview. I'll call you if I need anything more." Before I reached the door, he was sobbing.

I sat in my car in stunned reflection, fighting the urge to take one of my precious few pills to help me cope. Sorrow swept through my being. My daughter had been a kept woman. She was paid to provide sexual services for an older, married man. It added a whole new dimension to working your way through college. At lunch, Ronnie and her mother were apparently too embarrassed to tell me the true nature of our daughter's business relationship with Reggie.

My sorrow morphed into focused rage. I pounded on the steering wheel and exclaimed in anguish, "Ronnie, how can I investigate our daughter's murder if you keep things from me?" I vowed to confront her about this in our Wednesday breakfast meeting.

Caving to the urge, I swallowed a sixty mg Oxy with warm water from a stale bottle of water left in my car from who knows when. I wrote notes on a napkin while waiting for the euphoric high so badly needed. A 1980's era Chevrolet Impala with expensive 22-inch rims and low-profile tires pulled in next to me. A beast of a man wearing a dark blue hoodie and black stocking cap climbed out and entered the garage.

I returned my attention to finishing my notes until shouting from inside the garage got my attention. Ray and the big guy screamed at each other in anger. Ray pulled out his wallet and handed cash to the stranger. The large man ripped the billfold from Ray's hand, extracted more cash and tossed it on the floor.

As Ray bent down to retrieve his wallet, the other man kneed him in the face, nearly lifting him off the ground. Ray staggered before catching himself. The big man spit on Ray and then walked out.

Adrenalin trumped my fear. I sprung from my car and caught up to the behemoth at his car. A scraggly Fu Manchu moustache, together with his bulk and extensive tattoos screamed badass. "Hey, what the hell was that all about?" The words tumbled from my dry mouth, lacking any clout.

"Go home before you get hurt, dickhead. This doesn't involve you."

"You're not going anywhere. I'm calling 911." I pulled out my cell phone.

The man unzipped his hoodie and pulled the side back to reveal the biggest handgun I'd ever seen tucked in his belt. "I told you, asshole, this doesn't involve you. Butt out if you want to stay alive."

Racing heart in my throat, I backed away. The stranger opened his car door, jumped in and took off, spinning tires and leaving me in an acrid cloud of tire smoke. I ran into the garage to check on Ray and found him sitting with a shop rag held to his bleeding nose.

"Ray, you all right? Who was that guy?"

He picked up his wallet, confirmed his cash was gone and slipped it into his back pocket. "I'm okay. I appreciate your concern, but don't put yourself in the middle of this."

"What did he want?"

"They call him Mountain Mann. It's obvious how he got that name. I've had a little stretch of bad luck and owe his boss some money. I'm a little late paying it back. He just took all my cash, but I'm still about 5 g's in the hole. He wanted to make an impression on me. No big deal. I've got it covered."

"What are we talking about here? Gambling?"

"Yeah, gambling. Like I said, I've had a little run of bad luck and need to get out of this hole." Ray stared at me with determination. "Just stay out of it. It's not your problem." He needed help, but cash was one thing I couldn't help him with.

We said our goodbyes, and I left the building. I sat in my car and scribbled a short note to ask Ronnie about Ray's gambling problem and get her opinion if this might be connected in any way to Lorelei's murder. Lately, if I don't write things down, I tend to forget them. I'm not sure if it's old age or the Oxy.

CHAPTER 20

On the drive back to my motel, rain began to fall. The combination of reflected light off wet roadway, the rhythmic beat of the wipers and an earlier Oxy hypnotized me. I don't remember the drive to my hotel but somehow made it back. Not having heard the weather forecast, my umbrella remained in my warm, dry room while I became drenched by cold rain.

Focused on reaching my room, I didn't spot the squad car sitting in the parking lot, hidden by sheets of rain. I shook off some of the moisture and headed up the exterior stairs to the second floor. The torrential rain must have masked the sound of a car door opening and closing below. Standing at my door searching for the card key, I jumped a foot when someone behind me called out my name.

I fought to contain my rapid heartbeat and restart my breathing, all to the delight of a laughing Deputy Russo in uniform, holding a dripping umbrella. "Little on edge tonight, are we?"

"Damn it, Mallory! You scared the shit out of me! I had no idea you had snuck up behind me." My words sounded harsher than intended.

"Easy, Tanner. You need not bite my head off."

I tried to focus weary eyes on her while reeling in my anger. "Sorry, I'm tired. Didn't mean to take it out on you. I'm flattered you lowered yourself to come to my slum motel, but I'm too tired for company tonight."

"That's presumptuous. I'm afraid this isn't a social call. Sykes wants me to bring you in for questioning."

"Questioning? What about?"

"I'm not supposed to tell you, but Deputy Lowell knows you visited Lorelei's apartment, and he's not happy about it. He's got the sheriff wrapped around his little finger. So, here I am."

"Are you going to handcuff me?"

"It's a tempting offer, but I'll take a rain check."

I rode to the sheriff's office in the back seat of her squad car—regulations, you know. We talked, but it was superficial and strained. I dreaded the questioning awaiting me and sensed she did as well.

She led me to a small windowless room with two wooden chairs separated by a small wooden table. "Are you going to give me a ride back to my motel when we're done here?" I took the chair facing the door.

"Either home or the emergency room. Depends on how your interrogation goes, I guess." She grinned and shrugged her shoulders. The joke was so lame I couldn't force a smile. After she left, Deputy Lowell entered, carrying a paper tablet. He took up position beside me and glared at me. "You're in my chair."

I couldn't help but chuckle. "The chairs are the same. What does it matter?"

"Because, this is my chair."

I laughed out loud, sending him into a wild rage. He grabbed my chair and pulled it out from under me. I fell hard to the floor, aggravating my bad back. "What the fuck?"

"Get up and sit in the other chair. This one's mine."

As I picked myself up, I scanned the room for a camera or two-way mirror. Two cameras near the ceiling pointed at the two chairs with duct tape over the lenses. "What's the difference? The chairs are the same." I sucked in my pride and sat in the other chair. With harsh eyes locked on me, Lowell sat in *his* chair.

"You're sticking your nose into business where it doesn't belong." We locked stares for several seconds. "Apartment supervisor told me you snooped around the suicide scene. You want to tell me what you were looking for?"

"I wasn't snooping. Ronnie asked me to pick up a purse she had given Lorelei on her last birthday. It holds sentimental value."

He glared at me in silence. "It's my understanding you told Donald you were a private investigator looking into Lorelei Adams's suicide. What does that have to do with retrieving a purse?"

"Us PI's can multi-task."

"We both know you aren't a real investigator—merely a writer pretending to be a detective like in your book."

"Oh, you've read my book. Do you want me to autograph your copy?"

"Look, smartass, I don't buy your sorry excuse for showing up at the apartment. Your trespassing corrupted the crime scene. In fact, I understand you were there twice that day. Did you find anything we should know about?"

"You mean, like evidence Lorelei was murdered?" It became a staring contest while I pondered what to reveal about my visit. With foolish courage, I decided to go for it. "You mean like a bottle of barbiturates that would have provided a much easier route to suicide. Or empty trash cans even though a wine glass had been broken. Not sure how you view this, but it looks to me like murder and a cover-up."

He leaped from his chair and dove over the table, grabbing for my collar with both hands, but missing. The table collapsed under his weight and crashed on the floor. His momentum tipped me backward in my chair, smacking my head on the floor. He leapt on top of me. Light from the hallway exploded into the room. I heard the Sheriff's deep voice. "What's going on here?"

I pushed the deputy off me. He stood and pointed down at me, as I laid on the floor gasping for air. "I was just asking this asshole a few questions when he went psycho and attacked me for no reason."

I rubbed my aching head and rose to all fours but couldn't yet make it to my feet. "The hell I did! He assaulted me, Sheriff."

Lowell kicked me in the gut sending searing pain through damaged ribs and strained back. Sykes pulled his deputy away. I stumbled to my feet using the wall for support.

The deputy stuck his face in the sheriff's face and screamed, "I'm going to lock this son of a bitch up for assault."

"Deputy Lowell, you're over the line. Let's step out in the hallway 'n talk this over before ya do sumpin ya regret." After they left the room and shut the door, I collapsed into *his* chair and investigated the bump rising on the back of my aching head but found no blood.

Their arguing was loud enough to penetrate the thick door but not loud enough to make any sense of what was being said. After a few angry exchanges, their voices settled down.

Minutes later, the door opened, and Mallory entered. "You okay?" Her beautiful dark eyes showed concern.

"No blood at least, but I'm still seeing stars, my back is killing me, and my ribs may be broken. That animal needs to be chained up." In the distance, a door slammed.

"Don't push it, Tanner. Sykes got Deputy Lowell to drop his assault charge. Let it go at that."

"Assault? Hell, he attacked me. I should file charges against him for police brutality."

"Look, Tanner, don't make trouble. There aren't any witnesses and no video. It's your word against his, so who do you think the judge will believe?"

"You could be my witness." I explored her loyalty.

"I'm sorry, Tanner, but I didn't see anything and really need this job."

Small town justice at its finest. "Am I free to go?"

"Yeah. Consider yourself lucky. Lowell isn't used to having his authority challenged. He's really pissed, so you might want to cut your investigation short and go home while you still can." As she walked behind me, she noticed the knot on my head. "That bump looks nasty. You want me to take you to the emergency room?"

"All they would do is put ice on it and maybe wrap my ribs. I just want to go back to my room." I couldn't afford the co-pay for an emergency room visit anyway.

Despite regulations, I sat in the front seat of Mallory's squad car, but didn't feel much like talking, and it seemed she didn't either. Although the rain had quit, the roads remained wet. At my request, she stopped at a convenience store so I could buy a bag of frozen peas to put on my head. I also picked up a fifth of bourbon from the package store next door to deaden the pain and a bottle of water to wash down an Oxy. Back in the car, I cracked open the water and took a forty mg Oxy from my pillbox.

"What are you taking there?"

"Something for my headache."

"Didn't look like Tylenol."

"It's a prescription."

"Looked like an opioid. Do you have a drug problem?"

"No, the doctor prescribed it for my back. I told you I suffer from chronic back pain."

"You seem to take them a lot. Just be careful. Opioids are very addictive. Besides, you shouldn't be drinking alcohol on that stuff."

"Don't worry. I've got it under control. The bourbon's for tomorrow." Truth was, I longed to open the bottle right there, but waited for the solitude of my room.

She dropped me off at the CrossRoads Inn. As I walked around her car, she rolled her window down and spoke with a playful tone. "Guess you're not going to invite me in after our date tonight, huh?"

I needed information she possessed about Lorelei's death but struggled to keep my eyes open thanks to the Oxy. I leaned down and looked in the open car window to make eye contact. "Date? Strangely, I've had worse dates. Just for the record, if I had asked you in to share my bourbon, would you have accepted?"

"I thought the bourbon was for tomorrow night. Besides, you think I would step foot in that fleabag? Not had all my shots. Hell, there aren't enough shots in the world for that dive."

Her eyes turned somber. "Look, I feel bad about tonight. How about I make you dinner tomorrow night to make up for it?"

The idea of having dinner with a possible spy didn't seem right, but I accepted anyway. After all, I still needed to extract information from her.

It seemed strange that Mallory didn't pull out right away but watched me climb the stairs to the second floor.

CHAPTER 21

Light from the outside lamps provided the only illumination in my room. Flipping the wall switch repeatedly did nothing. I activated the flashlight function on my phone to produce enough light to enter the room safely. Each step created crunching sounds like broken light bulbs. The dim light from my phone revealed a scene of utter destruction. Bedding lay heaped in one corner, the mattress stood against the far wall with padding spewing from long gashes. Clothes from my suitcases were strewn about the room. Two table lamps lay smashed on the floor—the source of the crunching glass.

I ran back outside and down the stairs. Mallory was still sitting in her car in the parking lot leafing through paperwork. I tapped on her window to attract her attention.

Her window receded into the car door with a soft whine. "What's wrong?"

"Someone tossed my room."

"Tossed? You mean, searched?"

Her failure to get excited aggravated me. "That's exactly what I mean. Someone ransacked it."

Flashlight, note pad and pen in hand, she led me up the stairs. "Anything missing?"

"I haven't checked yet. I wanted to catch you before you left." A number of questions popped into my head. Why had Mallory sat in the parking lot so long after I left? Why didn't my sudden knock on her window startle her? Why was she so calm? Could she have known what I would find in my room and waited? Could she be in on it? After all, it did happen while I was in her custody,

She examined the door latch. "No sign of forced entry. Did you lock the door?"

"It locks automatically." Now that I thought about it, I wasn't so sure. I would check later.

"Don't touch anything until I get pictures." She directed me where to shine her flashlight while she snapped pictures using her phone.

After finishing the pictures, she jotted a few notes on her tablet. "Okay, see if anything's missing."

Fear exploded inside me. Where was my Oxy stash? The night stands lay broken and upside down. A panicked search confirmed my worst fear—the bottle of pills hidden underneath the nightstand was gone, only the tape remained. I dashed to the bathroom to check on the rest of my stash. The toilet tank lid lay on the floor in three jagged pieces. The Ziploc bag with Oxy was nowhere to be found. I fought back tears so Mallory wouldn't know how important those pills were to me.

She followed me into the bathroom. "What's wrong?"

"My pain pills. They're gone. They took my damn pills." My head throbbed, my back ached, and my ribs stung despite the Oxy I'd already taken. I craved another but didn't dare take any more in front of Mallory.

She jotted notes in her notebook. "How many and what dosage were they?"

"Various dosages, from twenty to sixty milligrams. There were maybe a dozen of them."

"Why varying dosages? A doctor would only prescribe one dosage of an opioid."

I realized I had made a mistake, varying dosages hinted impropriety. "Oh, they're all from doctors' prescriptions. I had some older lesser dosages lying around and brought them in case I ran out before returning home." That was pretty much true.

"Do you have enough in your pill box to hold you over until you can have your prescription transferred here and refilled?"

She must have spotted my personal pillbox earlier when I took an Oxy on the drive back to my room. It had been a huge mistake to let her see me take that pill.

"For now, but I will need to get more."

More. That was a problem. How could I get my hands on more? I had exhausted all of my prescriptions. Two doctors had already refused to renew prescriptions for fear I had a drug problem and had referred me to treatment. The Oxy stolen from my room was the only thing here I cared about. Now it was gone. Plotting how to get more pills consumed my consciousness. I needed more pills.

"Tanner." Mallory ramped up the volume to snap me out of my drug-craving trance. "Tanner, are you all right?"

"Yeah, sure."

"Shouldn't you check the rest of your things to see if anything else is missing?"

"It doesn't matter. I didn't leave anything of value here." Depression engulfed me and deepened my craving further.

Mallory phoned the front desk and asked the manager to come to my room.

A slender, grey-haired Indian man, barely five-feet tall, entered and spoke with a heavy accent. "Oh, my! What have you done here? You trashed my hotel. You responsible. I can't permit this kind of behavior here. You must pay for damage."

Dazed, I stared at him in silence, so Mallory stepped in. "Mr. Nole didn't do this. Someone broke into his room. I'm here to file a police report."

"I don't care who did this. Mr. Nole must pay. Cash, no credit card, no check. Cash only."

I didn't have that kind of cash, and what little I had left was needed to buy more Oxy.

CHAPTER 22

On Tuesday, an early morning sun peeked through the open curtain. As my head cleared, I took inventory. My back ached, and I convinced myself that was the sole reason I craved Oxy. It had been only seven hours since the last one. Due to my dwindling supply, I resolved to hold off until lunchtime. OxyContin is designed to be a time-release drug. Its manufacturer claims it to be effective for twelve hours, but it's common knowledge among frequent users that they're effective for eight hours at most, making it more difficult to stick to the prescribed frequency.

The seven remaining tablets in my pill case called to me, but I summoned enough constraint to shove them back in my pocket without taking any. It was too early to call my doctors in Savannah for an emergency prescription refill. TV didn't hold my attention, so I paced the room, itching all over like ants crawling on my skin. By seven o'clock, my will power faded. I chewed an Oxy to speed up and heighten the euphoria it created.

By seven-thirty, I felt invincible and set about calling my doctors. I began with the two who had last written prescriptions for me. The voice message at the first office directed me to press "5" and leave a message for the nurse, which I did. I described my case as an emergency and stressed my urgent need to speak to the doctor.

A nurse at the second office took down my information and promised to speak with the doctor. In desperation, I called two more doctors from years ago. The first refused to renew my prescription at any dosage. The next call burst my bubble. The nurse advised me the law prohibited a faxed script for a Schedule II narcotic like OxyContin. I would need to come in for an exam and pick up a signed paper copy.

Desperation overwhelmed me. I called local doctors in Talmadge, but the earliest appointment available was three weeks out. I scheduled it but didn't plan on still being here by then. I couldn't survive that long without an influx of pills.

Growing anxiety drove me to seek the closest immediate care clinic. They would want cash up front, but desperation trumped frugality. The nurse practitioner had my back X-rayed and prescribed Lorcet, a Schedule III mixture of hydrocodone and acetaminophen. A nurse practitioner in Georgia can't prescribe Schedule II drugs like Oxy. On the way to my car, I tossed the crumpled paper script in a trash can outside the door. I started my car and put it in gear before despair forced me to rethink my actions. Putting the car back in Park, I dumped the contents of the waste can on the sidewalk and retrieved my prescription, just in case.

CHAPTER 23

Earlier, on the way to the immediate care clinic, I had spotted large stainless steel letters on the side of a gleaming four-story brick and glass building spelling out Braun Enterprises, LLC. Any building in Talmadge more than two stories demanded attention, but the pure opulence of this one caught my eye. I decided to double back and pay Reggie a surprise visit. I had my doubts about the potential success of such a bold move, but at least it would distract me from my prescription dilemma.

A well-dressed, young black woman sat perched on a tall chair behind a high desk in the gleaming lobby. Horn-rimmed glasses and fifty extra pounds on her short frame screamed librarian. The name tag on the counter identified her as a receptionist.

"Good morning, Ayesha. What a lovely name for such a pretty lady. I'm Tanner Nole." We shook hands, and I held her hand longer than proper. "I don't see a ring which is certainly good news for me."

She pulled her hand away and blushed. "You're not half bad yourself. What can I do for you, Mr. Nole?"

"I'm here to see Reggie Braun."

"Do you have an appointment?"

"No. He told me to stop by anytime, and he'd break out of whatever he was doing to see me. We go way back."

"Okay, let me call his admin." Her tone signaled skepticism.

The call went unanswered, so she left a brief recorded message before returning her attention to me. "I'm sorry, but Mr. Braun's admin isn't at her desk. Why don't you take a seat until she returns my call?" She smiled and flashed her eyes.

"Okay." I leaned in close enough to smell her floral perfume and whispered in her ear. "I don't mean to embarrass you, but there's something green in your front teeth." I opened my lips and pointed to my upper incisors. She wiped her teeth side-to-side with her index finger and then looked at me with a big, open-mouth grin. "No. It's still there. Maybe if you used the mirror in the restroom."

"Thanks, Mr. Nole. Why don't you take a seat? I'm sure Mr. Braun's admin will be back soon. Mr. Braun can't do much without her." As I strolled to a nearby chair, she stood and pushed her chair back. After checking the otherwise empty lobby, she hustled to the women's restroom.

Before the door even closed, I dashed for the elevator and stabbed the call button. I assumed Reggie's office would be on the top floor to satisfy his ego. I willed the elevator car to show up before Ayesha returned. When it arrived, I dove inside and punched the "4" button. Nothing happened for what seemed an eternity. I pressed the close-door button several times in quick succession. The sound of the restroom door signaled time was running out. I caught a glimpse of Ayesha through the narrow crack of the closing doors and hoped she hadn't spotted me.

The elevator stopped at the second floor, where two women entered while chatting about some exotic dish they both adored and paying no attention to me in my little corner. The car stopped at the third floor, where they stepped off. A man in a gray golf shirt embroidered with "Braun Enterprises, LLC" got on. I nodded hello, and he returned the gesture before occupying the other corner in the back of the car. Bile bubbled in the back of my throat. I let the other guy exit before me. A quick sweep of the terrain revealed one person moving away from me down the long corridor and two standing, talking over a cubicle wall. In the open-office design, it was easy to identify Reggie's office. It and an adjoining glass-walled conference room consumed the entire end of the floor.

Hustling down the main corridor, I prayed silently for no one to stop me. The beautiful oak desk in front of Reggie's office stood vacant. A young, beautiful blonde approached from up the hall wearing a bitchy scowl. Her skin-tight top displayed ample cleavage, and a tight black leather skirt completed an outfit too hot for serious business.

To avoid her, I did a one-eighty and hustled down the hallway toward the sign marking the men's room. There I took refuge in a stall of the empty men's room.

Two men entered and used the urinals while babbling about a loan. After they left, I abandoned my stall, washed my hands and peeked down the hall. The blonde, I had seen earlier, sat at the desk in front of Reggie's office, speaking to a woman dressed in a security uniform. When she pointed in my direction, I retreated to my stall and locked the door.

Through a crack in my stall I saw the female security guard poke her head in. "Security. Anyone in here?

I will do almost anything to avoid vomiting, but these were desperate times. I bent over the commode and stuck my finger down my throat. Since I hadn't eaten in a while, the result was more noise and putrid smell than bile.

Heavy footsteps approached my stall. "I'm sorry, mister. Are you okay?" She gagged, likely from the sound and smell.

I spit in the toilet. "I'll be okay in a minute. Must've eaten something bad for breakfast."

"Okay. When you're feeling better, I need to talk to you. Oh, shit!" She turned and left the restroom gagging.

I ran to the restroom door and peeked out. The hot blonde knelt, laying paper towels on the guard's mess. She too gagged and plunged into the Women's restroom. Seeing a brief opening, I dashed for Reggie's office and found him alone sitting in a plush leather desk chair, typing on his laptop.

My heart pounded as I barged in. "Reggie, hi. My name is Tanner Nole. I'm investigating Lorelei Adams's death."

Reggie sprung to his feet. "What the hell?" His eyes popped, and his face reddened. "Get out of my fucking office. Nancy!"

"Not until you give me some answers about Lorelei Adams's murder."

Furled eyebrows bracketed a deadly glare. "Get the hell out of my office, now! Nancy! Nancy! Someone call security!" No one responded.

"Tell me about your business arrangement with Lorelei Adams."

Shock exploded across his face. "What the hell are you talking about? Who did you say you were?

"Tanner Nole. I'm investigating her murder and need some answers from you."

Still a bit green, Nancy stuck her head in the office. "Sorry to interrupt, Mr. Braun, but you need to leave for your lunch appointment at La Model."

Reggie looked to his admin for salvation from this threat. "Nancy, where the hell have you been? Call security and have this damned intruder thrown out! Now!"

She recoiled at the sight of me and scurried back to her desk.

I glared at the prime suspect in my daughter's murder. If I had had a gun, I might have shot him. "Reggie, we have a few minutes before security arrives, so answer one question for me. Did you kill Lorelei?"

The female security guard, still looking a bit green, burst into the room with pistol drawn. "Hands up! Now!"

Her gun quivered in her hand. I complied without question, for fear her weapon might accidentally discharge.

"Okay, okay. I'm going. Just don't point that thing at me."

"Turn and walk slowly." She fell in behind me, her gun pressed into my back. I gave brief consideration to spinning around and knocking the gun from her hand like on TV, but reason triumphed.

Nancy held the door for us. The security guard kept her gun trained on me until I got into my car and drove away. My heart still pounded two blocks later when I met Deputy Lowell racing toward Braun Enterprises with lights flashing and siren blaring. Too close for comfort.

CHAPTER 24

Foot heavy on the gas pedal and eyes fixated on my rear-view mirror, I expected to see flashing red lights from the deputy's car giving chase. That never happened. With time and distance, my heart rate slowed, and so did the car. While contemplating my next move, I noticed a sign for La Model restaurant. After a quick U-turn, I pulled in and self-parked where I could watch the front door while collecting my thoughts.

I shouted out in anguish and pounded the steering wheel with my fists. "What an idiot, barging into Reggie's office like that uninvited! What did I think I could accomplish?" I coveted another Oxy but strove to control my craving. Here I sat, waiting for Reggie to show up for his lunch appointment.

Realizing I was asking for trouble, I decided to leave, but a white Mazda MX-5 convertible cut me off and screeched to an abrupt stop at the valet stand. Reggie's hot-looking admin sprang from the car and tossed her keys to a googly-eyed valet. My eyes followed her catwalk strut to the door. The young parking valets enjoyed every wiggle of her firm butt, and all agreed they wanted some of that.

I re-parked my car and waited. A few minutes later, a blazing red Ferrari 458 Italia convertible pulled up. Reggie slipped the wide-eyed valet a few bills and hustled into the restaurant, talking on his smartphone the whole time. I hated this self-absorbed prick more than ever.

After giving Reggie time to be seated, I followed him in. The maître d' greeted me in a bad French accent. "Sir, do you have a réservation?" drawing out a nasal "o" and barely saying the "n".

"No, I'm looking for Reggie Braun. He's expecting me."

"That's odd. His admin only made a reservation for two."

"Oh, I'm not joining them for lunch, just delivering something."

"It'd be my pleasure to pass it on to Mr. Braun for you."

"No, I need to speak with him in person for a minute."

"I don't see any file." His fake French accent all but gone now.

I pulled the napkins with my notes out of my rear pants pocket and held them up for him to see. The maître d' squinted, and the creases in his forehead deepened. He glanced at his computer screen for reassurance. "Wait while I check with Mr. Braun. He is very private and does not like to be disturbed."

A party of three entered behind me. "Thanks. Why don't you seat your next party here while I run to the men's room? Where is it?"

"Down the hall, second door on the left."

I over-smiled and dawdled in that direction. As soon as the maître d' left his post to seat them, I doubled back and circled the restaurant until I spied Reggie. He and his lovely admin cuddled at a table in a secluded corner with more contact than justified by a boss/employee relationship. Reggie whispered in her ear, evoking a wicked smile. She laid her hand on his and whispered something back, precipitating a similar reaction from him. Get a room, I thought.

Closing to within two tables of the couple, I snapped two pictures using my cell phone before a waiter tapped me on the shoulder. "Can I ask what you are doing, sir?"

I turned my back to Reggie in hopes he wouldn't recognize me. The surrounding tables went silent. "Me? I'm just taking pictures of your table service here. My wife is really into that sort of thing, and she'll be very impressed with yours."

He displayed a look of disbelief mixed with disdain as I pocketed my phone and darted for the door.

The maître d' shouted as I breezed by his station. "Sir, I thought you had a delivery for Mr. Braun."

Over my shoulder, I said, "Just got a call from the office. They gave me the wrong file. I'll be back."

As I drove off, the maître d' stood in the doorway, recording my license plate number. I smiled and waved in an exaggerated manner to let him know I'd seen him. Pulling my phone out, I set it down on the console and patted it. "I've got leverage, baby. Now I can get that appointment to interview you, you rich son of a bitch."

CHAPTER 25

While returning to my hotel, I mentally kicked myself for getting nowhere fast. It was no wonder my police procedural was so awful. I knew nothing about investigations, and this one proved to be a lot harder than imagined.

When I reached the second floor of my motel, I spotted two suitcases sitting outside my door—my suitcases. When my key failed to unlock the door, I headed to the manager's office with a heap of Oxy-craving attitude.

I rang the bell on the counter twice, but no one responded. I slammed the bell several times with enough force to send it clanging to the floor where it rolled around.

"Okay, okay, I coming." The Indian manager's voice preceded him. "Oh, it's you."

"You're damned right, it's me! What the hell is my stuff doing on the floor outside my room, and why doesn't my key work anymore?"

"You been evicted."

"Evicted? I paid in advance for that room and have done nothing to get evicted. You better let me back in my room or I'll . . ." Without thinking, I reached across the counter for him.

He stepped back out of my reach. "I no want trouble. Leave now, or I call sheriff."

My arms fell to my sides in surrender. "Why the hell did you evict me?"

"You not pay for damage to room. I try charge your card and it rejected. You must go." His hand made a sweeping motion.

I noticed a gold plaque on the wall behind him. "This Hotel Owned and Operated by Braun Enterprises, LLC."

"Reggie Braun owns this hotel?"

"Yes and most other hotels in the county."

My head slumped forward in defeat. "He owns every other place in town, too? I've got nowhere else to go except maybe the YMCA or a homeless shelter."

"Mr. Braun not own YMCA but he major contributor and sit on board. There one place you could stay, but it not nice like this hotel. It called The Palace, on Turner Street just south of Temple."

"That was a bad part of town when I went to college here."

"Oh, it much worse now. Please take your stuff and go, or I call sheriff." I could feel his eyes on me as I slinked out of the office.

I gathered my belongings and tossed them in the trunk of my car.

The manager had said Reggie owned all the hotels, but if he didn't own The Palace, that wasn't entirely true. The Comfort Inn down the street might be another exception.

The Comfort Inn had a room but at twice the rate of my prior hotel. I decided I could afford it if I watched my money and accelerated the investigation to shorten my stay. When I handed the desk clerk my completed registration card, her gray eyes nearly popped out of her head.

She turned to her computer monitor and clicked a few keys. "Oh, Mr. Nole. I am so sorry, but that room is already occupied. It appears we have no rooms available." She tore up my registration and tossed it in the trash.

I chuckled. "Does Reggie Braun own this hotel?"

"I don't know who owns it. I just work here."

Over her shoulder was a gold plaque on the wall, with the words "This Hotel Owned and Operated by Braun Enterprises, LLC."

I conjured up my best puppy dog look. "I'm really desperate for a place to stay. Could you please just check again? An empty broom closet or something?"

"I'm sorry, sir, but you need to leave right now. If you don't, I'll be forced to call the sheriff." That had a very familiar ring to it.

As I left, I considered calling Maggie Mae and accepting her offer to put me up, but I couldn't overcome the dread of having her spy on me. I resigned myself to staying at The Palace. How bad could it be?

CHAPTER 26

The Palace was worse than I imagined. Dim light did little to mask its flaws. It hadn't had a good cleaning in a decade or fresh paint in the last two. The dilapidated structure seemed to defy the law of gravity. It reeked of stale cigarettes, but that seemed to be masking an even worse smell.

A sign advertising hourly rates set the tone. A tall, homely woman leaned on the counter, popping her chewing gum. She wore a bad blond wig, long fake eyelashes and caked-on makeup on an otherwise pale complexion. Although buxom, she didn't show any cleavage despite a skin-tight dress covered in red sequins with some missing here and there. "Hey there, good lookin. Can I hep you?"

Her flashing eyes and jutting Adam's apple distracted me. "I, uh, need a room."

"I'll bet you do, honey." A long black fingernail touched her lips as an exclamation point to her naughty grin. "I've got a special—second hour is half price. That is, if you can last that long." She gave me an exaggerated, playful smirk.

"No. No. I need a place to stay overnight . . . for several nights."

"Oh, you want a motel room? I think we have rates for that. Let me check." She called someone on her cell phone and got an answer. "We have a room available for you. How many nights?"

"What's the rate?"

"I'm shocked a big spender like you has to worry about money. It's $250 per night."

"What? It'd be cheaper to rent it by the hour."

She laughed and made a swatting motion with one hand. "Just messin with you. Its $99 a night plus tax, plus any optional services you might choose." Her eyes flashed above that naughty grin of hers.

It cost a little more than the CrossRoads Inn, but my options were limited—hell, they were non-existent. I held my breath when she ran my credit card, but by some miracle, it went through.

She handed me an old metal key like hotels used back in the '70's. "You're in room 219. There's an ice machine at the end of the hall, but it don't work."

I took the key from her. "What did you mean by extra services? Do you have a restaurant or a bar here?"

She waved a hand at me playfully and giggled. "Oh, you are cute, honey. No. I mean like . . ." She swept her hands down each side of her body and wiggled her butt. I could feel my face turn beet red. A clogged throat prevented a verbal response.

When I didn't accept, her face took on a pouty characteristic. "Guess I'm not your type. I can arrange other, uh, entertainment too. Whatta you into? Bet a good-lookin' man like you gotta kinky side."

Still unable to speak, I grabbed my bags and backed away. I collided with a short, chunky woman in a skimpy bright yellow dress that left little to the imagination. I dropped one of my bags and the key.

"Well, hello, there." She bent down to retrieve my key while making sure I got a look at her cleavage. "Ain't seen you roun here before. Y'all lookin for a date, sweetie? I be free in bout fifteen minutes. My nex customer's a quick one, if you know what I mean."

"I'm sorry. Wasn't looking where I was going. Thanks, but I don't need a date."

"Well, maybe later, sweetie. Believe me, I can rock your world." She handed me my room key along with a bright yellow business card that matched her dress. Stunned, I took it, gathered my bags and dashed for the safety of my room. Their rollicking laughter followed me up the wooden staircase to occupy 219.

I didn't expect much from the room. Still, it disappointed me. The bedroom was just that. It had only a bed. No phone, no tables, no chairs. Only one of three bulbs in the overhead light worked. The bathroom proved to be no better, and the last man to use the toilet had not bothered to lift the seat or aim. The linens were stained, dirty and stale.

I put my bags down and sat on the grungy bed to take in the room. It smelled of stale cigarettes, vomit and who knows what else. The bed in the next room squeaked in a steady rhythm as a woman screamed, "Oh yeah, baby. Give it to me! Give it to me!"

My surroundings depressed me too much to be doing what I had planned—scheduling appointments. The need for an Oxy overcame me, but I wouldn't dare drink any water from this room. I created a shopping list on one of my napkins—whiskey, bottled water, sleeping bag, earplugs, paper towels, toilet paper, soap, shampoo and a large case of Lysol. Scheduling appointments would have to wait. The rest of the afternoon would be spent getting my room to some level of toleration.

After shopping and making my room semi-habitable, I sat on the bed and admired my work. For some reason, my thoughts turned to Ronnie. Maybe I wanted her to somehow rescue me from this place. Depression turned to guilt. It was getting late, and I needed to shower for my dinner at Mallory's.

I considered canceling, but convinced myself I needed to pump her for information. It was for the good of the investigation.

CHAPTER 27

Eager to escape my depressing room I arrived at Mallory's house thirty minutes early. I drove on by and parked around the corner out of sight to wait. I hate people who show up early.

After killing time, I knocked on her door. Mallory opened it immediately as if she had watched my approach. The V-neck of her peach-colored sweater showed a modest amount of bra-less cleavage. Matching peach-colored silk pants completed the outfit. I didn't recognize her perfume but suspected it was loaded with pheromones. I began to question her motives.

"Mr. Punctuality, right on time. Did I see you drive by in your little red sports car about thirty minutes ago? What is it again?"

"It's a 1997 Ford Probe, and no, it wasn't me."

"I don't see many red Ford Probes running around Talmadge these days. It sure looked like your car."

"You don't see many because it's a classic, lots of other sports cars look like my Probe."

She grimaced. "You don't say. Come on in. Dinner's almost ready." A wonderful blend of tomato, sausage and hot bread emanated from the kitchen and merged with woodfire odors from the fireplace. "I hope you like lasagna. It's Nonna's recipe. That's what we Italians call our grandmother."

"I love lasagna." I struggled not to stare at this pretty lady and reminded myself how much younger she was.

"There's a bottle of Chianti on the table, and the wine opener is in the drawer on the end. You mind opening it?" She put soft jazz on her stereo.

Her wine opener was a simple corkscrew. Since I use a different type of opener and am not mechanically inclined, I struggled to open the bottle and ended up destroying the cork. To hide the evidence of my incompetence, I pushed bits of cork into the bottle and wiped out the loose crumbs remaining in the bottle's neck.

We enjoyed a wonderful meal under a cloud of tension. I was unsure how to extract the information I needed without giving up much in return. We nearly made it through the meal before Mallory discovered cork crumbs in her wine glass. Under expert interrogation, she extracted the story of the botched wine opening, which I blamed on inadequate tools and a dry cork. My embarrassment amused her and seemed to create a more relaxed atmosphere.

The tension broken, my defenses came down and we talked freely through desert. Could this all be part of her spy strategy?

She snatched our dirty dishes from the table and headed for the kitchen. "Why don't you stoke the fire while I clear the table?"

I stirred the embers and added one too many logs to the fire. I wanted to keep it going without attending it for a while. After admiring my work, I scanned her great room. "You have a great place here. Did you decorate it yourself?"

Dishes clanged on their way into the dishwasher. "No, that's not one of my strengths. Thomas, one of my friends, is a decorator and did this for me."

Looking about the room, I spied a brown leather valise lying on an end table and decided to have a closer look. Keeping one eye on the door to the kitchen, I studied it up close. The bag showed signs of wear that almost masked her monogram. After making sure she was still occupied in the kitchen, I unzipped it. "He did a nice job. Is he gay?" What a stupid question.

"Yeah, what difference does that make?"

Ignoring her question, I slid a document out and browsed it. In my shaking hand was a draft police report for Lorelei's death. I threw all caution to the wind and flipped through it. The report was composed of fifty-two pages including extensive photos. On the page titled *Conclusions*, I read the words, ". . . bullet entry wound on right temple." Thinking back to the pictures Ronnie had shown me, Lorelei was left-handed. I wanted to tear that page out but thought better of it. A missing page would incriminate me.

The dishwasher door slammed. "That should be enough for now."

I shoved the report back in the valise. The zipper jammed, so I dropped the valise back down on the table half-zipped and dashed for the sofa while trying to look innocent.

She paused for a moment as if she had detected my malfeasance, but then shook it off. "Nice fire. Bet you were a Boy Scout."

My pulse pounding in my head, I wondered how long she had been standing there and what she might have seen. "What tipped you off? Want to see my merit badges?"

She swept past me and inspected the valise on the end table as if she was suspicious. I prayed she wouldn't notice it was unzipped. She picked it up and shoved it in the hall closet and closed the door. "Brought some papers home to read but don't think I'll find time tonight."

There was an uncomfortable pause in our interaction. It seemed odd she brought this particular report home tonight of all nights. Maybe she wanted me to see it. Then again, maybe it was a trap. I needed to keep my guard up.

We took up on the sofa in front of the roaring fire and sipped Chianti. The reflected light off the fire added a glow to her big, round eyes. "You are a wonderful cook. Give Nonna my approval on that recipe."

She sat back, putting a little more distance between us. "So, how's your investigation going? Find any new clues?"

I pulled back, increasing the space between us further. My mind raced—she brought home the police report as if to tempt me and now she was asking me questions. What was going on here? My radar beeped red alert. "Why do you ask?"

"Just curious. After all, I'm a cop and helped investigate Lorelei's death, so questions pop into my head. I'm not sure why you're looking into it. Did you find anything we missed? Since the report isn't finalized, there's still time to make changes."

I searched her face for tells. Her eyes blinked more frequently than normal. The report in her valise looked finished to me. Was she a spy for Sheriff Sykes, Deputy Lowell or even Reggie? I wanted to mention the barbiturates I found in Lorelei's hidden drawer, but didn't feel safe enough to. "No, not yet, but I'm still looking. Is there anything new from your side?"

Her eyes grew cold. "You know I can't talk about an ongoing investigation. We've been through that." Her demeanor turned sour.

"I thought the investigation had ended, and her death was ruled a suicide. Something come up to cast doubt on that?"

"No, nothing new, but then I can't tell you that, can I?" Her mood seemed to lighten. "Until the final report's issued, it's officially an open case, even though we aren't investigating any further."

"So, when will the report be issued?"

"That's up to the sheriff. I'm just a li'l ole deputy. What will you look into next?"

An awkward silence ensued while I pondered her strange interest in my investigation. She was pumping me for information. That might explain why she asked me to dinner.

I decided to fish a little. "I tried to talk to Reggie Braun. He's a person of interest, you might say. That didn't work so well."

"Yeah, I heard about that. You're lucky he didn't want to call attention by pressing charges. I recommend you stay clear of him. How long you planning on staying here to do your investigation?"

"Just long enough." She knew about my attempt to question Reggie but held her cards close. "If you can't talk about the investigation, then tell me about Deputy Lowell. He's the lead investigator, right? "

She sat bolt upright, fear in her eyes.

After a pause, I pursued it further. "Well? What kind of deputy is he?"

She clasped her hands tightly in her lap and set her jaw. "He's not someone you want to mess with. He's ambitious and will do anything to get the sheriff's badge. With Reggie backing him, he's pretty much got a lock on it if the sheriff retires like he says he will. I think Sykes is retiring out of fear Lowell might somehow jeopardize his pension. You don't get rich being an honest county sheriff in Georgia, so he needs his pension to retire on. Lowell's dangerous and doesn't like you, so my advice is stay away from him."

She stood. "I know it's still early, but can we call it a night?" Her hands shook ever so slightly. "As I told you I did bring work home."

My mentioning Deputy Lowell seemed to spook her. Only minutes earlier she had claimed she wouldn't look at the report tonight, but now she was using it as an excuse to cut the evening short. Was she spying for Deputy Lowell? Was that the source of her discomfort?

At her door, I thanked her again for dinner and said goodnight. We both fidgeted like teenagers on a first date, unsure how to close this out. I took a chance and gave her a gentle, friendly hug. She seemed relieved by my choice and friend-hugged me back.

On the drive back to my room a car appeared to be following me. It stayed too far back to see if it was a car with a roof rack or a squad car. I kept an eye on my rearview mirror and turned at the next right. It too turned right. Each time I slowed, it slowed and remained the same distance behind, mimicking my every move. The next light turned yellow, so I accelerated hard and ran the light. The trailing car stopped at the red light and made a slow right turn. I still couldn't be sure if it had been a sheriff's car or not but felt relief when it turned.

I kept glancing in the mirror, but no other car followed for more than a couple blocks. While pulling into the motel parking lot, a sheriff's car went by at a snail's pace. The driver was a man, but I couldn't see who it was. The hair on the back of my neck stood on end. I entered my room, half expecting to find it ransacked, but it remained just the way I left it. No footprints showed in the talcum powder left on the threshold.

After a relaxing hot shower, I retired for the night, too fatigued to even brush my teeth. An image of a sheriff's car following me rang in my head. I worried that Lowell might have been following me and what that might mean for Mallory. Her eyes betrayed fear when I mentioned his name.

Tossing and turning inside my sleeping bag on top of the bed, sleep seemed impossible. For one thing, my body itched all over, a sign of opioid withdrawal. After a torturous hour, I gave in and took one of my precious Oxys but didn't chew it for fear the buzz might keep me awake. I yearned for the comfort of sleep.

After more tossing and turning, the itching subsided, and sleep finally engulfed me.

CHAPTER 28

Late the next morning raging back pain woke me. I grabbed my pocket pill holder to take an Oxy. After all, they were prescribed for back pain such as this. The few remaining pills gave me the resolve to return the case to my pocket without taking one. This would be day one of abstinence.

In the shower, hunger pangs struck. At Mickey D's I feasted on a Big Breakfast with Pancakes. For some strange reason, Amy had haunted my dreams last night. Her and her gothic friends taunted me with missing evidence from the investigation. Although I don't put much stock in interpretation of dreams, it made me question if she had been forthright in her responses to my questions. For one thing, she hadn't been forthright in the true nature of Lorelei's relationship with Reggie. I called her.

"Hello, Amy. This is Tanner Nole."

"Oh, hello, Tanner. I thought you had forgotten all about me."

"I thought of more questions. Is this a good time to talk?"

"Actually, I'm late for a meeting with one of my professors. It shouldn't take but fifteen minutes. How about we meet at Starbucks on Seventh Street in forty-five minutes?"

I agreed to meet her there despite my hatred for Starbucks. Love their coffee, but hate their prices.

With my tepid McDonalds' coffee in hand, I arrived ten minutes late, hoping she had already purchased her drink, so I wouldn't have to pay for it. My plan succeeded. She sipped on some fancy cappuccino drink costing nearly ten dollars.

"Thanks for meeting me. I thought of more questions." She listened while sipping her coffee in annoying little slurps. "What was the nature of Lorelei's relationship with Reggie?"

"I told you before. She was his mistress."

"How did Lorelei pay for her school and apartment? Her parents are on the verge of bankruptcy, and she apparently didn't have a job." As I said this, I realized in a way she did work.

Amy looked down at her hands and fidgeted in her chair. "Reggie was her sugar daddy." I cringed at those words. "He paid for everything—schooling, car, apartment, food and spending money."

"So, their relationship was a business arrangement."

She nodded affirmation as tears formed in her eyes.

"Why didn't you tell me about this in our first interview?"

Tears flowed heavier. She dabbed her eyes with her napkin without responding.

I pushed forward. "How are these licentious business deals consummated? Is there an app for making such connections? Does someone place an ad somewhere like on Craig's List?"

She rotated her coffee cup slowly in her hands. "I didn't tell you about their deal because I feel responsible." She turned away for a moment, and then looked me straight in the eyes. "I introduced them. This friend of mine, Missy Newman, graduated. She had the same business deal with Reggie. She had developed feelings for Reggie, not love, but a degree of affection. Apparently, he developed feelings for her because he offered to hire her to continue their relationship. She declined because her dream was to move to New York and work in the fashion industry. He didn't want to take no for an answer so she decided to help him find his next—uh—mistress to help him move on. She asked if I would be interested. It offended me, and I told her so. I could never prostitute myself for financial return, but it was easy for me to say no. My parents have tons of money.

"It was no big deal to her—just a business arrangement. When I started to leave, she laid a hand on my shoulder and asked if I knew anyone who might be a candidate. I told her I don't associate with those types of people.

"Later, I shared this bizarre conversation with Lorelei as one of those 'you won't believe what happened to me today' stories. To my surprise Lorelei expressed interest. I knew she had problems with money, but I didn't know how desperate she had become. She planned to drop out the next semester and work because she didn't have the money. She saw this as a solution to her financial problems.

"I resisted, but she badgered me until I agreed to call Missy. The three of us met for lunch the next day. The resemblance of the two was unsettling. Missy and Lorelei hit it off. But then everybody loved Lorelei."

I detected a hint of jealousy in Amy's tone. "Go on."

Amy seemed to draw new strength from within. "Missy decided Reggie would be crazy about Lorelei, so they arranged to meet with him in Missy's apartment. She was right, Lorelei beguiled him."

"And so that apartment became Lorelei's apartment?"

"At first, but when Reggie fell in love with Lorelei, he built out that luxury apartment on Maple Street and moved her there."

"Did Lorelei love Reggie?" I hoped the answer would be no.

Amy looked down at her hands. "Not at first, but I think she developed feelings for the sick bastard, kind of like Missy. Maybe it's something like Stockholm syndrome." She finished her coffee. "Is that all?"

Her mood changed. She looked toward the door as if plotting her escape.

"Just a few more questions. You said Reggie fell in love with her. Was Reggie the jealous type?"

Her eyes turned darker. "I know it bothered him when Lorelei and I spent so much time together, if that's what you mean."

"No, I mean, jealous of other guys?"

She sat back and paused. "He went off the deep end if he saw her with any other guy no matter how harmless the circumstances. He got very scary."

"So, he was jealous of Brandon?"

Amy's eyes almost exploded in surprise at the mention of Brandon. She rocked back in her chair and stared into the distance, looking like she might cry any second.

"Reggie went ballistic when he found out about him because he sensed Lorelei was madly in love with him. She feared for her life after he found out."

"What's Brandon's last name, and how can I reach him?"

"Fitzgerald. Brandon Fitzgerald." She took out her smartphone. "I'll airdrop his v-card to you."

I held up my flip phone and waved it. "Don't do that fancy phone stuff. Can you read me his number?" She provided it along with his email and apartment address, and I added it to my napkins. "Do you have his birthday, too?"

"Yeah, it's . . ."

"Just kidding." It seemed odd she had all this information on Lorelei's boyfriend saved on her phone. "How is it you know so much about Brandon?" Amy looked away as tears welled up in her eyes.

"He and I used to date, sort of. You see, I introduced him to Lorelei and then he dumped me for her."

My note-taking stopped so I could study her body language. "Didn't that damage your friendship with Lorelei?"

She dabbed the tears in both eyes with a clean napkin. "Yeah, it did, for a while. Lorelei felt bad about it, but she loved Brandon so. They were, like, soul mates. How could I deny her that? She was my BFF. She was special."

For some reason, she didn't convince me all had been forgiven and forgotten. "What about Brandon? Have you forgiven him?"

She folded her hands in front of her and studied them. "No. I guess not. It still hurts a lot." She wiped her eyes with her napkin.

"So, do you think Brandon could have killed her?"

"Brandon? No way! He's not like that. He worshiped her. Brandon couldn't hurt a fly." It was obvious Amy still harbored strong feelings for him.

"Was Reggie's wife aware of his arrangements with Missy and Lorelei?"

"Don't know about Missy. She confronted Lorelei at the student union about a week before her death. Lorelei said she reeked of booze and threatened to kill her if she didn't leave Reggie alone. Campus Security arrived and separated them. Lorelei had some nasty scratches on her arm but dismissed them as nothing. When Lorelei told Reggie, he promised to take care of it. I guess he did because Lorelei never mentioned her again."

Amy needed to leave, so we wrapped it up. After first resisting, she shared Missy's cell phone number. "Missy doesn't like to be reminded of her time with Reggie, so she may not talk to you. She's trying to put that chapter of her life behind her. I hear she's living a professional life now in the big city, if you know what I mean?"

I didn't know, but it didn't matter.

After Amy left, I finished my cold McDonald's coffee and caught a harsh glare from the barista. The more I thought about it, the more I believed Amy was still holding back information I needed. I realized all too late I forgot to ask her what she had remembered and wanted to tell me. She was a complicated young woman who bottled up a lot of guilt about many things. I now understood why she hadn't mentioned Brandon in our first meeting. Amy had motive, so I moved her higher on the suspect list

CHAPTER 29

After Amy left, I reflected on my daughter's licentious relationship with Reggie Braun, an older married man. Anger erupted inside me. Ronnie had not been a good mother to our daughter, and I wanted to let her know how I felt about it. I called her and scheduled a last-minute lunch date at the Waffle House near the college. Neither of us had a lot of money to spend on lunch and you always know what to expect at any Waffle House.

Before leaving, I called Brandon to schedule a meeting, but after ringing, it went to voice mail. I didn't leave a message for fear of scaring him off.

My body ached all over. I coveted an Oxy but didn't want to diminish my enmity toward Ronnie or abandon my new-found abstinence. I arrived before Ronnie and sat in the Waffle House parking lot to collect my thoughts. In college, we ate here often. Every Waffle House looks the same no matter when it was built. They must build new ones to look old. Fond memories chipped away at the edges of my anger. I pushed those memories away because I wanted to stay angry.

I dialed Brandon again. Ronnie parked and entered the restaurant. When the call rolled over to voicemail, I hung up and followed her in, anger festering inside me.

Ronnie had already taken a booth and was scanning the restaurant for acquaintances, something all locals do in a small town. She exchanged a small wave and nod with an elderly woman in the corner table. I slid in the bench across from her, resolved to resist her charm and warmth. She looked up with a polite smile that collapsed into a scowl. "Tanner, what's wrong?"

Words boiled up inside, ready to burst forth and punish this negligent mother. When I didn't respond, her attention returned to the menu on the placemat. "Can we order right away? I'm on a tight time schedule. The store's short-handed, and I need to get back."

I glowered at her while she studied the menu, a menu that hadn't changed in thirty years, and she knew by heart. "I think I'll eat light today." She recoiled when she looked up and noticed my dour face. "There is something wrong."

I took a deep breath to control myself. "Yeah, there's something wrong-*you*."

"What are we having today?" The waitress's gravelly voice escaped between gapping yellow teeth. Rail-thin, wrinkled skin hung on her, framed by thinning, unkempt gray hair held in check by a large barrette. If I didn't know better, I would have sworn this same woman had waited on us back in college.

Ronnie ordered a grilled chicken salad and un-sweet tea—healthy but odd choices in a Waffle House. I choked back my fury long enough to order a double cheeseburger with hash browns, scattered, smothered and covered.

"You need to watch what you eat, Tanner. You're going to bulk up and die young." Glaring at her, my outrage built. "You *are really* upset, aren't you? What is it?"

The dam burst. Words came out like a tidal wave. "I just learned our daughter slept with Reggie Braun, an older married man, for money. Is that why you think he killed her? Don't you think you should have told me about this? It's central to the whole investigation. What kind of mother were you anyway? Maybe if you had involved me in her life, things might have turned out differently."

I paused to catch my breath before my head exploded. Ronnie rocked back, face taut and eyes bulging. Her head reddened while waiting for the other nosey customers to return their attention to their meals.

She spoke softly, tensed muscles indicating she was trying to hold strong emotions in check. "You're right, Tanner. I should have been more upfront about things but feared you might think ill of her if you knew. I wanted you to keep an open mind about her. Is that so wrong?"

Her head slumped forward, and tears rained down her face. She removed her glasses and dabbed her eyes with a hanky from her purse. She took a deep breath before making eye contact. "I'm sorry I wasn't a better mother. It was a lot of responsibility raising her alone for all those years after the divorce. The meager child support didn't do much to support us, so I worked two jobs. I couldn't spend much time with her. She fell under the influences of her friends and took on their values. Lord knows, I tried. But you're only looking at the bad in her right now. Lorelei had a lot of good in her, too. She was kind and caring, always putting others first. She didn't want to be like me and work herself to death, so she went to college to make something of herself. Tim and I couldn't afford to send her, and her grades weren't good enough for scholarships. She would have done almost anything to go to school. When I learned about her arrangement with Reggie, I tried to convince her to back out of it, but she said it was too late. I sensed she was afraid of him. I hear he associates with some very bad people."

"And that's why you think Reggie killed her?"

"After Lorelei met Brandon, she tried to get out of her bargain with Reggie. He flat refused and went ballistic. There were rumors Braun Enterprises was bidding on several large government contracts. If the nature of their relationship came out, he would have had no chance for those contracts.

"It seems foolish now, but I didn't want you to think poorly of our daughter. I care what you think about her." She laid her hand on mine. My enmity subsided as if her touch drew it out of me. When we were dating, I never could stay mad at this woman. I felt empty—no love, no hate.

"Is there anything else you're not telling me?"

She paused for a moment before she resumed eating. "Were you aware Amy dated Brandon before Lorelei did?"

"Yes, Amy told me. I think she still harbors deep feelings for him. She says she forgave Lorelei for stealing him but didn't convince me."

"There may be more to that than you think. I don't know if I agree with her, but Mom thinks Lorelei and Amy were lovers before Brandon entered the picture."

I dropped the last half of my burger on my plate, splattering scattered, smothered and covered hash browns. "What? Did Lorelei have no morals at all? The more I investigate, the more trash I discover about her." My appetite gone, I shoved my plate away. "What kind of mother were you?"

A soft whimper escaped from Ronnie before she regained composure. Her face reddened, and her jaw tightened. "I'm sorry. I told you, being a single mother wasn't easy. You wouldn't know anything about that kind of responsibility. You just ran off to live your life without any worries." She tapped the table with an extended index finger in emphasis. "I did the best I could."

Fury erupted in me again, sending my blood pressure into the stratosphere. "How dare you turn this back on me! How dare you! Had I known about her, I would've done everything possible to help you raise a fine young lady and send her to college. You didn't allow me that opportunity."

"Sir." The short-order cook stood at our booth in a soiled apron. "Can you please hold it down? You're disturbing our customers. If you can't restrain yourselves, I'll have to ask you to leave."

A quick scan of the silent restaurant confirmed all eyes were trained on us. "I'm sorry. Can we get the check?"

The waitress jumped out from behind the cook and laid the bill on the table as if to encourage our departure. When they returned to their stations, I counted to ten to contain my anger before speaking. "Okay. Is there anything else you haven't told me?"

"No." Tears streamed from reddened eyes. We sat in silence while other patrons kept looking our way for the next outburst.

"Look, Ronnie, I'm sorry I jumped all over you. You're still hurting from your loss. Although I never knew our daughter, I too am grieving her and took it out on you. That's not fair." As I said before, I never could stay angry at this woman. She was my kryptonite.

Ronnie removed her glasses to wipe her eyes and took a deep breath to collect herself. When the tears stopped, she snatched the check off the table and stood. "I've got lunch."

She paid the tab at the register while I waited at the door. We walked to her car without a word spoken. She unlocked it, and I opened her door for her.

Her forced smile exhibited signs of shyness. "Oh, I almost forgot. I received the police report." She pulled it from her purse and handed it to me. I browsed through the four creased sheets of paper, which didn't take long. Where was the fifty-page report I saw at Mallory's house? The first page summarized the findings and concluded death by suicide. The last three contained a series of crime scene photos that clawed at my gut. I shook my head in disgust.

A puzzled look on her face, Ronnie asked, "Tanner, what's wrong?"

"This isn't the full report. There aren't any details here and no coroner's report, although the first page refers to it. The report should be about fifty pages long. This is a whitewash if I've ever seen one." Once again, the two of us were on the same team.

"Fifty pages? What do you mean?"

"I've seen the real report. It's at least fifty pages and has ten times more pictures. It said something about the possibility of foul play."

"Where did you see a longer report?"

I wasn't ready to mention my involvement with Mallory because Ronnie might question my motives. I clung to the hope of re-igniting things with Ronnie, but now I had stepped in it. "That's not important. What's important is that this report is part of a cover-up. If they issued this as a final report, then the case is officially closed."

We locked eyes in silence until it became awkward. The thin line between hate and love for this woman evaporated as strong feelings of affection overwhelmed any vestiges of anger. "Thanks for lunch."

She looked at me with a sad smile. "I'm sorry I held back on you about Lorelei's relationships. It's still a very sore subject with me."

She leaned forward and kissed me on the cheek and withdrew only a few inches as if waiting for me to make the next move. I grabbed her and clutched her close while kissing her hard on the lips. She didn't resist. In fact, I swear she slipped me tongue first, but that may be revisionist history. If I could have, I would have invited her back to my room.

After several minutes of passionate kissing, she pulled away. "I'm sorry. I shouldn't have done that. Please forgive me." Clearly, flustered, she dove into her car and tried to close the door, against my resistance. I leaned in and kissed her again. She accepted it willingly before pushing me away. "Really, Tanner, I've got to go or I'll be late." I knew she was lying because our lunch had ended early. Maybe she still loved me. I loved her so much it hurt.

CHAPTER 30

Brandon answered my next call. "Who is this? It's the third time you've called in the last hour." In the background, metal clanged and a television blared the Fox News channel.

"Hello, Brandon. Hope I didn't call you at a bad time. My name is Tanner Nole. You don't know me, but I got your number from Amy Hall." Even though I couldn't see him, I sensed him straightening up at the mention of her name. "I've been retained by Veronica Mason, Lorelei's mother, to investigate her death." He didn't respond, so I continued. "Could we meet this afternoon? I need to ask you some questions."

"I'm real busy today. Call me later in the week."

"I'm from Savannah and only in town for a few days. Both Amy and Lorelei's mother think it important for us to talk."

"I told you I'm real busy. Call me later."

"I understand you were very close to Lorelei. I'm guessing you know she didn't commit suicide. There's evidence she was murdered, and I need your help to prove it and catch her killer."

He paused for a minute. "Okay. I'm finishing my workout and about to head to the shower. Can you be at Hollinger's Gym in twenty minutes? I'll meet you in the snack bar."

Three college-age guys, each sitting alone, sipped large frothy drinks in the gym's beverage bar. The most athletic of the bunch was glued to his smartphone. I approached and asked if he was Brandon. He shot me a dirty look and said "no" in an irritated tone and returned attention to his phone.

A handsome, slender black man two tables over, stood. "Are you Mr. Nole? I'm Brandon."

Lorelei's boyfriend was black. I was okay with that, just surprised. People in small southern towns try hard to not show prejudices that still exist below the surface. I considered the issues a bi-racial relationship must have created for them and wondered if his color might explain part of Reggie's rage over him.

I joined Brandon at his table and eyed his frothy green beverage. "What are you drinking?"

"Kale and banana smoothie with protein powder. Want one?"

There were no beverages on the digital menu board for less than eight dollars. "No thanks. I've already reached my limit of kale for the day. As I said, I'm investigating Lorelei's death."

"Are you a private investigator?"

"No, I'm a writer, murder mysteries. Somehow Lorelei's mother thinks that qualifies me to be a detective." I spread my notes on the table and borrowed a pen from the person behind the register with a large plastic daisy stuck on top to deter it from being stolen. "I understand you were seeing Lorelei before her death. How serious was it?"

"Serious enough. We planned to get married after graduation."

"According to Amy, you broke it off before Lorelei's death."

"Yeah, I couldn't stand her being with that pervert any more. I mean, what's an older guy doing messing around with a college student? Have you seen his wife? She's gorgeous. He's not bad-looking and has tons of money. If he wasn't happy at home, he should have been able to get it anytime he wanted for free.

"She told Reggie we wanted to get married, so she wanted out of their deal. He went nuclear and threatened to have her expelled if she tried to leave him. He's a powerful man around here, so it scared her. To him, Lorelei was something he had paid for, and he wasn't about to give her up. She represented an investment to him, nothing more.

"That's what started our fight the afternoon before her death. She told me she couldn't break it off with Reggie before graduation and asked me to wait for her. I couldn't stand that sicko having his hands on her any longer. She needed to choose—him or me."

"I take it she didn't pick you."

"She claimed she needed us both—not words I wanted to hear. She begged me to let her finish school and then get married and move far away from Talmadge, start a family and forget about all this mess." He wiped his eyes on his shirt sleeve. "I told her I couldn't wait. My friends were needling me about my relationship with someone's paid mistress. It was bad enough that she was white. They couldn't understand why I would date a whore."

That word released a wave of heat inside me. I clenched my jaw and formed fists to maintain control by counting to ten in my head. It must have shown on my face because he watched my every move.

Tears erupted from his dark eyes. He looked around to see if anyone noticed and grabbed one of my napkins with my notes. To his surprise, I snatched it away and replaced it with a blank one. He wiped his eyes but kept them on me as if he feared I might strike him. "I'm sorry. I didn't mean to call her that. She just did what she had to do to get through school. I tried hard to be understanding, but it wore on me. I wish I could take it all back, but she . . ."

"Committed suicide?"

"No. She didn't kill herself. Lorelei would never have done that. She was strong, very strong. I'm sure she was murdered. You said you can prove it, right?"

"Where were you that night?"

"Home, writing a paper due the next day. I pulled an all-nighter."

"Do you have an alibi?"

Brandon flinched and timidly asked, "No. Do I need one?"

"You weren't planning on having dinner with her that night?"

"No. I told you I broke it off that afternoon. That was the last I spoke to her. I needed to wrap my head around a paper that represented half my grade for a course."

"Do you know if she planned on entertaining someone for dinner that night?"

"She didn't say anything about it. I remember she was busy cramming for a journalism test the following day, so she didn't have time to entertain."

"Did you know anything about a stalker?"

"Stalker? No. Oh, wait. She was creeped out by the apartment supervisor, Daniel, or something?"

"You mean Donald?"

"Yeah, that's it, Donald. He kept making suggestive comments and spying on her. Lorelei discovered a video camera hidden in her bedroom. When I confronted him, he laughed in my face and swore he knew nothing about it. He's weird, in a scary sort of way. She told her step-dad about Donald. He bought her a handgun, took her to the range and taught her how to shoot it."

"But she was killed with Amy's gun. They found no other gun in the apartment."

"Yeah. She made her step-dad take it back because she knew she could never use it. Guns scared her too much. That's why I knew right away it was murder. She couldn't use a gun, even on a pervert like Donald, much less herself."

"Do you think Donald might have killed Lorelei?"

He stirred his drink with the straw and paused for a moment. "Maybe. He's weird for sure. I doubt he's ever been laid."

"Who else might have wanted to kill her?"

"Reggie. Things were strained between him and Lorelei at the end. Maybe his wife. She knew about Lorelei. Tanya confronted Lorelei at the student union, and it developed into a catfight. University security showed up and separated them." He took a long sip. "Ray, her dad, maybe. He had a big fight with her just before I got there that day. She wasn't having the best of days."

"What did they fight about?"

Brandon's phone dinged. He checked it and laid it back down. "Ray wanted to borrow money from her. He was in hock to some bookie threatening to break his knee caps or something. The man has a major gambling problem. She felt sorry for him and agreed to loan him money, but then he laid into her again about her sinful relationship with Reggie and about her 'colored' boyfriend. She took the money back and threw him out. He became so upset he swore at her, and that's not something a Jesus freak would normally do."

I checked my notes. "I understand you were dating Amy when you met Lorelei. She said she introduced you two."

"I dated her a few times but broke it off a month before I started dating Lorelei. Amy's too needy and can be psycho sometimes. If I even talked to another girl, she accused me of cheating on her. It was never a serious relationship. She accused me of seeing Lorelei months before we broke up. Maybe she planted the idea of dating Lorelei in my head. I don't know. I'd have to think about that."

"Do you think Amy still loves you?"

"She still calls me late at night sometimes, but I don't answer any more. She left some very nasty voice messages, so I blocked her number."

"Were Amy and Lorelei ever more than BFF's?"

"You mean, like lovers? Not that I know about. They were very close, and Amy can get quite possessive and jealous. They may have experimented, if you know what I mean. That seems to be an in thing for co-eds these days, but I don't think it ever got to the point of them being, you know, lovers. Certainly not after Lorelei started dating me. She would have told me, I think." Brandon fidgeted in his chair. I wasn't sure if he was trying to convince himself or me.

My senses told me he was holding something back. I wasn't sure if his pride had been wounded by the thought of Amy and Lorelei as lovers, or there was something that might implicate him in all this. "Could Amy have killed Lorelei out of jealousy?"

"Amy? No, I don't think so. She can act certifiable sometimes, but I've never seen her turn violent. I know she's a gun nut, a card carrying NRA member and all." His phone vibrated, and he picked it up. "I'm sorry, but I've got class in ten minutes, and it's twelve minutes away. Anything else?"

"Not at the moment. Here's my business card. Call me if you think of anything else."

He turned it over in his hands. "Interesting. This is a bookmark promoting a book. I'm sorry, but I don't have time for recreational reading."

"I told you, I'm a writer. That advertises my book, but it also serves as my business card. You'll find my cell phone number on there. I'll be around for a couple of weeks."

"I thought you said you were only in town for a few days when you called me."

Busted.

Brandon was black. As he left, I wondered how Ronnie, Lorelei's two stepfathers and others in the community felt about that. Not everyone in Talmadge is as open-minded as me. Could racial prejudice somehow be mixed in with all this?

CHAPTER 31

A pop-up thunderstorm soaked my clothes on the short dash to my car. An older green Dodge pickup parked on the other side of my car honked its horn. The driver-side window rolled down with a whine. "Hey, Tanner. Jump in."

Tim Mason's glaring eyes penetrated the misty rain like twin searchlights in the night. A cold chill raced down my spine.

"We need ta talk. Get in." He leaned across and opened the front passenger door.

Dread flowed through my veins as I slipped into the seat. The first attempt to close the door failed with a metal-on-metal clunk. A second, more forceful attempt, succeeded with a loud screech. His truck reeked of cigarette smoke and stale whiskey. I hate smokers and couldn't believe Ronnie would put up with such a disgusting habit. I fought back a cough and pressed the button to roll my window down for fresh air, but it didn't budge.

"Been meanin ta fix that window, but you know how it is. Everythin takes money." After looking me over, he grasped the steering wheel with both hands and stared straight forward.

"What's up?" I asked but didn't want to know.

His grip on the wheel tightened. "You need ta go home 'n quit pokin your nose inta our business."

I decided to play coy. "Is that coming from you or Ronnie?"

His face reddened as he pounded the steering wheel with both hands. "That's comin from me, but I speak for Ronnie."

"Okay. But did Ronnie say she wanted me to stop the investigation?"

"I want you off the case. If I want you off, she wants you off."

"I'd like to hear that from her."

"Stay away from her. It's obvious you're still in love with Ronnie. I worry she may still have feelins fer you, too. She's dressin special every day an wearin a different perfume since you showed up. That lady's been the best thing ever happened ta me. I won't stand by while you swoop in 'n steal er back. I'm not askin, I'm tellin you. Leave town 'n never call Ronnie again."

"Does Ronnie know you're requesting I drop the case and leave town?"

His momentary silence told me volumes. She knew nothing about this conversation. "I don't care what Ronnie wants. Lorelei's gone 'n no damn investigation is goin to bring er back. You're stirrin a lot of people up 'n just makin trouble. I'll do whatever it takes ta keep her. It's best you leave town. Today!"

I don't know if it was a hunch or a hope, but I thought I detected something. "Are you and Ronnie having problems?"

His head whirled to face me, mouth open and eyes bulging. "Not 'til you showed up. Since then, it's been one fight after another. She says I'm just jealous. I reckon she's right, but I got good reason ta be. I don't need this. Promise me you'll stay away from her."

I paused for effect. "How was your relationship with Lorelei?"

The sudden change in topics appeared to catch him off guard because he didn't seem to notice I hadn't answered his question. "I loved her like

144

she was my own, but for some reason I never could live up ta her expectations. I suppose we got along okay, but she treated me more like the husband of her mother than a stepfather. She acted all sophisticated-like 'n looked down on me like some poor Southern redneck. Lord knows I tried ta be a father ta her. It just never seemed ta work."

"How did you feel about Lorelei's lifestyle choices?"

"It didn't really bother me, but it ate at Ronnie. She took it personal, made her feel like she'd been a bad mother. I couldn't stand the pain it caused Ronnie 'n I told Lorelei that."

"When did you tell her this?"

"The afternoon before she died. I went ta see her unannounced. She threw me out. Can you believe that?"

"Did Ronnie know you went to see Lorelei?"

His eyes watered. "Yeah. It caused a huge fight and things have gone downhill from there. I'd do anythin to keep that little lady."

What did he mean by anything? Would he commit murder?

He wiped tears with the sleeve of his gray jumpsuit. For the first time, I noticed a familiar logo on his left breast. "You work for Braun Enterprises?"

He sighed and dropped his gaze to his lap. "Yeah, so what? Half the town works fer the college, the other half fer Braun."

"Did someone at Braun Enterprises suggest you ask me to drop my investigation?"

"It's not what you think. Jobs are hard ta come by in this town. Things aren't exactly boomin. I need this job. Besides, I don't want you round Ronnie no more. If you know what's good fer you, drop the investigation 'n leave town, today."

"And if I don't?"

He turned and stared into my eyes. "If they don't get ta you, I will. It won't be pleasant. I guaran-damn-tee it. These are bad people you're pissin off. Promise me you'll drop the investigation and leave."

Time to play my Ace. "I'm sure you know I was Lorelei's biological father." I waited for a reaction, but none came. "I just found out last week. Now that I know, I have to see this through, not for Ronnie, but for me. Can you understand that? I can't just tuck my tail between my legs and run. I've been running away my whole life."

He chuckled and smirked before producing a flask and taking a big swig. "What makes you think you're Lorelei's father? Did Ronnie tell you that? I wouldn't believe everythin you hear. That little lady ain't the saint you think she is. I'd ask fer a damned DNA test before makin that claim."

My chest knotted. I fought for breath. What was he saying? Could Ronnie be playing me? I needed time to be one hundred percent sure. "Look. I need to wrap up some things today. Give me a day to think about it. Can I get back to you?"

He shook his head. "I hope you have that long. You're livin dangerously, my friend. Oh, and don't breathe a word of our little meetin ta Ronnie or you'll hope they find you fore I do." He took another long drink and put the flask back in his pocket.

When he started the truck, I took that as a signal our meeting had ended. As I unlocked my car, he drove off and yelled through an open window. "Tomorrow. No later or I'll come lookin for you."

I needed more than two days to explore the chemistry between Ronnie and me that had reappeared in the Waffle House parking lot. I gripped the steering wheel, took a deep breath and counted to ten. My hands shook. Until this last meeting, I hadn't considered myself in physical danger. I didn't so much fear Tim as I did the message he just delivered. The words, "These are bad people you're pissing off," echoed in my head. Could I, a lovelorn fool, ignore this new threat? Did I have the guts to see my investigation through in the face of danger?

After chewing a precious Oxy, I washed it down with a swig of tepid water from a bottle in my car. Abstinence would restart tomorrow.

After a few minutes, my hands stopped shaking enough to drive.

CHAPTER 32

Conflicting thoughts spun in my head as Tim headed south, the direction of Braun Enterprises. His threat scared me. What was I getting myself into? With all my being, I wanted to steal his wife, yet I felt sorry for him. He was as beguiled as me by Ronnie's charm. In a way, we shared a bond.

Kissing Ronnie had aroused feelings long repressed in me and apparently in her too. The knowledge that Ronnie and Tim were experiencing marital discord fanned my flames even more. On a wild impulse, I drove north to Talmadge Jewelers. I had ten minutes to catch Ronnie as she left work. I needed to confirm her passion for me was real and as strong as my fervor for her.

I parked near her car in the store lot and waited. She and a younger co-worker came out the back door and headed for their cars while jabbering away. My heart raced in anticipation, but I waited until the other woman got into her car before jumping out and calling to Ronnie as she unlocked her car. Her eyes opened wide with surprise, her brow wrinkled, and a half-smile broke over her face. She scanned the lot for potential snoops. "Tanner, what are you doing here?" Her face beamed.

"Ronnie, we need to talk. Can we go somewhere for a drink or dinner, maybe?"

"I can't. I've got to fix supper for Tim. Can this wait?"

"No. Lunch stirred old feelings for me, and I think it did for you too. I'm in pure agony and need to talk." My heart nearly burst with a longing to take her into my arms and lavish her with kisses. "Can we just sit in the car and talk for a few minutes?"

A woman exited the store, headed to her car. We fell silent, and Ronnie looked away as if that would make her invisible. Once the lady closed her car door, Ronnie looked at me with watery eyes and sighed in surrender. "Okay, but just for a few minutes and not here—too many prying eyes. Can we drive somewhere more private?"

I opened the passenger door for her as any gentleman would. "Tanner, please don't make a scene of this. Just get in and drive. Okay?"

Three blocks away, I pulled into the alley of a retail shopping center where they took deliveries. I shut the engine off and half-turned to her, my heart pounding in anticipation.

She stared straight ahead, her hands clenched, fidgeting. "You're right. We really do need to talk about what happened after lunch today. I've been distracted by it all afternoon, but have some clarity now. Tanner, I acted inappropriately. I don't want to lead you on. There'll always be a special place for you in my heart. But what we had in college is gone, and we can't go back. I'm not the person I was then. I'm married to Tim, so there can't be anything between you and me. I am sorry I gave you false hope earlier. Do you hate me?" With the back of her hand, she wiped the tears streaming down her cheeks and sniffled.

These were not words I wanted to hear and slashed me to the core. I took a deep breath. "Ronnie, I agreed to the Talmadge book signing for one reason—to re-connect with you. I didn't care if I sold any books. All I wanted was to see you because I love you as much as I did twenty years ago. I was a fool, and it tortures me to think how much I hurt you. My life has been empty without you."

She blew her nose into a tissue from her purse, making the same old squeaking noise that always brought a smile to my face.

I laid a gentle hand on the back of her neck. "Today when we kissed, I sensed you still love me, maybe even as much as I love you. You know in your heart we are meant to be together. I don't deserve it, but I'm begging for a chance to prove to you how much I've changed and, hopefully, win you back." Leaning closer, I stroked her hair.

The glow in her eyes validated my words. She smiled, placed her hand on my leg and shook her head. "Damn you. Why can't I get you out of my head? What am I going to do? I'm married."

"Give us a chance. One date, that's all I ask. If the magic's still there, we'll deal with it. If not, we part our ways and cherish fond memories of what we once had. Can you slip away tonight?"

"No. I told you I've got to go home and fix supper for Tim." She paused and took a deep breath. "He's going out of town after work tomorrow. He and some of his old college teammates are going to the game at Middle Tennessee on Saturday. It's too risky to go to any of the local restaurants, so I'll cook dinner. There are too many busybodies in our neighborhood who would question a strange car in our driveway, so I'll pick you up at your hotel, say about six? Oh, bring some white wine. I'll make a chicken dish I think you'll like."

Too embarrassed for her to know where I was staying, I asked her to pick me up at the Country Inn and Suites because, she'd assume I was staying there.

I laid my hand behind her head and pulled her to me. She did not resist, and our lips met. I slipped her tongue, and she accepted it willingly. After a few minutes, she pushed me away. "Take me back to the store. Tim doesn't like it when his supper is late."

"Are you and Tim having problems?" There, I played my trump card.

Her stolid expression confirmed what Tim had confided earlier. With opportunity, my heart soared to new heights.

I pulled around to the front of the strip mall where I noticed an empty sheriff's car in front of the boutique. Concern flooded my thoughts. Was someone following me? Focused on Ronnie, I hadn't kept my eyes out. I vowed to maintain a constant vigil from here on.

Ronnie asked me to drop her off a block from the jeweler's, so no one would spot us together. Driving back to my fleabag motel, I still tasted her wet lips and fantasized about tomorrow night, which seemed an eternity away.

CHAPTER 33

I somehow stumbled to the door to see who had interrupted my sleep. The peephole lens magnified the tarantula tattoo on a bald man's forehead, making it appear alive and ready to pounce. The tall, muscular guy pounded on the door again. A man in the next room hollered out, "What the hell's going on over there? Shut the fuck up! You're wrecking my enjoyment."

No sane person would open the door for such an ominous looking guy. I shouted back—emboldened by the heavy wooden door separating us. "Go away. You got the wrong room."

Through the peephole, I watched him press his ear to the door. "Mr. Nole. I'm Frank. I work nights here at the front desk. You need to come downstairs right away. Someone's trashed your car."

I paused, trying to weigh the merits of opening the door or going back to bed.

"Okay, man. Come down or don't. I don't give a fuck. Not my problem." He turned and left.

After a few minutes to calm my racing heart, I opened the door with extreme caution and gazed around. Hesitant steps became more resolute as I moved down the stairs. Halfway down, a quick scan showed the lobby to be deserted. Near the bottom of the steps, I spotted Frank behind the counter with his back turned toward me. I ducked and tried to slip out the door unnoticed, but the last step emitted a deafening creak.

Frank spun around. "Hey man, I wasn't sure you were coming down. They fucked up your car big time. You piss somebody off? I called the sheriff, but it'll take them a while to get here. They don't rush right over when we call."

"Thanks." I left to check on my car.

Frank was not wrong. The Probe was a mess—windows, headlights and tail lights all smashed, all four tires slashed, hood dented in. Inside, the foam padding bulged out of large slits in the upholstery. Fenders, hood and trunk were adorned with white graffiti. The paint felt dry to the touch, so this had not just happened. The phrases "Go home," "Your (sic) dead" and, my favorite, "Asshole" stood out in neon green.

"Somebody don't like you." Frank stood behind me shaking his head. He didn't appear as big and threatening as seen through the peephole. "Any idea who might have dunnit?"

"I have a pretty good idea. Did you hear or see anything?"

"No, but then I've been in the office working on paperwork. You don't hear much from outside, especially when Tijuana Joe is upstairs with a hooker. He's loud, but then you know what I mean."

A sheriff's car coasted into the parking lot. "What no lights or siren? I guess I don't rate around here." I looked over my shoulder to see Frank's reaction, but he had disappeared, possibly spooked by the arrival of law enforcement.

The squad car pulled behind the remains of my car, and Mallory climbed out with paper pad and cell phone. "Tanner, what the hell are you doing at a fleabag hotel like this? It's far worse than that other place you were staying."

"I got evicted. Turns out I was raising the caliber of their clientele too much." Disappointed she didn't laugh at my weak joke, I continued. "Actually, it turns out Reggie Braun owns every hotel in town and black-balled me. This was the only place I could get."

She did a quick walk around. "Guess some people don't appreciate a classic car like we do." She looked at me with a smile. My glare erased her smile.

"Any witnesses?" She took pictures with her smartphone.

"None I know of. The guy working the desk didn't see or hear anything. None of the patrons of this fine establishment will want it known they were here."

She looked around the parking lot. "Guess there's no security footage either. Any idea who might have done this?"

I chuckled. "You mean other than Deputy Lowell or one of Reggie's other henchmen?" I pointed to the word "Asshole" painted on the side. "His pet name for me. The message is pretty clear, too. He wants me out of town."

Mallory finished taking pictures. "Not that I want to see you leave, but you might want to give it some thought." She closed the distance between us and lowered her voice. "If it was Lowell, he can be a nasty opponent. He's accustomed to having things his way around these parts. The sheriff just looks the other way."

"What are you doing here, anyway? I thought you had an early shift."

"Working a double. One of our deputies had a baby. I mean, his wife had a baby. He's taking time off. Good thing I'm working. Two deputies closer to the scene begged off. You're not popular in these parts. My guess is your car, despite being a classic, is a total loss. I'll call a tow truck." She called it in on her police radio. "They can't pick it up until tomorrow morning. Can I see your registration and insurance cards?"

"Wait. Aren't you going to dust for fingerprints?"

"No, we don't do that for minor vandalism cases. Not cost effective."

"Minor! Not cost effective! Hell, this car is about all I own. I only have liability insurance, so there's no insurance to collect. I want to sue somebody for doing this."

A man and woman in a dark sedan pulled in, but then screeched to a halt, backed up and left in a hurry.

"Sure you do. Good luck with that. Insurance card and registration?"

I tried to open the passenger door, but the handle had been ripped off. I went in through the driver's door and produced the documents.

She looked them over. "You're going to need a car. Enterprise will bring one to you."

I flinched. Enterprise would need a valid credit card. I wasn't sure any of mine would work.

A high-rider pickup truck with a man and two lively women, all wearing cowboy hats, slowed, but they too sped off at the sight of the squad car.

Frank poked his head out the hotel door. "Hey, deputy, can you wrap it up? You're bad for business. No one's come in for the last hour. I gotta quota to make."

She waved acknowledgment at Frank and returned her attention to me. "Sure hate to see you in a place like this. Isn't there somewhere else you could stay?" Her eyes emitted warmth, her tone expressed compassion, but she did not offer to put me up at her place.

Maggie Mae had invited me to stay with her, but now that I was on the verge of scoring with Ronnie, I didn't need her mother looking over my shoulder.

CHAPTER 34

I awoke late morning. It had taken time to settle down after last night's vandalism even after breaking down and taking an Oxy. Resetting the clock, today was day one of abstinence. It required great effort to get up, dress and go down to the lobby.

The transgender who had checked me in the first night lounged on a sofa in the lobby, reading the newspaper and drinking something out of a coffee mug. She looked up, smiled and flashed her eyebrows. "Good morning Mr. Nole," she said in her deep, raspy voice.

"You remembered my name. I'm surprised with the traffic you get through here."

"Oh, we don't get many full-time guests here, if you know what I mean. The tow truck picked your car up about an hour ago. Man, they did a number on it. Who'd you piss off anyway?"

"I need to rent a cheap car. Any suggestions?"

"Enterprise will bring you a car."

"I need way cheaper than Enterprise. Is there a Rent-a-Wreck or something like that around?"

"Afraid not, but I know a guy who can get you a car real cheap." She batted her fake eyelashes at me. "What size and color you lookin for, honey?"

"Yeah, I bet you know somebody. I need something legit, not a hot car. I just want to rent it."

"Well now, that would be a different guy. How long you looking to rent it?" She stood, walked behind the counter, retrieved her purse and extracted a smartphone. It seems everyone but me has one these days.

"A week, maybe two at most. And, it's got to be cheap, cheap."

An hour later, a short, slender black guy with long dreads met me outside my hotel. A beautiful shiny, late model black Mercedes coupe sent my heart swooning. The guy spoke in a heavy Jamaican accent. "Hello. My name Kymani. I understand you wanna rent cheap car."

"Yeah, but I can't afford something like a Mercedes. I'm on a tight budget."

"No, no, that be my car, man. Here's car for you." He directed me to a reddish-brown Pinto with several cancerous holes in the body around the wheel wells. "This car for budget-minded. Just tuned up, so it run real good and get good gas mileage. Not burn much oil."

"A Pinto? Aren't they a death trap? Something about exploding gas tanks?"

"That only problem if you get rear-ended. Drive defensively, and you be okay, man."

I walked around and surveyed the car. If the paint hadn't been reddish-brown to match the rust, the car would have looked worse. The tires seemed to be four different sizes, and tread was in short supply. I doubt the car had been washed in years. The dirt very likely held the thing together. "I was hoping for something a little bigger."

"Bigger? I got bigger, but you say cheap, cheap. This cheap, cheap, man." Kymani laughed.

"How cheap is cheap?"

"Twenty-five dollar a day. You pay for gas and oil. Deal?" He held out his hand.

"Twenty-five dollars? I can rent something from Enterprise for that and a lot nicer too."

He bowed his head and chuckled. "Man, you not rent car long time. Enterprise forty, maybe feefty dollar a day. This good deal. It a classic."

I walked around the car a second time and shook my head in disbelief. This might be a classic, but it was no Ford Probe.

Kymani said, "Okay, man. I like you. For you, special deal, man. Fifteen dollar a day and bring back wid full tank. Deal?"

We shook on it. I gave him five days up front which nearly emptied my wallet. When I got in the car, a tear in the seat pinched my butt. The car reeked of cigarettes and joints. The gas gauge rested on empty. Fifteen dollars a day and bring it back full. What a deal!

CHAPTER 35

Returning to my room, I fretted over my critical financial state. Even on a near-starvation fast-food diet my cash would run out in three days, four tops, and my credit cards were all maxed out. The Palace would soon need another advance on my room, or I'd be homeless again. And, most of all, I needed to buy more Oxy.

A loan seemed the only option, but who would loan me money? Ronnie is nearly as broke as me and Tim would go ballistic if she helped out. Maggie Mae seemed to be doing okay, but I didn't want her having leverage over me. Reggie Braun was loaded, but I'd be the last person he'd loan money to. Maybe a bank, but I'd need a gun, a note and a disguise. Even a loan shark would deem me too high a risk.

Then it struck me—my old friend, Neena. I dialed her.

"Hey, Neena, this is Tanner."

"Tanner, how's the investigation coming? I hope you're calling to tell me you've finished and are coming back to work."

"Investigation's going great. I have strong evidence it was murder instead of a suicide. Now I'm trying to ID the murderer and should wrap it up next week." I doubted she was gullible enough to believe my bullshit. She knew me too well.

"That's great. We really need you back. The partners are asking when you'll return. Look, I appreciate your checking in, but I need to run. The waiting room is packed."

"Whoa, Neena. I need to ask a favor." Silence. "I need an advance on my salary. Expenses have been running higher than expected here, the price of progress, I guess. Say a couple of grand to tide me over until I get back. You know I'm good for it." Continued silence. "Neena?"

"Yeah, I'm still here. My hearing must be going bad. I thought you asked for an advance on salary you haven't earned yet because you're not here working like you should be."

"Your hearing is better than you think. About that advance?" Mentally I got down on my knees.

"Tanner, there's no way in hell I can go to the partners with an absurd request like that." Her voice sounded restrained, but that was only the second time I had heard her use a four-letter word.

"Neena, I really need the money. You see, I owe a bad guy, and if I don't pay him, I'm afraid of what might happen. I'm really scared."

She sighed. "What are we talking about here, Tanner? Gambling? Drugs? Prostitution?"

The drug question struck too close to home, so a different vice seemed better. "Gambling. I made a bet on a sure thing and lost. Guess I'm not much of a gambler, but I've learned my lesson. Please?" My begging tone disgusted even me.

"All right, Tanner, I can loan you twelve-hundred out of my own pocket, but that's all. And you better be back here a week from Monday, or I can't help you anymore. This is the last time I go out on a limb for you. Understand?"

I understood, but then she had said the same thing last time. Neena is a good heart. She just can't help herself when it comes to helping the down and out. And I qualified as very down and very out.

Neena wired me the money that afternoon. One problem solved, a growing list of problems yet to come.

CHAPTER 36

Fear of losing my menial job now motivated me to complete the investigation quickly. My success manipulating Neena emboldened me to take another shot at everybody's main suspect—Reggie Braun. The Pinto started with a loud back-fire and billowed black smoke. Memories of my violated Ford Probe elicited anger toward Deputy Lowell and prompted a side-trip to the sheriff's office on my way to Braun Enterprises.

To my pleasant surprise, Mallory manned the front desk. Heavy makeup failed to conceal bags under sunken eyes.

I gave her my best empathetic smile. "What are you doing working here? Don't you ever sleep?"

She smiled warmly. "Oh, Tanner, I do sleep. After I left you early this morning, it was straight home and to bed. Slept for four hours before starting my shift here about an hour ago. The real question is, what're you doing here?"

I pulled my shoulders back and extended my chest like a banty rooster. "I'm here to see the sheriff. I'm sure Deputy Lowell had my car vandalized last night, and I think you know it too."

She glanced around the office before speaking in lowered voice. "Not a good idea to accuse Deputy Lowell without proof. I don't have time to go to a funeral. Besides, the sheriff's not in today. He took the day off."

Deputy Lowell exited his office and headed for the back door without looking our direction. I turned to follow and confront him.

She jumped out of her seat and grabbed my arm to restrain me. "You don't want to do that. You don't have any proof, and that guy hates you already. I suggest you drop your investigation and go home before you get hurt."

"Is that a threat?"

"No, it's free advice, but that doesn't mean it's not good advice. Think it over."

It took me a minute to collect myself. "Okay, Mal. I'll give it some thought." She didn't look convinced, maybe because I'm not a good liar.

"Get out of here, and let me get back to work. Don't go Don Quixote and get yourself killed."

I needed to stay in the good graces of this potential information source, so acquiesced to her suggestion.

After I left the parking lot, Lowell pulled out in a sheriff's car, and I followed him at a safe distance. It was risky to shadow him, but he wouldn't recognize my new wheels. Excessive speed suggested he might be late for an important meeting. I tried to match his speed, despite the Pinto's violent vibration that blurred my vision and made me feel ill.

He pulled in to La Model, and the valet parked his Jeep next to a red Ferrari convertible I'd seen here before.

After self-parking, nose out for a quick getaway, I followed him in. My favorite maître d' stood guard at his podium, so I lowered my head in a lame attempt to sneak by. He called out, "Sir, stop! You can't come in here. Sir, you must leave immediately, or I'll call the sheriff."

I spotted Reggie sitting at his favorite table with Lowell, so I plowed on, maître d' in tow. "Don't bother. I see a deputy, so I'll speak to him for you."

The two at the table didn't see me approach from their blind side. Lowell spoke with confidence. "Don't worry. You know, I've got your back on this."

Reggie responded with emphasis, his expression one of determination. "Thomas, I'm telling you I don't know anything about that girl's death. I don't understand why you can't believe me?"

As I swung around their table, the maître d' and two waiters took up positions behind me. Recognition exploded on both men's faces. Lowell moved to stand, but Reggie took charge and motioned for him to sit back down. "Mr. Nole, you seem to pop up in the strangest of places. I'm beginning to think you are stalking me. Should the deputy here press charges against you?"

"I need to ask you a few questions about Lorelei's death. You do remember the young lady you corrupted with your money?" The commotion drew all eyes and ears in the restaurant. It became so silent I swore I heard the effervescence escaping from Lowell's Coke.

"I don't understand why this matter is of concern to you." Reggie's tone sounded dismissive.

"Because I'm . . ." I wanted to say, "Lorelei's father" but thought better of it. ". . .a friend of her mother and she asked me to investigate. She's convinced her daughter was murdered and the suicide thing is just a cover-up. After looking in to it, I agree with her."

Lowell started to come at me again until Reggie put a restraining hand on his shoulder.

"Deputy Lowell tells me, that besides being a trouble-maker, you are an author and a very bad one at that. He said you write murder mysteries, so you must have a vivid imagination. I'll bet you can invent all kinds of conspiracy theories, like a suicide that isn't a suicide and murders that don't exist. Take my advice and drop this nonsense before someone like you gets hurt. I suggest you go home and spend your time writing a better book."

My mind went blank for a few seconds before refocusing. On impulse, I blurted out. "Did you kill Lorelei?"

Reggie choked on his drink. Lowell sprung from his chair. Two waiters each grabbed one of my arms.

"Get him out of here." Reggie gave an exaggerated, dismissive wave of the hand.

"Wait! I'm not done with my questions," I pleaded.

"If you insist on interrogating me, call my administrative assistant and make an appointment. Goodbye, Mr. Nole."

"I've called her more than a dozen times, but she won't schedule a meeting. She always gives me some lame excuse."

The two hefty waiters grabbed me from behind and dragged me outside with the deputy following close behind. Outside, the waiters held me up, my feet barely touching ground. Lowell took a position in front of me. "Asshole, you must be one dumb son of a bitch. I've played nice up to this point. Now you're forcing me to get rough." He punched me in the stomach. I doubled over as pain shot through my gut, and air rushed out of my lungs.

Lowell leaned down to be face-to-face with me. I smelled his wretched breath. "Leave Mr. Braun alone, asshole. If you bother him again, I'll arrest you for harassment and disturbing the peace. I guarantee the sheriff won't intervene again. Our jail's not the friendliest place in town for assholes like you. It has a reputation in this part of the state. So, if you know what's good for you, pack up and go home while you still can. Comprenez-vous?"

I regained some composure until Lowell landed a second blow on my chin. He turned away and headed back in the restaurant shaking his right hand. The waiters dropped me and followed him, wiping their hands as if they had gotten soiled touching me. My body collapsed into a heap on the pavement.

A young parking valet approached tentatively. "Do you have a parking ticket?"

Unable to speak, I shook my head "no" and waved him off. I rubbed my aching jaw and fought for breath. He shrugged, pivoted and walked away. I spit blood on the sidewalk in defiance.

A stubby hand reached down to me. "Let me give you a hand there, Tanner." The unfamiliar voice came from a short, overweight white man in a well-worn dark gray overcoat with matching classic fedora. His brown eyes smiled through gray horn-rimmed glasses. He helped me up and caught me when I staggered. Once I stabilized, the mini Dick Tracy handed me a business card in the shape of a semi-automatic handgun.

Printed on the business card was "Wendell J. Sprat, Private Investigator, Sprat Investigations, LLP" followed by a Georgia license number, phone number and email address. He resumed speaking at a fast clip yet enunciated each word clearly. "I understand you are investigating a murder case where Reggie Braun is the prime suspect. I'm working a case for a client and suspect our endeavors might be closely aligned. Can I buy you a cup of coffee and explore how we might cooperate to our mutual benefit?" I stumbled a little, and he rushed to steady me. "I don't think you are in any condition to drive. My car is parked right over there." He pointed to an older boat of a light green Cadillac with a white vinyl roof.

Bells still rang in my head. "To be honest, I could use a drink more than coffee."

He drove up the street to a sports bar he knew. The bar's name was Hitters, an apparent play on the Hooters' brand, but the theme inside was quite different. The wait staff and bar-tenders wore conservative umpire shirts and black slacks in an obvious contrast to Hooters.

We sat at the bar, and I ordered a double-bourbon with water back. He asked for black coffee and continued his prattle with generous hand motions to highlight every statement. He pointed to my double shot. "I never touch the stuff. I drink coffee—morning, noon and night. PI's works long, odd hours. When I lay my head on the pillow, I'm out like a light switch. Caffeine doesn't affect me."

I disagreed with that last claim but kept it to myself. "So, Wendell, you're a licensed detective."

"Call me Jack. That's what all my friends call me. I just use Wendell on the card because it adds some class. Truth is that's not my license number on there. A friend of mine, who is licensed, let's me use it. Nobody in their right mind would hire an unlicensed PI. I'm working on my license, studying online, and am confident I'll pass the next test because I came close the last two tries."

I studied the card he'd given me. "Unusual business card you got here. I see you're incorporated as an LLP. That's impressive."

"The pistol shape differentiates my business card from my competition. The LLP makes me seem more, you know, professional. I plan to register as an LLP but haven't yet taken on any partners."

"Your card does stand out, but do people keep it? It doesn't fit in a business card file."

He waved his hand. "Nobody keeps business cards anymore. Everything's gone electronic. Hopefully, they enter my contact information into some app before they toss it."

I sipped my bourbon and followed it with a drink of water. "Wendell J. I assume your middle name is either Jack or John. Jack Sprat—isn't that a nursery rhyme? Did your parents have a sick sense of humor, or were they just cruel?"

"I had terrific parents. All my grammar school classmates teased me by calling me Jack Sprat. It was only funny because I've been overweight most of my life. I got tired of getting beat up every time I challenged them on it and finally just acquiesced. What can I say? It stuck."

I chuckled. "And your wife, if you are married?"

"I'm divorced, but it was ironic. I'm short and chubby, and she was tall and lean." He finished his coffee and pushed the cup forward for a refill.

I took another sip of bourbon. "You said you're working on a case that has something to do with my murder investigation. How did you know about my investigation?"

"Hel—lo." He slapped his forehead. "I'm a private investigator. I got sources. Our investigations have a point of intersection—Reggie Braun. I'm following him for his wife who is my client. She wants out of the marriage but signed a prenup. She's become accustomed to the high-life and needs leverage to break the prenup. You know, something like murder or adultery."

"If you are so wired in then you know Reggie had a licentious relationship with my daughter, Lorelei. I'm no lawyer, but I'd think that would be enough to contest her prenup."

"Wait a minute, Lorelei was your daughter?"

"I thought you were some hotshot PI. You didn't know I was her father, biologically speaking?"

"Well, I know now. Tanya didn't decide to divorce him until after your daughter's death. I started working the case a week later. Reggie did a good job staying on the down-low on that chapter of his life. Nobody in their right mind will testify against him, even Tanya's friends. It's been difficult dredging up concrete evidence on his affairs. Tanya thinks she's in love now and wants to marry her boy-toy. He's poor, so she needs Reggie's money. If Reggie goes down for murder, she's home free."

"Did I see you at La Model last Tuesday around lunchtime?"

"Nah, I had to work another case. I'm working Tanya's case on contingency and won't get paid until she gets Reggie's bucks. She claims he keeps her on a tight allowance. So, I do other work to stay afloat."

I showed him the pictures on my phone of Reggie having an intimate lunch with his admin.

Jack's eyes popped wide open. "Holy shit! That's his admin, what's her name? Nancy, that's it. Can you airdrop this to me? This is good, but it's not enough. Reggie'll just claim it was business. I'll need something more substantial, but this is a good start."

"Sorry, I don't airdrop. You said you want to work together to prove Reggie murdered Lorelei. Does Tanya think he did it?"

"To be honest, I think she wants to believe he did it, but isn't sure. I see remnants of doubt in her."

"I need to question Tanya. Is that something you can set up?"

"So, we're partners, then?" He took my nod as a yes and called Tanya. He scheduled a meeting at the Country Club restaurant in thirty minutes.

CHAPTER 37

Jack and I found Tanya Braun dining on the patio. An expensive white tennis ensemble highlighted her shapely petite frame and exposed a lot of, what appeared to be, well-engineered breasts. Sumptuous dirty blond hair, cut in a bob with blond highlights, framed a dazzling tanned face. Brandon referred to her as a looker, but she was striking.

The fit, younger man sharing her table reminded me of a romance novel cover. Long, sun-bleached hair draped to the collar of a loud Hawaiian shirt, half undone, exposing a muscular waxed chest.

Jack leaned into me and whispered. "Don't say anything about being a writer. I told her you're a PI from Savannah. Oh, and refer to me as Wendell rather than Jack."

Tanya ignored her doting tablemate and scanned the patio like a hawk in search of prey. Jack interrupted her search. "Hello, Mrs. Braun."

Disdain poured through expensive sunglasses. "Wendell, don't call me that, it reminds me I'm still trapped in my marriage. Just call me Tanya. How many times must I tell you?" Stunning eyes peered over the top of expensive sunglasses and scoured me up and down to the apparent consternation of her dining partner. "Oh, hello there. Who might you be?" She leaned over and whispered in her guest's ear. He shot me a killing glare, stood, kissed Tanya on top of her forehead, and left, his kale salad half-eaten.

She paused until he moved out of hearing range. "Wendell, you must introduce me to your scrumptious companion."

As Jack introduced us, she held her hand out, palm down like royalty expecting it to be kissed. Her expression soured when I shook the offered hand. She removed her sunglasses and undressed me with her eyes. I now understand how a woman feels when a man looks her over—violated and cheapened.

"My horoscope said pleasure aligns with expressive Mercury, and this certainly is a pleasure." She winked. "Take a seat, boys. What's your sign, Tanner?"

"Aries, but I'm not into astrology." I consciously avoided checking her out by maintaining eye contact so as not to encourage her.

"I'm a Sagittarius. We're both the fire element. How delicious." Tanya worked an app on her smartphone. "Oh, interesting. Your horoscope says a new influence will enter your life." She did a seated version of a curtsy and set the phone down. "Wendell tells me you are investigating the death of that slut my husband kept."

Her disparaging reference to my daughter drove me to verbally accost this woman and storm out, but I overpowered the urge by counting to ten silently. "That's right. Lorelei's mother retained me to investigate her death. She questions that it was suicide."

I lost concentration for a moment, and my eyes dropped to her cleavage. A self-induced mental cold shower reestablished my focus.

She caught me looking, winked and smiled. "What makes her mother think it might have been murder?"

"I'm not at liberty to say at this stage of the investigation. Do you have information that supports suicide?"

Tanya twisted her hair around her index finger. "That girl was under a lot of stress. It was written all over her face."

"When did you meet her?"

She flinched and studied me as if looking deeper than before. "Oh, a week or two before her death, she called and asked me to meet her at the student union. I'd been pressuring Reggie to end it and kick her out. Can you believe it? She asked me to back off and let her finish her education. I told her to go to hell."

"I understand things got a little heated that day."

She laughed and waved her hand in a dismissive gesture. "What? You think I killed her?"

I shrugged my shoulders, and her face became serious.

"I'm not a murderer, Mr. Nole." If she had been attracted to me, it seemed to evaporate. "Okay, I may have raised my voice and called her names, but I do that even with friends. She took it surprisingly well. Hell, in a way, I felt sorry for her."

It appeared she could lie without any outward tells. That worried me. "How long did you know about his relationship with Lorelei?"

"Since it started, a couple of years, I guess. And I knew about Missy before her and Bonnie before that. He didn't try very hard to hide his indiscretions from me. He gets pleasure rubbing my nose in them. Because of the prenup, I couldn't do anything more than bitch about it, and believe me, I did."

"Did Lorelei express suicidal tendencies when you spoke to her?"

"I don't know. How do you tell if someone is suicidal? She shared that her fiancé dumped her because of her relationship with Reggie. I urged her to break it off with my husband and mend things with her guy before it was too late. She said she wanted to but couldn't until she finished college. She needed Reggie's financial support. If I could have, I'd have given her the money. Reggie keeps me on a tight financial leash, so he would have known. That man can be very scary sometimes."

"Is he capable of murder?" Jack asked.

"Yeah. That's one reason I hired Wendell. Reggie wanted me out of the picture, and it scared me. If Wendell uncovers anything, he'll let me know. Sorry, darling." She shrugged and smiled at Jack. "I didn't mention it for fear you'd charge me extra for protection services."

"You were saying you think Reggie is capable of murder."

"Yes. That man's ambition and ego are unbounded. He will do anything for money—kill me, one of his sluts or anybody who crosses him." She showed me a catty smile. "Or even kill you if you get too close to the truth. That's why he keeps his college buddy in the sheriff's office so close—to cover his tracks."

A chill ran down my spine. "Did Reggie have any other women other than the college students he kept?"

"Reggie always has at least one other on the hook at all the times. Nancy, his new admin, is the latest."

"And how is it you know about his other women?"

"I told you. He doesn't try to keep them secret. He'd love for me to divorce him so he can find someone younger and prettier while hanging on to all his money."

"Prettier than you?" I heard myself say. Jack shot me a dirty look.

Tanya perked up, leaned in and batted deliciously long eyelashes at me that signaled I was back in her good graces. "I simply adore this guy, Wendell."

Avoiding her beguiling blue eyes, I struggled to regain focus. "Does Reggie know about your boy toy?"

She sat back and glared, contempt showing on her face. "That is my tennis coach you're referring to. You're being very presumptuous." She looked around. "Yes, Reggie has his suspicions, but I doubt he really gives a damn other than hoping I divorce him under our prenup so he can be free and stay rich."

"So, you hired Wendell to find dirt on your husband?"

"It's one way to break the prenup. I told you he's a dangerous man."

"Do you know where Reggie was the night of the murder?"

"Yeah, he was with me. I remember because he appeared agitated but wouldn't say why. He couldn't sit still and stayed up into the wee hours of the morning."

"Did you ask him what was wrong?"

"Oh, sure. We still talk, and on occasion, share our bed. He said it was just business, and I wouldn't understand."

"Did you believe him?"

"Let's just say he rarely brings his work home. He's too exhausted by his whoring around."

"So, you were home that night?"

"My tennis instructor got sick, so Reggie carried in Chinese takeout, if I remember."

Tanya had taken control of this interrogation. I needed to knock her out of her comfort zone. "Did you kill Lorelei?"

Tanya's eyes opened wide. A fake laugh escaped as she laid her hand on her heart. "Me? You think I could kill someone? Oh, I see—motive. Jealous wife kills husband's mistress to save marriage. There's nothing in our marriage worth saving. I've moved on, you might say. Besides, I would need to kill half the pretty, young women in Talmadge to stop that prick from running around."

"I need to interview Reggie, but he's hiding behind his admin who won't give me an appointment. He and Deputy Lowell have strongly suggested I drop my inquiry and go home. I know your marriage is strained, but do you have enough influence with Reggie to set up a meeting with me, without his deputy friend intervening?"

"Does this mean our meeting is over? We were just getting to know each other." She patted my hand and smiled. "I can't get that prick to take out the trash." She looked away in thought. "I'll see what I can do. Maybe if I bitch enough, he'll do it just to shut me up."

"I'd appreciate it. Can I get your number in case I think of more questions?"

As Jack and I stood, Tanya did also. "Only if you give me your number." She stepped close, and our eyes connected, her powerful eyes hypnotizing me for a second. Standing on her toes, she pressed her augmented breasts against me and kissed me hard on the lips. Paralyzed, I couldn't resist even if I had wanted to.

"Have Wendell give you my personal number. Call me if you need anything more—and I do mean *anything*." She winked, and a seductive smile broke across her face. She rummaged through her purse, producing a gold lipstick case. A flash of sunlight reflected off something metallic in her purse.

"Do you carry a gun in your purse?"

Her eyes turned cold. "Yes, I've got a carry permit. What of it? I told you Reggie can be scary at times."

"Do you know how to use it?" Jack and I made eye contact.

She slung her bag over her shoulder and stood tall. "You damn bet I do. But that doesn't make me a murderer." She turned and walked away, one foot in front of the other like a runway model. All the men's eyes on the patio fixated on her swaying, tight ass.

Jack grinned ear to ear on the drive back to the restaurant to retrieve my car. "Wow. She never acted that way around me. Can I be your wingman?"

"Don't you think she was just trying to manipulate me?"

"Maybe. So, what do you think? Did Reggie do it? What about Tanya?"

"She provided an alibi for Reggie and set up an alibi for herself. I'm not ready to rule him out as my top suspect, but the list is growing."

"That's not a good sign. What's next?"

I shrugged my shoulders. "Follow the women, I guess."

Chapter 38

I called Reggie's office to schedule an appointment, but his admin said he would be out of town for two weeks and suggested I call back then.

Next on my list was Amy to see if she had another number for Missy. She didn't and suggested calling the college alumni office.

Despite shifting position every few minutes, my back ached on the drive to the alumni office. Ford must have researched medieval torture chambers when designing Pinto seating. A quick stop to gas up at a convenience store provided an opportunity to buy bottled water for taking an Oxy. With my stash reduced to three, acquiring more Oxy would be my next priority. Abstinence sucked. I convinced myself I wasn't feeding an addiction, simply moderating pain.

A gleaming, glass-sided building housed the alumni office. A plaque near the door listed donors for this recent addition to the campus, and of course, Reggie and Tanya Braun topped the list. An older black woman, tall, slender and sporting curly hair without a hint of gray, met me at a high counter. Her mannerisms projected warmth and sophistication. "May I help you?" A nasal accent revealed she was not native to the South.

"Good afternoon. I love your new building. It's gorgeous."

She beamed a proud smile. "We have our alumni to thank for that. They are so generous."

"I'm Melissa Rohrbach's uncle, Tanner Nole. I'm in town for a meeting and dropped by only to discover she's already graduated. Haven't stayed as close as I should, I guess. Someone from her sorority told me she moved to New York City, which, by coincidence, is where I'm headed next. Would you mind looking up her phone number and address so I can contact her while in the city?"

"I'm sorry . . . Mr. Nole, was it? We aren't allowed to share that information. We have a strict policy of protecting students' and graduates' personal information. I hope you understand." Her vocal pace and inflections hinted at New York City roots.

"Oh, I understand, and I wouldn't ask you to break any rules. But you see, Missy and my daughter were close growing up. My Cynthia recently succumbed to cancer, and no one has been able to contact Missy to let her know. We don't have much family anymore, so it would be a huge help to me and to Missy too."

Warm eyes, coupled with the frown on her face, indicated I had touched her. "I am so sorry for your loss. My son, Demetrius, died of cancer a year ago, so I understand your pain." She paused and broke eye contact, which gave me hope. "I truly am sorry, but I can't violate Missy's privacy. I hope you understand."

Summoning a sad, puppy dog face, I tried to shed a tear. "Sure, I understand." I turned to walk away but then spun back. "Could you at least verify that my information is correct—that she is living in New York? That wouldn't be divulging personal information because I already have it."

She thought for a moment and glanced over her shoulder. "I guess there's no harm in that." She sat down to a computer on a desk opposite the counter and keyed in her password.

Despite standing on my toes and straining my eyes to see over her shoulder, her password remained secret.

She returned to the counter, showing a broad smile. "Yes, she does live in New York City." She lowered her voice and gazed around the office. "Soho. I grew up in New York."

A middle-aged, frumpy-looking woman standing in the doorway of an inner office shined a dirty look my way. "Mabel, sorry to bother you, but can you step into my office when you're through there?"

"Yes, Mary. I'm just about done helping this gentleman."

Mary scowled and returned to her office

I thanked Mabel and said goodbye, but took my sweet time reaching the door. Over my shoulder, I saw her step into the other lady's office. A quick survey confirmed no one looking. A few cautious steps to Mabel's computer and a quick scan of the room confirmed no one could see me from this position. Hitting a key, the screen came back to life, requesting a password.

I'm not into computers, so I write my passwords down. I hoped Mabel did the same thing. A quick check under her desk phone, stapler, pencil holder and computer keyboard came up empty. Same for her desk drawers.

Still in her boss's office, I heard Mabel's voice. "I'll jump right on that."

My heart raced. Time was running out fast.

My eyes focused on a framed picture sitting on her desk of a younger Mabel with a young black man in graduation cap and gown. "Demetrius." Furiously I typed it and hit 'Enter.' "Invalid Password" stared back at me. Despite raging nerves, I keyed it in again, slower and with greater care. The screen returned to Missy's contact information where Mabel had left it.

She appeared to be a neat freak as there wasn't a scrap of paper on her desk. Mabel's boss said something inaudible, but the tone bore a stamp of finality. My time had run out. I retrieved my napkins from my back pocket and scribbled down her phone number.

I dove for the office door, jogged down the hall and out the front. Mable had to notice the office door closing after me and her screen active. Who knew? Maybe she would call security or the sheriff. I flogged myself for giving her my real name. If I wanted to act like a detective, I needed to smarten up.

Sitting on a campus shuttle bus bench two blocks away gave me a chance to catch my breath and let my back relax before calling Missy. She answered on the first ring. "Hello, Missy. I got your number from Amy Hall. My name is Tanner Nole."

Doubt dominated her words. "Amy doesn't have this number. Who did you say you are?"

"Tanner Nole. I'm a private investigator retained by Lorelei Adams family. I don't know if you heard, but Lorelei was recently murdered."

"Oh, my God! What happened? Was she mugged or something?"

"No, someone killed her in her apartment. The sheriff ruled it a suicide, but the family believes she was murdered."

A campus shuttle pulled up and stopped, muffling her tear-laced words. It sounded like she mentioned Reggie. The shuttle driver motioned for me to board. After a dismissive wave of my hand, he drove away, and the noise subsided. "Missy?" The line was dead. I called her back hoping it had just been a call drop. It went to voice mail. My message begged her to call me back while trying to make her feel guilty for putting Lorelei and Reggie together. Had the call dropped, or did she hang up? Had she said something about Reggie when the bus drowned her out?

CHAPTER 39

While talking to Missy, I noticed a prominent pain clinic ad on the shuttle stop shelter wall. It appeared to be an ad for one of the pill mills for which Florida and Georgia are infamous—just what I needed. The ad invited drop-ins, so Central Georgia Pain Clinic became my destination.

My image of a pill mill was a hole-in-the-wall storefront in a bad neighborhood with hordes of people waiting in long lines around the building. Instead, Central Georgia Pain Clinic featured red brick and expansive glass in a new medical complex near the hospital. A very sanitary smell and bright lights added to an air of legitimacy. Twenty people waited in a room sized for at least twice that many.

Although they advertised "Walk-ins Always Welcome," the very young receptionist must not have received the memo. "Are you sure you want to wait? We're really backlogged today. Thursdays are always busy here."

It was already Thursday? I had lost track of time. Tomorrow was my date with Ronnie, so I needed more Oxy.

"Sir?" The receptionist exuded condescension. "Do you want to wait, come back another day or schedule an appointment?"

My thoughts returned to real time. "How about tomorrow?"

"Are you kidding me? Fridays are the worst. Best day is Wednesday."

"I can't wait that long. Do you have *any* openings tomorrow?"

"*Sir*, you aren't listening. Fridays are our worst day. We're already overbooked, and there's a long waiting list." The "sir" dripped with condescension.

Some people shouldn't chew gum, and this lady fit that category. She swapped her large wad to the other side and popped it in an annoying fashion. "First opening is two weeks from today at 7:30 AM. You want it?" Without waiting, she started keying it in.

My vanishing Oxy supply wouldn't make it through the weekend. "That's two weeks from now. *You're* not listening. I'm in a lot of pain here." The chicle-queen giggled like she heard that from every patient, which she probably did. "I must warn you. When I'm in this much pain, I'm not responsible for my actions. I can go kind of loco."

She stopped typing, suspended chewing and watched me with pensive eyes while her hand felt for the deskphone. "Sir, are you threatening me?"

"Look, I'm sorry. I didn't mean to frighten you. I just want you to be a little more empathetic because I'm in a lot of pain here and can't wait two weeks to see a doctor. Can't you overbook one more for today or tomorrow?"

"All of our patients are in serious pain, so I can't put you ahead of those already on our waiting list. Do you want the appointment, or do you want to wait today?" She popped her gum as if to emphasize her question. Her hands hung over the keyboard.

After reviewing my lack of acceptable options, I answered, "I'll wait. Any idea how long?"

She frowned, popped her gum and deleted the record she had started. "We close the door at five, but see patients up to six o'clock. There's no guarantee we can see you today. Sit down and fill out this paperwork." She handed me a stack of papers.

After finishing the extensive paperwork, I tried Missy again, but it rolled to voice mail. It was pointless to leave her another message because she knew I wanted to talk to her.

A quick scan of the waiting room revealed a sorry bunch of people with drawn wrinkled faces. New people checked in with the receptionist, and others left with papers in hand. The crowd waiting with me turned over twice. I looked at the receptionist who gave me a smile that said, "Getting you back, asshole." Resigning myself to a prolonged wait, my attention shifted to my investigation notes.

"Mr. Nole. Mr. Tanner Nole!" The woman's voice woke me from an unplanned nap.

The waiting room had emptied except for an older woman, wearing loose gold scrubs, holding open the door to the back.

"Oh, yes. Sorry." The clock above the reception desk showed it was five to six. The since departed gum-chewer had been true to her word. The nurse checked my weight and guided me to an exam room, where she asked a long list of medical questions. She recorded each response on a tablet. I condensed my history as I had done on the paperwork earlier to omit any pattern of opioid abuse. She checked heart rate and blood pressure, all the steps of a legitimate medical practice. I was beginning to question the potential for success with this pain clinic.

A middle-aged dark-skinned man, with shaven head, hurried into the room. The nurse excused herself and closed the door.

"Mr. Nole, I am Doctor Abegunde Olanrewaju." The heavy accent seemed to be African. He smiled at my reaction. "You can just call me Dr. Olan. What can we do for you today?"

I explained my chronic back pain and the need for more OxyContin because mine was stolen in a motel burglary.

"I understand. Are you addicted to opioids?"

I feigned surprise. "No, of course not. I just need it for pain management."

"Have you tried alternative pain management approaches?"

It took intense concentration to understand his tortured words. "Sure. I've tried all of them, but none worked. Only OxyContin can help."

"What alternatives did you try?"

I tried to remember alternatives doctors had suggested, and I ignored. "I don't know—aromatherapy, hypnotherapy, massage."

"How about chiropractic or biofeedback?"

Chiropractors always seemed like quacks to me. I'd never heard of biofeedback. "Oh, yeah, sure. I tried those too. Didn't work."

He studied my paperwork and then checked his wristwatch. "Okay. I will write you a prescription."

He keyed into his laptop and paused. "Sorry. I cannot fill your prescription yet. You refilled only three weeks ago and show a history of heavy usage."

They were using the Georgia Prescription Drug Monitoring Program that tracked opioid prescriptions. My heart dropped. This wasn't a Georgia pill mill after all.

He wrote on a prescription pad and handed it to me. The instructions were to take four Tylenol every four hours and the name of a chiropractor, his address and phone number.

"This is a good chiropractor. Your liver function is not good, so don't take Advil or ibuprofen. If you are still in pain in two weeks, come back and I will work you in."

I had come up dry again and didn't know where to turn next.

CHAPTER 40

On my way to my car, my phone rang. It was Missy returning my calls. "Hello, Tanner, sorry about cutting you off earlier. My fiancé walked into my office. He doesn't know about my past and never will. So, you see, I can't get caught up in this thing. Oh, I feel so bad for Lorelei. She seemed nice."

I sat on the hood of my Pinto. "Thanks for calling me back. When we lost the connection, you were saying something about Reggie."

"I was saying I hope Reggie didn't do it."

"Is there some reason to suspect him?"

"Oh, no. I didn't mean to implicate him. In fact, I can't imagine him doing it. He was always so sweet and thoughtful. I remember once when I had a spider in my apartment. He caught it, took it outside and let it go because he didn't have the heart to kill it."

This didn't seem like the same Reggie others had spoken of. "Did any of your disagreements turn physical?"

"No. I mean, we argued from time to time, but what couple doesn't? It never got physical or anything close. Besides, the make-up sex was amazing."

That seemed to contradict what Tanya had told me about my prime suspect. "Amy said she thought you were in love with him. Is there any truth to that?"

The phone went silent for a minute. "Yeah, I suppose at some level I did love Reggie. It hurt to leave him behind, but he was married, and I had this great opportunity in The City."

"Was there ever talk of you two getting married?"

"No, absolutely not. From the beginning, I understood our relationship would end after graduation, and I would move on. It was simply business."

"Did he ever say anything about divorcing Tanya or his prenup with her?"

"He talked a lot about his wife, and not in a good way. He was so unhappy. I think it helped him to have someone he could talk to. He did mention the prenup more than once but never said anything about wanting to break it. Oddly enough, he seemed satisfied with the status quo."

"How well do you know Amy?"

"Not real well. I didn't have much time for friends with school and Reggie and all. If I recall, she and Lorelei were tight. Why?"

"Did Amy ever express harsh feelings toward Lorelei?"

"What? Do you think she might have done it?" Neither of us spoke for a while. "You know, I remember Amy blowing up once. I don't remember what about, but it seemed trivial to me. She kind of flipped out. Another friend had warned me she could be a little unstable at times. Sorry, Mr. Nole, but I need to get off the phone. My fiancé will be back any minute. Please don't call me again. Lose my number. I don't want anything from my past life to catch up to me now. I made a clean break."

CHAPTER 41

I arrived at the Bored Room, Jack's favorite haunt, forty-five minutes early. I fought a strong urge for an Oxy and decided a few stiff drinks would have to do since this was my first day of opioid abstinence.

The bartender, an attractive black woman, in her mid-thirties, wiped the bar in front of me, exuding a warm, friendly smile. She had once lived in Savannah, so we traded stories and laughed a lot while I ate a greasy burger and equally greasy fries with a side of two bourbons. In fact, we were laughing when Jack walked in and saw her rest her hand on my wrist.

"Looks like the party started without me." A hostile look hinted disapproval. "I'll take coffee, black—like my women."

The bartender met Jack's grin with a scowl before leaving to pour his coffee.

"What is it with you and women? They seem to fall all over you—first Tanya and now this broad." He leaned back to get a better look at me and then leaned in and sniffed near my neck. "Must be your pheromones. Then, again, I could stand to lose a few pounds, but you could too. You're not that much better looking and don't smell any better than me. What's your secret?"

The obvious difference was height, weight and hair, but I wasn't going there. "No secret. Like I told you before, they all seem to want something from me. Back in Savannah, I struggle to even get an online date."

Ignoring Jack, the bartender gave me a big warm smile when she delivered his coffee, turned and left to get me another bourbon.

"Damn. Maybe I don't want to be your wingman. When I'm with you, women don't know I exist." Jack took a sip and winced. "Coffee here is boiling hot and strong, too." He glanced at the two empty glasses in front of me and gave a little shake of his head. "Let's talk about the investigation while you can still talk."

I summarized my findings to date while he asked questions—good questions. Jack's wave to the bartender for a coffee refill seemed to go unnoticed. He shrugged it off.

"What do you think?" I asked.

"It's clear Lorelei was murdered, and the sheriff's office is trying to bury the whole matter. Given that, I would say your biggest problem is too many suspects. You're trying to whittle that list down one-by-one until the last man or woman is standing, and that would be the murderer. Problem is, your approach takes too much time. I'd work from the top down. Divide the suspect list into two groups—prime candidates and secondary suspects. I'd put Reggie on top of the primary list. Although circumstantial, the bulk of the evidence points to him despite his alibi. He and the deputy seem to be joined at the hip, so I'd add the deputy to the primary list, too. Everyone else would go on the secondary list. Concentrate your time on the primaries and work the secondary suspects to fill in the gaps. You'll get there a lot faster."

"What about Amy and Tanya? You'd put them on the secondary list?"

"Absolutely. For one, this crime has the mark of a male perp. Women may tear someone to shreds verbally, but they don't like to get their hands dirty. Tanya doesn't have the money to hire it done. I know because she's behind paying me. Does Amy have that kind of money?"

"She says her parents are loaded, but she doesn't dress like a princess, more Gothic and she works at the Barking Owl Pub part-time."

"Have you verified that her parents are rich? Question everything you hear and take nothing for granted."

The bartender brought my drink. "Thanks, ma'am. Oh, and how about a coffee refill for my pal here?" Her eyes narrowed into a dark scowl targeting Jack for a moment before she took his empty mug away and returned it full of hot, steamy coffee.

Jack watched her walk away. "What did I do to that bitch? If looks could kill, I'd be dead." He shook his head and chuckled. "All right, back to the investigation. Here's a few pointers. You need to get your hands on that longer police report. If you've got some pull with that lady deputy, I'd work that angle."

I shared my suspicions she might be a spy. In his opinion, if she was spying on me, that made her an even more valuable asset, but I should be very careful.

"First thing, you've got to interrogate Reggie. Has Tanya set that up yet?"

"No. I've been putting off calling her. She makes me very uncomfortable."

"Well, jump on that right away. She seemed to have the hots for you. In fact, I'm surprised she hasn't called you. She called me to get your phone number. What about video? Does the apartment have any video cameras?"

Security cameras. I felt ashamed for not thinking about video cameras. These days there are cameras everywhere. "I don't know, but I'll check."

"Also, check around the neighborhood for any cameras on other nearby buildings."

I added these tasks to my To-do list napkin and returned it to my pocket. My hand touched something foreign. I showed Jack the sandwich bag holding the fancy safety pin. "Oh, yeah. I found this when I searched the apartment. I doubt it has any significance, but it seemed odd for

Lorelei to have such an expensive-looking safety pin. Maybe it was a gift from Reggie."

Jack took the bag and scrutinized the pin inside. "This isn't a safety pin. Look, it doesn't have the normal little loop at the bottom. This is an earring."

"An earring?"

"Yeah. I've seen punksters wear them. You know, they wear screws, nails, skulls, all sorts of weird shit. Was Lorelei into punk or Goth?"

Mentally, I retraced my search of her apartment. "I don't recall seeing any punk or Gothic clothes in her wardrobe. Oh, wait. I found one punk-type outfit in the dress-up section."

"Dress-up section?"

"Yeah, it appears Reggie's into sexual role-playing. There was one whole rack of sexy women's costumes—a nurse outfit, a police uniform, French maid costume and so on, including leathers for a dominatrix. This might go with that."

"Kinda kinky. Didn't see Reggie as that sort of freak." He studied the safety pin earring. "Did you find another of these? They typically run in pairs."

"No, the jewelry had all been removed by someone." I made a quick note on a bar napkin and saved it with the rest.

Jack fiddled with his empty coffee mug. "Oh, man, if that's evidence, you shouldn't have taken it. Chain of custody, you know. Judge would throw that out in an instant."

I felt stupid. A rookie error I vowed not to make the next time.

The bartender exchanged Jack's empty coffee mug for a full one and smiled at me. "Are you still doing all right, handsome?"

KEN L. BURKE

I declined another drink. Jack took a sip of the fresh coffee and spit it out. "Oh, that's terrible. Tastes like shit. You put something in it?" He tried another small sip and spit it back into the cup. "Salt! You put salt in my damned coffee." He set the mug down and pushed it toward the bartender.

"Are you crazy? I did no such thing. I'll get you another cup. You know what? You've got bad manners. I bet you're a racist."

"Racist?" Jack lunged forward with a jerk, almost scooting off his bar stool. A sweeping hand knocked his cup off the edge, splashing scalding hot coffee on the bartender.

Eyes bugging, she stepped back and assessed the damage. "You, son of a bitch. That's boiling hot. You did that on purpose."

Jack rocked back on his bar stool. "Look, lady, I'm sorry. I didn't mean to spill it. It was an accident, I swear."

Her eyes reached out to the front door, and she waved her hand over her head. "Hey, Tom. Show this racist bastard the door."

A huge white guy with shaved head and strapping muscles approached us in an instant and cupped Jack's upper arm between large paws. "Sir, would you please come with me?" Jack offered no resistance as the bouncer escorted him to the door. Without thinking, I fell in behind.

"Sir?" The bartender called out to me. "Your bar tab?"

"Oh, yeah, sorry." I returned to the bar, and she handed me the tab. "Sorry about my friend. He's a little high strung. I think he drinks way too much coffee." I threw sixty dollars on the bar. "Keep the change."

By the time I got outside, Jack had disappeared, either in anger or shame. I stumbled toward my car and stopped to open the door. A grating voice came from directly behind me. "Hey, asshole. Nice wheels you got there. Did something bad happen to your car?"

191

Alcohol-glazed eyes focused on a beaming Deputy Lowell in street clothes.

I sobered up. "You know damn well what happened. You had someone vandalize it."

"Careful now with your wild accusations. I'm a man of the law. Someone makes up bad stories about me, I sue them for slander." He stepped close, trapping me between him and the car. "I smell alcohol. Don't tell me you're about to get behind the wheel. And I bet you're on Oxy too. Oh, no. I forgot. You don't have any more of that because it got stolen." He let out a loud, sick laugh. Go ahead and drive. I got a nice warm bed waiting for you at the office."

"Out of my way! I'll Uber it."

He laughed. "No Uber driver in his right mind would pick up a rider in this neighborhood this time of night."

"Then I'll walk back to my hotel. It's just up the street."

"You mean the Shit Palace? That must be ten, twelve blocks. You don't look in that good of shape, asshole. But if that's what you want, go right ahead." He stepped back and made an exaggerated sweeping motion with his left arm toward the street.

I relocked the car door and started down the street.

The sheriff chided me as I walked away. "Bundle up. Might get a bit chilly walking. Oh, and be careful. The Shit Palace is in a bad neighborhood. You should see the crime statistics. No one in our office will go there. Be real careful now."

His taunts sent a sudden chill through my body. I buttoned my coat and wrapped my arms around myself. The farther I walked, the dimmer the street lights and the colder the night. I had never owned a gun, but decided at that very moment to buy one.

A dog barked behind me. I looked back and spotted two large figures wearing hoodies closing on me fast. I stepped up my pace and looked back again. They too had sped up and were still closing.

I tried to run, but it sent shooting pains up my back. I stumbled but caught myself.

Nearing the next corner, two more figures stepped out of the darkness wearing ski masks. In a half-jog, I crossed to the other side of the street. One figure ahead and one behind also crossed. I froze in the middle of the street, boxed in. My spinning head searched for an escape. The four closed in and circled like a pack of coyotes. One pulled out a two-foot piece of pipe, one held a baseball bat and the other two produced knives. My heart racing, I nearly fainted.

From behind, a car raced toward me with bright headlights, horn honking in long repeated blasts. I shaded my eyes from the blinding headlights. My pursuers spread to escape the onrushing vehicle. My legs refused to respond to my commands, stranding me in the middle of the street. A large car squealed to a halt inches from hitting me. A short figure jumped out and fired a gun into the air. My assailants disappeared into the night from which they came.

"Jump in, buddy." My unknown rescuer slipped back into the driver's seat. I weighed my options. I could take my chances with the four thugs or risk getting into this car with a stranger who came to my rescue. I chose the car.

As I jumped in, my savior spoke. "What the hell are you doing walking in a bad neighborhood like this at night? Halfway home, I realized you were too intoxicated to be driving, so I circled back."

I gave the driver a big smile. "Thanks, Jack. You're my hero."

CHAPTER 42

My body shivered and my teeth chattered, more from adrenalin crash and Oxy withdrawal than night chill. Jack ran the car heater at full blast to alleviate my shivers. Abstinence sucked. I gagged down an Oxy dry, something I abhor doing.

"Hey, don't barf in my Caddy. Here, drink this." He handed me a McDonald's Styrofoam coffee cup. The cold, bitter coffee dislodged the stuck pill. It went down but unsettled my alcohol-laden stomach. Between loud belches, I said, "God, how do you drink that stuff black?"

"What was that you took?"

"A pain pill for my back. Running always aggravates it."

"You shouldn't take that stuff with alcohol in your system. It could kill you. You sure you don't have a drug problem?"

My chattering stopped, but the shivering persisted. "No, I don't have a problem. I told you, it's for my bad back, the doctor prescribed it."

"Okay, just saying, it's not a good idea to mix alcohol and opioids. During the investigation, you need to lay off those pills and alcohol to keep your head straight. Stick to coffee, like me."

"Oh, I've cut way back on the pills. You should be proud of me."

Neither of us spoke for several blocks. "I lost most of my pain pills when they trashed my room at the CrossRoads Inn, so I'm running out. It's too soon to refill my prescription. You know where I could buy some?"

He glanced at me and sighed. "You mean on the street? Sure you don't have a problem there? Sorry pal, I don't travel in those circles. I deal with infidelity cases mostly."

Jack turned into The Palace parking lot. "Man, this place is a real shithole. How can you sleep here? I'd ask you to stay with me, but I'm between places at the moment and staying with my sister and brother-in-law. With their kids, there's just not room. I sleep on the couch as it is."

"I understand. Thanks again for saving me back there. I owe you." I jumped out and watched him leave before heading into the lobby.

My friend, the transgender, manned the counter, reading a cheap romance novel.

I must not have been walking as well as I thought. "Good evening, Tanner. It appears you've been doing a little drinking tonight. Celebrating something special?"

Inspiration struck me. I leaned against the counter to steady myself. "Maybe you can help me."

"Oh, finally. What'll it be? Woman, man, threesome, moi?" She performed that gesture again, running her hands down the sides of her tight-fitting red dress.

"No, no. Nothing like that. I suffer from back pain—an occupational hazard with dentistry. I'm running out of my prescription pain meds and can't get any more for two weeks. Do you know where I could get my hands on some OxyContin? You know, just to carry me over."

"Oh, Oxycotton. I know a guy. He can get you anything you need— Oxy, ludes, acid, meth, crack, weed, or my favorite—ecstasy. Name your poison."

"I just want Oxy, for my back."

"Sure you do." She located the contact on her phone and wrote it down for me.

I stumbled back to my room, collapsed on top of my sleeping bag, and fell into a deep sleep.

CHAPTER 43

Propped up on her bed, I watched Ronnie enter the bedroom. Light from the open bathroom door formed an aura around her negligee-clad body. I admired her figure during her sultry stroll to the bed. Hard pink nipples protruded behind the sheer, hot-pink fabric. At bedside, her nightgown slinked to the floor, revealing her loveliness. I scooted over to make room, and she glided in beside me. We stared into each other's eyes before kissing passionately. Her hand sought my firmness.

Knock, Knock, Knock. Ronnie sat bolt upright and covered herself with the sheet. "Oh, shit! It's Tim. He's come home early."

I blinked and shook my head to clear it. As the fog withdrew, I found myself alone on top of my sleeping bag in my dive hotel. The knocking came again, louder this time.

I slipped out of bed to answer the door. Once up I realized I was fully dressed in wrinkled clothes from yesterday.

I disengaged the security lock and opened the door. Through blinding light from the hallway, I could make out a biker-looking man with extensive arm tattoos standing in the doorway. He smelled homeless and his dark-brown oily hair confirmed his need for a good bathing.

"What do you want?" I asked.

"Pack your shit and get the fuck out. You've been evicted, dickhead." His voice had the character of rough sandpaper.

"Evicted? I'm paid up. What the hell?"

"Hey, retard. What part of evicted don't you understand?" His voice sounded angrier.

"Are you the manager? I need to speak to the manager."

"He's the one who told me to throw you the hell out. I'll be back at noon, and you better not be here, or I'll toss your ass on the street. And that's if I'm in a good mood. You don't wanna see me get pissed off. People get hurt real bad." He turned and clomped down the stairs.

After splashing my face and taking a swig of warm bottled water, I slipped down the stairs. No one manned the counter, so I poked my head in the office. The hairy guy who had just shadowed my threshold was searching through a beat-up gray file cabinet with his back toward me.

I resigned myself to relocating once again. Either Reggie had bought The Palace, or the sheriff's department had threatened to shut the place down. It didn't matter, either way, I had nowhere to go.

After walking back to last night's bar and retrieving the Pinto, I loaded my few possessions into the car and bade The Palace goodbye with mixed feelings. It was a disgusting dump but had been one step above being homeless, which I now was. Besides, I would miss the colorful characters there.

My phone showed a missed call and a voice message. Ronnie's message reminded me she would pick me up at the Country Inn and Suites at six tonight and changed the order to red wine. Rib roasts had been on sale, so the menu changed.

Here I was hooking up with Ronnie tonight when I smelled and looked like shit. It had been two days since my last shower. I made a mental note to call Jack and see if I could shower at his sister's.

Since I was so grubby, lunch was fast food—Bojangles' spicy fried chicken and dirty rice. I hate eating in the car, so I went through the drive-thru and then took it inside to eat in a far corner. A table of young people pointed at me and joked among themselves. One held their nose as they walked by, inciting raucous laughter from their friends. After they left, I savored the sweet tea and tried to ignore my aching back.

A call to Jack went unanswered, so I left a message. Next, I dialed Tanya. "Hello, handsome. Have you been avoiding me?"

"No. I've been busy with the investigation and all. Say, did you talk to your husband about meeting with me?"

"Oh, so that's why you called. I'm disappointed. I did speak to him. He flat refused, but I'm still working on him. Wait a minute, I have an idea. He and I are having lunch at the country club tomorrow, so why don't you show up around one and join us?"

"Are you sure? He hasn't been too happy when I've shown up uninvited in the past. Will Deputy Lowell be there?"

"Reggie might get upset, but he won't make a scene in front of his country club friends. He has a reputation to maintain. Deputy Lowell shouldn't be a problem. He doesn't fit in with that crowd."

Meeting this way made me uncomfortable. I knew Lowell would be only one phone call away for his benefactor. "Okay, I'll be there at one tomorrow. Thanks, Tanya. I appreciate you going out on a limb for me like this."

"Thank you, Tanya. That's all you've got to say? When can we get together so you can *show* me your appreciation? After all, I'm taking a big risk for you here."

She made great eye candy, and a guy like me would be lucky to score with her, but my heart still belonged to my Peaches. "My schedule's up in the air at the moment. Let me call you next week and schedule something." I needed to string her along until after I met with Reggie. That was too important to blow.

I next called Sharique, the Oxy source from the transgender at The Palace. My palms sweated, and the veins in my neck pulsed. This would be my first drug deal. I didn't know anything about it.

"Yeah?"

"Is this Sharique?"

"Who the fuck is this?"

I didn't recall the name of the transgender who gave me his or her number. "This is Tim Mason." I finally got smart enough to use an alias. Lacking creativity at the moment, I panicked and used the name of Ronnie's husband. Maybe that was Freudian. "I got your number from a common friend who works at The Palace. She said you could get me some OxyContin."

"Oh, you mean, Magnolia. Sure. What dosage ya lookin for?"

"Sixty milligrams. How much is it?"

"Wow! Sixties. You a heavy hitter, man! Ain't got but forties. They be forty dollars."

"Forty dollars? For how many?"

"Forty dollars each. You a fuckin' Fed or sumpin?"

"No. I'm just new to the street scene. Where do I meet you?"

"So, this ya first drug deal, eh? I'll be at Twentieth and Central tonight. Any time 'tween dark 'n two AM. Come alone, bring cash and 'n no pocket rocket."

"I'll be in a car, not on a motorcycle."

"Say what? Hey man, yo is green. A motorcycle is a crotch rocket. A pocket rocket is a gun. Don't bring none. See you t'night."

"Wait! Don't hang up. I can't make it tonight. What about tomorrow night?"

"Same place, same time." Click. The call ended. At forty dollars a pop, I was thankful for Neena's loan. I couldn't afford very many but, fortunately, only needed enough to get me by for a little more than a week until I could refill a prescription.

A second call to Jack went unanswered. Time was running out for me to get ready for tonight's date. I resigned myself to a spit bath and dressing in the bathroom sink here at Bojangles.

After several loud unanswered knocks on the restroom door, a female employee unlocked it and stuck her head in. She caught me standing in the middle of the single-person restroom wearing only underwear and socks. She pulled back out of the opening and hollered in. "I'm so sorry to interrupt you, but are you okay? People have been complaining you've been in there a long time. Can you please finish and vacate the restroom? Customers are waiting."

In seconds I threw on clean clothes, tossed my dirty ones in the outside pocket of my roller bag, and exited the restroom. All eyes in the now busy restaurant followed me. Several angry men shouted profanities as I hustled out the door, pretending not to hear them.

Since I hadn't finished prepping, I stopped at Arby's on the way to the Country Inn and Suites. Teeth now brushed and hair combed, copious amounts of cologne covered any residual odor. I washed down my next-to-last Oxy. Couldn't let back pain inhibit the highly anticipated sexual activity awaiting. I craved my Peaches even more than the drug.

Once finished, I admired my reflection in the mirror and told myself I looked good despite my circumstances. Tonight would be a big night. I had waited so many years for this and now the time was here.

CHAPTER 44

With barely enough time to pick up wine and beat Ronnie to the Country Inn & Suites, I pushed the Pinto harder than it was designed to be driven. It vibrated at speed, and its bald tires screamed of abuse on every turn. More than once the car came very close to spinning. After racing into the package store and purchasing two bottles of wine, I ran the gutless car air conditioner at full blast, hoping to cool off. My heavy application of cologne could only mask so much.

Ronnie's SUV sat under the awning at the hotel's front door as I drove in. I went around the hotel to enter through the back door and make a grand exit from the hotel lobby. The back door was locked, and since I wasn't staying here, I didn't have a key to unlock it. Plan thwarted, I drove around to the front. After parking, I charged the front door, pretending not to see Ronnie sitting in her car. She lowered her window and yelled to catch my attention.

Feigning surprise, I slipped into the passenger seat. "Sorry, I'm late. I left the wine in my car and went back to grab it. Didn't see you pull up."

"Two bottles of wine? You planning to liquor me up and take advantage?" Our eyes locked as did our smiles.

Unsure if she expected a kiss, I played it cool for the time being. "Not taking anything for granted." I felt like a nervous teenager on his first date.

Conversation became sporadic and strained during the trip to her house. Her pensive face suggested she felt as anxious about tonight as I did. My stomach churned.

As she turned onto her street, she asked, without taking her eyes off the road, "Do you mind ducking down so the neighbors don't see you? They're real nice people, but a bit gossipy."

My apprehension deepened. "Sure, no problem." But it was a problem. I felt like a juvenile delinquent, sneaking into the neighborhood to commit illegal pranks. Being a a people pleaser, I complied with her request.

She pulled into a garage so neat it could only belong to a deviant. As the garage door closed, she laid a gentle hand on my shoulder. "You can sit up now."

Awkwardness blanketed the two of us as we entered the house. I so wanted to kiss her but waited for a signal she wanted me to. I set the wine on the dining room table and checked out her house. Two places were set across the width of the table, rather than the length. "Where can I find a wine opener to let these breathe? I hope you like a good Cab." I didn't know if I had purchased a great wine or a terrible wine. Not being a connoisseur, I normally rely on the store clerk but didn't have time tonight.

"Cabs are my favorite. Center drawer on the buffet."

The opener was a fancy thing with a lever I'd never seen before. My mechanical skills are atrocious, but I needed to master this and not destroy the cork to protect my male ego. After ten minutes of fumbling with it, Ronnie entered the room carrying two plates of luscious smelling food. "Need some help?"

"No, I got this."

She left the room and returned with a gravy dish. "Let me help you. I really need some wine, and the food is getting cold."

I yielded, and she opened the first bottle of wine in a flash. Embarrassment didn't help my male ego or my deepening anxiety. "Aren't you going to open the other bottle, so it can breathe, too?"

"I'm not much of a drinker anymore. Besides, I'm not sure I trust myself with you if we drink two." She grinned, and her eyes reached out to me saying a silent "kiss me." So, I did. Our passion burned hot as our lips locked for several glorious minutes. I felt her tensions wilt away. Mine didn't.

She pulled back. "Wow! I'm not sure I trust you with wine either. Let's sit down before the food gets cold."

"You've gone to a lot of trouble, but it smells so wonderful."

We ate a delicious meal of rib roast, roasted potatoes and carrots all drowned in rich beef gravy with biscuits to soak it all up. I ate slower than normal. Fatigue set in as alcohol met Oxy.

Her bare right foot touched and caressed my ankle. When I failed to respond, her foot worked up my leg to my crotch. Her foot rubbing me felt good but did not excite me as much as we both expected. I removed my right shoe and returned the favor. I could sense her enjoyment at my touch, which aroused me.

Ronnie pushed her food around more than eating. I cleaned my plate until it shined like it had just come out of the dishwasher. She emptied the wine bottle into my glass, filling it to the very brim. "Drink up."

"Filled it a little full, didn't you? Got a straw?" Fearing movement would spill red wine on the white table cloth, I bent down and sipped from the glass sitting on the table. "That was delicious."

Ronnie stood and collected her plate and silverware.

Anxiety grew. I felt trapped and questioned if I wanted this to happen. Was I feeling guilty? I studied her fireplace. "Maybe I should start a fire."

Ronnie massaged my shoulders from behind. It felt wonderful. My tension lessened, but fatigue filled its place. If I relaxed any more, I might doze off. I stood, took her into my arms and held her tight. Our tongues intertwined for a long moment, her breathing louder and faster. My erection pressed against her stomach.

She broke off the kiss and smiled. "Maybe you should build a fire."

The fire blazed after thirty minutes of effort. I joined Ronnie on the sofa, and my anxiety returned. This moment had finally come following years of daydreaming about it, and now I dreaded it. I gazed into her eyes.

Her smile seemed an invitation, so I leaned in to kiss her, and she met me halfway. I pulled her to me, and she wrapped her arms around me. It was a long kiss. Her breathing became heavy when I nibbled on her ear. She slipped me her tongue, and I responded. My inner voice screamed at me, "This is wrong. Think about what you're doing here. Think about Tim."

I became hot, more from the blazing fire than our kissing and hugging. She slid backward on the couch pulling, me down on top of her. More out of obligation than desire, I unbuttoned her dress, slipped it off her shoulders, and made quick work of her bra. Fondling her breasts didn't arouse me as much as when we were in college. Was it guilt or the combination of opioid and alcohol?

As I nibbled on her nipples, her hand slid down to my crotch. She pulled away and pushed my head back. "You're not hard. What's wrong? Don't you want me?"

Any lust in my heart drained away, replaced by heavy guilt. I got off her and sat up. "I'm sorry, Ronnie."

She sat up, her breasts still exposed. "What's wrong?"

When I didn't answer for a moment, she re-hooked her bra and buttoned her dress. Tears rolled down her flushed cheeks. "I thought you loved me."

"I have always loved you and always will."

"Funny way of showing it." Her sobbing touched my soul.

"I'm sorry, Ronnie. It's not you, it's me. I shouldn't have drunk so much wine." I couldn't tell her I had also taken an Oxy.

But that wasn't the true reason for my inability to see this through. I wanted her more than I have ever wanted a woman in my life, but somewhere along the way, I had grown a conscious. Having met Tim a couple of times made him real. Pictures of her with Tim, hanging on the walls, further drove home the point. I couldn't seduce his wife. Besides, having sex with Ronnie would have changed everything—for the worst. If she left Tim for me, it would hurt her as well as Tim. If she didn't leave him for me, it would still cause her pain if she still loved me. Moderate pain and suffering now would avoid greater pain and suffering later.

I wanted to take her in my arms and make her suffering go away, but I knew I couldn't.

I grabbed a hand towel from the kitchen and gave it to Ronnie to wipe her tears while repeating how sorry I was and reassuring her this was not her fault.

After a few moments, she collected herself and stood, avoiding eye contact. "I'll get my purse and take you back to your hotel."

If I could have walked to the hotel, I would have.

CHAPTER 45

The drive back to the Country Inn & Suites seemed an endless odyssey. Ronnie's restrained sobbing interrupted long periods of echoing silence. I wanted to crawl into the ashtray and hide.

For the first time since puberty, I had failed to perform. "Ronnie, I'm so sorry. It must be the wine mixed with my pain meds for my back. I really did want you." Without thinking, I had mentioned my opioid use.

She sniffled and stared straight ahead through the windshield. "Are you still an addict?"

Her question knocked the wind out of me. How did she know about my drug problems in Savannah? Who was feeding her information?

"No. I don't have a drug problem. I take pain pills for my back. My back ached so bad I worried about being able to perform tonight, so I took a pain pill. I guess I overcompensated."

I had so anticipated our planned tryst. Excitement and anxiety had resonated through my being for two days. But when Ronnie picked me up from the hotel, an eerie silence had dominated the drive to her house as if we foresaw things not working out. We had both placed a lot of pressure on ourselves not to disappoint the other, but in the end, I did just that.

I reached across the car and touched her shoulder. "Ronnie, I'm so sorry. I do love you so very much, but I can't have you like this."

Her gaze locked onto the road, tears dripped off her face. "If you really loved me, you would have gotten hard."

"It's not you. It's me."

Looking back, I had obsessed on my Peaches—the young, spirited college girl. Over the past twenty years of separation, we both changed and matured. I was in love with a mirage I had created from fond memories embellished over time.

I felt guilt for wanting an affair with her and pressuring her into it.

"It's not . . . just that." Outbreaks of sobbing disrupted Ronnie's words. "I'm feeling . . . guilty, too. I shouldn't . . . have done this. I've never . . . cheated on Tim."

My guilt intensified. "Ronnie, I am so sorry I hurt you when I left after college. I've been in love with you since that day. When I came back, I pushed you hard because I wanted to make amends and pick up where we left off. But now I can see how selfish I've been." My eyes watered. Despite my words to the contrary, I now questioned the magnitude of my love for her, which made me feel even worse.

I rested my hand on her thigh. She turned, smiled and laid her hand on mine. "When we kissed the other day at Waffle House, it stirred a lot of old, suppressed emotions. Lorelei's death left a gaping hole in me. Maybe I'm trying to fill that hole with you. I need time to process all this. I hope you understand." She offered what I needed most—time to sort through my feelings for her.

She pulled up to the hotel's front door and looked down rather than meet my gaze.

"I am so sorry, Ronnie. I do love you." A strong urge swelled up in me to wrap her in my arms, lavish her with kisses and tell her it would be all right. Jumbled emotions swarmed inside me.

"Please, just go." She buried her face in her hands and cried aloud.

As I entered the hotel, I sensed her eyes on my back. The men's room off the lobby provided refuge until she left. I sat on the toilet, holding my head in my hands. Despondency, together with Oxy and wine, created intense fatigue. I dozed for a second, nearly falling off the toilet seat. A quick shake of the head reinitiated cranial blood flow enough to collect myself. I needed a jolt to revive me. Maybe the answer was my last Oxy to create its brief euphoria.

On the walk to my Pinto, a quick check of my phone showed a call-back and message from Jack. It said he was going to bed early but promised to call me in the morning.

Where would I go now? No hotel in town would take me in. I considered staying up all night, but intense fatigue vetoed that idea. If I drank coffee to stay awake, I'd need to pee every hour, and I didn't have a bathroom. I pulled to the far corner of the hotel parking lot and parked under a burned-out light. My jacket served as a blanket, my arm as a pillow.

I fell asleep in minutes, but the long night stretched out forever. An aching back woke me every thirty minutes or so. A change in position relieved the discomfort enough to permit sleep for another half-hour. By daylight, I could no longer find any comfortable position. I reached for my last Oxy but needed a drink to wash it down. At McDonald's, I dined in, ordering a large black coffee and two sausage breakfast burritos. The booth provided a welcome change in seating position after the long night in the Pinto. I poured bourbon into my coffee and took my last Oxy.

Jack called as I enjoyed a free coffee refill. I told him I had been kicked out of my hotel room and spent the night in my car. He felt sorry for me, but couldn't ask his sister to put me up. She had already threatened to throw him out. Since he couldn't afford a place of his own, he didn't dare do anything to jeopardize his accommodations.

I told him about my scheduled meeting with Tanya and Reggie. He wanted to be there but had a conflict he couldn't get out of. He suggested the two of us meet for drinks that evening to brief him on my meeting.

Call waiting showed Amy was calling. It seemed odd she would call me so early in the morning, so said a quick goodbye to Jack and answered her call.

CHAPTER 46

"I'm sorry, Mr. Nole. Did I call too early?"

"No, not at all, Amy. I'm just finishing breakfast. What's up?"

"I couldn't sleep a wink last night." Her words sounded forced. "When we spoke the other day, I forgot to tell you what I had called about, and now it won't let me go. Something happened between Lorelei and Professor Robinson, who teaches ethics, which is totally ironic."

I waited for her to continue.

"Lorelei was struggling in his class last term--I mean, really badly. It was bumming her out, so she set up a meeting with him to see if she could earn extra credit to improve her grade. He offered to change her grade in return for sex."

The fatigue from last night's lack of sleep evaporated in a whoosh. "Did he know about her deal with Reggie?"

"No, I don't think so. You see, Lorelei's not the first girl he's made such an offer."

"Do you know if she agreed to go through with it?" Consistent with Lorelei's recent history, it would not have been a surprise to hear she had.

"No, Lorelei exploded and threatened to report him to the Regents. He called her bluff and said no one would believe her without proof. Lorelei needed to talk to someone, so I came over. She told me what happened and asked for advice. I confessed I wasn't surprised, because he had propositioned me with the same deal last term. She screamed in relief and exclaimed how we had him by the balls if we went to the Regents together. They would have to believe the two of us."

Amy paused, probably to garner enough courage to continue. "I told her I couldn't. She asked why, but I refused to tell her. She kept pleading and pleading for me to join her in nailing the son of a bitch. She wore me down until I confessed I had taken his deal. Last term Professor Robinson bumped my failing grade to a 'B' in return for sex. I took a pass on a request for a second encounter in exchange for an 'A.' She surrendered to my begging and promised not to tell anyone what I had done out of desperation to pass the class. I don't know which was worse, the shame of what I had done or the loss of Lorelei's respect.

"She asked around for other victims and found several, but no one had the courage to join her in filing a complaint. Several had already tried and suffered serious reprisals. She resorted to writing a letter to the university president, documenting her experience and alluding to other unnamed victims. She asked me to proof it for her."

"Did she send it?"

"Somehow, Dr. Robinson learned she was up to and called her. She accused me of telling him, but it wasn't me. He claimed she misunderstood him, and they could clear this all up. She agreed to meet with him again and asked me to go with her, but . . ." Amy shed tears. "I couldn't do it. I was chicken. I hate myself for not stepping up." Her crying intensified. "She might still be alive if I had agreed to go with her."

"So, do you know if she ever met with him on her own?"

"I'm not sure. I thought I saw Dr. Robinson drive away on my way to her apartment the night I found her dead. The image of him driving off haunted me all night."

Her revelation blew my mind. "Amy, think hard now. Did you see the professor, or didn't you?"

She sobbed and spoke in a near whisper. "Yes . . . maybe. I don't know. I can't be sure."

"Okay. I understand. Would you be willing to tell someone at the university about your experience now?"

The crying became hysterical.

"Amy, you're going to be okay either way. Take a deep breath." I paused until she calmed a little. "Would you be willing to speak to the dean or someone at the college if I go with you?"

After a few sniffs, she regained composure. "I'll think about it, but I'm not sure I can. If my parents found out, they'd cut me off."

After the call, I sat in utter disbelief. Could Lorelei have been murdered by someone I hadn't considered a suspect until now? Someone obscure like one of her professors? I borrowed a pen from the cashier and wrote Professor Robinson's name on a fresh napkin and circled it twice before adding this napkin to the note file in my pocket.

Jack's admonition from the other night popped into my head. In his opinion, I had way too many suspects. Well, I just added one more to the list.

CHAPTER 47

The inferno raging inside me distracted me from preparing for my critical meeting with Reggie Braun. The image of some dirty old man propositioning my daughter in exchange for a grade ruled my thoughts.

I couldn't wait for Amy to decide if she would go with me to the dean. I called her back and she volunteered to look up the professor's office hours online. It didn't show any on Saturdays, but my pent-up rage couldn't wait until Monday. Under intense prodding, Amy broke down and confessed she knew where he lived. Too cheap to pay for a hotel room, he lured Amy into his wife's bed while she was away nursing her ill sister. This additional information further deepened my hate and disdain for this predator.

Mrs. Robinson answered the door of a white two-story colonial in an upscale neighborhood where doctors, lawyers and college professors lived. She was attractive for a woman in her early sixties, dressed as if expecting company. Her mannerisms were prim and proper, just what I would expect of a professor's wife. "May I help you?"

"Is Professor Robinson in?"

"Oh, my. Was he expecting you?"

"No. When we spoke on the phone, he suggested I stop by next time I was in the neighborhood, so here I am."

Widened eyes expressed surprise to the point of shock. "That is odd. He maintains a rigid schedule and dislikes surprises. Drives me batty with it, he does. I'm surprised he didn't tell you he sometimes schedules student conferences on Saturday mornings."

"Is it common for him to meet students on a weekend?"

"Weekends, evenings. He says he must work odd hours to match the lifestyle of his students. You know how they are. May I tell him who called?"

"Yeah. Tell him Stephan Hall stopped by to see him. I'm the father of one of his victims, I mean, students—Amy Hall. She raves about the smell of your hand soap in the master bathroom. I doubt your husband has ever mentioned her to you, but you might want to ask him about their extra-curricular activities."

I called Amy back for directions to his office. My phone supports GPS, but I don't know how to use it. She too thought it unusual the professor would have student conferences on a Saturday since they were not posted online.

Once in the building, I stopped in an open copy room and stole a business envelope and a clean sheet of copy paper. With a borrowed ink pen, I scrawled on the top sheet:

To whom it may concern:

Dr. Marvin Robinson is a sick pervert and a prime suspect in the murder of Lorelei Adams.

He preys on young co-eds by trading grades for sexual favors.

He thoroughly disgusts me!

The Late Lorelei Adam's Father,

Tanner Nole

After addressing the envelope to the University President in my most girlish handwriting, I folded the note and sealed it in the stolen envelope.

The professor's office door was closed, and the shade drawn. A knock elicited no response from inside. The door was locked, so I knocked on it and then pressed an ear to the door. I heard faint rustling inside, so pounded on the door with my fist and shouted, "Professor Robinson, I know you're in there. Your wife told me you were here. Answer the door, or I'll keep pounding and shouting until you do come out."

The lock clicked, and the door opened a crack. The office was dimly lit as if I had interrupted a nap. He opened the door enough to poke his head out while blocking the opening with his body. "I don't know who you are, but I am not to be disturbed when my door is closed. I'm in the middle of something right now, so please leave, or I'll be forced to call security." He pulled his head back in, but my foot prevented him from shutting his door.

"My name's Tanner Nole. My daughter was Lorelei Adams, a former student of yours I'm investigating her death and need to ask you a few questions."

His face drained of color, and his eyes became saucers as if he had seen a ghost. He said in a broken voice, "I'm sorry, I don't remember a student by that name. I've taught a lot of pupils and can't remember them all. Good day, sir." He tried again to close the door. I slammed my shoulder against it like an offensive lineman executing a block. The door swung open, knocking him deeper into his office. Wrinkled and unbuttoned, the professor's white dress shirt looked as if he had slept in it. His hands served as suspenders holding up unbuckled Dockers.

Something moved in the shadows of the darkened office. I clicked on the desk lamp, sending a shadowy glow about the room. A young woman with short black hair clutched her clothes in front of her. She stared at me and trembled like cornered prey. I located the switch to the overhead light but let her quickly dress before throwing it. The brighter light reflected off a pale complexion, contrasted by black lipstick and eye shadow. Large gothic crosses hung from ear lobes with multiple earrings. Her pale complexion flushed with color. She took a step backward, bumping into a bookshelf.

I sneered at the decrepit-looking old man in front of me. No woman, not even his wife, would want to sleep with such a loser. "You keep it kind of dim in here for a student/teacher conference, don't you think? It's hard on dirty old eyes."

I felt pity for the young woman slumped in her corner shedding tears. "Do you remember Lorelei Adams?"

Terror filled her eyes. She shook her head "no" as she slid into her black leather boots.

"It's okay. I'm not going to hurt you. In fact, I'm here to help you. Your conference is over for today, and you need not reschedule, or for that matter, even show up for Dr. Robinson's class anymore this term. Don't worry about your grade. Dr. Robinson is about to give you an 'A'. I promise. You may go."

The young lady slinked toward the door with dark eyes glued to me and fled in a wild dash. I shoved the professor who collapsed into his desk chair, nearly tipping it over.

He sat upright, assumed a supercilious pose, and glared at me. "I don't know who the hell you are, but you have no right to barge in here like this and assault me. Now get the hell out of here, or I will call campus security."

"I told you. I'm Tanner Nole, Lorelei Adams' father. I understand you propositioned her much like you did that poor thing who just left. How many other victims of your lust are running around campus damaged by your heinous actions?"

"How dare you? I never touched Lorelei or any other student for that matter."

"So, you do remember Lorelei? I don't believe you when you claim you didn't proposition her or touch that student that just left. I reached down, snatched black thong panties off the floor and held them up for inspection. I suppose this is yours. So you cross-dress, too? Kinky. Very kinky."

"I haven't a clue how those got there. They're certainly not mine. Now, please leave." He reached for the desk phone but dropped it when I slapped him across the face. He took a tissue from a box on his desk and wiped a trickle of blood off his mouth. "You struck me. That's assault."

Leaning down, I grabbed him by the collar with both hands and met his eyes in a glare, only inches away. "Lorelei wrote a letter to report your perverted solicitation to the college. Is that why you killed her—to shut her up?"

His jaw dropped, and his eyes widened. "I didn't kill her. She killed herself."

"So you admit you do remember her. Well, it turns out the sheriff got it wrong. She was murdered, and I'm looking for her killer. I think you killed Lorelei because she was going to expose your deviant acts."

He pulled back, eyes nearly popping out of his head, his body shaking. "No, no. I didn't do anything. I never touched her. I could never hurt one of my students. Lorelei received a far better grade than she deserved." Tears ran down both cheeks, and a sob escaped from somewhere deep. "Please leave me alone."

"You never hurt a student, huh? What do you call extortion for grades and sexual assault? Lord knows how many coeds you've scarred for life." I felt disgust for this sexual lowlife. Despite his denials, he was clearly guilty of sexually assaulting female students.

I pulled the envelope out and tossed it on his desk.

He picked it up and studied the addressee. "What's this?"

"It's a letter Lorelei wrote to the university president exposing your inappropriate behavior toward her and endorsed by three more of your victims. I found it in her apartment."

The professor regained composure and sat up straight, a signal the balance of power had shifted, a sign my bluff was failing. "So then, why are you here and not at the president's office?"

"Because I haven't yet decided what to do with this. My decision will depend on what you say in the next two minutes. I have an eyewitness account placing you at the scene of the murder that night."

A gasp escaped his mouth. "You what? They're lying."

"So, you admit you were there the night she was murdered?"

"Oh, no. That's impossible. I attended a committee meeting that evening. Here I can prove it." He spun around and touched his laptop keyboard. The blank screen came to life, playing a video of a woman performing oral sex on a well-endowed man devoid of pubic hair. The professor attacked the keyboard to make the video disappear and flipped through several screens, stopping on what appeared to be an online newsletter. Satisfied, he rolled back and pointed to the screen.

I browsed over his shoulder. A newsletter article showed a group photo of Professor Robinson among colleagues, all looking very scholarly. The caption referred to a committee meeting on the date Lorelei died. The clock on the wall showed 6:23. He couldn't have been anywhere near the crime scene that evening. Disappointment flooded over me.

He plucked the letter and scissors off the desk. "Are you convinced now?"

I snatched the scissors from him and waved them in his face. "You may not be a murderer, but you are a sexual predator. Swear to me on Lorelei's grave you will stop abusing your students!"

"I swear. I can stop. I'll get help."

Without a word, I tossed the scissors in his lap and left. The sound of an envelope being ripped opened, followed by a sick laugh, traveled down the hall.

Satisfaction warmed my soul. Later I would report the good professor to the dean. And then there was the suspicious wife waiting for him at home. I did it for Amy—and my daughter.

CHAPTER 48

When I reached my rental car, I crossed Professor Robinson's name off the suspect list. Jack would be proud of me. A suspect eliminated.

At the Talmadge Country Club, I stopped at the valet stand and awaited service. Three valets tried to ignore me. I coughed loud enough for them to hear. The loser in a quick game of Rochambeau slunk over to take my keys while his buddies laughed and poked fun. My cold stare silenced them, but only for a minute.

Inside, the restaurant teemed with activity. My sheepskin jacket, blue jeans, and light blue sport shirt stood out among the khaki pants and preppy sweater crowd. A short Hispanic hostess with long wavy hair studied me as if I were homeless. "Sir, may I help you with something?"

"I'm a guest for Reggie Braun." I stood straight and attempted to put forth a facade of sophistication.

"Is he expecting you?" Her grimace said she was not buying my act.

"Tanya, his wife, invited me to join them for lunch. Can you please point me in their direction?"

Latin eyes surveyed me, and her authoritarian face mutated to a look of skepticism. "*Sir,* please follow me." Her over-enunciation of the word "sir" dripped of disdain. She sent a subtle signal to a large Nordic man in a white suit wearing an earpiece like a CIA agent. She guided me through the restaurant, the guy in the suit in tow. Reggie and Tanya dined alone at a table for four on the patio.

Tanya made eye contact, smiled warmly and motioned for me to join them. Reggie turned to see who had caught her attention. He sprung to his feet, knocking his chair over backwards, crashing to the floor. "What the hell are you doing here? You *are* stalking me! Get this bastard out of here. Now!"

The big guy in the suit stepped forward and grabbed me from behind. Tanya stood and laid a gentle hand on his shoulder. "It's all right. I asked Mr. Nole to meet us for lunch."

"The hell you did!" Reggie's eyes glowed red as he tossed his napkin down on the table.

The big guy maintained a tight grip on me. "Mr. Braun. Do you want me to escort this gentleman to the door?"

Tanya moved around us to confront her husband. "Reggie, I'm sorry. I didn't realize you two had met. I asked Tanner to stop by." She glared at me. "You didn't tell me you were stalking my husband. You used me." Her glare became a playful snarl.

The security guy bruised my ribs, carrying me toward the door in a bear hug. "Wait, Reggie, tell Tanya about your lunch meeting at La Model on Tuesday."

"Stop!" Tanya's outburst drew the members' eyes to her. A robust smile suggested she loved the attention. "Please, let Mr. Nole go. Tanner, would you please join us as my guest?" Reggie's glare nearly burned holes through her as the hostess righted his chair for him.

Tanya returned her husband's scathing stare with an overly sweet smile. The security guy released me and stepped away. Wearing a self-righteous smirk, I brushed myself off and walked in front of my assailant to a chair Tanya pulled out for me. She dismissed both the security guy and hostess with a flippant wave of her hand.

Once settled, Tanya leaned forward and stared into my eyes. "So, Tanner, tell me about La Model."

Reggie peered at me through slits for eyes. In a subtle gesture, he shook his head "no" and slid his index finger across his neck in a slashing motion.

My face flushed. "Last Friday? Oh, yeah. I ran into Reggie having—ahh— a business lunch. I rudely interrupted him, so he asked some friends to show me the door. That's it. Not really much to tell." I glanced at Reggie for affirmation. He dropped his head slightly and shook it, wearing a look of disgust on his face.

"And who was this alleged business meeting with?" Tanya loured at Reggie.

Ignoring Reggie's murderous stare, I said, "I didn't get her name, but she was a frumpy looking lady in an expensive business suit and appeared to be delivering a sales pitch. Maybe a banker?"

"Frumpy looking?" Tanya asked. "You sure it wasn't little miss Good Body? What's her name? Your new assistant? Nancy, that's it, Get-in-Her-Tight-Pants Nancy? Enough!" Tanya sprung to her feet and snatched her purse off the table. "I'm going for a tennis lesson. You two boys can both go to hell as far as I'm concerned."

Every man on the patio gawked at Tanya stomping off in her skin-tight white dress ending halfway up her thigh. That is, all the men, except her husband, who focused instead on finishing his martini and ordering another. The waiter asked if I wanted to order.

Reggie waved him off. "Mr. Nole is not going to be here long enough to eat or drink anything."

The waiter left, and Reggie leaned toward me, wearing a smug look. "I bet you think Tanya is hot for you, don't you?"

"Oh, no. I have no interest in Tanya, at least not in that way. My only interest in her is as a source of information." I hoped my attempt at sincerity appeared more real than it felt.

He sat back, his face taking on a look of contempt. "Don't flatter yourself. She flirts and comes on to any halfway decent looking guy. Hell, I've seen here nearly kill an octogenarian in a wheelchair who thought he was going to get laid. She's a prick teaser. She enjoys getting men hot and bothered and then throwing cold water on their fantasies." He took a long sip of his martini and set it down. "The only exception is that damned tennis partner of hers. I can smell his cologne on her when she comes home."

He seemed to reflect on that for a moment, then chugged his drink and chomped on the olive. He leaned in. Expecting to hear a confession, I leaned in, too. "If you ever speak to my wife again, you're a dead man. You hear me? I pretty much run this town. In a way, the sheriff's department works for me. But then, a smart guy like you already knows that."

I winced at such a bold threat from my number-one murder suspect. Borrowing a pen from a passing waiter, I scribbled a note on a cocktail napkin.

Reggie fell silent for a full minute. I guessed he was replaying his words in his head. "So, tell me again why you are so anxious to speak with me."

"To ask you about Lorelei's death. I tried to set up an appointment, but your admin keeps blocking me. When I get frustrated like that, I tend to become aggressive. That's why I took matters into my own hands and crashed your office that day and then again at your lunch with Deputy Lowell."

A dreamy smile broke out on Reggie's face. "Lorelei. Yeah, she was something else." A quick shake of his head seemed to bring him back to the present.

All I could think about was this slimeball violating my daughter. I fought hard not to reach over the table and choke the haughty son of a bitch.

He held his empty glass above his head to signal the waiter for another. "The service around here sucks. Okay, you've got my attention. You've got five minutes, so ask away."

Limited on time, I decided to go to the core of the issue. "Do you think Lorelei, killed herself?"

He shifted in his seat and rubbed his chin. "The sheriff classified her death a suicide, and I see no reason to question him. I really did care for that girl and would hate to think someone murdered her."

I wrote on my cocktail napkin and asked, without looking up, "Did she seem suicidal to you?"

He scratched his nose and stared into the distance as if he needed to give it thought. "No, I didn't see any signs of it. Lorelei was full of life—go, go, go, a female Energizer Bunny. She was special. Did you know her?"

My eyes filled with tears. "No, I wish I had. I hear she took after her mother, someone very special to me." Our eyes met in a momentary bond. "I've been told you wanted to marry Lorelei. Is that true?"

Reggie's eyes went dark, his jaw clenched and his eyes scoured the people around us as if to see who might be listening. "Yeah, I did fall in love with her and even asked her to marry me, but she refused. Turns out she had some guy on the side, that she claimed was her soul-mate and wanted to marry him, not me. Love's a bitch. I was willing to give up half my business to my piranha of a wife to marry Lorelei. Love makes a man stupid." His drink arrived, and he took a gulp.

"Who might have wanted her dead?" I watched intently for any tell. I saw nothing.

"First of all, I told you I accepted it as a suicide. I'm not ready to concede she was murdered." His words slurred.

"All right, humor me for a moment. Let's say, hypothetically, that Lorelei was murdered. Do you think Tanya could have killed her?"

Reggie chuckled softly. "If you're asking, 'Could she kill someone?' yes, she could. I sleep with one eye open. If you're asking 'do I think she murdered Lorelei?', the answer is no. Tanya wants a divorce, but she can't initiate it because of our prenup. Truth be told, she wanted me to divorce her and marry Lorelei. That would have broken our prenup, and she would walk away with half my money. One thing my lovely wife can't do is poverty."

"Where were you the night of Lorelei's death?"

He took a quick scan of the room. "I was with Nancy. I remember because the sheriff woke me when he called to tell me about it. Why? Did Tanya tell you I stayed home?" He took my silence as a yes.

"And Nancy will vouch for you?" He now had two alibis but had just contradicted Tanya's. Somebody was lying

"Sure, but stay away from her." He waved his index finger at me. "And not a word about this to Tanya. That's just between us." The alcohol seemed to be loosening his tongue.

I paused to collect my thoughts. "What about Deputy Lowell? Do you think he could have killed Lorelei? He's the investigator on the case and seems to want to declare it a suicide and brush it under the rug. Maybe he has something to hide."

"Deputy Lowell. What in god's name would make you think he might have killed her? What motive would he have had?" Reggie sat up and wiped his mouth with the back of his hand. "Oh, I get it. You think he might have done it to please me because he wants me to back his campaign for sheriff. He's a deputy—a servant of the people. He wouldn't want to jeopardize his chances to become sheriff. I admit he does look out for my interests, and in return, I take good care of him—nothing illegal, of course.

"But do I think he killed Lorelei? No. I certainly didn't ask him to, if that's what you're getting at. It's strange, though. He seems to think he's doing me a favor by declaring her death a suicide. I keep telling him I had nothing to do with it, but he doesn't seem to be listening. If he ruled it a murder, I'm afraid everyone would be looking at me as the prime suspect." He looked off into the distance and gulped the rest of his drink.

Reggie motioned to the waiter for his check. "I have to go. You should try the food here sometime. It's pretty good for Talmadge. As for you and me, we're through. I don't want to see you again. If I do, it won't go well for you. Remember, I have influence in the sheriff's department. Am I making myself clear?"

"Yeah, I understand. Thanks for your time."

The security guy stood behind my chair breathing fish breath down my neck. Reggie gave him a nod, and he hustled me out of the restaurant.

CHAPTER 49

I checked my phone while waiting for the valet to retrieve my Pinto from the lot full of Mercedes-Benzes, Audis, Lexus's, Land Rovers and exotic sports cars, some costing more than I made in my best year practicing dentistry. My only message was from Ronnie: "Tanner, I tried calling you at the Country Inn and Suites, and they said you're not registered there and never were. What gives? Call me back. Ple-e-e-ease"

Standing in the open doorway of my rental, holding my key, the valet cleared his throat to attract my attention. Sporting a sneer, he brushed the back of his pants as if ridding himself of Pinto cooties. Guilt drove me to take out a twenty-dollar bill to boost his opinion of me. Amused by his continued cootie-ridding dance, I realized a valet at a country club expected exorbitant tips, so my twenty would not impress him. Seeking revenge for his earlier rudeness and subsequent exaggerated behavior over the questionable cleanliness of my ride, I stiffed him. For him, it became a self-fulfilling prophecy. The valet didn't expect a tip from someone like me, so they treated me rudely and, thus, got no tip. Sneering down his nose, he dropped my keys on the pavement, kicked them into the grass and stormed away.

My lingering embarrassment from last night's fiasco made Ronnie the last person I wanted to speak to, but her elongated "Please" in her message stoked my guilt. I stopped at Captain D's for lunch since Reggie hadn't let me eat at the country club. While dining on a fish and shrimp combo, I struggled to muster enough courage to return Ronnie's call. Before I finished, she called again. I forced myself to answer.

"Tanner, what gives? I thought you were staying at the Country Inn and Suites. Where are you?" After a long pause, "Tanner? You there?"

"Yeah, I'm here. I'm sort of between hotels at the moment. Seems Reggie owns every hotel and motel in town, and has black-listed me. I got evicted from two different places."

"You got kicked out of the Country Inn and Suites?"

"Not exactly. They wouldn't let me check in at all. I let you believe I was staying there because I felt embarrassed about the slum where I was staying. Even they asked me to leave. I think Reggie bought that place just to have me evicted."

"Tanner, you sound paranoid. I wish you could stay with Tim and me, but that's probably not a good idea. Why don't you stay at Mom's? She did offer to put you up."

I had declined Maggie Mae's offer for fear she would try to drive a wedge between Ronnie and me. That now seemed more a blessing than a problem. Better yet, it was free. "You think the offer still stands?"

"I'll call her and double-check. Get right back to you."

Later that afternoon, I arrived at Maggie Mae's. Any lingering apprehension about staying with her evaporated with the welcoming fragrance of baking bread. After moving into her guest bedroom, I took a quick shower to wash off layers of grime. My new hostess cooked fried chicken with mashed potatoes, gravy and green beans, lavished with country ham bits—simple, but one of the top ten meals of my life. We sat and talked for a long time after supper. Maggie Mae proved to be a hoot once I got to know her. Her spunky nature helped pick me up.

Now I needed to score some serious Oxy.

CHAPTER 50

A three-quarter moon rose on my drive to make my first illicit drug purchase. My destination, Twentieth and Central, lay deep in a section of town avoided by college students in my day. By the looks of things, this area had deteriorated even further since then. Only half the street lights worked, casting eerie shadows obscuring shady characters lurking in the creases. Fear overcame resolve and forced my right foot down on the accelerator to escape. A few blocks later, my craving for Oxy reclaimed me, and I slammed on the brakes. Sitting in the middle of the street, I struggled to regain control of my nerves.

A loud horn blast from behind, startled me. My heart pounded in my ears. A huge, bald black man gave me the finger as his gold Lincoln Navigator veered around me, hip hop music blaring through open windows despite the chill in the air. I didn't belong in the hood. Fear and reason compelled me to get the hell out while I still could.

My craving for Oxy overruled self-preservation. Almost on its own, the car turned around.

A bright-red vintage Camaro, sporting wide tires, rough-idled at my destination. A tall, thin black man wearing a do-rag leaned in through the passenger window from the sidewalk. I guessed he was Sharique, the drug dealer.

I had never witnessed a drug deal, but this looked like what I expected. Both the driver and the guy on the street glared my direction as I crept by peering back at them. I hoped they were simply checking out my classic

Pinto. But after circling the block, both the Camaro and the guy in the do-rag had vanished. "Shit!" I pounded the steering wheel. "I spooked him. Damn! Now what?"

My hands shaking too much to drive, I pulled over and parked where the Camaro had sat. A county deputy in a squad car crept by, eying my car and likely recording my license plate number for a check. I prayed Kymani had a clean title on this car and no outstanding tickets.

After about ten minutes, my resolve wore thin, and I put the car in gear to leave. Someone tapped on the passenger window, nearly causing me to soil my pants.

I leaned over and cranked the passenger window down. The guy in the do-rag poked his head in and scanned the interior with his eyes. "Don't know who you are but, but no pig would be caught dead in this piece of shit. Who the hell are you and what you want?" At least, I think that is what he said in a heavy ghetto accent.

"Are you Sharique?"

"Depends. Who the fuck is you?"

"I'm Tanner Nole. I called yesterday about some Oxy."

"You sho you not a cop? Maybe one with self-esteem issues, drivin this death trap on wheels? You actin suspicious-like 'n all—drivin by slowly and then doublin back as the po-po show up. Hell, you sho got the attention of that county Mountie. You lucky I came back."

"Well, I appreciate it." I sounded like the idiot I was. "Yesterday you said I could get forty-milligram Oxys for forty dollars each. I'll take ten." When I reached for my wallet, Sharique jumped back from the window, ducked and drew a pistol from his waistband.

"Sorry. Just reaching for my wallet." I held my shaking hands up to show my lack of a weapon, certain I had soiled my pants just a little this time.

Sharique tucked his gun back in his waist-band and peered around to see if anyone had spotted his weapon. He poked his head back in the window and scanned the interior a second time as if a threat might have appeared out of nowhere. "Whew. Thought you was goin for the heat there. Man, don't make no sudden moves like that. You get plugged for that roun here. We cool, but I got no Oxy."

As a writer, I wanted to correct his double negatives and fractured grammar but refrained. "What? Yesterday, you said you had forties."

"That was yesterday. This's today. Got cleaned out. You whities can't get enough of that shit. But, know what? This bein yo first drug deal and all, tell you what I gonna do. Here's a sample of sumpin better. You like em, I got more." He passed me a small Ziploc bag containing three round blue pills.

I held it up in the dim light and inspected its contents. "These look like Fentanyl."

"Yep. They way better'n Oxy. Try em, and you'll be back for more. I guaran-damn-tee it." That seemed to be a popular phrase in Talmadge these days.

"Fentanyl's dangerous. People die buying this crap on the street."

"No, no. Those dumbasses got contaminated Fentanyl, made in China, or someplace like that. This pure stuff, made in the good ole US of A, like they use in hospitals 'n all. Trust me. This can't hurt you 'n you'll love the high. Better'n any ol Oxy any day."

"When will you get more Oxy?"

"Couple days, maybe a week. That shit's movin fast. Can't keep up with demand. Call me in a few days." He reached in to retrieve the Fentanyl, but I pulled it away.

"You're sure this is good stuff?"

"Swear on my Mama's grave, that good shit. You'll see. Call me if you need more."

"Sorry to hear about your poor mother. You have my condolences."

"What? Oh, yeah. She not dead yet." He returned to the shadows to wait for his next customer.

As I drove off, mixed emotions flowed through me—relieved I had survived, yet frightened by the ordeal—elated to have the drugs, but uneasy about it being Fentanyl—eager to take the drug, but fearful of something new and potentially dangerous.

Halfway back to Maggie Mae's I realized I was cold and shivering. In my haste, I had failed to roll the passenger window back up. Reaching across to crank it up, I nearly hit a parked car. Blue lights flashed behind me. "Shit!" Busted on my first drug deal.

I shoved the bag with the three blue pills down inside the front of my pants. No cop with any self-respect would find them there, short of a strip search or drug-sniffing dog. I pulled over and rolled my window down. Through a cloud of despair, I looked up at the lovely eyes of Deputy Mallory Russo—the one deputy I wouldn't mind strip searching me.

"Tanner, you lost? Wouldn't expect to find you in this neighborhood. Been drinking a little tonight, have we?" Her Southern drawl was music to my ears.

My heart raced. "Nary a drop. I was rolling up the passenger window. It's a crank window and slips down every now and then."

"Crank window? Didn't think they still made them. Oh, yeah. I forgot. You're into vintage Fords. At least I think this rust bucket is a Ford. Still, I'm gonna need you to step out of the car."

I complied with several field sobriety tests, certain I would easily pass. In the final one, I had to touch my nose with alternating index fingers with arms held out away from my body. While breezing through this exercise, my bag of blue pills shifted and slid down my leg. I torqued my body to stop the bag's progress down my pant leg.

Mallory's face showed a half-smile/half-frown. "There's obviously something wrong with you, but you don't appear to be intoxicated. Okay, you're free to go. Please pull over next time you need to roll a window up."

"All that's wrong with me is my back. It's killing me. I can't stand straight tonight."

When a smirk turned into a smile, she dismissed me and headed for her car. Halfway, she stopped and turned back toward me. "Do you like veal? I make a mean veal scaloppini. Another of my Nonna's recipes,"

"I love veal scaloppini and am falling in love with Nonna, even though I've yet to meet her."

"Tomorrow night, my place, say around seven?"

"See you then. I'll bring Chianti."

Continuing on to Maggie Mae's, all I thought about was how much I craved an Oxy. I needed it more to relax my tension than ease my aching back after tonight's adventures. But I didn't have any left and wouldn't for several days. I retrieved the Fentanyl from my pants leg but couldn't muster the courage to try the dangerous drug.

Instead, I drank myself to sleep that night.

CHAPTER 51

Ray called Sunday morning and asked me to stop by the shop around two. He wouldn't tell me why, which piqued my curiosity.

A few minutes past two, I arrived at Central Georgia AutoWerks. The bay doors were closed, but a door to the dimly lit office stood ajar. I poked my head in and shouted out for Ray, but heard no response. I stepped into the office to look around and was greeted by a mixture of grease, gasoline and oil vapors.

A sound like clapping came from the bay area. I went in and looked around but didn't see anyone. I heard the clapping sound again coming from the far side of the other bay. Moving deeper into the service bay, I spotted Mountain Mann pinning Ray against a red pickup and slapping him hard with the front and back of his hand. Without thinking, I snatched a large wrench off the workbench and snuck up behind the abuser. Lofting the wrench high, I took aim for his head. As I swung, he pivoted to his right and deflected the blow with his right forearm. His block dislodged the wrench from my grasp and sent it clanging along the floor.

Mountain cried out in pain and clutched his right arm to his body. The fire in his eyes shot fear down the length of my spine. Towering over me, he backed me against a car sitting in the first bay, pinning me between him and the car. I broke to my left. With his good arm, he grabbed me and tossed me down like spiking a football. His bulk came crushing down on top of me, shooting pain through my compressed ribs. I struggled to breath under his weight. Two quick punches with his left hand sent pain shooting through the right side of my face. The taste of blood erupted in my mouth.

He lifted himself to his knees and delivered a pile-driver blow to my chin. Darkness closed in from the edges. He stood up and kicked me in the gut. I coiled up into a little ball waiting for the next blow, but it didn't come.

The beating stopped with the sound of a metallic click. Looking up through tears, I saw back Ray aiming a handgun at my attacker. "Okay, Mountain. That's enough. Put your hands up where I can see them."

Mountain raised his good arm above his head but struggled to raise his bloody, injured arm. "Be very careful there, Ray buddy. Don't do anything stupid, man." He spoke in a soft but confident tone.

"Keep your hands up and no sudden movements." Ray stepped back but kept the gun trained on him. "Tanner, you okay?"

I staggered to my feet and steadied myself on the car. Unable to speak, I gave him an affirmative nod.

Mountain's injured arm drooped to his side. "Ray, you're a smart guy. Don't do this. You're just digging yourself a bigger hole, amigo. Put the gun down or prepare to get hurt bad."

Ray steadied his aim. "Tanner, search him for weapons, but be careful."

Patting him down from behind, I found a pistol tucked in the back of his waistband and a knife in a sheath at his ankle.

Mountain half-turned and gave me a nudge. A gunshot exploded in my ears. The bullet ricocheted off the floor and struck an oil drum. A trickle of smoke snaked from the barrel of Ray's gun. Dark oil poured from a small hole in the drum.

Mountain's body stiffened and froze in place. I trained his gun on him and backed away, my hand trembling. He glared at me, displaying no sign of fear. "Careful there, asshole. That thing could go off if you're not careful. Listen to me. You don't want to get your sorry ass involved in this. This freeloader owes TLC twenty G's in gambling debts. He's been running a couple of months behind on payments. I'm just collecting a debt for him. Maybe you can help out a little, say a couple grand or so. Otherwise, Ray's living on borrowed time. Comprender?"

Ray's clenched mouth became a straight slit of determination. "You need to get the heck out of here, Mountain. I'll get TLC his money. I just need a little more time. Now go on and get out of here."

Mountain made a brush-off movement with his head. "Humph. Fuck you."

Ray's hand shook as he motioned him toward the door keeping his aim on him. "Get the fu . . . Go on, get out of here, Mountain."

The thug gave a dismissive shake of his head. "You two are making a big fucking mistake here. Think about it. I'm a pussycat compared to TLC. He's got a nasty temper. I'll be back, and you better fucking have TLC's twenty G's. And add an extra five for my trouble. Let's call it a service fee. And as for you . . ." He looked directly at me and held up his injured arm. "Watch your back. I'll be looking to even the score with you."

Ray opened one of the overhead doors. We trailed Mountain out the open raised door with both our weapons trained on him. He cradled his right arm in his left and swore at us all the way to his car. While driving away, he glared at us and slid an outstretched index finger across his neck in a slashing motion.

After Mountain drove out of sight, Ray cleared space on a workbench and set his gun down. A gentle hand on my shoulder, he looked at me with tender eyes bounded by a reddened, swelling face. "Sorry to get you involved in this, Tanner. You look a mess." He went to the restroom and returned with wet paper towels for both of us. "Here, wipe the blood off your face."

"Is this why you called me?"

"No, I didn't know he was coming. I can't get TLC's money, so I'm leaving town. I asked you to stop by so I could tell you something you should know."

"You keep a gun on you all the time?"

"Normally not, but lately, yes. Sometimes the Lord's protection alone is not enough. The gun's not registered. You see, I'm a convicted felon, so I can't legally own or carry a handgun." He saw my stunned expression. "Didn't know about my record, did you?"

He was right, I didn't. His revelation aroused new suspicions. "What were you convicted of?"

"It wasn't a big deal, just a bar fight over a bet. Yes, I have a gambling problem and a drinking problem, too. I'm a weak man. I pray to the Lord every day to deliver me from my temptations."

"You said you asked me to come because you remembered something to tell me concerning Lorelei's murder."

"It's about that hood, Mountain Mann. When I couldn't pay my debt to his boss, Mountain mentioned Lorelei and how she seemed to be doing pretty well. He suggested I get the money from her. I told him to leave her alone or else. He laughed and said it'd be a shame if such a pretty girl got hurt. His threat shook every element of me. I had to tell her, so that was why I stopped by the day she died."

"I went to warn her to be careful and offered to give her my gun, but she declined the offer. She asked if there was anything she could do, so I asked her if she would loan me some money. She blew up and threw me out—her own dad."

"What happened then?"

"I had a big bet riding on a sure thing, so I went to a bar I frequent to watch the game with some buddies. When my team got creamed and didn't cover the points, I got drunk. Don't remember much after that until I woke up in my car in the parking lot late that night."

"Is there anyone at the bar who could vouch for you?"

"What? Oh, you think I killed her? How dare you! I loved my stepdaughter very much and could never hurt her."

"I'm just asking."

"I go to that bar a lot. It's called 'The Hooch,' after the Chattahoochee River. The bartender should remember me being there. Look, I've got to hit the road. Mountain will be back and won't be alone. You better get out of here and lay low for a while, too. Sorry you got sucked up in my mess."

I offered Ray the handgun Mountain left, but he waved me off. "Keep it. You might need it." That he thought I needed a gun spooked me.

I would later check with the bartender at The Hooch who confirmed Ray had been at the bar that night but staggered out early around six o'clock after some heavy drinking. His alibi not holding up, Ray remained on the suspect list.

After I left, Ray lowered the overhead door. Wet paper towel pressed to my throbbing, bloody face, I walked back to my rental car. The altercation had aggravated my back, causing a noticeable limp. Such severe pain justified a Fentanyl trial.

As I neared my car, I heard what sounded like firecrackers going off nearby. Strange dinging metal sounds seemed to surround me. When shattered Pinto window glass showered me, I realized someone was shooting at me and ducked behind the car.

My heart beat hard enough to escape my trembling body.

CHAPTER 52

Bullets struck my car, sending shards of glass raining down on me. I scrunched down and covered the back of my head with my hands to protect myself. Mountain Mann's handgun slipped out of my waist-band and fell. I plucked it off the pavement and rose to a crouching position, ready to return fire. Weakened legs and shaking hands prevented me from discharging the weapon. The sum of all fear experienced in life prior to this did not equal the terror owning me now.

Gunfire erupted behind me, coming from the door of the shop. The sniper fire shifted to the building. From the open office door, Ray was shooting in the direction of the sniper's position, drawing the sniper's fire away from me.

Ray shot several quick rounds, forcing the gunman to duck behind a dark car across the street. When Ray paused, the gunman took the offensive, forcing Ray to duck back inside for cover. The sniper's barrage shattered the security glass in the door, but the internal wire mesh held the remnants in place. Unsure how long Ray's ammunition would last, I searched for better cover.

The shooting ceased for several minutes. I feared Ray might have exhausted his ammo, but then he poked his head out the door, fired off three rounds. The sniper did not return his fire. The sound of a car door slamming drifted from across the street a second before its engine came to life and tires cried out in abuse. Through cracked and shattered car windows, I watched a bullet-ridden black Chevy Impala speed away.

"Tanner, you okay?" Ray shouted from the shadows of the office.

Self-inspection revealed no serious injuries. A chill ran through me resulting in uncontrollable shaking. "Yeah, I think so. How about you?"

"Yeah, I'm good. I'll call 911."

A trickle of courage took root in me. Holding my gun in both hands the way they do on TV, I peeked over the roof of the Pinto and scanned the landscape for any other threats, but none remained.

"Sure you're okay?" Not realizing Ray had walked up behind me, his words nearly caused a heart attack. "Did you know you're bleeding?"

I didn't. A quick survey of my head found a few cuts from flying shards of automotive glass. I'm a wimp when it comes to seeing blood. My knees buckled, and I slid down the side of the Pinto and collapsed on the ground. A quick assessment determined my cuts to be minor. Ray bent down and helped me up.

My rental car was a mess. Three of the four side-windows suffered hits, but the back window survived unscathed. The windshield had imploded into a million beads of glass, one headlight was shattered, and the sheet metal had several bullet holes. Coolant and oil leaked beneath the car. "Shit! Kymani's going to be pissed. I can kiss my security deposit goodbye."

Ray reached in his pocket and produced a Ford-logoed key. "Here. This is to the blue pickup in back. It's a beater but runs like a top. Where I'm going, I won't need it for a while."

I accepted the key and thanked him as sirens grew louder in intensity. Ray tapped me on the shoulder. "Better give me that .38, so the sheriff doesn't find it on you. Knowing Mountain, it's likely hot. I'll hide it under the seat in the pickup for you to have later."

Ray paused at the office door, picked up his shell casings and pocketed them.

The sheriff's car and another squad car, lights flashing and sirens blaring, screeched to a halt sandwiching the Pinto in. Guns drawn, Sheriff Sykes jumped out of one car and Mallory out of the other. After a quick survey of the crime scene, they turned their attention on us.

Sykes pointed his gun at me. "Freeze and put ya hands on the back of your head, asshole."

I complied without hesitation. The sheriff made a slow, cautious approach and then swung around behind me. He holstered his gun, hooked one foot around my ankle and patted me down. "Ya armed, son?"

"Hell no, I'm the victim here, not the shooter. You should be chasing the shooter instead of harassing me. He left in a full-sized older black Chevy."

"Oh, so, you're an expert on proper police procedure now that you're a private dick? Let the professionals do our job, and ya stick to writing. Anyone hurt?" He examined my minor injuries but didn't exhibit any concern.

I assured him neither Ray nor I suffered any serious injury, but avoided mentioning the possibility the shooter could have been hit. That would have implicated Ray having a gun illegally. Lights flashing and siren wailing, an ambulance sped onto the scene. Sykes told them to rest easy for a few minutes while they sorted things out.

The turmoil of flashing blue and red lights drew a crowd. The sheriff holstered his weapon and approached the growing throng of bystanders. "All right, all y'all, back up and stay out of the way. There's nothing here to see. This is an active crime scene, and I'll lock up anyone who gets in my way, so I recommend y'all go back to whatever ya was doin." The crowd retreated a few feet without leaving and soon reclaimed the real estate they had ceded. The sheriff and Mallory stretched red police tape between trees to better corral the restless audience. The sheriff returned to continue questioning me while Mallory worked crowd control.

Ray returned and joined the discussion. Scowling, the sheriff studied our injuries. "Ya two look like ya been in a bad fight. Want to tell me what happened? Any idea who the shooter was?"

We both answered that it was an unknown male assailant. Beyond that we couldn't provide a description other than his car—a black older Chevy Impala.

As the crowd became bored and dwindled, Mallory joined us. Her eyebrows drew together when she noticed my bruised and bloody face. I forced a brief smile despite the pain it caused. The sheriff scowled at our silent interaction.

I took the lead. "We were in a fight, but not with each other. Mountain Mann paid Ray a little visit. I came to Ray's defense, but Mountain got in a few punches before he left."

Ray shot me a dirty look and shook his head no.

"So, Mountain did that to your face, Ray? Are there any other witnesses besides this guy? Mallory, take some notes here. I want ya to take the lead on this."

She took out pen and pad. We made momentary eye contact. She shook her head no.

"Mr. Nole here was telling me how Mountain took shots at him."

"No, no. That's not what I said. Mountain was gone before the shooting started."

To Ray's chagrin, I related the whole incident with Mountain Mann but withheld any mention of our guns.

As I finished, the sheriff scowled, looked down and shook his head. "Ray, ya wanna add anything to this cock 'n bull story?"

Ray shook his head. "Honest, Sheriff. That's the way it came down. After the altercation with Mountain, I didn't see anything until the shooting started, but Tanner pretty well covered it."

"From the looks of that door, the perp shot at you, too. You hit?"

"No. Guess he wasn't much of a shot."

Sykes scratched his head. "The shooter had the two of ya pinned down, unarmed. So what scared him off? Sounds to me like he had easy pickins."

Ray and I stared at each other, looking for an answer to an obvious question. After an uncomfortable minute, Ray looked away, so I offered an answer. "Maybe he ran out of ammo or didn't want to kill us, just scare us, which I assure you he did."

"Do I understand ya want me to believe two pantywaists, without any weapons, chased off a badass like Mountain and scared off a sniper who had ya two pinned down? Smells like seven-day-old fish to me. What am I missin here?"

I realized my error in omitting both guns but couldn't introduce either to the story now without throwing the whole tale into doubt. "I don't know. Maybe Mountain thought we got the message, or maybe he knew the sniper was outside waiting."

My ideas seemed lame even to me. I considered walking back the story and mentioning Mountain's .38, but Ray shook his head again. I was getting that a lot lately. "Honest, Sheriff. That's the way it happened."

"Ray, ya wanna press charges against Mountain?"

Ray did not hesitate. "No. It'll just make matters worse."

The sheriff looked at me. "Mister Nole, ya wanna press charges?"

Although I really wanted to, I followed Ray's lead and declined.

244

"Well then, if I was y'all, I'd try to stay away from Mountain. He's not one to mess with. Mallory, finish up here and see if you can make any sense out of this cluster-fuck. Ask around and see if ya can get a better description of the shooter. Oh, and talk to Mountain. That is, if ya can find him, but be careful. He's one powerful, dangerous thug."

The sheriff glared into my eyes. "Ya seem to be making a lot of enemies roun here, Mr. Nole. Somebody's goin to get hurt, and I don't need that kinda trouble. We'd all be a damn sight better off if ya hightailed it out of town before someone shoots yar sorry ass." With that, Sykes left.

Mallory inspected the damaged Pinto and snapped pictures with her smartphone. She collected twenty-one shell casings from the parking lot across the street. "Looks like a 223, probably from an assault rifle. Either the gunman was a bad shot or you're one lucky dude."

After thirty minutes of interrogation, Mallory put away her notes and called for a tow truck to impound the Pinto as evidence. A customer showed up to pick up their repaired car, so Ray excused himself.

She brushed my right cheek, and I recoiled in pain. "Wow. Mountain really did a number on you." She located a tissue in her pocket and dabbed two small glass cuts on my face. "You're bleeding on your arms too." She handed me the tissue for the cuts on my arms. "All right, Tanner. What really went down here?"

Despite uncertainty as to whose side Mallory was on, I decided to take a chance. Maybe I could get some information out of her. "Off the record?"

She put her pad and pen away, looked at the ground, and shook her head. "I knew it. Okay, off the record."

I filled her in on Mountain's gun but withheld that Ray also had a weapon. I trusted her, but only so far. In this version, I played the hero returning fire.

"Tanner, you don't want them to catch you with that gun. It's not registered to you, and you don't have a carry permit. Besides, it's likely hot. If you give it to me, I'll run a trace on it. We might pin a stolen weapons charge on Mountain. We've had a peck of trouble putting him away."

I relented and retrieved the weapon from Ray's pickup as he drove off in a Mazda sedan waving goodbye. I handed the gun to Mallory and walked her back to her squad car.

"Got to go back to the office and write this up before I can leave for the day. Need a lift back to your hotel?"

"Thanks, but Ray loaned me his old pickup."

"Okay." She slipped into her car. "We still on for dinner tonight?"

"They'd have to shoot me to keep me away. Oh, shit, they almost did."

She laughed. "You silver-tongued devil, you. Seven o'clock, and don't be late because veal can't sit."

As I drove back to Maggie Mae's, I shook uncontrollably. I pulled over to let the trembling subside.

The blue pills in my room at Maggie Mae's called to me. Last night I had feared taking such a notorious drug. Drug addicts took Fentanyl, not someone like me needing it for chronic pain relief. Still, I rushed home to take a Fentanyl for my nerves, swollen, bruised face and aching back.

CHAPTER 53

Singularly focused on my aching back and throbbing face, I burst into Maggie Mae's house on a mission. Maggie Mae set aside her needlepoint, rose from her recliner and followed me into the kitchen. Her eyes sprang open and her jaw dropped. "Oh, my word! Tanner, what happened to your face? Did you get in a fight or something?"

"It's nothing. I just need to take a pill and lie down for a few minutes. I'll be okay."

With a bottle of water from the refrigerator, I headed for my room to retrieve my Fentanyl. Maggie followed me like a dog nipping at my heels. "Tanner, how did you get hurt? You need medical attention."

"I'm okay. Just leave me alone." Shooting pain always puts me on edge. "I need to leave for a dinner date in an hour. Just leave me alone."

She recoiled, her eyes wide and mouth agape, giving her the appearance a gray-haired owl. "Are you and Ronnie going out tonight?"

Her nosey question pissed me off. "No. It's *not* Ronnie. I'm having dinner with a friend."

Her eyes softened, and her mouth hinted a smile of approval. "You sure you don't want ice for that face? What's your date going to think with you beat up and all?"

"She's already seen the damage." I stopped and counted to ten in my head to calm myself. "You know, an ice pack would be nice. Thanks."

I located the little bag of blue pills in the bottom of my suitcase, downed one pill and guzzled the rest of the bottle of water.

Maggie Mae returned to the shadowy room. "Here's your ice pack and some Tylenol."

"Already took something for the pain." I stopped and smiled at her. "Look, Maggie Mae, I'm sorry I snapped at you. My face hurts, but it's my back that's really killing me."

"How'd you get so banged up?" Her eyebrows drew together, deepening the lines in her already wrinkled forehead.

"I wrecked my rental car." That was close to the truth—the Pinto was a wreck. "Don't worry, I'm okay. Going to lie down for about thirty minutes for this pain pill to kick in. If you don't see me in forty, please wake me."

"Sure." Maggie Mae smiled at me like my mother did when I was ill.

If the drug failed to work magic, I would have to call Mallory and cancel. I didn't want to because I really needed to ask her about the longer draft version of the police report.

Later I learned Maggie Mae found me on the floor, lips and fingernails blue, barely breathing and called 911. I was in and out of consciousness and confused, so memories from that point on are shrouded in fog.

Ironically, Mallory was the first responder on the scene. It likely shocked her to discover tonight's dinner guest was the "unresponsive middle-aged Caucasian male" in the police call. Recognizing the urgency of my situation, she began CPR. "Tanner, it's Mallory. What did you take? You appear overdosed on something? Is it OxyContin?"

Mallory disappeared for a few seconds before jabbing me in the right thigh with a needle and returning to CPR. In the distance, a siren grew louder and then went silent.

"Tanner. Tanner. Can you hear me?"

I struggled to maintain consciousness, but darkness held me in its throngs and prevented me from speaking as if paralyzed but still alive.

Two paramedics rushed in and started oxygen. One checked vital signs and called them out to his partner. "BP is 80 over 40, and pulse is 32." He continued to examine me. "Constricted pupils, blue fingernails and lips. Looks like an overdose." He looked at Maggie Mae. "Any idea what he took?"

She was too flustered to answer. Mallory found the plastic bag with the two remaining blue pills on the dresser and held them up for the paramedics to see. "Looks like Fentanyl. Damn it! He took street Fentanyl."

"That explains a lot." They put me on the gurney and started an IV. He checked my vitals. "42 over 22 and pulse is 19. We're losing him."

Everything went dark.

The next thing I heard was the paramedic saying, "65 over 44 and pulse is 37. The Narcan you gave him is working."

Mallory held a weeping Maggie Mae close. The paramedics continued monitoring vitals while repacking their equipment. "Sir, we need to take you to the hospital for treatment."

I regained enough consciousness to understand the paramedic and to realize I could not afford an ambulance ride and emergency room. "No. I don't want to go to the hospital. I'm okay." I met Mallory's eyes with a focused stare and willed her to back me up on this.

Without looking up from their packing, one paramedic said, "You need to be in the hospital. You came dangerously close to dying and aren't out of the woods yet." He picked up a load of equipment and headed for the ambulance.

Mallory touched the arm of the other paramedic to get his attention. "Chuck, look. We've been friends since grade school. I have to ask a favor. I need you to leave this guy here and record this as a false alarm. I've had paramedic training. Maggie Mae and I can take care of him and watch him closer than the hospital would. This is the first time he's OD'd, so give him a break. Besides, you owe me."

He studied her before shaking his head. "I can't believe you're calling in your marker for this loser. Sure you know what you're doing? What're you going to do about the Narcan you used? You're required to record it."

"Yeah, I'm sure on this one. I'll just break the syringe and say it leaked out in the car. It happens sometimes. Can you take care of this with your partner?"

He looked away. "Yeah, Tommy's not going to be too happy, but he'll get over it. Just remember, Mallory, this is it. No more favors."

"Oh, and not a word of this to the sheriff or Deputy Lowell. Okay?"

After Chuck nodded, he looked down and shook his head. When his partner returned, he took him aside and murmured to him. Tommy reacted with disbelief and argued, but relented in the end.

They lifted me off the gurney and set me on the bed, propping me up with pillows. Daggers in his eyes, Tommy spoke in a gruff, angry tone. "I don't know what's going on here or what you have on Chuck, but you need to be in a hospital. You came very close to checking out of this world. Get some help. I don't want to see you again on another call. Understand?"

"I don't need help. This won't happen again. I swear."

"Yeah, right." Tommy shook his head and helped Chuck collect the rest of their gear and carry it to the ambulance. Chuck returned one last time to make sure they had retrieved everything. He confronted Mallory as she sat on the edge of the bed, stroking my hair. "I hope you know what you're doing. Here take this. Give him a second dose if he needs it." He handed her a Narcan syringe.

Ronnie rushed in the open front door, nearly colliding with Chuck as he left.

"Oh, my god. Is he all right?" she asked.

"I wouldn't say he's all right, ma'am, but he's alive—at least until the next time he OD's."

I learned later Maggie Mae had called Ronnie, who dropped everything and rushed right over. Ronnie sat on the bed next to me and held my hand while her mother stood over us and briefed her. Ronnie's eyes teared up. "Oh, Tanner, are you all right? What happened to your face?"

Maggie Mae let Mallory answer. "Tanner got assaulted this afternoon, came back here and overdosed on what appears to be street Fentanyl. Not the best of days."

"Fentanyl?" Ronnie asked dumbfounded. "I thought you took OxyContin. Where'd you get Fentanyl?"

"I bought it from a friend of a friend. He promised me it was hospital grade. I didn't want to take it, but my face and back hurt so bad I had to take something strong enough to kill the pain. I'm out of OxyContin, so that's all I had." Fighting against the fog in my head, I slurred my words.

Mallory's face reddened again, this time in anger. "Oh yeah? Well it almost killed you. You need to be in the hospital, but I called in a favor to keep them from taking you. If the sheriff knew he would insist I arrest you for possession of a narcotic. Despite your denials, Tanner, you have an opioid addiction and need help."

"I keep telling you, I don't have a problem. I suffer from severe back pain, and I take pills, prescribed by my doctor, to manage the pain."

Mallory's face hardened. "Tanner, this is not a prescription drug. This is street Fentanyl. Who knows what's in there? If you're not an addict, why are you buying street drugs?"

"I ran out of OxyContin and can't renew my prescription for another week or so. I needed something to tide me over."

"But Fentanyl?"

"I couldn't buy Oxy because apparently there's an opioid problem in Talmadge. Fentanyl was all I could get."

Ronnie stroked my face and cried. "Tanner, if you're running out of your prescription before you can renew it, you have a drug problem. You're addicted. You need help—professional help."

"Please don't touch my face. It hurts like hell."

"So, what happened to your face?"

I didn't feel up to talking, so Mallory filled both ladies in on the earlier events at Ray's garage and made me sound like a hero.

Thirty minutes later, I passed out, and Mallory injected the second Narcan. An hour later, the Narcan sent me into withdrawal, giving me a terrible case of the shakes. Mallory took charge. "Okay, ladies. Let's get him up and walk him around. It promises to be a long night."

CHAPTER 54

The following morning was dark from overcast clouds, so I slept late. Normally six hours is the most I can sleep before severe back pain wakes me. After nine hours in bed, not only my back ached, but my whole body, especially my abdomen. The bedsheets, damp from night sweats, provided evidence the second dose of Narcan had sent me into opioid withdrawal.

The only thing that could ease suffering this severe would be an Oxy, but I had none. Desperate for relief I, I decided to take half a Fentanyl to tide me over. A quick, but thorough search failed to locate the little bag of blue pills, leading me to the conclusion Mallory must have confiscated them. That would be the cop in her. That left me to tough it out on booze and Advil until I felt well enough to buy more Oxy from Sharique.

Despite weak and wobbly legs, the enticing smell of frying bacon lured me to the kitchen. Maggie Mae labored over the stove singing, her back toward me.

"That smells wonderful," I said

She let out a scream and jumped, sending her spatula flying. Hand on her chest, she took deep breaths. "Tanner, you about gave me a heart attack." Her shoulders relaxed a little as she caught a breath. "After the rough night last night, I thought you could use a good breakfast. I sure can." A normally prim and proper Maggie Mae looked mussed and disheveled with dark bags under her eyes and no sign of makeup.

I retrieved the spatula for her. "What's for breakfast? It smells grand."

"It's closer to lunch, but I thought you might need comfort food because Lord knows, I do. I'm cooking bacon, eggs and fresh biscuits with sausage gravy. We'll call it brunch to justify all that food. Hungry?"

"Famished." I was hungry despite my stomach roiling.

"It's about ready. Grab some coffee and sit down. I made it extra strong because I thought you'd need it if you ever got up." She served me a plate heaping with hot food.

"When did Mallory and Ronnie leave?"

"They left about three. We put you to bed a little after two. The three of us were too keyed up to sleep, so sat and talked." Without waiting for her to sit down with a smaller plate of bacon and eggs, I started cramming food in like a homeless person.

Hard eyes glared at me. "Seems you have the makings of a love triangle."

"What do you mean?" Hunger trumped etiquette. I talked with my mouth full.

"It's obvious you and Ronnie have feelings for each other. I sensed it the day you stopped by and ate lunch with us. To be honest, I invited you to stay with me so I could keep an eye on you. Then last night, I found out you had a dinner date scheduled with that nice young deputy. Are you chasing after her too? She seems a might young for you."

After pondering a minute, I swallowed and said, "It's not what you think. Mallory's like a little sister to me. Besides she has information I need for the investigation. That's all there is to it."

"I think Mallory has feelings for you, not just as a big brother."

"I assure you she doesn't think of me as a love interest. She's made that very clear, and besides, she's been spying on me for Sykes. That's likely the only reason she invited me to dinner—to pump me for information while I'm trying to do the same to her."

"Maybe, but I saw something more. She didn't have to stay and take care of you last night, but she did. Besides, did you hear her beg the paramedics not to tell anyone about your overdose? She could have easily told the sheriff herself. Doesn't sound like a spy to me."

My foggy brain struggled to make sense of Maggie Mae's words, which confused me even more about Mallory's role in all this.

Maggie Mae looked me straight in the eye. "Are you still in love with my daughter?"

I wanted to lie to her, but my brain didn't function well enough to respond with anything other than the truth. "To be honest, I've always been in love with Ronnie, even after I left. She's very special and will always hold a warm place in my heart. In fact, she's the only reason I came back to Talmadge. The book signing was an excuse. I'd heard she divorced and hoped we could pick up where we left off."

"Pick up where you left off? You skipped town without any explanation, never to be heard of again until now."

Her words were battering ram thrusts to my gut. "Maggie Mae, you're absolutely right. I was a jerk, and I regret what I did."

"What worries me is she still has feelings for you. I had to force her to leave this morning. Tim has been very good for her and worships the ground she walks on, so please don't sabotage that. You screwed up her life once, and I won't stand by while you do it again. It took her years to get over you the first time."

As if on cue, Ronnie burst in the front door and followed her nose to the kitchen.

"Honey, weren't you scheduled to work today?" Maggie Mae asked.

Ronnie paused at the kitchen doorway and stared straight ahead. Her lower lip quivered, but no words came out.

"Honey, what's wrong?" Maggie Mae rose, rushed to her daughter and wrapped her arms around her.

"He's moving out." Tears erupted from bloodshot eyes.

"What do you mean? Tim? Tim's leaving you?"

"His buddy saw Tanner and me kissing at the Waffle House parking lot the other day after lunch. Somehow Tim found out Tanner came over for dinner Friday night while he was out of town." She sobbed. "He waited for the right moment to confront me. Then, last night, when I got your call about Tanner, he begged me not to come. He threatened to divorce me if I did, but I had to come. Tanner needed me." She bawled. "Now he's leaving me. Oh, Mom, what can I do?"

Maggie Mae's face turned white, and her mouth gaped, looking like she had been struck by lightning. The discovery of my covert dinner with her daughter confirmed her suspicions of my intentions.

My attempt to slip away unnoticed was foiled by Maggie Mae. "Where do you think you're going, Tanner? You're a major contributor to this situation and need to take part in our discussion. Let's sit in the living room and talk." I left half my delicious breakfast uneaten despite not feeling full. My stomach did not react well to the heavy breakfast and the coming inquisition.

They sat on the love seat, and Maggie Mae put her arm around her grieving daughter. I sat in an upholstered rocker opposite them and rocked vigorously while struggling to keep my breakfast down.

Maggie Mae broke the ice. "Ronnie, I sense you're in love with Tanner."

Ronnie began to speak, but her mother silenced her with a wave of her hand. "Let me finish. I saw it that first day when he joined us at your house for lunch. It's obvious he's been stoking those feelings for his own benefit. I know you and Tim have had problems since Lorelei's death, but do you still love him?"

Ronnie gave me a deer in headlights look and sobbed. She hung her head. "Yes, despite our troubles, I do still love him."

"Are you in love with Tanner?" Maggie Mae asked.

Ronnie paused. "I know I shouldn't after what he did, but yes, I am. I realized it the day of his book signing. I guess I have always loved him. I'm so confused."

"Well, let me help un-confuse you, then. Did you know Tanner has been seeing that attractive young deputy from last night? In fact, his little episode spoiled their plans for a romantic dinner at her place."

Ronnie turned toward me, her face showing a tortured expression as if in physical pain. "Tanner, is that true? You're dating her? She's so young."

Flushed with undeserved shame, I looked at Ronnie. "No, no. I told your mother she was wrong. Mallory and I are friends out of convenience. She appears to be spying on me, and I'm trying to pump her for information for my investigation. There is no budding romance there on either's part."

Ronnie's face tightened, drawing her brows together. "Tanner, you haven't changed, always looking for something better. It's still all about you and what you want."

Shifting position eased my back pain. The sweats returned, bolstered by nausea, another sign of withdrawal. "Ronnie, I still love you just like I told you the other night. I've always loved you and always will. But it doesn't feel right, because you're married. I told you I've developed a conscious."

"Be honest with me. Are you in love with Mallory?" Ronnie wiped her eyes with a small wad of well-used tissue.

I looked away to reflect. It was true that Mallory was very attractive, but my focus still was the investigation, not romance. Besides, Mallory was too young for me. Still, confusion stirred my brain. "I told you, I'm just trying to pump her for information. There's nothing there. Honest."

"Is she why you couldn't get an erection Friday night?"

Maggie Mae gasped, a hand covering her gaping mouth and eyes bulging.

I chose my words with great care. "It's been rough for me the last few years, and I've become a very lonely man. It's sad, but my fondest memories were when we dated in college. Fantasizing about us reuniting kept me going through some deep, dark patches. I told you the other day, I had come back hoping to reconnect with you and live out my fantasy. When I saw you again, my love for you seemed real. Tim told me you were having trouble, and I saw my opportunity, so pursued you. I shouldn't have, but I did.

"Thursday, when we kissed outside Waffle House, it felt right. I wanted you more than I've ever wanted anyone else. But Friday night, when we went to take things to another level, I couldn't get Tim out of my head. It just didn't feel right anymore."

"So, what do we do now?" Ronnie held her head in her hands.

Leaning forward, I cradled my head in my hands too and reflected on how I should respond. Our eyes met. "I don't want to hurt you, Ronnie, but we have both evolved and moved in different directions. We can't regain what we had. I realize that now. Times are different and we're different. You're married, and from what your mother has told me, happily married—at least until Lorelei died. Ronnie, go back to Tim. He loves you, and that is where you belong. If it will help, I'll talk to him and tell him it was my fault. I pushed too hard and took advantage of you being in a vulnerable place."

"You would do that for me?"

"Absolutely." I doubted I could keep that promise. My tendency is to avoid conflict at all costs. But, at that moment, I felt magnanimous.

The two of them hugged and cried. Over Ronnie's shoulder, her mother looked at me and gave me a single nod of approval.

Ronnie broke from her mother's embrace and went to the bathroom to fix her makeup. Maggie Mae hugged me. "Thank you, Tanner. I know you're still very much in love with her, so it took a lot of courage to do what you just did."

I fought back tears. "You have no idea how hard that was. Ronnie is my soul mate—always has been and always will be."

She took a deep breath. "I think it best you make other living arrangements. You two need distance. Will you abandon the investigation and go home?"

"No. I'm committed to finishing it, as much for my sake now as for Ronnie's. My daughter's killer is out there somewhere, and I won't rest until he's behind bars. It's the least I can do for my daughter."

Ronnie reappeared with limited makeup. "I called Tim. He's coming home so we can talk. I've got to go. Thanks, Mom. Thanks, Tanner."

She gave me a friend-hug, and rushed home to the other man. I asked Maggie Mae for Advil and took four. Not only did my back and abdomen ache, I now had a throbbing headache. I raced to the bathroom, not knowing whether to sit or lean over the toilet. Diarrhea won the battle. I fought to keep the Advil down but eventually, that failed too. Opioid withdrawal is a bitch.

When my stomach settled down, I packed my bags and hit the road, once again homeless.

CHAPTER 55

Mallory called as I left QuikTrip, having purchased gas, soda crackers, water and Tums. Ignoring the voice inside my head screaming to let it go to voice mail, I watched my finger accept the call.

"How are you feeling'?" Mallory's voice exhibited a concerned tone that touched something dormant inside me.

"Living the dream. Did you take my Fentanyl?"

"Yeah, and flushed it down the toilet to destroy the evidence. You wouldn't dream of using that stuff again, would you?"

I answered with silence.

"You're addicted to opioids, aren't you?"

"No, I experience chronic back pain and take prescription pain medication for it."

"No, Tanner. I'm telling you. You have a problem, and you need to seek professional help."

I needed to steer the conversation in another direction. "Thank you for what you did last night. I understand you stayed until after two."

"You almost died, Tanner. I saved your life. If you don't get help, next time you could die. I'm telling you as a professional, you need help. Promise me you'll do something about it when you get home."

"I promise." I didn't believe it and wondered if she did.

"Go home, get clean."

"Does this mean we're not rescheduling our dinner?"

"No. I don't think that would be a good idea after all that's come down. I've got enough on my plate with Deputy Lowell looking over my shoulder."

"Be honest. Were you only inviting me over for dinner so you could spy on me?"

Her long pause seemed to confirm my suspicions.

"Look, Tanner, it wasn't like that. The sheriff knows Lowell has you in his crosshairs and that you have had run-ins with Reggie Braun. He asked me to keep an eye on you for your own good. That's it."

"What about Deputy Lowell? Were you reporting back to him to?"

"Absolutely not. As a matter of fact, I never reported anything back to the sheriff. I just kept an eye on you, but I do like you. You're like the big brother I never had, and I enjoy talking with you."

"So, you don't have a crush on me?"

"What? Are you kidding?"

"For some reason, Maggie Mae thinks you do. I told her she was wrong."

"As I said, I like you, but I'm not interested in a romantic relationship."

Although I never believed there was any chance of a romantic relationship between the two of us, the confirmation of that fact still hurt nonetheless. The dark sky matched my mood as rain began to fall.

CHAPTER 56

A soft rain fell as a classic Cadillac pulled into the Talmadge Extended Stay motel, its headlights reflecting off dark wet pavement. It pulled up next to me, and I slid into the passenger seat. The car reeked of pine from a green tree cutout dangling from the rear-view mirror. I didn't know they still sold them.

"Jack, thanks for coming. I really appreciate it. Here's cash for the room. Ask for one near the back door, so I can avoid being seen going through the lobby. Reggie owns this place, so there's probably a picture of me posted at the desk."

"Yeah, yeah." His tone and stoic expression confirmed I had inconvenienced him. Snatching the cash from my hand, he hustled into the hotel hoisting a dilapidated umbrella to provide some protection from the rain.

Ten minutes later, he returned with a key card. "They gave me room 115. From their floor map, it's near the back door, as you requested. Even though I paid cash, she insisted on having a credit card on file, so I gave her mine. Don't rack up a lot of bills with room service or steal the towels."

"Room service? At an extended stay hotel? Hell, I'll be lucky to have maid service once a week. Thanks, Jack. I owe you one."

"Technically speaking, you owe me three. I saved you from those four goons the other night and set you up with Tanya Braun. By the way, how's the investigation coming?"

"Slow, but I have eliminated one of Lorelei's professors from the list." I failed to mention that he had been added to the list and then eliminated for a net change of zero. "Now, I'm focusing on my number one suspect. Problem is he has two alibis—his wife and his current mistress. I'm pretty sure his wife is lying, but I haven't confirmed the other yet. It's still a long list. Like you said before, I have too many suspects." I felt like I was kissing up to him because I had inconvenienced him. If he was even a mediocre PI he sensed it.

He glanced down and shook his head. "Did you get your hands on the security videos from the apartment like I suggested?" His tone reminded me of a skeptical parent.

My face blushed. "Not yet. I didn't feel well this morning, so slept in, but am planning to look into security videos right now."

"From my experience, that is where you need to go next. Quit chasing the suspects around. All right, I gotta go. My sister's cooking meatloaf tonight. It's my favorite, and she doesn't like it when I'm late."

We shook hands. "Thanks again, Jack." I love meatloaf, but the thought of it made me nauseous. My new first day of involuntary abstinence.

As I left his car, he offered advice in an agitated tone. "Do yourself a big favor and look at the security video."

"Thanks, Jack. I appreciate you coming out in the rain to help me out. Can I buy you lunch tomorrow to thank you? How about we meet at the Barking Owl Pub near campus?"

"Sorry, but I have to go to Atlanta in the morning. How about a rain check?"

Sure, I'll give you a call."

264

As I carried my things in the hotel through the back door, my body trembled, and sweat poured off me. A gurgling stomach sent me rushing to the bathroom to dry heave.

I lay down with a cold rag on my head. An hour later, my stomach settled enough to eat some soda crackers with a Tums chaser.

After an hour of TV, the crackers seemed to settle okay. My muscles ached all over, but I dared not take Advil for fear of messing up my stomach again. A hot shower made the aches tolerable, so I went to bed early only to toss and turn, seeking a comfortable position for my back.

After forty-five minutes of sleep, I awoke, soaked in heavy sweat. Anxiety clutched me in her grips, preventing any further sleep. As I paced the room, my heart raced to the point I feared it might burst. With every passing minute, my resolve to stay clean waned.

When nausea returned, I vowed to score some Oxy, but limit my intake to the level prescribed by my doctor. A call to Sharique went unanswered, so I left him a message and resumed pacing.

It was only thirty minutes but seemed like days when Sharique called back. "You rang?"

"Sharique, this is Tanner Nole, you gave me some Fentanyl the other night." I failed to use a pseudo-name again.

"Oh yeah, I remember, the newbie. I weren't lyin bout the Fenty, right? They's on special, twenty-five a pop. How much yo want?"

"No, that stuff nearly killed me. I'm sticking with Oxy. Did you get any?"

"Sorry, man. Fenty not fo everybody. You's in luck, though. Just got some Oxy in today. Got some forties. They be sixty bucks each. How many?"

"Sixty dollars! Last time you said forty dollars a pill for sixties."

"What can I say? It's a sellers' market. Want 'em or not?"

I counted the dwindling cash in my wallet. "Okay, okay. I'll be there in about thirty minutes."

"Still drivin that piece of shit Pinto?"

"No, it's in the police impound. I'm driving an old blue Ford pickup now."

"Whoa, forget it, man. If the po-po breathin down yo honkie neck, yo too hot for me."

"No, it's not like that, I was the victim. Someone vandalized my car. They're holding it as evidence." It took another five minutes of discussion to calm him enough to sell me the drugs.

On the drive back from a successful buy I rationed myself to only one Oxy despite craving more. I chewed it to get it into my bloodstream faster. By the time I reached my room, my pains had diminished to a tolerable level.

After another shower, the craving worsened and resolve weakened. I compromised with myself and took half a pill. Euphoria soon flowed through my body. After an hour or so, the buzz diminished, and drowsiness overtook me enough to drop into the comforting arms of uninterrupted sleep.

Chapter 57

The room clock showed 9:48 AM. The one and a half Oxys taken the night before had knocked me out for eight hours. I might have slept longer if not for the raging back pain and a heavy craving for more Oxy. I opted for two ibuprofens to preserve my small supply of the precious drug. A cold shower pushed the cobwebs away, but the ibuprofen did little to diminish my pain and nothing for the Oxy craving. I doubled down with two more ibuprofen.

Having not eaten since brunch yesterday, I was famished. Driving through Chick-Fil-A made for a change of pace. As I ate and drove, Jack's recommendation to view the apartment security video dominated my thoughts. I mentally kicked myself for not following up on the video before now. Maybe I had been drawing out the investigation to be with Ronnie, but now I was anxious to find my daughter's killer and bring him to justice.

Three buzzes on Donald's apartment intercom went unanswered. A quick tour around the building identified three security cameras—the front door, rear door and resident parking lot.

Returning to the front door, I buzzed Delilah Morgan, the elderly lady in apartment 1D, to whom I'd spoken twice before.

She answered in a sharp tone after the second push. "Stop ringing my buzzer. Takes an old woman time to reach the intercom. Who is it and what's so damned important?"

"Good day, Mrs. Morgan. Sorry to bother you, but this is Tanner Nole. We've spoken before about the death of your neighbor, Lorelei Adams. You're an important witness in the case, so I need to ask you a few more questions if it's convenient."

"No, it's not convenient. Now go away and stop bothering me."

"Do you own a gun, Mrs. Morgan?"

"What? Why did you ask that?" Her voice rose to a glass-breaking pitch.

"To make sure you're safe. We haven't found Lorelei's murderer yet and have reason to believe he might strike again. I want to make sure you're protected."

"You said he. Couldn't it have been a woman? I heard two women arguing just before the gunshot."

"You see, that's why I need to talk to you." A large truck passed, drowning out what she said next. "I can't hear you for all the street noise. Can you please buzz me in? Won't take but five minutes, I promise."

I yawned and shook my head for clarity while awaiting her response. She buzzed me in and met me at the open door to her apartment. "Come in, but I can only give you two minutes. 'The View is coming on. Oh, my. You don't look well, and all banged up, too. Can I serve you some water or tea?"

Sweat flowed from my pores, and my muscles hurt all over. Spicy chicken rolled in my stomach. "No, thank you. I'm okay. I just didn't sleep well last night. You said you heard two voices the evening of the murder, both female. Is that correct?"

"Actually, I'm not sure. One was definitely a woman. The other could have been a woman with a low voice or a man with a high-pitched voice. Or, it might have been just one voice I heard. My hearing's pretty good for my age but it's not perfect anymore."

"What was the tone of their voices?"

"What'd you say?"

Not perfect? She was downright hard of hearing. "How did they sound—angry, bossy, happy, sad . . .?"

"One voice sounded angry. That was the one I'm not sure about. He, or she, raised their voice. The other was definitely a woman and seemed to be trying to calm the other person."

"Can you tell me what they said?"

"I'm afraid not. I heard their voices but could only understand a word here and there. It doesn't matter. I've forgotten anything I heard."

After several fruitless questions, it sounded like the building's front door closed.

"I guess that should do it. After all, you need to get to 'The View'." I opened her door, and the sound of an interior door closing came from down the hall. I stepped into an empty hallway. "Okay. Bye, and thanks, Ms. Morgan."

A harsh scowl fell across her face as if she wanted me to stay and watch The View with her. I gave her a warm smile and closed her door to see if Donald had returned.

After twice pounding on his apartment door, a faint voice leaked through the door. "Damn it. I'm in the bathroom. Hold on for just one damn minute." Minutes later, Donald appeared at his door, drying his hands on a towel. "Oh, it's you. How the hell do you keep sneaking into the building? I canceled Lorelei's building access card and changed the lock on her door."

"Sorry to bother you, Donald, but I need to review the security tapes for the night of Lorelei's murder."

Color drained from his face. His eyes bulged, and his body tensed. "Murder? What do you mean, murder? She killed herself."

"I have proof Lorelei was murdered. Someone made it look like suicide. I'm tracking down the killer."

Donald fidgeted in quick jerking motions reminiscent of a squirrel. "But—but—the sheriff said she killed herself." His higher pitch reeked of confused irritation. I wondered if his voice might be mistaken for a woman's at a distance.

"Well then, you have no reason to not let me see the surveillance videos for that day."

"I—I can't. That would violate our residents' privacy." The guy was sharper than I thought.

"That video is evidence. If I have to, I'll get the sheriff involved and subpoena them. They might charge you with obstruction of justice. Could mean real jail time. Ever done time, Donald?"

Through blinking eyes, he scanned the room. "My boss would be pissed if I let you see them without his permission, and he's on vacation this week." Perspiration beaded on his forehead.

"All right then, who's his boss? Maybe you could get approval from him."

He wiped his hands off on his faded blue jeans. "I'm not sure, maybe Mr. Braun. I understand he owns the building, but I can't bother him. He's a busy man."

"Don't worry. Reggie and I go way back. Let's call him."

Donald nearly passed out when I whipped out my flip phone and called a stored number.

After one ring, I heard Jack Sprat answer, "Tanner, what's up?"

"Hello, Nancy." Covering the microphone as if I didn't want 'Nancy' to hear, but spoke loud enough for Jack to hear me. "That's Reggie's admin. She's quite a looker."

"Tanner, you been drinking again? What's going on?"

"This is Tanner Nole. I met with Mr. Braun last week, and he told me to call him if I needed anything. So, I'm calling because I need a favor. I'm at his apartments on Maple Street with Donald Wirth, the building supervisor."

"What the fuck are you doing? Who the hell is Donald Wirth?" Jack sounded on the verge of hanging up.

"I asked to view the security tapes for Lorelei's apartment building. Donald says he needs Reggie's approval to let me see them."

"Oh, I get it. You want me to pretend to be Reggie. Smart. Okay, let me speak to him."

"That's right. His immediate boss is out of town. Can you put Reggie on the phone? Great. Nancy, you're an angel."

"She's no angel. She's a gold-digging slut." I couldn't dispute Jack on that point. "And you didn't say 'please' either."

Suppressing a laugh, I handed my phone to Donald. "Hello, Mr. Braun? This is Donald Wirth. I supervise your apartment buildings on Maple Street. Sorry to disturb you, but this guy here is investigating the death of Lorelei Adams and wants to view the apartment's security video. I told him no unless you authorize it. Okay, I'll help him."

Struggling to maintain a straight face, I took back my phone. "Thanks, Reggie. I appreciate it."

"Hey, Tanner, copy the video files onto a DVD or a memory stick or something so you can take more time to look at them later. That is, if they're still there. Security videos are erased at some point to conserve memory."

My heart plunged at the suggestion the videos might have been lost. "Sure thing. Talk to you soon."

Donald was as stupid as I first thought. He fell for our childish ruse.

"I access the surveillance records from a desktop in my apartment but I need two Benjamins for my trouble." I took out my phone and started to redial Jack. "Wait, what are you doing?"

"I'm calling Reggie back. I'm sure he'd like to know he has an extortionist on his payroll."

"No, don't." His face morphed from wide, panicked eyes to a forced smile. "I was just kidding. Can't you take a joke?"

We both knew I had him right where I wanted him. His apartment was less than half the size of Lorelei's and very basic. The appliances were all Hotpoint rather than Bosch as in Lorelei's apartment. It was a different world than her grand apartment.

Chapter 58

Donald led me to the second bedroom in his apartment, which served as an office. He borrowed a chair from his dining area for me to watch over his shoulder before plopping down in his desk chair. "I assume you want to view the tapes from the day of Lorelei's suicide. You're lucky. We only keep them for thirty days. Day after tomorrow, they'd be gone."

We started with the backdoor camera covering the resident entrance. When he got to the correct day, he paused the video and gave me a brief tutorial before we switched seats. Donald's chair squeaked as he fidgeted behind me.

On the screen, Lorelei left the building early morning dressed like a typical college student carrying a backpack. From the pictures in the police report, I realized these were not the clothes she had been killed in. My heart ached at the sight of her.

Shortly after her departure, Brandon slipped out the residents' door. He had lied. He had spent the night with her. Why would he lie about that? I borrowed a yellow legal pad and a pen from Donald's desk to record the people going and coming and the time of day. I started with Brandon and added a large question mark to remind me to follow up with him.

I sped up the frame rate as residents left throughout the morning. Donald gave me their names and apartment numbers for my notes. None seemed to stand out.

Lorelei returned late afternoon. I stopped and replayed her entrance. Freezing her image on the screen, a lump formed in my throat as I admired my beautiful daughter. I snatched a tissue from the desk and dried my eyes, trying hard to contain the heartache. Feeling Donald's eyes staring at me, I sucked it up. "These monitors give me eye strain."

"She was one great piece of ass, wasn't she?" His crass declaration made my blood boil. I sprung from the chair, ramming it back into Donald's legs.

"Ouch! What the hell?" He took a martial arts stance, ready to take me down.

I wanted to hurt this guy. Instead, I stared at him and silently counted to ten to regain self-control.

When I didn't attack, he relaxed his stance and rubbed his knees. "I ought to kick your sorry ass. What the fuck got into you. That hurt like hell."

"I'm sorry, but you disrespected the dead, which happens to be one of my hot buttons." He had disrespected my daughter, but I couldn't tell him that.

I sat back down and so did he. Despite a strong yearning to replay the video of Lorelei once more, I trudged on.

With his help, I continued recording residents' names and the corresponding times. This routine was becoming monotonous until late in the afternoon when Lorelei left the apartment again wearing the same clothes as before.

It started raining. An umbrella hid the face of a woman entering the building and Donald hadn't a clue who it might have been. The same problem repeated itself with a very well-dressed man a few minutes later.

Donald suddenly perked up for some reason. He had appeared on the screen coming from the parking lot wearing sweats and carrying a gym bag. A woman in a long raincoat and matching umbrella hurried to catch up to him. She sidled up to him at the door, and they appeared to flirt. When she folded her umbrella I noticed bright red hair and that she was wearing dark sunglasses on a gloomy day. She grasped his arm and whispered in his ear. He unlocked the door and held it for her. She pecked him on the cheek as she passed, generating a large, sick grin on his ugly face. He paused for a moment, transfixed.

After the door closed, I froze the video and turned to Donald. Beads of perspiration glistened on his forehead. "Who's the pretty redhead, a friend of yours?"

His nasty grin reappeared. "That's Destiny, one of my girlfriends. Pretty hot, huh? Yeah, I'm hitting that." He puffed out his chest in pride.

"That's great, but what's her last name?"

"Why? You want some of that too?" He laughed, and I gave him a dirty look. "Her name's Destiny Childs."

That was rich! I wondered if he was making it up as he went or was just too stupid to realize she had given him a fake name. Rarely am I good at detecting lies, but I knew for sure he wasn't telling me the truth. Restarting the video, residents appeared to be returning home for the day.

The rain had stopped by the time Lorelei returned carrying several full grocery bags with fresh produce visible in one.

For the next hour, residents returned home, and left again. Among them was Donald's red-headed girlfriend. She must have been late for an appointment because she zipped out the residents' door and nearly jogged toward the resident parking lot.

We zipped through another hour's worth of video with nothing of note, and moved on to the front-door camera. There were few visitors that day. Ray and Brandon visited that afternoon, as they had testified. Donald proved to be of no help in identifying any of the other visitors. Then, after the time of Lorelei's death, the activity at the front door picked up, starting with a parade of first responders rushing into the building—paramedics, Mallory, Deputy Lowell and the coroner. Tears filled my eyes when they carried out a black body bag containing my daughter. Thirty minutes later, Mallory departed with Amy to take her home. Over an hour later, Lowell was the last to leave. I guessed he had stayed behind to sanitize the crime scene and stage it to look like a suicide. Oddly enough the sheriff never appeared.

Tears again streamed down my cheeks. Although I had never met her, I felt strong love for my late daughter. Collecting myself, I shifted to the parking lot camera, which only covered about half the lot. Cars came and went in conjunction with the resident traffic at the back door.

Donald soon became restless. "Look, I've got clothes in the laundry downstairs and other things to do. You seem to have this thing mastered. Don't touch anything else while I'm gone."

After he left, I paused the video and searched the desk for digital storage medium and found a USB flash drive. After plugging it into a USB port on the computer, I deleted all the files on it to make room and began exporting video from the three cameras.

With the copying in progress, I turned my attention to searching Donald's messy apartment. Clothes were strewn throughout the master bedroom. Among his clothes were black leather pants, vests and caps. One desk drawer held a mass of Gothic earrings modeled after nails and screws as well as Gothic crosses with fake diamonds. My heart rate quickened with anticipation, but a quick search failed to find a safety pin earring like I found in Lorelei's apartment.

One pile of clothes on the floor differed from the others. It was composed of expensive name brand men's clothing. It seemed odd to find expensive outfits heaped on the floor while cheap clothes hung in his closet. The finer clothes didn't appear to fit Donald, size-wise or style-wise. Why would clothes, not fitting Donald, be piled on his floor? Under these clothes were several pairs of expensive Italian shoes, also too small and expensive for Donald. These were the clothes and shoes a wealthy man might wear. And then I recalled the empty section or Lorelei's closet. These were likely Reggie's clothes.

I found a gun safe hidden in the back of the closet, tall enough to hold long guns. After a few frivolous attempts to guess the combination, I gave up. Hell, I didn't know if the combination was composed of three numbers or four.

After completing the search, I returned to the security computer to find the copies had completed successfully. I started the video of the parking lot camera and quickly became bored. Residents came and went coinciding with the back door camera traffic. I sped up the frame rate until I recognized a car entering the lot—Reggie's Ferrari with the top up. I stopped and backed up to watch it again. I couldn't actually make out the driver's face, but it had to be him. There couldn't be two of such an exotic sports car model in Talmadge. The car entered the lot about twenty minutes before the time of death and parked in a portion of the lot not visible on camera.

I checked my notes on the back door traffic. The well-dressed man with the umbrella had to be Reggie. I sped up the frame rate until his car left the lot and noted it was about forty-five minutes later. This video blew Reggie's alibi all to hell. At last, I had found my murderer.

But then I realized I hadn't seen footage of Reggie leaving the building. How had I missed that? I returned to the back-door video to search for Reggie's departure.

The apartment door slammed shut, sending a chill down my spine. The flash drive lay in plain sight on the desktop. I snatched it and slid it between the pages of the legal pad I had been using.

Donald poked his head in the room. "Find anything?"

I tried to appear innocent. "Nothing of note."

"You about done? I need to leave."

"I'm not quite finished, maybe thirty more minutes."

"No, you're finished now. You've seen the videos. There's nothing there. Now get the hell out of here. I told you I've got to be somewhere."

I headed for the door.

"Hey, where are you going with my paper?"

"It's got my notes. Here." I set the pad down, took out a twenty and stuffed it in his shirt pocket. "Buy yourself a whole package of legal pads." I reclaimed the borrowed pad and strode to the door. The flash drive slipped out, but I caught it with my other hand in mid-air.

"Hey, wait."

My back toward Donald, I froze, certain he had spotted the flash drive.

"Don't go cheap on me. First time I helped you, you gave me a hundred dollars."

Over my shoulder, I said, "That's all I got. Twenty will have to do."

"Well, don't come back looking for any more favors, asshole." He slammed the apartment door behind me. My armpits and forehead dripped with perspiration. I took a deep breath to calm myself.

I had all the proof I needed to nail Reggie. He had shown up just before Lorelei was murdered. I hadn't seen what time he left, but I could find it later on my copy of the video. Everybody had been right. Reggie murdered my daughter.

CHAPTER 59

Reggie entering the apartment building around the time of Lorelei's murder played over and over in my head. A feeling nagged me. Had I missed something in the video—something very important? Distracted by my thoughts I paid no attention to my speed.

A short bleep of a siren broke my concentration. Piercing blue lights flashed in my rearview mirror causing my heart to skip a beat. I slowed and pulled over. The squad car parked behind me, lights flashing. My stomach sank when I saw Deputy Lowell approach. I tossed the flash drive in the glove box for safekeeping.

My sweaty palm made it difficult to roll my window down. Wearing a stoic expression the deputy said, "Well, well, well, it just keeps getting better. You should have left town when I told you to, Mr. Nole. Do you know how fast you were going?"

The situation demanded a quick decision how to play this—kiss-his-ass diplomacy or kiss-my-ass obstinance. Deputy Lowell deserved obstinance, but jail time would impede a confrontation with Reggie. "No, sir, I confess I wasn't watching my speed, but I'm sure I wasn't much over the limit."

He laughed. "I guess fifty-three in a thirty-five zone isn't much to someone from Augusta."

"I'm from Savannah, not Augusta." The words escaped before I could catch them.

The deputy's eyes glowed red as he yanked my door open and grabbed me by my shirt and tried to pull me out, but the seat belt constrained me. In a single motion, he produced a hunting knife and slashed the seatbelt. He grabbed me, pulled me out of the pickup and stood me beside the hood. For such a small man, he demonstrated surprising strength. "Okay, asshole, spread them." He slammed me down on the hood while his foot moved me into a spread-eagle stance.

My face stung from the impact with the truck's hood, and blood trickled from my nose. "Hey, what the fuck? Last time I checked speeding isn't a capital offense."

"If you know what's good for you, you'll shut the hell up." He frisked me and tossed the paltry contents from my pockets on to the hood—wallet, flip phone, hotel room key, change and my napkins with notes.

"Now, what the hell we got here?" He examined my scratchings on the napkins. Fortunately, my writing is indecipherable to anyone else. He wadded up the napkins and tossed them on the hood.

During a quick search of my wallet, he withdrew my room card key and tossed the billfold back on the hood with my other things. "How'd you get a hotel room, asshole? Reggie owns every hotel in town and has banned you. Extended Stay, huh? I'll just hang on to this to find out how you got a room." He stashed the card key in his shirt pocket. "Where are you hiding your drugs, asshole? I know you got some because you're a junkie. They in the truck, or maybe your hotel room?"

"Drugs? I don't know what you mean. Honest."

"Opioids. You're hooked on that shit, aren't you?"

If he was behind the burglary of my first hotel room, he knew I took OxyContin. Or maybe Mallory told him. I worried he might know about my clandestine drug purchase and subsequent Fentanyl overdose. He pretty well had his finger on the pulse of all that goes on in Greene County.

"I used to take OxyContin for back pain, but don't need it anymore."

"Sure, you don't." He chuckled and shook his head. "You stay put while I check the truck." He pushed me hard, targeting my back with an elbow thrust

A stabbing pain shot through my spine. "Hey, you can't do that without a search warrant."

"Don't need one. I got probable cause." He tossed a small plastic bag containing a hemp-like substance onto the truck hood with my pocket contents.

He jerked my hands behind my back and cuffed me. He led me to the backseat of his car and banged my head on the door jamb, likely on purpose. His vehicle reeked of stale cigarette smoke.

Circling stars clouded my vision while he searched Ray's pickup. I prayed he wouldn't find the flash drive in the glove box. Search completed, he scooped my things off the truck's hood and returned to his squad car, his face distorted in frustration after not finding any opioids. Somehow, he must have missed the video flash drive in the glove box or had pocketed it without saying anything.

He slid behind the wheel. "Registration says that's Ray Adam's truck. Did you steal it from him?"

"Ray loaned it to me after my rental car got shot up. You know about that, I'm sure. Been meaning to ask you guys if you have any suspects from that sniper attack yet?" The bullet-proof glass separating us gave me bravado. He turned and glared with fire in his eyes. Fear surged through me as he swore, opened his door and started to exit the car. Locked in his back seat I had no way to escape.

He grabbed my door handle but must have thought better of it because he stopped and got back in the driver's seat. "There you go being a smartass again. That smart mouth of yours is going to get you in serious trouble. Speaking of Ray, you heard from him lately? Word is, he left town after your encounter with Mountain at his garage, something about a gambling debt with TLC. You know how to get in touch with Ray?"

"No. Haven't spoken to him since Sunday. If you want to call him, his number is in my phone."

Lowell dropped my pocket change in his cup holder and tossed my wallet on the front passenger seat. He opened my phone, found Ray's number and called. After a minute of silence, He closed my flip phone. "His number's been disconnected. Got another number for him?" I didn't.

The deputy called dispatch and requested a tow truck to impound Ray's truck. "Guess you'll be spending the night at my place tonight. You've been busted for possession of a controlled substance, looks like more than two ounces. That's a felony. I told you several times to get the hell out of town. Maybe next time you'll listen."

"You know that's not my weed. You planted it. I saw you."

Lowell chuckled aloud. "If it's not yours, how do you know what it is? Who do you think the judge is going to believe—you or me? Oh, and did I tell you the judge and I play poker every Friday night?"

"If you're arresting me, you need to read me my rights."

"Thought you were a washed-up dentist, not a lawyer." He faked a laugh at his own humor. "Look, I told you before. Reggie and I run this county. You have no rights unless I give them to you. There, I read you your rights. Happy?"

Rock music blared from the car speakers and Lowell sang along, despite knowing only half the words and faking the rest. He sang about two octaves off-key in a falsetto that could have been mistaken for a girl. I fought my cuffs, hoping to free my hands enough to plug my ears.

After booking me, the deputy threw me into a spartan, empty cell furnished with a cot, toilet and sink. Although the building couldn't be five years old, the cell smelled like a urine-soaked locker room with a tacky floor.

I insisted on my requisite one phone call, but Lowell reminded me I had no rights in this county. Sitting on the cot with my head in my hands,

I wondered how to survive this mess. I spent the evening pacing and fretting. I tossed and turned most of the night because the rock-hard cot killed my back. I longed for two Oxys to blunt the agony but would have settled for a Fentanyl to permanently put me out of my misery.

CHAPTER 60

After finally falling asleep, glaring lights illuminated the jail. A deputy hummed Judy Garland's famous "Good Morning" song as he approached. "Morning. Got some breakfast for you." I hated this man. His nasal dialect sounded northeastern, certainly not Georgian—probably a damn Yankee. And, he was way too cheery for my sullen mood.

Through the bars, he handed me a grease-soaked wrapper and a Styrofoam cup of dark liquid. The wrapper held a cold, stale breakfast biscuit with bacon, egg and cheese that might have been a decent sandwich yesterday, or whatever day it had been prepared. The coffee was hot but tasted like dregs from yesterday, reheated. I didn't dare ask for cream and artificial sweetener. After choking down half of each, severe nausea set in. It could have been the food and/or opioid withdrawal. It didn't matter.

"Will I see the judge today? Can I call my lawyer?" I didn't have a lawyer or the money to hire one, but he wouldn't know that.

"Deputy Lowell said no phone calls. Nothing's happening until Monday since the judge is on vacation. I'll scare up some old magazines or something for you to read—can't promise much."

Under different circumstances, I would have chewed this guy up one side and down another. My back hurt from the terrible bed, my face hurt from being slammed on the truck hood and my head ached from hitting the squad car door frame. I craved Oxy to prop me up until I could confront Reggie. Anxiety had set in, so I just wanted to get it over with

284

and go home. I sweated profusely, a sign of the dreaded opioid withdrawal.

The deputy either forgot his promise or ignored my request for reading materials. With nothing to do and unable to fall asleep, I paced my cell, tears welling up in hopelessness. My resolution strengthened when I spotted a security camera. I couldn't give Lowell the satisfaction of seeing me break down.

It seemed like days but had only been hours when the deputy finally returned.

"Hey, where's my reading materials? Can I have some ibuprofen or aspirin for my back?"

"You made bail."

"What? Bail? Who posted my bail? I don't know anybody with money."

"Hey, look, I'm just doing what I'm told. You want out or not?"

In the lobby, Ronnie and her mother greeted me. "Oh, Tanner, are you all right?" Ronnie raced to me, putting her face so close to mine I thought she might kiss me. I wanted her to, but she didn't.

Her lined and pallid face begged for makeup, her mussed hair for a brush. She wore faded blue jeans and a loose-fitting black sweatshirt that did nothing to improve her look. I smiled at Maggie Mae who, by contrast, appeared dressed for church or a funeral in a dark blue satin dress, her hair up in a bun and enough makeup for both of them.

"Tanner, are you sure you're okay?" The lines on Ronnie's forehead deepened. "What happened to your face? Were you in another fight?"

"I haven't been in any fights. My face met up with a truck hood, compliments of your glorious sheriff's department. Did you bail me out? How'd you find out I was here? Where'd you get the money?"

Ronnie looked over both shoulders before she leaned in to whisper in my ear. "Mallory called me. She said you'd been arrested for drugs and speeding. Mom loaned me the money to bail you out. Tell me it's not true about the drugs."

The deputy sat at the duty desk in the lobby, shuffling paper. "Mr. Nole, I need you to sign your release forms."

Standing in front of the desk, I signed the papers presented to me. "What about my personal items?"

The deputy took back the forms and scanned the paperwork. "Let me check." He left the room for a brief moment. On his return, he tossed a manila envelope on the desk and shoved another clipboard with another release form at me. "Sign here verifying you received your personal items, one antique cell phone, and one worn brown leather billfold."

"What about the keys to my room and truck?"

"The pickup is being held for evidence until we determine whether or not you stole it. I show no record of a room key."

I slid the flip phone in my pocket and opened my wallet. My credit cards and ATM card were there. "Hold on. There was a couple hundred dollars in here when you booked me. Where's my damn money?"

The deputy browsed my paperwork. "Notation here says there was no money in the wallet when you were booked. Deputy Lowell thinks you used it to buy the marijuana he found on you." His sly grin told me he knew otherwise. He held out the form for me to sign.

My blood boiled, but I signed the form anyway. "I'm signing this under protest." I wrote something to that effect in the margin on the form.

The deputy chuckled, took back the paperwork and initialed it in the proper places. "You're free to go, Mr. Nole. Just be at the courthouse on Monday morning for your hearing. Ten o'clock sharp. You don't show, Deputy Lowell said he'll come looking for you, and you won't like it."

I grimaced and shook my head, sick of Southern small-town politics.

My rescuers escorted a haggard shell of myself to the car. Ronnie slipped behind the wheel, Maggie Mae took the shotgun and I sat in the back seat. "I want to thank you, ladies, for bailing me out. That place was driving me crazy. It may take a while, Maggie Mae, but I will pay you back every cent."

Ronnie slipped the key into the ignition but didn't start the car. She stared forward out the windshield. "Tanner, I can't believe you got busted for possession. First OxyContin, then Fentanyl and now marijuana. You have a serious drug problem. What other things are you into?"

My head drooped as I collected my thoughts. Then, meeting her eyes in the rearview mirror, I said, "Ronnie, like I told you before. I don't have a drug problem. I suffer from chronic back pain, so the doctor prescribes OxyContin for me. I only took Fentanyl because someone stole my OxyContin from my hotel, probably Deputy Lowell. For the last time, I don't smoke weed." At least I hadn't since I arrived in Talmadge. "That deputy has it in for me and planted grass to frame me. He wants me off the investigation, and now I understand why."

Both ladies turned in their seats to make eye contact with me.

"I have proof Reggie was at Lorelei's apartment when she was killed. I have it on video. Oh, shit! The flash drive is in Ray's pickup at the police impound. Luckily, Deputy Lowell didn't find it. Damn. How can I retrieve it?"

Ronnie said, "We've got to have that video. Maybe Mallory could get it for you, or do you still think she's a spy for her boss?"

I replayed my phone conversation with Mallory in my head. She admitted she had been spying, but swore she wasn't anymore. "I don't feel comfortable asking her when I'm uncertain I can trust her."

Maggie Mae turned to Ronnie. "Maybe you can ask her. You and Mallory seemed to hit it off the other night when Tanner OD'd. Maybe she'd do it for you."

Ronnie stiffened. "Whoa! Hold on a minute. I'm not comfortable with that. We're not friends, just acquaintances with a common problem— Tanner."

Groggy from lack of sleep and opioid withdrawal, her sarcasm went over my head. "But, you've got to. That flash drive holds the evidence to break this case wide open and nail Reggie, along with his buddy, Deputy Lowell, for covering it up. Don't you want to catch your daughter's murderer?"

Maggie Mae patted her daughter's hand. "Ronnie, he's right. You've got to do it. I didn't believe you at first when you said Lorelei had been murdered, but if Tanner has real evidence, we've got to retrieve it before Lowell finds it."

Ronnie agreed to call Mallory despite body language signaling reluctance. Late for work, she promised to call Mallory once she got settled in. She dropped us off at Maggie Mae's so I could borrow her car. Maggie Mae had lost her license a couple of years ago but couldn't bring herself to part with it.

She handed me Lincoln keys and led me into the garage. There sat a battleship-sized classic car. I'm not sure if it was brown or the heavy dusting made it look that color. Maggie Mae smiled with obvious pride. "This is a 1984 Lincoln Town Car. It was Edgar's pride and joy. I couldn't bring myself to part with it. It's only got 34,000 miles on it. Get in."

I slid behind the wheel and was surprised when Maggie Mae slipped into the passenger seat. "Wait a minute. What gives?"

"I'm going with you. Maybe I can help because the Lord knows you need it. If Lorelei was murdered, I want to help catch her killer. Crank this baby up and let's roll, time's a-wasting."

The heavy dust inside the car made me sneeze three times in quick succession.

"Hope you didn't catch something in that jail. Now fire this beauty up. It's crying to be driven."

The engine turned over but didn't fire. After several failed attempts, I got out to look under the hood. It seemed the right thing to do despite knowing nothing about cars. Maggie Mae slid over into the driver's seat and cranked it again while I watched under the hood. It turned over slower than before as the battery gave up the ghost. I was ready to admit defeat when the engine sprang to life. She slid over to the passenger side, and I assumed the driver's seat.

"It's a little temperamental when it's been sitting." Maggie Mae spoke with pride. "You got to pump the gas pedal to get it started. It has a carburetor, you know."

With that, we headed to the headquarters of Braun Enterprises to confront my daughter's murderer.

Chapter 61

"You're not very talkative." Maggie Mae broke my concentration.

"Sorry. I'm trying to devise a way to sneak by Reggie's office security. They'll be watching for me after my last intrusion."

"You need a disguise. Taylor's Western Wear is ahead on the right. They'll fix you up in no time."

"I'm broke. Deputy Lowell stole my cash, and my credit cards are maxed out."

"Pull over. I'll spring for it. Shouldn't cost much to change your look, and Lord knows your wardrobe could use some help."

From Taylor's clearance section, we selected a dark brown cowboy hat, tan faux leather jacket and dark sunglasses. On the way to the register, I paused to ogle a gorgeous pair of cowboy boots. I've never worn cowboy boots or even thought about buying them, but these were boots to admire, like fine art.

A young Hispanic clerk stepped forward. "Try them on. They're made by Lucchese." He stroked them as one would a prized horse. "Finest boot made. Got a pair myself." After cozying up to me and looking around, he spoke under his breath as if someone might be listening. "I can give you a good deal on these. They're marked $1,290, but for you, $799, today only. Try them on, and you'll never wear any of your other boots again."

"Let's go, Tanner." Maggie Mae called from the checkout lane. "I ain't made of money and time's a-wasting. Nobody will look at your feet if you're dazzling them with your bullshit."

I smiled at the clerk, shrugged my shoulders and retreated to the register.

At Braun Enterprises, we parked in a handicap spot near the door. The car had a handicap plate, but the tag had expired two years ago. After donning the hat, jacket and sunglasses, I admired myself in the rearview mirror. Satisfied, I turned to Maggie Mae, seeking approval.

"You look good." She handed me a red bandanna. "Here put this on. It'll draw attention from your face."

"I didn't see you buy this." She smiled from ear to ear. "Wait. Don't tell me you stole this?" She shrugged and winked. "Maggie Mae, you're going to hell."

Surprisingly, Ayesha still manned the receptionist's desk. It was a miracle they hadn't fired her after my last visit, so I was sure she'd remember me. It was a good thing I had changed my look.

We initiated our plan. As I bypassed Ayesha's desk, she was answering Maggie Mae's call from my cell phone.

"What? Ma'am, I can't hear you? Can you repeat what you said? Excuse me, ma'am. I need to put you on hold for just a sec." Click. She spotted a cowboy approaching the elevators. "Sir, stop. Do you have an appointment? You need to sign in." Her phone rang again. Per my instructions, Maggie Mae had hung up and redialed. Next, Maggie Mae entered the door and approached the reception desk to add to the commotion.

Ayesha paused to consider her first move—take the incoming phone call, challenge me, or greet Maggie Mae at her desk. By the time I became her highest priority, an elevator door opened, and I dove into an empty car. Repeatedly pressing the button for the fourth floor, uneasiness erupted in my stomach, more representative of a swarm of angry yellow jackets than butterflies. The door glided shut before Ayesha could stop me.

Unlike my last visit, the executive floor teemed with activity. It reminded me of the fervency of a Wall Street trading desk like in the movies. No one paid attention to a solitary cowboy ambling down a busy hall.

Nancy would also remember me from before, so the plan was to look away as I snuck by her desk. That plan failed when I couldn't help but check her out in her tight white sweater with plunging neckline. Instead, I tipped my hat and gave her a flirting smile as I shot past, unable to look away.

"Sir, you can't go in there. Wait." She chased after me on my way into Reggie's office.

Still distracted by Nancy's cleavage, I collided with Reggie in his doorway, talking on his cell phone as he was stepping out. My cowboy hat tumbled to the floor, and my sunglasses went askew, unmasking me.

Reggie's eyes popped open with recognition and his face turned beet red. He stopped and spoke into his cell phone. "Marvin, something's come up. Call you back in a few minutes." He hung up and slipped the phone into his pants pocket. "What the fuck are you doing here? Nancy, call Security and then the sheriff. How the hell did you get out of jail?"

That he knew of my arrest stunned me, but then Deputy Lowell kept his head half up Reggie's ass most of the time. I slid my hand inside my coat. Reggie's eyes nearly popped out of his paling face. He extended both hands in front of him as if he might push me away. "You don't want to do this. Nancy, call 911. He's got a gun."

Nancy screamed.

I was shocked by Reggie's reaction to my innocent act until I realized he thought I was going for a gun. I changed my tactic to take advantage.

"You're right. I don't want to hurt you—at least not yet. First, why did you lie to me? You were there when Lorelei was murdered. You either killed her or know who did."

"What the hell are you talking about? I went away with Nancy that night."

She glared at him as if to say, "Shut up! That's our little secret."

My head shook in disbelief. "No, I saw you."

"What do you mean, you saw me? Were you there?"

The frumpy female security guard, who had evicted me last time, appeared at Nancy's desk.

Through tears, Nancy shrieked, "Do something! He's going to shoot Reggie!"

Brushing a dazed Nancy aside, the guard drew her handgun, aimed and shouted in her best police voice. "Freeze. Remove your hand from your jacket slowly, and then drop your weapon, or I'll shoot."

My bluff called, I carefully withdrew my hand, clutching my ink pen. "Don't shoot. I'm not armed. I was just taking my pen out to make notes, and Reggie overreacted."

The guard didn't seem to care. "Drop the pen. Now, put your hands up in the air and stay very still." Remembering how her gun hand shook the last time, I complied without argument.

Reggie doubled over, clutched his chest and gasped for air. His hysterical admin/lover raced to his side in panic and attended to him.

The security guard frisked me. "He's not armed. He was just bluffing." One hand pressed her gun into my back while the other grasped my arm to steer me.

Reggie regained composure and raised a hand in a stop signal. "Wait. I want some answers before you escort him out. Can you two give us a minute—alone?"

Nancy shook her head and dabbed at her mascara-streaked eyes. "Reggie, what are you doing? He's dangerous. Wait till the sheriff gets here. Please."

Reggie ushered Nancy and the guard out of his office and closed the door. The two ladies watched through the glass like tourists gawking at zoo animals. The guard's gun hand dropped to her side. Nancy clutched herself with crossed arms and rocked side to side.

His back to the ladies, he spoke in a soft tone. "You said something about seeing me at Lorelei's when she died. What did you mean?"

"I've got the security video from Lorelei's apartment building. You showed up a few minutes before her death and went in. You were there when she was killed. What happened? You have a fight and kill her in anger?"

"But that's not possible. I wasn't there. I told you I was in Atlanta. Nancy can vouch for me."

"Just like your wife lied for you about being at home with her that night? Does Tanya know you are a murderer? Is that why she covered for you?"

"Who knows why Tanya does anything. I'm telling you, you're mistaken. I never went to Lorelei's apartment the day she died. I was in Atlanta like I said. Can I see this security video you're talking about?"

I realized my mistake. I should have waited until I had the copy in my hands before confronting Reggie. I was in so deep at this point I had to keep the pressure on him with what I had. Maybe he would confess. "I saw the video yesterday on the apartment security system. Your apartment manager, Donald Wirth, is a witness." Donald hadn't really seen that part of the video, but I tried to make my case more convincing than it sounded.

Despite Nancy's best efforts to stop her, Mallory burst into Reggie's office, her weapon drawn. The security guard followed her in.

"What's going on here?" Mallory appeared dazed and unsure how to handle the situation.

Reggie waved her off. "Ladies, put your guns away. This guy's harmless. He's a major pain in the ass, but harmless."

She appeared confused until Reggie gave her an emphatic nod. The security guard followed suit and holstered her weapon also. Realizing I might live through this, I let out a sigh.

Reggie paused and shook his head. "I'm sorry. What's your name again? With all the excitement, I've forgotten."

"Tanner, Tanner Nole."

"That's right." He pivoted to Mallory. "Tanner here claims he saw security video of me at Lorelei's apartment about the time she died. Did anyone at the sheriff's office review those security tapes?"

Mallory cleared her throat. "No. Deputy Lowell told us not to bother since the evidence pointed to suicide, clear and simple."

Reggie motioned to his dazed admin. "Nancy, call and ask if we still have the security videos from my apartment building on Maple Street the night of Lorelei's suicide."

Nancy stood immobile, eyes wide and mouth agape. When Reggie motioned for her to leave, it broke the spell, and she went to call.

He turned his attention back to me. "Now, why again are you so obsessed with the idea that Lorelei was murdered? Deputy Lowell investigated it and swears the evidence supported suicide."

"It's quite simple. Suicide victims, especially women, rarely use a gun. As you probably know, Lorelei hated guns. I found a prescription bottle in her nightstand full of phenobarbital, a 'sleeping pill' rarely prescribed anymore, because of its popularity in suicides. Yet she didn't choose that route."

Reggie interrupted me. "Oh, yeah. I remember now. Lorelei had trouble sleeping, something about some creep stalking her. I doubt she ever used it. She was very health conscious, so abhorred medications of any kind."

If felt good to know my daughter had taken care of herself. "Second, if someone shoots themselves in the side of the head, they normally use their dominant hand. Lorelei's wound was on the right side."

"And Lorelei was left-handed," Reggie said

"Third, a neighbor overheard arguing just before the gunshot, so Lorelei was not alone. There was hostility in the one voice. Based on the security video, that was you." I pointed at Reggie and wondered if his angry voice could be mistaken as a female voice by an elderly woman with poor hearing.

Mallory's eyes popped and her mouth dropped.

"That's preposterous. I keep telling you it wasn't me." Reggie's blazing eyes and flaring nostrils were akin to an angry bull preparing to charge.

"Finally, there's this." I held the safety pin earring up for all to see. "This earring was found in Lorelei's bedroom near where she died. I couldn't locate a matching earring, so the killer may have dropped it."

Reggie sneered at me. "As you can see, I don't wear earrings, and that's not anything Lorelei would have worn. She had good taste. I should know—I paid for it." Reggie spoke with apparent pride.

Nancy entered the office. "I spoke to the apartment supervisor. He said they only keep security videos for a week, and then they are automatically erased."

Reggie turned to me. "When did you supposedly see this security tape of me entering the apartment building?"

I could feel all eyes bearing on me. "Uh, yesterday. The supervisor's lying. Yesterday he told me they keep them for thirty days. I'm telling you I saw it at his apartment yesterday." Confusion ran amok in my head.

"How is it possible you saw me when the recording was erased three weeks ago?"

The room spun, and my knees nearly buckled. I looked to Mallory for help, but she shook her head as if telling me I was on my own here.

I had a copy of the video, but couldn't say anything about it because it was in the glove box of Ray's pickup at police impound. If I divulged that, Reggie would tell Lowell to find it and destroy it. I searched for a reasonable lie.

"Okay, that's enough." Reggie's face tensed and his eyes shrunk to pinholes. "Deputy, take this mental case away."

Mallory looked at Reggie. "Do you want to press charges?"

"Can't you just book him on something without me having to get involved? Work it out with Deputy Lowell." Reggie flicked his hand like he was shooing a fly away.

Mallory handed me my hat and then clutched my upper arm to lead me away. Blaring alarms and piercing flashing lights erupted, sending chills down my spine from sensory overload.

Reggie shook his head. "What more can go wrong today? Nancy, check on that fire alarm. This is *not* a good time to be evacuating."

Everyone waited anxiously for Nancy to find out what was happening. Racing for the stairs, employees filled the halls, forming a visual and audial wave of humanity.

A pale Nancy returned, shaking. "There's a fire in a storeroom on the first floor near the back of the building."

Reggie sighed. "All right, let's play it safe and evacuate."

Mallory and the security guard escorted me to the hallway, where we merged into the throng of anxious employees streaming to safety. The guard fell behind in the swirl of humanity. Glaring sunshine blinded us when Mallory and I exited the stairwell door.

She caught my attention. "Tanner, make a break for it. If I take you in, who can guess what Deputy Lowell would do to you?"

"Yeah, but what'll happen if you show up empty-handed? Lowell will be expecting you to bring me in."

As if on cue, the brown Lincoln screeched to a halt in front of us. A grinning Maggie Mae poked her head out her open window. "Quick, Tanner, jump in. We'll make a run for it."

With a sweep of her hand, Mallory motioned for me to escape. "Go on. Do like the lady says. Scram."

"Has Ronnie called you about the copy of the video in Ray's pickup?"

"Yeah, but I haven't had a chance to look for it yet. I'll go by impound on my way back to the office. Who knows, I may not be working there for long after this." She forced a smile.

"Thanks, Mallory. I owe you big time." I raced around the car and jumped in. Maggie Mae burnt rubber as we pulled away. I swear I heard her giggle under her breathe like a kid at an amusement park.

We met three speeding fire trucks followed by a sheriff's car, in a menagerie of flashing lights and wailing sirens. Fortunately, the deputy didn't recognize me in my cowboy outfit, riding in a classic Lincoln with an expired tag.

At a safe distance from the scene, I begged Maggie Mae to pull over and let me take the wheel.

"What? I'm not a good driver? I saved your sweet little ass, didn't I?"

"Yeah, you sure did. Did you start that fire back there, too?"

Pride burst across her beaming face. "Yeah, that was little ole me. When Mallory showed up and ran in the building, I knew the jig was up. I bummed a cigarette from a smoker at the back door and waited for someone to exit so I could sneak in before the door closed. I started a little paper fire in a bucket in a storeroom that was more smoke than fire. Clever, don't you think?"

I grinned at her with a new-found appreciation, and she smiled back with a youngish gleam in her eyes.

"This here's Miss Bonnie Parker," I said, hamming it up. "And I'm Clyde Barrow. We rob banks."

We laughed so hard my sides hurt.

Being on the lam, we stayed off the main road and drove back streets to my motel. My hands shook, and nausea returned. I needed an Oxy from my stash back in my room. I prayed Deputy Lowell hadn't cleaned me out again now that he knew about my motel room.

CHAPTER 62

A slender girl with chopped-off brown hair manned the hotel desk. She looked young—barely college age. Large, owl-like brown glasses completed her bookworm look. Clashing with her orange smock, Monica's green name tag identified her as Assistant Manager. I chuckled to myself at the generous title.

She looked at me with an exaggerated smile. "May I help you?"

"Yes, I'm so sorry. It's embarrassing, but I seem to have misplaced my room key. I'm in Room 115, Sprat. Wendell Sprat."

She checked her terminal. Her dull brown eyes grew to fill her oversized frames. "Mr. Sprat. According to our system, you checked out earlier today."

My heart sunk. "That's odd because I paid through the weekend and have been gone all day. I know I didn't check out before I left, so there must be a mistake. Please check again."

She bit her lower lip and worked the keyboard with aggression. "There's a note on your account saying you were checked out by management."

"What do you mean checked out by management? Do you mean evicted? I told you I paid through the weekend, in cash I might add. So why would someone at this hotel evict me? I don't understand."

"I'm so sorry, sir." Her face blushed. "It appears you did pay through the weekend, but there are no notes saying why management checked you out. This wasn't in my training."

"Where's my stuff? Did you put it out on the street, or give it to Goodwill? I want my damn stuff, now!"

Her shoulders tensed, her face tightened and her lower lip quivered. Fingers that had glided over the keys earlier now became clumsy. "It says your personal property is in the luggage room. Give me a minute to check on that for you."

"What about a refund? I paid through the weekend. I want my damn money back. You have no excuse for throwing me out on the street."

Monica tried calling someone on the phone, but no one answered. Shaking, and with tears in her eyes, she concentrated on the terminal and struck the keys hard. She stood erect and tried to smile as she spoke in her best customer service voice. "You are correct. You are due a refund of $226.92. If you show me your ID, I can give you cash."

If I showed her my ID, she'd see right away I was not Wendell Sprat, who had checked in to the room. I ratcheted my voice down and spoke in an emphatic, but restrained, tone with a hint of sarcasm. "Well, you see, here's the problem. I must've left my wallet in my room. That's why I don't have my room key or my driver's license. Now, if you will please bring me my luggage, I can show you my ID, that is if someone here at the hotel hasn't ripped me off."

Despite watery eyes and a sniffle, she agreed to take me back to the storeroom. I had her right where I wanted her. We each carried a bag to the front desk area. Laying one on the counter-top, I opened it and searched it.

When the phone rang, Monica jumped as if the Grim Reaper had tapped her on the shoulder. She excused herself and took the call, likely happy to get away from me.

Per our plan, Maggie Mae was calling to create a diversion. I closed my suitcase, set it on the floor and lifted the other one up on the counter. The clerk spoke into the phone. "I'll check the luggage room for it, ma'am. Can I put you on hold while I check? Won't take but a minute." She placed the call on hold. "Sir, will you be okay while I check on a bag for this lady?"

I nodded assent.

When the clerk stepped out of sight, I swept around the counter and pressed the cash drawer release. Grabbing a stack of twenties, I crammed them in my pocket. Running back around the counter, I slammed my suitcase shut and yanked it off the counter. It hadn't latched, so its contents spewed everywhere. I madly crammed clothes back into the bag. Clothes hanging out prevented it from latching, so I tucked it under one arm to hold it closed and grabbed the second bag with my other hand. The bags banged both sides of the opening automatic door as I sprinted for the parking lot.

Maggie Mae screeched to a halt in front of me and hit the remote release for the trunk in what was becoming a familiar scene. I tossed my bags and loose contents inside, but in my haste, the trunk didn't latch. As she screeched out, Maggie Mae nearly struck the confused clerk who gave chase on foot. Speeding down the street, the trunk lid bobbed up and down as clothes took flight.

We both laughed hysterically. I caught my breath enough to speak. "I'm Clyde Barrow. This is Bonnie Parker. We rob banks . . . and cheap motels."

We laughed harder than before. Clothes continued to blow out the open trunk until a pothole created enough of a bump to latch the trunk lid.

CHAPTER 63

We stopped for a late lunch at IHOP. Maggie Mae went in to get us a table while I searched my luggage for the little bag of Oxy I'd hidden under the lining. I located a loose spot in the lining, but the bag of Oxy was not there. Despair swept through me at the thought that someone had taken my Oxy again. I dreaded the prospect of buying more. Thanks to my larceny, I now had the necessary cash. Unfortunately, that cash made me a marked man, rapidly running out of time.

My hands shook, sweat slithered down my back and bile erupted in my throat. I became a child on the verge of bawling. Two furious searches through my clothes, strewn about the trunk, dashed all hope the pills might have fallen out into the trunk. My body screamed for Oxy, overwhelming me with despondency out of fear the small bag of pills had blown out of the trunk with my clothes. I scoured my cerebrum for any possible alternative explanation. In desperation, I checked the first suitcase a second time.

Maniacal laughter sprang from my entrails when my fingers contacted the little plastic bag with the magic pills tucked under the liner in a different corner than I expected. A gawking elderly couple hustled into the restaurant in an apparent attempt to stay clear of the crazy man foraging in the trunk.

I sat across from Maggie Mae, who studied her menu as if she would be tested on it later. The hostess tried to seat the elderly couple from outside at the booth next to us, but they insisted on sitting far away. They winced when I showed them my best maniacal smile.

A long sip of iced tea washed down a badly needed Oxy. Despite a strong urge for two, I limited myself to one to maintain clarity and to preserve my dwindling supply of the precious drug. As long as I had control, I wasn't an addict.

After ordering, I counted my self-service refund. "Oh, shit! There's four hundred dollars here. I only meant to take two-hundred twenty to cover the refund they owed me."

"You think the sheriff's gonna care whether you took one dollar or five thousand? You shouldn't have done it. You crossed a line and made me an accessory. You're digging yourself a deeper hole. It's only a matter of time until the sheriff or, worse yet, Deputy Lowell finds you."

I moved the cash to my billfold to give it some semblance of legitimacy. "Yeah, you're right. I shouldn't have taken the money. Didn't plan to, just got riled up for the clerk's sake as part of my act and then got carried away."

After a long sip of her sweet tea, Maggie Mae sat back with a somber face. "After lunch, let's go by your motel and return the extra $180." She stared at me without expression. Stunned, I searched for a response.

She erupted into laughter. "Just kidding. You should've seen your face go white. Since you got that extra cash, lunch is on you."

By the time I settled the check, the Oxy had kicked in. Nausea subsided, and my back pain moderated.

As we left the restaurant, I spotted a police cruiser and froze. Maggie Mae must not have noticed it because she kept walking and talking. The car crept by, did a U-turn and zipped into the parking lot. I called out to warn Maggie Mae, but she kept walking and talking as if I was right behind her. When she spotted the cruiser, she froze, stranded in the open.

The squad car parked behind the Lincoln. I held my breath, and my heart rate spiked. When Mallory's lovely head appeared over the car roof, I nearly collapsed in relief.

The three of us huddled between the two cars, where Mallory handed me my flash drive. "Didn't think I'd ever find it. I was ready to give up when I felt the edge lying in a crack in the very back of the glove compartment. That's why Lowell didn't find it when he searched Ray's truck."

"Have you seen the sheriff yet?" Maggie Mae asked with a frown.

Mallory let out a soft chuckle and looked away. "No, not yet, but I'm sure Lowell filled him in. Lowell and the sheriff kept calling over the radio, so I turned the volume down. Then they blew up my cell phone, so I turned it off to avoid him. I'm on my way to see the sheriff and take my lumps. Wish me luck."

We did, and I thanked her. She didn't seem to be listening, as her mind likely shifted to her imminent inquisition from her boss.

"You two better get going. Did you really rob a hotel?"

I shook my head. "Not exactly. They owed me a refund, so I took it upon myself to make it happen."

"Be careful. Lowell put out a local APB on you and this car. The sheriff wanted to escalate it to the state patrol, but Lowell stopped him to keep a lid on it for now. Turn off your cell phone, so they can't track you either and buy a burner phone. Oh, and ditch the car. Everybody's searching for it. This classic land yacht stands out like a sore thumb."

As we waved goodbye, I asked Maggie Mae, "You have a cell phone?"

"Heaven sakes, no. Why would I need one of those? All I'd get would be sales calls, and the buttons are so tiny. Some phones don't even have buttons anymore."

I turned my phone off and removed the battery, just to be safe. On the way to stash the car, I purchased a pre-paid phone at a dollar store and activated it.

We drove to Enterprise Rental Car seeking alternate transportation. Maggie Mae lusted for a red Mustang convertible on display out front. With effort, I convinced her it would not be the best car for maintaining a low profile or for her hairdo.

All my credit cards were maxed out, and Enterprise wouldn't take cash. Since Maggie Mae paid for it, she insisted we rent a full-sized car. They gave us a bland, white Camry.

When Maggie Mae laid eyes on it, she labeled it a death trap on wheels. She couldn't believe the rental car company classified this as full-sized. She insisted on exchanging it for a specialty car, but I convinced her we didn't have time. Still, the transaction took over an hour. Nothing in Georgia moves fast.

Maggie Mae drove her Lincoln, and I drove the Camry. We stashed her classic car in the hospital parking deck because she insisted her baby be covered. Besides, we figured no one would take notice of a car sitting several days in patient parking.

On the drive to Jack's office, she ranted about the piece of dog crap the Japs made. In her words, "They just don't build cars like the Town Car anymore."

I agreed.

CHAPTER 64

Jack's office was located on the seedy side of town where potholes, peeling paint and rusting metal burglar bars proliferated. Jack's light green Cadillac sat alone in the parking lot behind his building. Nobody hangs around such neighborhoods after five o'clock.

Half the office spaces on the first level were boarded up. A sign at one door advertised a half-dozen businesses, including "Sprat Investigations." The exterior door opened to a small, musty landing illuminated by a single bare light bulb. A straight, narrow unlit stairway rose before us. With each squeaking step the light from below grew dimmer. Clutching the loose, wooden handrail, Maggie Mae struggled up the stairs looking as if she might collapse any second. She couldn't understand why Jack's office had to be on the second floor. Didn't he have any older clients?

The fire door at the top had been blocked open, allowing light from a hallway to illuminate the top steps. The stairway opened to a dank hallway unfolding on our right for the length of the building. Halfway down the hall, we passed a unisex bathroom. Our guard up, we jumped at the sudden muffled sound of a toilet flushing in an otherwise silent, lonely hallway. Jack's office was the last one on the left. A knock on his door elicited no response other than an echo in the empty hallway. A second knock fared no better, so I tried the door. To my surprise, it opened.

"Hell-o-o-o. Ja-a-ck." Silence.

We entered a brightly lit, but deserted secretarial office. A second callout went unanswered. Maggie Mae clung to my arm like a frightened child. Moving as one, we passed through the neat, vacant small office to the larger, cluttered office behind it. A gray metal desk, piled with books, files and newspapers, dominated the small office. A wall of black and white photos gave it a nostalgic look. A dozen pictures hung on one wall, appeared to be client photos. Some appeared happy and others not so happy. A grouping of colored pictures on another wall showed Jack smiling at the racetrack with winning tickets in hand. Jack was a gambler. It showed in his eyes.

A noise in the outer office alerted us Jack had slipped in and now sat at the secretary desk, typing away with his back to us, oblivious that we were there. The dusty office made my sidekick sneeze. Jack whirled around, pointing a revolver at her.

I froze, but Maggie Mae stood her ground. "What in tarnation do you mean by pointing that thing at us? It might go off and shoot one of us. Who knows? You might could shoot yourself. Now, put that thing away before somebody gets hurt."

Jack blushed and laid his gun on the desk. "Sorry. You scared the shit out of me. Don't go sneaking up on me like that. As you may have noticed, this ain't the best neighborhood, so I work with my gun in my lap." He looked at Maggie Mae. "Who are you and what are you doing here?"

"On your lap, huh? Better be careful you don't shoot your dick off." I waited for a smile but got none from either of them. "Sorry, Jack. We knocked, but you didn't answer. It wasn't locked, so we came in. This is Veronica's mother, Maggie Mae. She's helping me with the investigation."

"Lord knows you could use help. Take your coats off and hang them over there." His black trench coat hung on one of three coat hooks adorning the wall near the door. "You got the video you want to view?"

Jack snatched the flash drive from my hand. "It's sticky what'd you do, spill something on it?"

"It must have picked up something in the glove box."

Jack inserted the drive into one of the computer's USB ports. A few clicks later, the computer came to life. The screen displayed a long list of files. He scratched his head. "I view video files on here all the time." He pointed to a list of filenames on the screen. "When you exported this from the security system, it copied a lot of other files. They do that, so you can restore everything, should the system's hard drive crash. We're looking for files ending in '.AVI'." He double-clicked a file.

An error message popped up. "Cannot read file. Incorrect file type or data may be corrupted."

I slammed the desk. "Shit!"

"Hold on. Let me try a few things." Each effort yielded the same result. "We're not beaten yet. Let me try to open it with a video player program I have." After fifteen minutes of futile efforts, he gave up. "Sorry, buddy. I can't get these videos to run. You need an IT guy or someone who works with video."

He called his IT guy but got a voice message saying he was at a Vegas conference and wouldn't return until Monday. Jack handed the flash drive back to me. "Sorry, Tanner. To view this video, you may need to take it back to the system at the apartment building or find a good video guy."

"I'm sure the university has computer techs who could crack this. I just need to find one of them. Wait! Amy! She said she's a computer major. Maybe she'll know what to do."

I called her on my new burner phone, but she didn't answer. I put the battery back in my regular cell phone and tried again.

"Hey, Mister Tanner. Did you, like, just try to call me on some other number? I don't answer unless I recognize the number."

"Please just call me Tanner. Mr. Tanner makes me feel old. No, it wasn't me, must have been a telemarketer. They call me all the time. Say, I need help viewing video files from a security system. You know anything about that?"

"For sure. You, like, remember I'm an Information Systems major, right? How about we meet at the computer lab tomorrow, and I'll take a crack at them."

"I'm kind of pressed for time. What if we came by your apartment in twenty minutes? Could we view them there?"

Her long pause indicated she didn't want me coming by or else was not interested in helping me. "You said we. Who's with you?"

"Me and Lorelei's grandmother." It sounded weird when I said it.

"What? Why do you, like, have Lorelei's grandmother with you? That's kind of strange, isn't it?"

"It's a long story. I needed her car, so she's tagging along." Maggie Mae glared at me.

"I'm, like in the middle of cramming for a midterm. I should be done about ten. How about you come by then?"

That was two hours from now—too long. The sheriff and his deputies were hunting me. The last of the sand was passing through the hourglass. Time to bring this investigation to a quick close while I still could. "Look, Amy, I'm running out of time. Could you please do this right now? Do it for Lorelei."

Her voice dripped with reluctance, but she agreed.

We arrived at Amy's apartment fifteen minutes later. I handed her the flash drive.

"Whoa. What's on this thumb drive?" Amy wiped it with a tissue while her laptop booted. I took up position behind her.

Maggie Mae hung back, showing no interest in computers. "Lovely apartment, Amy. Mind if I nose around a bit?"

Amy focused on her computer. "No, go ahead. It's a bit of a mess due to midterms."

She inserted the flash drive and worked the keyboard like an accomplished maestro. "Where'd you say this drive came from?"

I hadn't said. "It's a copy from the security system at Lorelei's apartment."

Amy's head jerked around, her mouth gaping. She studied me with wide eyes. "How did you get these?" Her staccato delivery, laced with an accusatory tone, caught my attention and reminded me it had been Amy's gun that killed my daughter.

"Donald, the apartment super let me make a copy for my investigation."

Her brows drew closer, and her face tightened. "Give me a minute." Her movements became slower and more erratic, exhibiting less confidence now. "The system, like, uses AVI format for the videos. That's a Microsoft format commonly used for security systems, and all." Efforts to open the file failed, generating error messages similar to those Jack encountered. "The data files are encrypted by the system. You use a codec to unlock them, much like a key. Codecs are proprietary, so I can't open these files. Sorry."

My head drooped in disappointment. "Thanks for trying." I retrieved the drive from her. "Come on, Maggie Mae. We're done here."

She popped out of the bedroom, holding something up. "Look what I found." Maggie Mae held out diamond safety pin earring.

Amy's face burst into rage. "Hey, what are you doing going through my things, old lady?"

Maggie Mae flinched at the insult. "I found it in your open jewelry box. It was laying there on top."

"No, it wasn't. I never leave my jewelry box open. You were going through my things. What the hell is the meaning of this?" She turned on me. "Is this really a copy of video from the security system, or was that an excuse to gain access to my apartment, so your partner could snoop around?"

I pulled the earring from my shirt pocket and compared it to the one in Maggie Mae's hand. It matched. "I found this one in Lorelei's apartment. How do you explain this?"

"I must have lost it when I visited her. Okay? I've been looking all over for it. Where'd you find it?"

"In Lorelei's dining room, where you murdered her."

"Are you insane? I didn't kill Lorelei. She was dead when I arrived. Finding her freaked me. I might have dropped it then, or some other time I was visiting. I've been looking all over for that earring. Let me have them."

She reached for the earrings, so I pulled them back. "Sorry. I've got to keep these for evidence."

After a short, heated argument over the earrings, Maggie Mae and I left with them as an angry Amy threatened to call the sheriff. Not the first time I've heard those words on this trip.

Dejection overwhelmed me, and I longed for an Oxy. I had just lost my major piece of evidence—the security video. Now, another piece of evidence fell into question.

We knew Amy had been at Lorelei's that night. The video recording showed her entering the building, she was the one who found the body, and she called 911. Although it was possible she dropped the earring that night, it could also have happened during an earlier visit. Did she murder my daughter? I couldn't be sure.

As we drove away in silence, Maggie Mae looked upset. No destination in mind, I drove aimlessly.

Maggie Mae broke the silence. "Now what?"

"Oh, shit!" I cried out.

In the rearview mirror, I could see a police cruiser with lights and siren closing on us fast. My pulse rate jumped. Bile collected in the back of my throat. I considered making a run for it.

CHAPTER 65

My heart beat nearly out of my chest at the sight of the flashing lights and the eerie sound of the police siren. Without conscious thought, my foot pressed hard on the accelerator. As the sluggish Camry accelerated, the officer laid on his horn. I let off the gas and pulled over to concede to the inevitable. Time had run out. I'd been busted.

The sheriff's car passed by and continued on, paying no attention to a bland-looking Camry.

"Oh, my!" Maggie Mae laid a hand on her chest and gasped for air.

My hands shook on the steering wheel, and a sudden chill shot through my being. Three cleansing breaths did little to ease the symptoms.

Maggie Mae leaned toward me with worried eyes. "You okay?" Receiving no response, she continued, "I could use a drink. How about you?"

Despite a powerful craving for another Oxy, I didn't want to hear about my supposed opioid addiction from her. Alcohol would have to do for now.

We went to the Barking Owl Pub, where Amy had taken me that first night. The normally popular college hangout was deserted. I headed for a table but realized Maggie Mae had peeled off and taken a seat at the bar. Bar stools provide little to no support for a bad back, but I joined her without complaint. Sitting with a lean to the left relieved some of the stress on my lower back.

Jake, Amy's bartending friend, greeted us. "What can I get you?"

Suddenly, I was starved. "What've you got to eat?"

He looked at his Smartwatch and scowled. "Kitchen closed ten minutes ago, but let me check." He walked over and poked his head in the serving window. "Are you still cooking?" He got his answer and returned. "I got good news and bad news. The fryer's still hot, but the grill is off. You can order anything on the menu, as long as it's fried." Jake leaned over the bar and spoke softly. "It's safer to eat from the fryer here, if you know what I mean."

Fried shrimp sounded good, but then common sense dictated you don't get good seafood in a college bar in the middle of Georgia. "How about chicken fingers and fries? And a pint of Sweetwater 420, please."

Maggie Mae passed on food. She groused that someone her age can't eat fried food after six. Instead, she ordered a Cosmopolitan, because she'd heard Oprah drinks them.

"You got it." He delivered my food order to the window and returned with my pint in a frosty glass. "You look familiar."

Two large, quick swallows of the ale soothed my dry throat. "I came in here with your friend, Amy, last week."

"Oh yeah. Now I remember." His smirk confirmed he still suspected I might be a dirty old man despite the cougar sitting next to me. "How do you know Amy? You a *good* friend, relative or something?" He peered at Maggie Mae to catch her response.

"No. I'm . . ." I got a dirty look from my partner. "*We're* investigating the death of Lorelei Adams. Did you know her?"

"Oh, yeah. She was real tight with Amy. Sweet girl, but out of my league. Didn't she kill herself?"

I knew better but needed to talk after losing the evidence that would have cracked this case. Bartenders, even in a college bar, are good listeners. "There's some question whether she committed suicide or was murdered. This is Lorelei's grandmother, and I'm a friend of the family."

He paused from washing glassware and looked at me with puzzlement. "So, which was it, suicide or murder?"

Maggie Mae kicked me under the bar, but a long guzzle of beer loosened my tongue anyway. "Her mother is adamant that she didn't kill herself. I . . . I mean, *we* have done some investigating and found strong evidence of foul play."

I emptied the glass and pushed it toward him. He took it and returned with a frothy head running down the side.

"You have any suspects?" he asked.

"Yeah. Actually, too many. I've got surveillance video from Lorelei's apartment the night she died. It points the finger at one suspect in particular. Problem is I can't seem to view my copy of the video. Amy tried to help but couldn't. Something about encryption and codec and proprietary software." I slurred my words.

"Amy's in some of my classes. She's a little moody for my taste, but sharp when it comes to computers. I'm surprised she couldn't open them."

I imbibed further. "You an IT major?"

"Yeah. Not as smart as Amy, but I can hold my own."

"What did you mean you're surprised she couldn't run the video?"

"Because the files are compressed, not encrypted, and the codec for the compression is normally found in the file header. You can download the decompression software for that codec from the internet."

His words echoed in my head, so I pushed my half-full mug away. "Is this something you could do?"

"Sure, if you have the video with you. It's a slow night. The security system in the office should have no trouble running your videos."

He asked the other bartender to fix Maggie Mae another drink. Jake and I went to a cracker-box sized office with stuffed manila folders piled on the desk, floor, safe and everywhere. Pinned up documents and yellow sticky notes covered the walls.

"Bit tight in here, but it shouldn't take long." He took the flash drive. "Something's been spilled on this drive. It's all tacky." He inserted the drive into the security system computer and worked the keyboard. The screen went blank. "That's odd."

He repeated his actions with the same result. "There's nothing on this drive."

"What?" My mind exploded. "That can't be. We found a whole list of files using Amy's computer."

He clicked a few keys, but the screen went blank each time. "Sorry, but this drive's been wiped clean."

"Could someone have deleted the files?"

"No. When you delete a file, it doesn't erase the data. It's still there. Deleting only erases the pointer to that record on the flash drive. I checked, and this drive has been wiped clean as a new one. If there was video, it's gone now."

"Is it possible Amy accidentally wiped it?"

He paused. "No. You'd have to do it intentionally. It's not a normal thing." He handed me the drive, and I put it in my pocket. "You said you copied that video from a security system. You should be able to make a new copy."

"I can't. The video has been erased on the security system."

My shoulders drooped on the way back to the bar. I wondered why Amy would wipe the drive. The murderer would want to destroy this key evidence, but the video implicated Reggie, not her. Maybe she was in this with Reggie and was protecting him. Maybe it wasn't a coincidence that her gun fired the deadly shot, and she discovered the body. Could she be having an affair with Reggie? I hadn't confirmed her parents supposed wealth as Jack had recommended.

What was that tacky substance on the drive? Despite Mallory's claim to be on my side now, she did still work for the sheriff and with Deputy Lowell. Could she have done something to it?

When I returned to my seat at the bar, I found Maggie Mae nursing her drink in danger of falling off her bar stool. Between lukewarm, greasy bites of my meal, I told her we still couldn't view the video, but withheld my suspicions Amy may have destroyed the evidence.

"Where's that leave us?" she asked.

"Nowhere. Without that video, I've got nothing. It feels like someone set me up, but I don't know who or why."

Jake must have heard my last statement. "In the office, I told you that when a file is erased, it only destroys the pointer to the file. The file data on the original security system is likely still on its hard drive."

He had my interest. "If you had the security computer, could you recover the data?"

"Can't promise anything, but I'd give it a shot for you." A new customer sat down at the bar several seats over, and Jake shifted his attention to him.

It was grasping at straws, but this had become my best opportunity to crack the case. Despite the late hour, I committed to a new mission.

Using my burner phone, I called Mallory.

318

"Oh, Tanner. Thank God you called. I don't have your new number. Whatever you do, don't go back to Maggie Mae's or to Ronnie's. We have their houses under surveillance. They found the Lincoln at the hospital parking lot and towed it in. The sheriff has us all working overtime looking for you. We know about the rental car."

"How did you find out about that?"

"It wasn't hard. Enterprise is the only rental company in town, and you used your driver's license."

"What about Lorelei's apartment? Is it under surveillance, too?"

"Oh, yeah. I'm sitting in the parking lot here, eating a cold Arby's sandwich."

"I need to get my hands on the apartment's security system. My copy of the security video has been wiped clean, so I need to get my hands on the original."

"At Reggie's office today, his secretary said the video has been erased on the security system. What good would it do to get your hands on it?"

"I have a computer whiz who can extract the video even if it's been erased. I need that video, and I need it now before Lowell hauls me in again."

"What's the plan? Bust in there and just take it? That's trespass and theft at the very least."

I hadn't thought it through yet. "I don't know. I'll offer the building supervisor money. He seems to respond to cash. I know this isn't fair to ask you, but are you going to arrest me if I show up at the apartment building?" There was a long pause. "Mallory?"

"Yeah, I'm still here. Tanner, I'm hanging on to my job by a fine thread. If I let you visit the apartment building without picking you up and Lowell finds out, he and Reggie will make sure I never work in law enforcement again."

"It's a big ask, but I need to borrow that security system. Let's call it retribution for spying on me for Sykes."

"Damn you! That's hitting below the belt. I told you I did it for your own good." After a prolonged silence, she said, "All right. Park down the street and sneak in the back way. How are you going to get in?"

"The same way I always do. I'll sneak in when someone goes in or out."

"Maybe you can follow the apartment supervisor in. He's been carrying heavy boxes out to his pickup like he's moving."

Maggie Mae dozed off but awakened with a jerk when she started to slip off the bar stool. She shook her head. "Where are we going next?"

"Lorelei's apartment, to steal their security computer."

"Can you take me home on your way? I'd really like to see this through, but I'm exhausted. I hate to admit it, but I can't hold my liquor anymore. Wouldn't want you to take advantage of me." Her wink brought a smile to my face.

After hearing that both her and Ronnie's houses were under surveillance, she acquiesced. A deep breath seemed to perk her up a little.

While driving, I planned my next moves. My body chilled and shook. Was it fear, withdrawal or both? I decided it was both and wondered if I could physically pull this off.

Donald had a gun safe so likely had a gun. Therefore, I needed one to level the odds. Physically, I was no match for Donald, so a handgun would be a great equalizer.

CHAPTER 66

In a small college town like Talmadge, only one store sells guns after ten PM—Walmart. To my dismay, they only sell long guns that cannot easily be hidden. Some creativity was required to properly arm myself. I chose a pocket knife, Umarex air pistol, and pepper spray. Although this air pistol only shoots BB's, it looks enough like a real handgun to fool most people. For the knife, I chose a Kershaw assisted-opening pocket knife, the closest thing to a switchblade sold legally. The small can of pepper spray might buy the seconds needed to open the knife or turn and run.

Returning to the car, I found Maggie Mae so soundly asleep she didn't stir the rest of the way to Lorelei's apartment building. When I parked, I spotted Mallory's squad car among residents' cars in the parking lot. Per her suggestion, I parked up the street. I decided to let Maggie Mae stay in the car and sleep. Besides, she would be much safer here since I didn't know how Donald would respond to me.

At this time of night, there would be no resident traffic to follow into the secure building. Mallory was correct. Someone had blocked the outside door open. Inside the building, Donald's apartment door also stood ajar. I slipped in unnoticed and scanned the living room. Packing paper and heaps of clothes littered the floor, bordered by moving boxes along the walls. Most were taped shut, others stood open, half-filled. A quick scan of the clutter in the living area revealed no sign of Donald. The sound of packing tape came from the master bedroom. I poked my head in the door and spotted Donald, back toward me, lifting a box marked fragile. My entering the room must have startled him, because he dropped his box, shattering its glass contents.

He assumed a warrior's stance, ready to strike. "What the fuck are you doing here? You got me fired, dickhead. I knew I shouldn't let you see that security video. Which one of your sick friends posed as Mr. Braun on the phone? I know for a fact it wasn't him *because he's the one who fired me.* You made a copy of that video, too, didn't you? I checked the logs. Good thing Mr. Braun didn't find out or I'd be running for my life."

"This may not be a good time, Donald, but I need to see the video again."

He chuckled and shook his head. "There ain't no damn video. I erased it so it's gone."

"It was there yesterday. You and I viewed it."

"You didn't see any video because it got written over weeks ago. Now get the hell out of here before I throw you out."

The two pints of high-gravity beer at dinner scrambled my brain enough for me to question if I had actually seen the video or merely imagined it. I searched my cloudy memory until clarity struck like a bell. "No, I did see it here yesterday. I saw Reggie come and go about the time Lorelei was murdered. It proves he did it."

To my surprise, he was quick for such a beefy guy. Donald grabbed the back of my jacket collar before I could reach any of my weapons. Thanks to his apparent years spent in the free-weight room, he lifted me off the ground and carried me out of the building. He tossed me on the front sidewalk with all the care shown a bag of refuse. "Now, get the hell out of here before I kick your stupid ass." He wiped his hands off and headed back in.

The tumble on the hard sidewalk torqued my back, sending shooting pains down my legs. After a moment's repose, I decided nothing was broken and pushed the pain to the back of my consciousness by promising myself an Oxy as soon as this was over.

Fool that I am, I picked myself off the walk, marched around back to resident entrance and re-entered the building with a moron's confidence. Donald was packing an open box in the living area. He must have thought so little of me, he didn't consider I might return to confront him.

Intent on his task of packing, he didn't seem to notice when I snuck by him heading to the second bedroom. Without warning, Donald tackled me from behind and pinned me to the floor. My BB gun pressed hard into my aching back. I freed a hand and went for the can of pepper spray already going off inside my pocket. The spray burnt my skin like the worst sunburn imaginable. The slippery can made recovery difficult and, having Donald on top of me didn't help. I managed to pull the slimy can out of my pocket, but it slipped out of my hand, numbed by the intense burning. I frantically searched the floor for it.

Donald pulled my arm back farther than it was intended to bend. On the verge of surrendering, I located the small, slippery can and unleashed the rest of its contents in the general direction of Donald's face.

He screamed, released his hold and rubbed his eyes like a crazed animal. I pushed his writhing, coughing body off me and clawed my way to a crouching position. In triumph, I rolled to my feet and spiked the spent can like a football in an end zone. Ignoring my burning skin, I resumed my mission and scooped the security computer off the desk. Cable connections resisted my efforts to make off with it. A harder yank sent the monitor tumbling to the floor with a loud cracking noise and sparks flying. Still, the computer did not come free of its entanglements.

I tugged with all my weight. The computer came free with a lurch, throwing me off balance. As I stumbled to regain equilibrium, Donald reached out and tripped me. The hard fall on top of the computer case knocked the wind out of me.

After a minute of gasping for air, my lungs began functioning again and the panic of suffocation passed. I sat up and pulled my BB gun out of my belt. Donald towered over me with an assault rifle, pointed at my head. Tears rolled over his blotchy, reddened cheeks. He blinked profusely and coughed with the vigor of a four-pack-a-day smoker. "Toss that gun over here, handle first, or I'll blow your fucking brains out."

Considering the huge imbalance in firepower, I tossed my BB gun at his feet. "Now, Donald, you don't want to make a mess. If you get brains all over the apartment, the landlord won't return your security deposit."

He retrieved my gun and laughed. "Hell, this isn't even a real gun. It's like bringing a knife to a gun-fight. On your feet and put your hands up." Little did he know I still had a knife.

I slowly stood and raised my hands over my head. Holding his rifle in his right hand, he aimed the BB gun at me in his left and fired several quick shots.

Two struck me on my jacket, stinging a little. In defiance, I suppressed an outcry and kept my hands up.

Scowling, he pelted me with half a dozen more BB's. Most missed my jacket and struck my thin shirt. Those less padded stings felt like an attack of killer bees. "Shit! That hurts." Three red spots appeared on my shirt, where high-velocity BB's at close range broke the skin. I ignored the BB stings and the moist, fiery sensation of pepper spray on my pants, now contacting my testicles.

"Nice rifle you got there, Donald. Is that what you used to shoot at me outside Ray's garage?" When he failed to respond, I continued. "So, it wasn't Reggie who murdered Lorelei. It was you. Did Reggie pay you to do it?"

His red-splotched face showed panic. "I didn't kill anyone. Honest. It wasn't me. I didn't do it." He tucked the BB gun in his belt near his belly button and wiped tear-filled eyes with his left sleeve. Prepared to pounce, I watched for an opening, but his gun never strayed from its bead on me.

I bought time, hoping for an opportunity to present itself. "You were stalking Lorelei, weren't you? That's why Amy loaned Lorelei her gun, the one you used to kill her in cold blood."

"Damn you! That spray burns like hell!" He wiped his sleeve over his face but froze when I moved ever so slightly. "I told you I didn't kill her, and I wasn't stalking her either. Sure, I asked her out a few times, but that haughty little bitch thought she was too good for me. Hah! Too good for me? She was just a high-priced whore for old Reggie. She threatened to have him fire me. I wanted to kill her, but she did me a favor when she shot herself."

Sudden rage overruled common sense. Head lowered, I charged him with reckless abandon. He pulled the trigger, but his gun failed to fire. I bounced off him as he swung the rifle in a sweeping motion that connected with my face in a sickening crack. My body collapsed on the floor with a loud thud. My world closed in as blackness consumed me.

I came to, lying on the floor next to a sofa in the living room with both my hands and feet bound with clear packing tape. A strip of tape over my mouth functioned as a gag. The front of my T-shirt felt damp from an aching, bloody nose. My head throbbed, my chest and abdomen stung, my back ached and my groin was afire. I craved an Oxy. A swollen nose full of drying blood made breathing difficult.

The apartment door was closed. Donald paced the floor, his clothes dripping and soggy shoes squishing with each step. It appeared he had jumped in the shower with his clothes on to flush the pepper spray out of his eyes and face.

Every few minutes, he paused, wiped his face with a towel and swore under his breath. Frequently checking his watch suggested he was waiting for someone or something to happen.

The packing tape prickled everywhere it contacted my reddened skin. An attempt to cry for help yielded only a garbled, muffled sound. He stopped pacing and glared at me with flames shooting from bloodshot eyes. Again, I tried speaking through the tape. He leaned down and ripped it off my mouth with a quick jerk.

"Damn, that hurts. I can't breathe through my nose. I think it's broken."

"All right, I'll leave the tape off, but keep your damn mouth shut. You don't, I'll blow your head right off. See, the safety's off now." He showed me the right side of the weapon as if I knew what to look for.

"So, what happens now, Donald? Are you going to kill me and make it look like a suicide the same way you did with Lorelei? You're not bright enough to have done it alone. Who else is in this with you? Reggie? Sykes? Deputy Lowell? Amy? Professor Robinson? Brandon?"

"I don't know any Brandon, and who the hell is Professor Robinson? I told you I didn't kill her."

I sprung my trap. "But you admit it was murder, not suicide?"

Donald froze and paused as if deliberating. "I didn't kill her. She killed herself. That's right, she shot herself. I couldn't shoot anyone."

"But you shot at me. You tried to kill me."

He paced at an agitated gait for a moment and then stopped to face me.

"You're right. I was the one who shot at you, but I really didn't try to kill you. I couldn't kill anyone. Believe me. I just wanted to scare you off."

"So, you lied to me. You're not really as bad a shot as you told me you were." A female voice drew my attention to Maggie Mae standing in the door. Although familiar, the voice was not hers.

CHAPTER 67

Maggie Mae fell forward into the apartment and collapsed in a heap on the floor next to me.

A redheaded woman, wearing rubber gloves and sunglasses, stood in the doorway brandishing a semi-automatic handgun. "Look what I found running around outside." She wore an evil yet beautiful smile. "So, Donald, I guess you're not as bad a shot as you led me to believe. You really didn't try to kill old Tanner here like I ordered you to, did you? Guess I shouldn't have sent a boy to do a woman's job."

Donald's grimace reminded me of a kid who had dropped his ice cream cone. "No, really. I tried to shoot him, but the gun bounced around when I fired. I'm a good shot, I'm just not familiar with assault weapons."

Maggie Mae collected herself, sat straight and looked me over. Tears streamed down her face. "Oh, my word. Tanner, what happened to you? You're all bloody. Are you all right?"

I assured her I was okay, but her reaction told me I was no better a liar than a writer.

"Sorry, Tanner, I woke up and saw how late it was, so came looking for you. Didn't see her come up behind me. Who is she?"

It was the woman from the security video walking in with Donald that night. When she removed the sunglasses, her wig shifted, revealing streaked blond hair. "It's Tanya, Reggie Braun's wife. I should have known."

Tanya waved the pistol between Maggie Mae and me. "Enough of the chit-chat."

"What are we going to do with them?" Perspiration rolled down Donald's tense ashen face. The assault rifle swayed in his shaking hands. "They can testify against us. Not sure about you, but I don't want to go to jail. How'd I let you suck me into this mess?" He shifted his weight from one foot to the other, like a child needing to urinate.

"It wasn't that hard, Donald." Tanya motioned with her gun. "Okay, Mabel, get up and sit on the sofa. Donald, you have any more of that packing tape to bind her up?"

"My name's not Mabel." She rose in defiance and plopped down on the couch. "It's Maggie Mae, Lorelei's grandmother. What's wrong? You afraid of a little ole southern peach like me? Gottta tie me up?" She held out her hands for taping in a show of defiance.

Tanya shook her head and chuckled. "Okay, whatever. She's right, Donald. Don't bother taping her up, but if she makes a peep, shoot her." She gave Maggie Mae a sadistic grin and winked.

The knife in my front pants pocket was our only hope, but I had to sneak it out without being seen. Conversation presented the only distraction available. I needed to keep Tanya talking. "So, you were the redhead on the video walking in with Donald that night. The two of you killed Lorelei. Why?"

Donald shook his head, his eyes became pinholes. "I told you I didn't kill her. I wasn't in on anything."

Tanya sneered, but her eyes smiled. "Okay, it was me. Turns out old muscle-bound Donald here doesn't have the balls for it. Too many anabolic steroids, maybe? Makes one stupid."

Maggie Mae's face lost all color. "Oh, my. Why did you do it?"

328

"Well, you see, Mable, I couldn't stand Reggie sleeping with your granddaughter anymore. I know all about his string of co-eds he's stashed away on the side for years. It's his fountain of youth, I suppose. I had learned to live with that. Lord knows I've had my own little transgressions, if you know what I mean. But the fool fell in love with this one. A wife can sense that.

"I begged Reggie to end it. The bastard laughed and asked if my backswing had improved since I found my new tennis coach. Reggie knew I wouldn't divorce him because our pre-nup would have left me high and dry. He couldn't ask me for a divorce because he used my name and signature on some questionable business loans. The fool doesn't realize how much I love him."

I worked the knife until it fell out of my pocket onto the carpeted floor. No one seemed to notice. I reached between my legs, retrieved the knife, and opened it in slow motion. Slight as my movements were, they drew scrutiny from Tanya. She pointed her gun at my head.

I froze. "Sorry. Just a leg cramp. So you scheduled to meet Lorelei in her apartment that night."

Tanya's gun hand relaxed as she continued. "Not exactly. I called her up, posing as a temp calling on behalf of Reggie. I told her he had something important to tell her and wanted her to fix dinner for them, and would six o'clock be okay?

"I knew Reggie would be in Atlanta that night so he would be out of the picture. I waited outside Lorelei's apartment until she left to shop for groceries and then persuaded Donald to let me into the building."

"How did you know Donald? Was he spying on her for you?"

"I met loverboy here that night walking into the building. I had borrowed Reggie's car because the key to her apartment was on that key ring. I snooped around while she was shopping and found a gun. When I saw how nice her apartment was, I realized how much Reggie loved her. There was only one way to end this.

"I sat at the dining table with the handgun I found in her closet. I didn't know it belonged to Amy, but that worked in my favor because it threw suspicion on her.

"Reggie's slut came in carrying groceries. When she spotted me, she dropped one bag. At my invitation, she placed the other one on the kitchen counter and sat across from me at the table. I promised her that when I left tonight, her relationship with my husband would end one way or another.

"She spotted the handgun sitting on my lap through the glass table and begged me to let her live. She swore she didn't love my husband and rejected his marriage proposal. She claimed to have a serious boyfriend and promised to break it off with Reggie.

I knew she was lying. That gold digger had her hooks into him and would never give up her sugar daddy. If she told him about my visit to her apartment, he might kill me or, more likely, hire someone to do it. He's capable of that."

Tanya gazed into space for a prolonged moment as if her thoughts had taken her captive. Hands between my legs, I sawed at the back of the tape on my ankles.

Tanya shook her head and peered at me. "Without thinking, I aimed the gun at her and pulled the trigger, but it didn't go off. The safety was on. She fainted, collapsing on the table. I had planned to frame Reggie for her murder, but in that moment, realized I still loved him too much to see it through. I couldn't let her off the hook, so decided to make it look like she shot herself.

"Before I was ready, she started coming to and I panicked. I pressed the gun to her temple, disengaged the safety and pulled the trigger. The gun powder residue on my arm and my fingerprints on the gun posed problems. I rubbed my hand on hers to transfer some of the powder residue. After wiping my fingerprints off the gun with her napkin, I staged it in her right hand."

Donald stood transfixed as if hearing this story for the first time. A tear rolled down her cheek. Her eyes turned cold, and nostrils flared.

Having sawed through the tape on my ankles, I began working to free my wrists, a much more difficult task to conceal. I had to keep Tanya talking. "How does Donald fit into this?"

Tanya glanced toward Donald and chuckled. "He showed up and saw me put the gun in her hand. He nearly stroked out before I could calm him down. I made a deal with him to help me clean up and complete the staging of a suicide."

"How much did you pay him?"

"It cost me plenty, but I didn't really get my money's worth."

Donald eyed Tanya like a tiger studies its prey. "Mrs. Morgan knocked on my door repeatedly. I got out of the shower and wrapped a towel around me to see what was so damned important. She claimed she had heard a gunshot, I didn't believe her because she's so hard of hearing. She kept nagging me so I threw on my robe, grabbed my master key and went to check things out.

"No one answered Lorelei's door, so I used my master key. Tanya was leaning over the body, putting the gun in Lorelei's hand. The scene disturbed me—blood on the table and more blood pooling on the floor beneath her head. Tanya pointed the gun at me and threatened to kill me if I didn't help her."

I had to buy more time. "How'd you get the sheriff's office to cooperate in declaring it a suicide? Despite your efforts, the evidence still pointed to murder."

"They really didn't help *me*. Lowell jumped to the conclusion Reggie had killed her and covered it up by concluding it was suicide. Good old Reggie didn't question the conclusion because he wanted to believe it was suicide and not murder."

"So, Reggie was in Atlanta while this all happened?"

"I don't really know where he was but he spent the night with his secretary, Nancy."

Suddenly I realized what had bothered me about the parking lot video from that night. Reggie's car showed up on the parking lot video but parked out of range of the camera. I assumed he was the man with the umbrella, but I never saw Reggie leave. Now I realized I hadn't seen him at all, only his car. Tanya had driven his car that night.

"Why didn't you destroy the video evidence?"

"Brainiac here was supposed to but forgot. When I found out you had viewed the video, I told him to erase it. When he called back to tell me it was done, he let it slip you had made a copy. It became necessary to find your copy and destroy it too."

"So, Amy wiped the flash drive clean for you. What leverage did you hold over her?"

"None. Donald took care of the jump drive. Amazing what a little Coke will do to computer chips".

"What do you mean?"

"Deputy Lowell told me they had searched you and your room but were unable to find your copy of the video. I guessed it still had to be in the truck. I helped the good deputy live out one of his sexual fantasies in the back seat of an impounded Porsche while Donald snuck in and searched your pickup. He found the jump drive in a crevice in the glove compartment, soaked it in his Coke, and then returned it to the glove box. Sounds like it worked."

"So, you paid Donald to help cover up the murder and destroy the copy of the video."

"Yeah, I paid him a bundle to help me stage the suicide and then keep his mouth shut. But that wasn't good enough for him. He's been blackmailing me ever since. And tonight he called me complaining Reggie fired him and he needed money to carry him over until he found another job. And guess what? He told me to wear the red wig and come prepared to fuck his brains out."

She pressed her gun against Donald's head, relieved him of his assault rifle, and then set it on a table. She nuzzled up to him. "You ready for me, big boy?" As she rubbed his groin with her free hand, her eyes grew large. "Whoa! You are a big boy. Too bad." She smiled and shoved her gun against his mouth. "Open up big boy."

His eyes snapped wide open. With her free hand she removed the red wig and tossed it aside, revealing her dirty blond hair tied in a tight bun behind her head. "Sorry, Donald. No fantasy sex for you, not tonight, not ever. I don't do freaks."

Donald shook. Tanya forced the gun barrel in his mouth and pulled the trigger. Blood shot from the top of his head, splattering moving boxes and the walls. His eyes became hollow, and his body went limp. Tanya guided his collapse onto the sofa next to Maggie Mae who screamed and clutched her chest as if having a heart attack. Her face turned porcelain white, and she passed out. Her head fell back, but she remained sitting upright.

"So now what happens?" I asked.

"You don't get it yet, do you? This is going to look like a murder/suicide. Donald shoots the two of you and then takes his own life. I'll leave a note from him, confessing to Lorelei's murder and revealing how sorry he is. You two were getting too close to the truth, so he killed you. Afterward, guilt drove him to take his life rather than stand trial and be executed. Pretty clever, huh?"

Tanya wrapped Donald's limp right hand around her gun and aimed it at Maggie Mae's head. "I'm learning to stage this better. This time there will be plenty of powder residue on the shooter's hand." She labored to pull the trigger with Donald's limp, large paw between her petite hand and the gun.

There was no time to free my wrists. Planting my feet, I pushed up from the floor toward Tanya, leading with the knife in my bound hands.

My shoulder struck Donald's arm as the gun went off. The bullet went wide, striking the sofa next to Maggie Mae's head.

The knife hit something solid, knocking it out my hands and sending it flying. Off-balance, I tumbled over Donald's legs. His body slid off the sofa onto the floor, and he ended up on top of me. Pain shot through my back.

Spinning away, Tanya fell on top of a box and lost her grip on the gun, which bounced off my back on its way to the carpet. She reached her left arm out to the wall and caught her balance. Blood ran down her right arm from a knife wound.

She collected her wits and dove into the pile with Donald's body and me, scrambling to recover her pistol. We scuffled for the gun, but my bound wrists proved to be too much of a disadvantage. She recovered her weapon and pressed the barrel against my forehead. I conceded the match and rolled into a seated position on the floor.

Tanya stood over me with her back toward the sofa. She shifted the gun to her left hand. Blood ran down her injured right arm. She wiped it on her pant leg before refocusing her attention on me. Despair overwhelmed me, draining all my resistance.

She pressed her bleeding arm against her leg. "Damn, that hurts, you mother fucker." I closed my eyes and waited for the end. "I'm going to enjoy putting you away, you son of a bitch."

I heard a loud thud behind me just before Tanya's gun discharged and sent a flash of burning heat down the side of my head. In the midst of my struggle with Tanya, Maggie Mae had regained consciousness and clubbed Tanya with a heavy table lamp. The blast from the gun singed my head, but the errant bullet missed. Maggie Mae had saved my life, barely.

I lay on the floor, blinded, dazed, ears ringing like a bell tower. Through the fog in my eyes, I saw Maggie Mae standing over me, her lips moving in an agitated manner, but I couldn't hear anything for the ringing in my ears. Everything seemed to move in slow motion. With great difficulty, she helped me up.

By the time I was able to stand, Tanya had recovered and held her gun in her left hand, eyes struggling to focus. She wobbled and took aim at me. Before she could shoot, the doorframe splintered, and the apartment door swung hard against the wall. Mallory burst into the room with her service revolver gripped in both hands. She took aim at Tanya who still had me targeted.

"Freeze, or I'll shoot." Mallory's commanding voice peeked through the ringing in my ears.

Tanya turned her wavering gun in the general direction of the deputy.

"Drop it now, or I'll shoot! I mean it!" Mallory started to pull the trigger.

Tanya let her gun fall to the floor before letting out a big sigh and slouching in defeat. I heard later her first words were, "I want my lawyer."

CHAPTER 68

A ten-foot statue of Lady Justice adorns the main entrance to the Greene County courthouse in Talmadge, Georgia. Her blindfold signifies true justice is blind. The scale she holds represents the weighing of evidence and is in balance to portray that the evidence should stand on its own. Sometimes in rural Georgia, justice isn't blind or equal. The rich and powerful rest their thumb on the scale like a crooked merchant.

I expected to be the star witness in Tanya Braun's trial for the murders of Lorelei and Donald. I was never subpoenaed because there was no trial. Deputy Lowell refused to change the findings on his investigation into Lorelei's death, and Sheriff Sykes went along to keep the peace. It remains categorized as a suicide.

Tanya cut a deal with Reggie and the justice system for Donald's murder. In a pre-trial hearing, Deputy Lowell's poker-buddy judge committed her to a mental institution for one to three years. I understand her mental health facility is nicer than many vacation resorts. In exchange, she agreed to an uncontested divorce with minimal alimony. Braun Enterprises removed her name from the questionable loans, and no evidence remains that her name was ever there. With measured improvement in her sanity, she could be free in a year or so to find another rich husband to keep her in the lifestyle to which she's become accustomed.

While being booked into the county jail, I threatened to take my story public. Face to face, in hot putrid breath, Deputy Lowell made me a solemn promise. If I talked, he'd make sure I went to prison for ten years on a long list of charges—the hotel robbery, resisting arrest, trespassing at Braun Enterprises, sexual assault of Tanya Braun, grand theft auto of Ray's pickup, possession of a controlled substance, obstruction of justice, speeding and even jaywalking and littering. If, however, I kept my mouth shut and promised to never set foot in Greene County again, I could walk away a free man.

With Ronnie's concurrence, I chose the deal. To my surprise, she was okay with Lorelei's death remaining a suicide, officially. She, Maggie Mae and Tim all knew the truth, and that proved to be enough for them. I, on the other hand, had trouble letting Tanya get off so easy. In the end, my love of sunlight trumped any need for revenge.

Our deal done, I was released early on Saturday morning. Ronnie and Maggie Mae picked me up and we met Tim at Waffle House for breakfast.

After the waitress took our order, Ronnie produced a small package wrapped in silver paper with large gold bow. My surprised reaction seemed to please her. "Tanner, we are so thankful you investigated Lorelei's murder. We didn't get to see Tanya convicted, but *we* know the truth. It took a big commitment of your time and placed a big financial burden on you. I wish we could pay you for what you did. Still, we want to show you how thankful we are for your efforts. It isn't much."

Inside the package was a prescription bottle with the label half torn off. Inside were six round gray tablets with "15" embossed on one side and "OC" on the other—15 mg tablets of OxyContin. Ronnie beamed with pride at her gift. "They're left over from some surgery I had last year. Might tide you over until you get some help with . . . you know . . . your problem. Promise me you'll sign up for rehab the minute you return home."

She remained convinced I had a drug problem, so this represented a bold and generous gesture on her part. I didn't have the heart to tell her I was resistant to such a small dose and would need all of them to make a decent dosage for fear it might sound like I was an addict.

A smiling Maggie Mae pushed forward a second small package, wrapped the same as the first. Choked up and unable to speak, I opened it. Inside were car keys and an envelope. The envelope contained a hundred-dollar bill and an executed pink slip for a classic Lincoln Town Car. She explained the money was for gas to get home.

Tears welled in my eyes. "Thank you, Maggie Mae. You are very special."

"I know the investigation left you flat broke and without transportation. I can't drive it anymore, and it's just collecting dust and rotting there sitting in the garage. Tim drove it here, so it's waiting for you in the parking lot. Treat my baby good." Maggie Mae patted my hand.

"Thanks. I appreciate how much that car means to you. I promise to take great care of it."

Their gifts touched me. It took a minute and great effort to rein in my emotions enough to continue. "Look, Tim, I apologize for being a jerk. I came back here thinking I was forever in love with Ronnie and wanted—no—*needed* to win her back. It became an obsession. I pushed her hard and didn't play fair. What happened is my fault. Turns out, I was in love with a memory, and they only live in the past. In life, there are no do-overs. One can only live the present, remember the past and look forward to the future. You've got a great woman here, and you're obviously good for her. I hope I didn't mess things up for you two."

Tim and Ronnie held hands on top of the table and smiled as their eyes met. It hurt to see the old sparkle return to her eyes for another man.

Tim spoke first. "Thank you, Tanner. I appreciate your honesty. I need to apologize to you, and to Ronnie, for being so difficult. Lorelei's death has been hard on our marriage. But we've talked, and we're committed to making it work. We plan to renew our vows this spring, and we'd like you to come."

"Thanks. That would be great." Even without my agreement to stay away from Talmadge, I would not come back for their renewals. I'm still healing from the loss of my Peaches.

As I left Waffle House in my new four-wheel land yacht, Mallory called my burner phone. I pulled over and stopped before answering. Georgia has a hands-free law, and I did not want any run-in with local law enforcement.

"Hey, Tanner. I called to say goodbye. Wish I could've seen you off in person, but things are just too hot at the moment. Lowell is keeping a close eye on me."

"Don't worry. I understand."

"Let's stay in touch. I've been wanting to visit Savannah. You can be my personal tour guide. And call me if you come back to visit Ronnie and Maggie Mae. We'll get together."

"Sure thing. You've got my number." Maybe it was the false pretense under which our friendship started—me pumping her for information and her spying on me. "Keep your head down and take care of yourself. And, thanks."

"Thanks? You mean for saving your butt?"

"Yeah, for that—and for keeping me from getting too lonely."

"Stay in touch."

"Sure. And you call me too."

They were hollow words. I didn't expect either of us would call the other.

Someone knocked on my car window. My heart pounded in my ears as I rolled my window down. "Morning, Deputy Lowell. Something wrong?"

"License, registration and insurance."

Maggie Mae's registration and insurance card were in the glove box. I handed them and my driver's license to him.

"This insurance card expired four years ago." He crumbled the card and tossed it in the open window. The paper wad bounced off my forehead and fell to the floor. "Got a new one?"

"Not yet. As a matter of fact, I was on the phone with my insurance agent when you pulled up. She's changing my insurance over from my Ford Probe to this car."

"Says here, the car is registered to Margaret Mable Tobias. You steal this car, asshole?"

"No, she gifted it to me. Here's the title signed over to me." I handed it to him.

After looking it over and pocketing the hundred-dollar bill, he returned the envelope to me. I prayed I had enough gas in the tank to get home.

"Tags are expired, too."

"I know. I just got the car today and will go to the tag office the minute I get back to Chatham County."

He glared for a minute that seemed more like twenty, before tossing the registration card on my lap. "Okay, asshole. I'll let it slide this time, but I never, ever, ever want to see your ugly face in this county again. You understand me? I'll toss your ass in jail and throw away the key. And that's if I'm feeling compassionate."

"Don't worry. I'm as glad to leave town as you are to see me go." He returned to his car, sat and waited for me to pull out.

I paused for a few minutes hoping he would leave first, but it was clear he wanted to sure I was leaving town. The starter ground when I tried to start an already running engine. My hands shook as I put my left turn signal on and pulled away from the curb.

I needed the Oxys Ronnie had generously given me, but now didn't seem to be the best time to indulge.

EPILOGUE

Upon returning to Savannah, I discovered I'd lost my job managing the dental practice. Out of desperation, I started a limousine service using the Lincoln Town Car and am making decent money. People adore the classic Lincoln. I'm now three months into a twelve-step program and doing well.

I speak to Maggie Mae a couple times a month. She keeps me up on the local news and gossip in Talmadge. Tim and Ronnie renewed their vows and even went on a short honeymoon. She said they appear happy and I'm delighted for them.

Maggie Mae ran into Mallory at the store the other day. She asked about me and told Maggie Mae to tell me, "hey." Hey is a Georgian's way of saying hello to a friend. She told me Mallory appeared to be on a date with a very nice-looking man. I am happy for her.

No one has heard from Ray Adams since he left town. Rumors range from TLC putting out a hit on him to being on a mission trip in Africa. Who knows?

Mountain Mann got busted for beating a man who turned out to be a distant relative of Reggie's. From the picture in the local paper, the arresting deputies worked him over pretty well.

Amy and Brandon will graduate soon. I haven't received an invitation to their graduation and don't expect to. I couldn't go back, even if I wanted to.

As for me, I've met a woman, and we've dated a few times. We're taking it slow, which is fine with me. I'm not yet healed from my past relationships, but I'm working on it.

Documenting this sordid tale made me realize how much I enjoy investigating. In fact, Jack Sprat convinced me to study private investigation online. I call him from time to time seeking help with my coursework. This time next year, I hope to have my PI license.

I'm glad to finish writing this story. It is better written than my novel and will likely be the best thing I ever write. Sadly, I will never experience the thrill of seeing this published.

I provided copies to my lawyer, accompanied by a letter with explicit instructions. Should I die of unnatural causes or under questionable circumstances, he will deliver copies to the Atlanta Journal Constitution and the newsrooms of all four major Atlanta TV networks. I sent an extra copy of my written story to Deputy Lowell for late-night reading. I don't trust him, so this "book" is my insurance policy.

Documenting my story also renewed my passion for writing. I've authored several short stories and can see improvement. Someday, I hope my private investigating will give me a good storyline for another novel.

Overall, life is good, or at least, good enough for me at this stage in life. It's amazing how things look different when you set your expectations low. Victories come more often but taste just as sweet. I guess, when you're at the bottom, there's no way to go but up.

All this, and I still need an Oxy. Badly!

ABOUT THE AUTHOR

Ken L Burke

Ken grew up in a small village in west-central Illinois. At a young age, he became an avid reader and crafted stories in his head while doing chores such as mowing, raking and picking strawberries. He earned a BS degree in Mechanical Engineering from the University of Illinois. Ten years later, he received an MBA degree from Governor's State University while working full time.

He began his career at Chrysler Corporation as an aerodynamicist. For the next twenty-three years, he worked for ARCO, a major oil company later acquired by Amoco. There he worked in a broad range of areas including product development, administration, IT, retail marketing, sales and electronic payments. The remainder of his career he spent in sales, marketing and business development, primarily in the electronic payments industry.

After forty-one years, Ken retired to fulfill a life-long desire to write fiction. He joined the Carrollton Writers Guild and began writing short stories and novels in multiple genres. *Too Many Suspects*, a mystery/thriller, is his first novel to be published. *Those Who Hunt Us*, a science fiction/thriller, is scheduled to be released later this year.

Ken and his wife of forty-eight years live on a small lake west of Atlanta, GA, were they enjoy boating, fishing and entertaining their two children's families, including five grandchildren. When not writing, Ken reads, tours Civil War battlefields and enjoys auto racing on TV, in person and on his racing simulator.

Visit Ken at KenLBurke.com and sign up for his email list to keep up on future book releases. You can also follow his Facebook page @KenLBurkeAuthor. Contact Ken by email at Ken@KenLBurke.com.